GENTLE TRUST

The thought of Anna Lowell was keeping Jordan awake. If he wasn't going to sleep, he'd have a drink. He rose from the bed ———————————— s, then opened his desk d ———————————— brandy and a cup.

He heard a faint ———————————— imper. He eased to the do ———————————— to the landing and closer ———————————— or was cool to his bare feet ——— ——— of tallow and burned wood. He put his ear to her door and listened. She was crying!

Taking a deep breath, he rapped gently on the door and opened it at the same time. By the shadowed moonlight he saw her bolt upright at his intrusion. He opened the door wider and whispered, "Anna, it is I, Jordan."

He closed the door behind him and walked over to her, lowering his weight onto the edge of the bed. "I heard you crying and came to check on you."

She sniffled, wiped her eyes with the back of her hands, and pulled the sheet up to her neck. "You shouldn't be here," she said.

"Tell me what has you weeping in the dark night." He reached out and brushed her hair away from her shoulder so he could see her creamy skin. Then she dropped the covers. The gown she wore had a scooped neckline, and the soft moonlight enhanced the beauty of her neck and throat.

Slowly, he slid his arms around her and pulled her close to him, letting his hands massage the muscles in her back. She moaned her pleasure and fitted her face against his throat in a way that was so natural it made him tremble. Her breath fanned his heated skin. Jordan warred with himself. He had no right to pursue this course when her emotions were running so high. But God help him, he wanted her. He'd just hold her like this and be content, he told himself. He wouldn't kiss her. No, he couldn't do that. It would put him over the edge. He was too close as it was. But then her lips parted and pressed a moist kiss at the base of his throat and he was lost . . .

GLORIA DALE SKINNER
TENDER TRUST

ZEBRA BOOKS
KENSINGTON PUBLISHING CORP.

This book is dedicated to the memory of my father-in-law, Clyde Skinner, and to the memory of my nephew, Randy Nellums, a young man who took time to stop and smell the roses.

ZEBRA BOOKS

are published by

Kensington Publishing Corp.
475 Park Avenue South
New York, NY 10016

First Printing: March, 1993

Printed in the United States of America

Chapter One

Connecticut, 1780

Anna hummed as she shoveled ashes over the bright red coals in the fireplace. She held her long cotton skirt tightly between her knees so the hem wouldn't get caught in the few remaining embers.

Lowell Tavern had had a busy night. The warm July weather was bringing the men of the township out every evening for a drink, some talk, and the latest news from travelers.

With the fire properly banked, Anna straightened from her stooped position and looked about the dimly lit taproom. Her father was coming from behind the bar, tying his money bag to his belt as he did every night.

"Did you lock up, daughter?" he asked as he approached her.

"Not yet, Papa," she said with a bright smile. "Did we do well tonight?"

"Very well." He patted the full leather pouch. "Soon we'll make a trip to New York and meet one of the big sailing ships. I'm told the finest cloth is bought immediately for the women of New York and our salesmen get only the leftovers. It's time for

5

us to go and find something worthy of my only daughter. Would you like a dress made of silk?"

Anna picked up the skirt of her dress and rubbed the plain homespun material between her hands, thinking about the soft, luxurious feel of silk. "Oh, Papa," she whispered. "I'd love it for my wedding dress. Can we go next week so I'll have enough time to have it made?"

Levi chuckled and brushed his long beard. "No, not next week, but perhaps by the end of the month."

"I'm so excited I don't think I can wait."

"Well, you'll have to, daughter. Now, you lock the front door, and I'll get the back, or it will be daylight before we can get to bed."

Anna watched her father walk through the arched doorway that led to the kitchen. Hugging her arms tightly to her chest, she imagined how her wedding dress would look.

Laughing lightly at the wonderful thought, she hurried to the front of the taproom. As she reached for the lock on the nailspiked Deerfield door, it swung open, knocking her aside. She caught herself from falling backward and gasped at the man standing in the shadowy doorway. His black clothes blended with the darkened opening.

Even though the candles were low, Anna immediately recognized the heavily whiskered man as one who had been in the tavern earlier that evening. Levi had thrown him out for making rude comments to her.

"We're closed," Anna said firmly, straightening the fichu that draped her shoulders. Her cheeks felt hot as she remembered the man's crude remarks. He remained silent now, and his dark eyes shifted from the

6

depth of the room to her and back again. He stared for so long a feeling of unease settled over her. He wasn't a large man, not much taller than Anna, but his stocky build indicated strength. He was also dirty and smelled of liquor and unwashed clothes.

From the age of twelve, Anna had known how to escape unwanted attentions from men. Her father had taught her early to be firm and strong and never to appear weak or afraid of any man.

She took a deep breath, lifted her chin, and fixed her determined blue eyes on his face. "I told you, we are closed. Now, leave before I call my father to throw you out again."

The only sound she heard was his heavy breathing. Anna's skin crawled with apprehension as he continued to watch her. Most men backed down immediately when they saw she wasn't afraid. She knew he was trying to decide what approach to take. He obviously hadn't expected her to be so firm when her father wasn't around to protect her.

At last Anna heard Levi shuffling back into the taproom and with a sigh of relief she turned toward him. Her father would make this difficult man leave.

"So it's you again." Levi walked to the doorway. He towered over the stranger. "I'll not serve a man who makes advances toward my daughter. If you're looking for a bed for the night, you'll have to go elsewhere. Now, off with you before I give you the trouble you're looking for."

When Levi started to grab the man, he suddenly stepped deeper into the shadows of the doorway and pulled a long-bladed knife from his waistcoat. The tarnished metal glinted faintly in the feeble light of the taproom. Anna gasped with alarm. Levi took a steady step backward.

7

"Just give me that money bag you have tied around your waist." He spoke quietly, holding the knife in one hand and beckoning Levi forward with the other. His small squinting eyes didn't waver from Levi's face.

Levi gave Anna a quick glance as if to assure himself he had to obey the stranger and give up their earnings without a fight. Then, slowly and with care, Levi untied the purse and handed it to the man.

As the robber reached for the heavy pouch with his empty hand he took a step forward and thrust the long blade into the center of Levi's stomach, lifting the knife up before pulling it out.

Levi's surprised grunt trailed into a soft groan as he sank slowly to the floor, his shaking fingers trying vainly to stanch the blood oozing from his stomach.

Anna screamed and caught hold of her father's shoulders as his knees hit the hard floor, but his dead weight knocked her backward.

"Papa!" she screamed again, and looked up in time to see the wild-eyed stranger lunge for her. She let go of her father and rolled away, her long, full skirt twisting and tangling about her legs.

Terence jerked awake and lay still in his bed. Had he heard his sister scream, or was he having a nightmare? He strained his ears for sounds other than his own breathing and heard the shuffling of booted feet. Another scream reached him. It was Anna!

He bounded off the bed, his bare feet hardly touching the cool wood floor. When he reached the stairs, he descended cautiously and peered into the dimly lit room. His eyes grew wide with horror at the scene before him. His father lay motionless on the braided rug in front of the door, his hands, folded across his stomach, covered in blood. A few feet away, Anna fought with a man.

Terence was only eight years old, and he knew he would be no match for a full-grown man. He had to get help. He bolted back up the stairs, across the landing, and down the steps that led into the kitchen. His nightshirt clung to his legs as he ran past the archway leading into the taproom and toward the back door. With trembling fingers he threw the latch and disappeared into the moonless night.

Anna tried to stand, but a rough hand grabbed her ankle and jerked her to the floor. The hard jolt knocked the breath from her lungs, and she gasped to regain it. She screamed again as a heavy body pounced on her and a hand covered her mouth. She tried to bite the foul-smelling palm, but the man held her too tightly. An intense pain shot through her as a beefy fist slammed into her side. She was sure a rib was cracked or broken. Pain and fear mingled, and she thrashed wildly.

"Quiet! Be still and I won't hurt you," the man said between raspy grunts.

After what he'd done to her father, she didn't believe him. Panic welled inside her. She had to get away from him. She had to warn Terence and see to her father. Kicking harder, bucking under his pressing weight, she fought to shove the man away.

When he took his hand from her mouth, a scream started deep in her throat, but it never came out because his fist struck her face just below the eye. Anna moaned loudly and went limp for a few seconds, then anger replaced fear and pain. She pulled her knee up and jammed it into her attacker's crotch.

He gasped harshly before striking another hard blow across her face with his open palm. The room spun and Anna lost her strength. Sparks flashed before her eyes, and blinking didn't make them go away.

The awful man pulled at her skirts, but she was too stunned to fight. She was shaking her head, trying to clear her eyes, when she realized the sparkles she saw were glimmers of candlelight reflecting off the brass cuspidor at the base of the bar. Her hand closed around the thick lip of the heavy container. She lifted it and swung with all her might, hitting the man on the side of his head. Spittle flew from his gaping mouth, his eyes widened in surprise, and the jar covered both of them with its foul contents. His inert body fell heavily upon her.

Anna pushed him off her chest and struggled to her knees, trembling. Clutching the bodice of her torn and soiled dress, she rushed to her father. Tears, mingled with spit from the cuspidor, ran down her cheeks, and her stomach lurched in revulsion as she wiped the mixture with the back of her hand.

She lifted her father's head into her lap. His eyes were open, but empty of life. Dark red blood had saturated the front of his shirt and waistcoat. "Papa?" she whispered. "Are you all right, Papa?" She pressed a trembling hand to his forehead.

Anna jumped when, seconds later, Eli Dudley and Parks Winchell rushed through the taproom door, carrying a long-barreled musket and a large piece of firewood.

Anna looked up at Eli. In a barely audible voice she asked, "Is Papa going to be all right?"

Eli laid down his weapon and knelt beside her on the rug. He put the tips of his fingers to Levi's throat, then waited a few moments before shaking his head. "It's too late, child. There's nothing to do. He's dead."

Anna cradled her father closer to her breast. "No!" she whispered desperately, and kissed the top of his head. Eli was wrong. Her father couldn't be dead. He was taking her to New York to buy silk for her wedding dress.

"Let me in! What happened!"

Moss, the cantankerous old man who helped around the tavern, pushed Parks Winchell aside and took in the scene—Anna's torn dress, her father, the stranger with his breeches twisted about his knees.

Hope stirred within Anna. "Moss, you've got to help me. They say Papa's dead." The words tumbled from trembling lips, and tears streamed from her eyes.

Eli scrambled away as Moss knelt beside Anna. After a moment, he reached over and closed Levi's eyes. "It's the truth, Anna. God's seen fit to take your papa home."

Moss pulled Levi away from Anna and laid him gently on the floor, then scowled at Parks and Eli as he helped Anna to stand. "Why are you two blubbering idiots standing around like you're touched in the head? Can't you see what needs to be done?"

"What can we do?" Parks spread his hands and dropped them.

Suddenly, Anna felt light-headed again. Her left side ached and her bruised bottom lip burned, but she ignored the pain. Her father was dead! How was she going to tell Terence? She brushed her long, tangled hair away from her sticky face and looked down at the man who had killed her father.

At that moment, Benjamin Jarvis and his mother, Althea, hurried through the open taproom door.

11

Benjamin rushed to Anna, and she fell sobbing into his outstretched arms.

Benjamin patted the back of her head but remained quiet while her body heaved against his chest. She pressed her face close to his warm neck, wishing he'd hold her tighter, wishing he'd tell her everything was going to be all right.

"What happened here?" Althea demanded, clutching her wool shawl around her full figure. Her dark brown eyes darted quickly around the room, gathering in every detail of the sordid scene. Her long, unbound gray-streaked hair spread across her shoulders like a shroud.

Parks was the first to speak. "It appears that stranger over there came in and robbed Levi." He pointed to the man. "That's Levi's money bag sticking out of his pocket. Then, I guess, Anna came in and he decided to—er—a—"

"Rape her," Althea finished in a strong voice as she bent over Levi's body.

Anna's sobs stopped abruptly and her head popped up. She wiped her eyes with her hands to clear her vision. What was Benjamin's mother saying? That man had killed her father, but he hadn't raped her! She pushed out of the safety of Benjamin's arms and looked at the pinch-faced, sharp-nosed woman who was examining the stranger sprawled on the floor.

"Is that man dead?" Althea asked.

"Appears to be," Eli answered.

"He's dead?" Anna asked as a cold chill shook her body. "I—I hit him only once. How could that kill him?"

Moss walked over and picked up the slimy brass cuspidor. "Did you hit him with this?"

12

Anna nodded and glanced at Benjamin, hoping he would say something, do something to defend her. But all he did was to pull uncomfortably at his shirt and look away.

"Must've cracked his skull," Moss answered.

She hadn't meant to kill him! Anna winced and her knees buckled. If Benjamin hadn't caught her under the arms, she would have hit the floor.

"I don't think this is something you should be seeing," Moss told Althea in a sober tone as he stepped between the woman and the dead men.

Numbly, Anna watched Moss take off his tattered coat and cover her father. She squeezed her eyes shut, and her hands tightly clenched the front of Benjamin's shirt. Her father was really gone. And she had killed a man. What was she going to do?

Althea paid no attention to Moss. She stepped over Levi and stood before Anna and Benjamin. Anna felt Benjamin stiffen.

"How did it happen, Anna?" Althea demanded. "Did you kill that man, after he killed your pa and raped you?"

"No!" Anna screamed, coming out of the protection of her fiancé's arms. She looked at Benjamin's worried expression and then at Althea's accusing one. "He didn't rape me! He only tried to. I hit him on the head before he could do anything." Her voice trembled. "I—I didn't mean to kill him. I wanted only to get away and see to Papa."

Althea gave Anna a hard, unyielding look. Anna knew Benjamin's mother hated her. She'd made that clear on a number of occasions. The only reason she'd agreed to let Benjamin marry her was because she was the innkeeper's daughter and would bring a good dowry.

13

"Don't lie to me, Anna Lowell," she said shrilly, taking a step closer. "The proof is right before my eyes. What little of your dress is left is in shreds and covered in virgin blood."

Anna looked down at the front of her dress. "No, it's my father's blood," she protested fiercely, holding the material together with trembling hands. She looked to Benjamin for help, but he was standing quietly, watching her with dark eyes and pursed lips while his mother tried to ruin her. Didn't he believe her?

"Then why are the man's breeches around his knees?"

Anna's attention returned to Althea. "I—I don't know. He must have unbuttoned them when he hit me. I was stunned for a moment." As she spoke, Anna realized her lip was swelling, slurring her words.

"Mama, perhaps this isn't the time—"

Althea ignored her son's feeble protest and pushed him aside, stepping closer to Anna. They were equal in height, but the older woman had a much larger frame. "Now, Anna, you must tell the truth. No one will blame you. There's proof that man attacked you."

"Yes, he did attack me," Anna said truthfully, wiping her tearstained cheek. Once again she looked to Benjamin for help. Their eyes met, but he looked quickly away. Anna's chest tightened. He wasn't going to help her.

"There!" Althea turned to the three men who still stood silently around the taproom. "She's admitted it."

"But he didn't *rape* me," Anna insisted in a stronger voice, not taking her eyes off the woman

14

who wanted to ruin her reputation. She knew what Althea was trying to do, and she wouldn't let her. Althea had never wanted Benjamin to marry her, and now his mother thought she had a good reason to prevent the marriage.

In desperation, Anna turned to Benjamin, and this time he didn't look away. His worried expression had been replaced by an accepting sadness. She couldn't understand why he wasn't fighting for her. He stood so straight, so silently, that Anna wanted to shove him just to see him move.

The pain in her side threatened to take control, but she denied it. "Benjamin, I swear he didn't touch me in that way. He only tore my dress and hit me a few times. I didn't mean to kill him."

Anna needed Benjamin's reassurance. She needed to know he believed her even if no one else did. His deep-set brown eyes scanned her face, and the sides of his nose flared with each breath, but he didn't touch her again.

Suddenly Benjamin faced his mother and said, "I believe her when she says she wasn't r—"

Benjamin couldn't even bring himself to say the word. To Anna it seemed that he didn't really believe in her innocence.

"You're a fool," Althea stated firmly. "All you have to do is look at her. This isn't the first time her father has had to fight men to preserve her honor. She's bewitched men for years—you're a perfect example." Glaring, Althea pointed a stern finger directly at her son, then turned to confront the other townsmen who had heard the news and were now gathering in the tavern. "Anna has caused the death of two men. She's a doxy. She brings shame to the town, and something needs to be done about her."

"No! I'm not!" Anna protested. Her hands tightened into fists even as they held her dress together. "You have no right or reason to say such things about me."

Moss pushed his way between the two women, shorter than both. "I've heard enough of your accusations, Althea. You know Anna's not a loose woman. Now, go home before you get yourself in trouble."

"Humph," Althea grumbled, not taking kindly to being told what to do by the old man.

"Eli, you and the others take Levi and the stranger out of here so I can clean up. Benjamin, you and your mama go home. I'll stay the night with Anna and Terence." Moss looked around. "Where is that boy, anyway?"

"My house," Parks called out to Moss. "He's the one who ran over and told me a man was attacking Anna."

"Send him on down here when you get back. We might as well tell him about his pa tonight."

Anna held her side and winced. How had her brother gotten to Parks Winchell's house? How was she going to tell Terence? What were they going to do without their father?

Benjamin turned a sympathetic face to Anna and took hold of her hand. "Get some rest. I'll be back in the morning. Things will look better then."

"How will they be better? Her father's dead, she's been raped, and she's killed a man. I say she should be run out of town."

Althea's words stole the comfort out of Benjamin's touch. Anna felt like scratching his mother's eyes out. How could so mean a woman have such a nice, mild-mannered son?

16

"You're the one who's going to be run out of town," Moss said, as he picked up a poker and started for Althea. "I said for you to get out of here!"

Althea screeched and grabbed Benjamin's arm, dragging him out the door with her.

It was all a horrible nightmare, Anna thought as she watched Eli and Parks lift her father and carry him away. Her ears rang, and for a moment the room spun. Still holding her side, she sank into a nearby chair. She had to pull herself together. She had to tell Terence about their father.

"I'm not posing as a minister," Jordan Kent told the man who sat across the table from him in the crowded tavern.

"You don't have a choice. Washington asked specifically that you do it."

Jordan picked up his ale and drank deeply before returning the tankard to the table. "Did I come all the way over to this miserable section of Boston for you to tell me this?" He wiped his lips with the back of his hand, his lace cuff tickling his clean-shaven cheek. "I agreed to go to this town, be the schoolmaster, and do a little spying. You didn't say anything about my playing the part of a minister. That's a crazy idea, and no one would believe it anyway — I don't quite live the part." He took a long look at a heavy-bosomed serving maid to press his point.

"Oh, you won't be playing," the expensively dressed man assured him in a confident voice. "Everything has been arranged. We're going to have the church ordain you tomorrow, so all will be legal and proper."

"Hell and damnation! You must be out of your mind, Virgil." Jordan pushed away from the table, ready to take his leave.

"Jordan, please." The other man grabbed his wrist. "Do be quiet." He looked nervously about the crowded room. "Someone will overhear us, and you know how dangerous that could be. Sit back down."

Jordan jerked free of the man's grip and wondered whether he should refuse to hear another word. He gazed balefully at his friend and colleague before resettling himself in the chair. He'd known Virgil for the better part of ten years and could tell he was serious about this matter. Did Washington really want him to pretend to be a minister? Jordan laughed inside. Him, a minister! He liked women and ale too much even to consider the idea. He could never be that good . . . could he?

"I agreed to find out what I could. If there's a spy working the Boston Post Road, I'll find out who he is, but why do I have to become a minister to do it?" Jordan protested. "Washington must be mad. And ordaining me . . . sacrilege."

"You must. People will tell a minister things they won't tell anyone else. No one will suspect. It's the perfect foil." Virgil brushed his thinning hair with his hand.

Jordan weakened further. Maybe it would work. Virgil was certainly right about it being the perfect disguise. But could he pull it off? He drank from his ale again. Why not? Hadn't he put on a red coat and posed as a British officer in New York six months ago? The role of a minister should not be so much harder.

Virgil leaned across the table. His voice grew softer and his green eyes narrowed as he slipped

18

some papers into Jordan's hand. "Here are the letters of inquiry I made on your behalf. You'll need to be prepared to leave by the end of the week. Upon your arrival in Georgetown, you'll stay in the Lowell Tavern, where you can get to know the townspeople and hear all the news of travelers."

Frowning, Jordan stuffed the papers in his coat pocket and asked, "Why Lowell Tavern?"

"The owner's been known to shelter British soldiers, which is enough to make him suspect. Recently some of our men came into possession of a letter that was bound for Clinton."

"And?" Jordan prompted.

Virgil glanced about the room. "The ink was smeared, but it was clear that Clinton was ordered to send a Mr. John Anderson to Lowell Tavern at once."

Jordan was thoughtful for a moment. "I don't recognize the name."

"We're not supposed to. It's a common alias. But Clinton will know who he is, and I'm certain another letter will be sent. We need to have you established at the tavern before Mr. Anderson arrives."

"And I'm to find out whom Anderson is to meet and what information they exchange?"

"Exactly." Virgil leaned back in his chair, a satisfied smile lighting his pale face.

Jordan stood and this time refused to be detained. The fair-haired maiden had just given him the nod. She was ready for him. He picked up his tankard and finished his drink before looking back at Virgil. "Tell Washington I'll go—and that he'll owe me a big favor for this one."

Chapter Two

"I'm certain there's no letter for your father, Lydia. I would have remembered seeing it." Anna reached behind the bar in the taproom and took out the small stack of mail that had arrived earlier in the day. Mail didn't come every day, and it was never regular.

Anna sifted through the letters anyway, keeping her face down so her friend wouldn't have to stare at the ugly bruise still covering one side of her face. Moss had checked her ribs and assured her nothing was broken, but her side still hurt when she took a deep breath.

"P-Papa's anxious to hear from his brother in B-Boston," Lydia told her. "He was qu-quite ill last time there was n-news. Maybe we'll hear s-soon."

"I'll watch for a letter and send Terence over with it immediately."

Lydia touched Anna's shoulder with a gentle hand. "Oh, d-don't do that, Anna. As long as P-Papa is expecting c-correspondence, he will let me c-come to the tavern."

Anna looked up at Lydia's smiling face. A wave of warmth washed over her. The two of them had been friends since they were old enough to talk.

She smiled. "In that case, I won't send Terence. I want you to come every day."

Lydia laughed lightly and her dark brown eyes glistened. "P-Papa wouldn't let me c-come that often. He likes to c-come in the evenings and enjoy a-a drink."

Saddened, Anna turned away from Lydia and put the stack of mail back in its box behind the bar. Her father had liked a drink in the evenings, too. As soon as the doors of the tavern were locked for the night, Levi would get out his account book and pour himself a tankard of mulled elderberry wine and sip it while he posted his figures.

"I-I did-didn't m-m-mean t-to remind y-you of—"

"It's all right, Lydia," Anna calmed her friend with a soft voice and a brief smile. "Don't feel bad. Papa's been in his grave little more than a week. It's only natural for everything to make me think of him."

Through the years Lydia's stuttering had improved greatly, but when she got upset or excited the nervous habit became more pronounced. She lost all control when she tried to hurry her words.

Lydia wasn't as tall as Anna, and she would have been as pretty except for her protruding front teeth. Anna constantly tried to reassure Lydia by telling her how pretty she was, although she knew Lydia didn't believe her.

"I wish I c-could help." Lydia's big brown eyes filled with compassion.

"You have helped me more than anyone. You didn't believe Althea Jarvis when she kept telling everyone I'd been raped. You didn't blame me for killing that man. You let me talk when I needed to, and that was more than—" Anna cut her sentence short. She didn't want Lydia to know how coldly Benjamin had treated her since her father's death. "Anyway, you've been very good to me and to Terence. I couldn't find a better friend anywhere."

"How is Terence?"

Anna was glad Lydia accepted the change of subject so easily. "He's doing much better than I expected. Did I tell you he ran for help that night?" When Lydia nodded, she continued. "Moss has been so good in helping Terence adjust to Papa's death. He agreed to stay with Terence in Papa's room, and he has even taken over some of Papa's chores. I don't think I could bear being alone in the tavern all night. With the good weather coming, travel will pick up and we'll have strangers in the tavern the rest of summer."

What she really wanted to say but couldn't, not even to her best friend, was that she hoped Benjamin would want to move the wedding date up and marry her so he could help her run the tavern. She had no problem in continuing with her own duties, but she had also taken on most of her father's responsibilities as well.

"Is there n-nothing I can do to ch-cheer you?"

"Just having you as my friend cheers me." A smile came once again to Anna's face. "I've written to Major John Andre. I haven't heard from him in several months now. But I know he will answer my letter, and he will make me feel better. He has such a nice way with words."

Lydia looked dreamily at Anna. "He is very h-handsome, and he does write beautiful p-poetry."

Anna walked from behind the bar to stand beside

Lydia. "The first time he came to the tavern, I was only twelve and I was enchanted by him. I remember Papa thought I was ill because I was so besotted."

"But now you have B-Benjamin," Lydia reminded her.

Anna took a deep breath and then grabbed her side, as pain reminded her how sore her ribs still were. She was certain she had a cracked rib.

"Yes, I have Benjamin," she answered, but she was beginning to doubt if even that was true.

Benjamin had been the most eligible man in their small community and she the most sought-after young lady when they'd become engaged last fall, shortly after Anna had turned eighteen. Benjamin was handsome and made a fair living. From the first time he'd come calling, the townspeople assumed they would marry. Benjamin's mother was the only one who didn't favor the prospect. Althea never had a kind word for her, although Anna had hoped that would change after they were married.

"M-Mama said I shouldn't tarry. I-I have to go. But don't s-send Terence with the letter when it c-comes."

Anna smiled. "No, I won't. I'm so glad you came." The two hugged, and Anna felt comfort from Lydia's light embrace.

"I'll be back in a c-couple of days."

Anna watched Lydia walk out the door and had started for the kitchen to help with the noonday meal when a stranger walked into the taproom. Anna tensed. He was a large man, taller than most of the men she knew. Her heartbeat quickened. Travelers were common at the tavern, but she still

23

hadn't recovered from the shock of being attacked.

The stranger's clothes were clean and expensive, and his face was handsome. A plain black ribbon held his queue in place at the back of his neck, but his brown hair wasn't powdered, and a frown marred his aristocratic features. Anna watched him take in every detail of her face. He was staring at her and she knew he was wondering how she had gotten the frightful bruise on her face. She was getting used to such prolonged looks, but that didn't mean she liked them.

Anna lifted her chin slightly. "May I help you?" She kept her voice steady, which helped her to shake the brief moment of unease.

"Yes," he answered as his blue eyes met hers. "I'm Jordan Kent. I was hoping you could tell me where to find Eli Dudley. I believe he's expecting me."

"Oh, yes, of course," she replied. This elegant man in cream-colored breeches and black leather boots with silver buckles running up the sides was no one to fear. "Reverend Jordan Kent. You're going to be our new minister."

"Yes, minister and *schoolmaster,*" he responded smoothly. "In his letter, Mr. Dudley suggested Lowell Tavern would be the best place for me to stay until I find permanent accommodations."

Anna wondered briefly why he emphasized the word "schoolmaster," but she soon forgot that because he was so handsome. There was nothing in his appearance to indicate he was a man of God. She knew it wasn't right for her to be so instantly attracted to this man—not when she was engaged to Benjamin.

"I just arrived in town. If you don't mind, I'd like to get settled before I see Mr. Dudley."

"Certainly. I was told to have your room ready. Just a moment." He was making her uncomfortable with his staring. "Let me call for someone to stay in here while I take you upstairs." Anna went to the door leading into the kitchen and called, "Moss? Terence?"

"They're both out chopping wood," Glynis, the tavern cook, called back.

"Then, Glynis, would you please come here?" Anna walked back to stand before the minister, noticing that his expression had softened. She tried to suppress the strange sensations that tightened her chest and affected her breathing when she looked at him. He was too appealing to be a minister, and she shouldn't be attracted to any man but Benjamin.

Glynis shuffled into the taproom, wiping her flour-covered hands on a long white apron. She was buxom, and her gruff voice matched her size. She seldom smiled, and Anna was sure it was because she had a front tooth missing.

"What can I do for you, Anna?" she asked.

"Would you please stay and watch the front while I show our new minister to his room?" she asked.

"I've bread in the oven." The heavyset woman continued to wipe her hands. Glynis didn't acknowledge the minister, but Anna thought nothing of it because she was a peculiar woman. She had worked at the tavern for a year and knew how to cook and clean, but she didn't say much.

"I won't be long." Anna held up the hem of her dark gray skirt and climbed the narrow stairs, acutely aware that the Reverend Kent was right behind her.

Three small bedrooms lay on each side of the staircase. The rooms on the right were kept for Anna, Terence, and Moss. The other rooms were for overnight travelers and boarders. How long, she wondered, would this latest boarder stay—this man who stood so close to her that she could feel his shallow breath on the back of her neck?

"Will this room do?" she asked, and stood aside to allow him entry. "It's a little bigger than the others." But standing beside the impressive man, Anna suddenly realized just how small the room really was.

She followed his gaze, looking over the room with him. A one-man bed with a lightweight quilt sat flush against the far wall. A pine chest, topped by a pitcher and basin, rested in one corner beneath a hand-sized wall mirror. Beside the chest stood a straight-backed chair. Curtains of coarse brown cotton fluttered around one tiny window.

"This will do quite well," he answered as he placed his satchel on the foot of the bed.

Anna took a step backward. She wished he wouldn't look at her as if he were trying to see inside her. "Meals are served all day. When you're ready to eat, just go to the kitchen and tell Glynis and she'll get you a plate."

"When do you eat?" he asked.

His question surprised her. "Ah—I usually eat twice a day—midmorning and early evening."

"By the looks of you, you've been missing a few meals."

Anna's back stiffened. She thought he was being

rather forward, for a minister. He was right, though. There was so much work to do she often didn't have time to eat.

He was making her nervous and she wanted to get away. "I'll leave you to get settled in. If you need anything, just let me know."

"Yes, there is something—I do a lot of writing, preparing for school and my sermons. Is there a small desk I could use, or perhaps a place where I might purchase one?"

"Oh, I'm sure I can find one for you. I'll see to it before the day's out." She backed out of the room and hurried down the stairs.

She heard the shakiness in her voice and knew why: the town's former minister had been older, and not pleasant to look upon, but this one was so handsome and appealing he had her heart hammering like an ironsmith and her stomach in knots.

As she rounded the corner of the taproom she saw Benjamin waiting near the door to the kitchen. He was impeccably dressed, as usual, his hair perfectly arranged. A smile brightened her face and lifted her spirits. His presence relieved some of the tension that had taken control of her body. She had seen Benjamin only once since her father's interment. At last he'd come to spend time with her, to comfort her.

She brushed a hand down her apron to smooth the wrinkles and said, "Oh, Benjamin, I'm so glad to see you."

He looked nervously toward the cook, then back to Anna, and asked, "Can we talk alone for a few moments?"

"Of course." Her heartbeat quickened, her eyes

widened. Perhaps he was finally going to tell her they would go ahead and be married before their wedding date. She turned to Glynis and quickly dismissed her with a thank-you.

When the cook was gone, Benjamin faced Anna. "I've made some decisions I think you should know about." He stood in a rigid stance in front of the fireplace, his hands clasped together behind his back. A worried expression creased his brow and thinned his lips.

"What, Benjamin? Tell me what you've decided." Pain returned to her side as her breathing increased in tempo. Why was he going about this so slowly?

Benjamin remained still, but looked away from her. "There's been a lot of gossip about you — us — for the past few days. What I'd like to do is put it all to rest as quickly as possible."

Anna's spirits soared, her throat went dry with relief. He was going to marry her. Thank God! "Yes, I'd like that, too."

He pursed his lips and started pacing back and forth the length of the fireplace. Abruptly, he stopped and said, "I think we should sell the tavern, find someone to care for Terence, and get married immediately."

Anna gasped, her eyes widening. "Sell the tavern? Find someone to care for Terence?" She took a step forward. "Benjamin, whatever do you mean? *I'll* care for him. He's my brother."

"I'm sorry, Anna." He finally looked at her, his deep-set eyes piercing her, his sharp nose flaring with each breath. "We simply don't have room for Terence at my house. I'm sure you have a relative who can take him in and care for him properly. I'll help you see to it."

This wasn't Benjamin talking; it was his mother. This was Althea's plan. Benjamin loved her and would never ask her to sell the tavern or give up Terence. Suddenly Anna felt dizzy and leaned against one of the low-backed armchairs that circled the tables in the taproom.

"Your mother told you to do this, didn't she?" Her breathing wasn't coming any easier, and the pain in her side seemed sharper.

"No," he said, but his voice lacked conviction, and he moved restlessly back and forth in front of the fireplace.

Anger replaced shock and coiled tightly inside Anna. "Your mother has never wanted us to marry. She's never liked me. She agreed to the marriage only because my father owned the tavern and she knew you'd get a large dowry."

Benjamin grabbed her shoulders roughly and Anna flinched as his fingers dug into her soft flesh. She was reminded of the man who had attacked her, and for a moment, she struggled to break away from Benjamin.

"That's not true. You know we have plenty. I don't need your dowry. The clocks I make sell very well in Philadelphia and Boston, and I now have a customer in New York."

"You can't ask me to give up the tavern or Terence. I thought you loved me."

"I do love you. Why else would I go against . . . why else would I marry you?"

His hands bit firmly into her arms, but Anna ignored the pain. "How can you expect me to give up my brother? He's all the family I have left."

29

"Mama and I will be your family." He tried again to persuade her. "We don't have room for Terence."

"We will if we live at the tavern after our wedding." Desperation caused her words to tumble swiftly from her lips. "Benjamin, I need you to help me manage the tavern. Terence is too young, and Moss is too old. With your help, I can make Lowell Tavern the best on the Boston Post Road."

"Manage the tavern?" Astonishment widened his brown eyes. His fingers tightened on her arms. "I don't know anything about the ins and outs of a tavern, Anna. I'm a clockmaker."

"You can learn." She clutched the front of his ruffled shirt and balled the material into her hands. She didn't like begging, but what else could she do? Her dreams were slipping away.

Benjamin jerked away from her and stepped back, his brown eyes searching her face. "Learn? To manage a tavern? No, I can't." He shook his head. "I simply can't. There's too much work to do here. Besides, I have three clocks under commission." Benjamin pressed the back of his hand to his lips and sighed.

"Yes, there's a lot of hard work, but I won't have to give up Terence if we live here." Anna rubbed her arms where Benjamin had held her.

The plea in her voice didn't go unnoticed as Benjamin's expression softened. He made an effort to smile as he took hold of her hand. "If we are to marry, you'll have to go along with what I say. You've just admitted you can't manage the tavern properly on your own, and I don't want any part of it. This is a prime location, and I'm sure we can

30

find a buyer quickly. Now, about someone to care for Terence—"

"Never!" Anna bolted away and turned on him with fierce anger. "I'll never give up Terence. How dare you ask me to give up the brother I've cared for since he was six months old? And this tavern was all Papa had to leave us. I won't sell what took him most of his life to acquire."

Benjamin was clearly surprised by her vehemence. His face whitened. It was obvious his mother hadn't told him what to say if Anna didn't agree to go along with his plan.

"Uh—well, you'll have to, if you want to marry me. There'll be no compromise in this matter, I assure you, Anna." He nervously pulled on the stiff cuff of his shirt sleeve.

Anna took a step toward him and Benjamin backed away. "If my brother is not welcome in your home, neither am I. Go tell your mother that."

"Leave my mother out of this," he said, regaining some of his self-confidence. "Don't be childish, Anna. Surely you're welcome, and so is Terence. We simply don't have room for him. We'll find him a good home, even if we have to use some of the money from the sale of the tavern."

Anna felt cold. Her anger turned to bitter disappointment. She'd known Benjamin was a weak man, but until now she hadn't known just how weak. She'd always thought she would have enough strength for them both, once they married. Now she knew his mother had influenced Benjamin's life too long; Anna knew she could never be happy with him.

In his own way, she knew Benjamin loved her. He

simply couldn't defy his mother. Anna lifted her shoulders, standing tall despite the protests of her bruised body. "I relieve you of your promise to marry me, Benjamin. Tell your mama that Terence and I don't need either one of you. We'll do quite well on our own. You can go now. We have nothing more to say to each other."

"Anna, this is madness. You can't continue to manage this tavern on your own. You're only eighteen. It's too busy. There's too much work to be done."

"I can and I will," she stated firmly. "It's not uncommon for a woman to manage a tavern."

"You're not a woman yet, Anna. You're still a girl. You can't make it on your own. Merchants will cheat you, customers will lie to you. Be sensible about this."

"I am being sensible. My father taught me well." She heard the unusual shrillness of her voice, and she continued to rub her arms. "I'll never do what you asked."

"What will you do if someone tries to rob you again?" he shot back quickly. "Will you kill again?"

Anna gasped. For a brief moment he had gotten the better of her. She brushed her hands down the front of her apron, waiting for her breathing to slow. "That bothers you, doesn't it? The fact that I killed that man."

"Of course it does. Doesn't it bother you?" he asked, his voice troubled.

"Very much," she answered quietly. She bit her bottom lip to keep it from trembling. "I didn't mean to do it. I only wanted to get away from him and tend to Papa." The fight had gone out of her. Without realizing it, Benjamin had let her know how he really felt. He hadn't forgiven her for killing that man. Although he didn't say the words, she read in his eyes that he didn't really want her for a wife, now that her reputation was blemished. She turned away from him.

"Anna, that man tried to rape you. He—put his hands all over you. Can't you see that it's not safe for you and Terence?"

She turned somber eyes on him, wishing he wouldn't remind her of that night. "We have Moss." A vision of Jordan Kent and how strong he looked flashed across her mind. "And the new minister is also living here now." She swallowed hard. "I'll be quite safe with both of them here."

"They will be no more protection than your father was. Don't act foolishly." Benjamin walked to the door, then turned around. "I'll give you a few more days of trying to run the tavern. I think you're going to change your mind about all this." He closed the door quietly behind him.

Cry. Yes, all she wanted to do was cry. For losing her father, for losing Benjamin, for killing that stranger. She walked to the bar at the far end of the taproom, plunked her elbows down on it, and rested her head in her hands. Why shouldn't she cry? She owed it to herself. She hadn't cried at her father's graveside services or later when she was alone. Surely if anyone deserved to cry it was she.

"Can you tell—"

"Oh!" Anna gasped, and spun around quickly, her heart pounding with fear. "How dare you sneak up on me."

Jordan's eyes questioned. "I didn't sneak up on you."

Anna held her side. "Yes, you did. My back was to you. I couldn't see you or hear you. Don't ever do it again!" Her outcry was harsh and accusing, but she couldn't help it. He'd almost caught her crying, and he'd nearly scared the breath out of her.

"I think you're overreacting. I walked into the room in a normal manner." His voice was gentle, and concern showed in his eyes.

Pressing the folds of her apron, Anna moved away from the imposing man. What had possessed her to speak to a minister in such a way? He hadn't really done anything wrong. How could she have yelled at the Reverend Kent?

"I'm sorry; please forgive me. I'm a bit jumpy these days."

"It's all right. No harm done. I'll remember to announce myself next time."

Why did he forgive her so easily? He should admonish her for the outburst and tell her to watch her tongue. Why did he look at her so closely? Surely he was used to the bruise by now. Others stared at first, but quickly became accustomed to it. And now it was fading, not as bad as a couple of days ago.

"Thank you," she murmured. "I'll see to it that I don't forget my manners again."

"As I said, no harm done." He smiled at her, and she warmed to him immediately. "If your father's around I'd like to talk with him about payment on my room."

She looked down at her hands. Too much had happened. She couldn't concentrate on figures right now. All she wanted was some time to herself. "My father died recently. Can we discuss payment later? I—I have several things to do. I d-don't have the time right now." What was wrong with her? This man had her stammering like Lydia.

"I'm sorry to hear about your father. Would you like to talk about it?"

His kindness renewed her anguish. Hadn't she wanted Benjamin to say those very words, to look at her this way, to make her feel the way this man did?

She lowered her lashes and shook her head. "No, thank you. Everything is fine."

"All right. If you can tell me how to get to Mr. Dudley's house, I'll be on my way."

"Anna, Anna!" Terence ran into the room, his long queue bouncing on his back. "There's a woman out by the garden. She wants to know if you will buy some berries from her."

"Terence, mind your manners," Anna reprimanded. She brushed loose hair away from his forehead and a smudge of dirt from his cheek before turning him to face the minister. "Reverend Kent, this is my brother, Terence." The two shook hands.

"I'm pleased to meet you, Terence."

"I'm pleased, too, sir." Terence's bright blue eyes shone as he looked up at the tall man.

"I was just asking your sister where Mr. Dudley lives. Do you suppose you could show me his house?"

"Certainly, sir." Terence spun toward his sister and asked, "May I?"

"Of course." Anna smiled and touched his cheek lovingly. Terence was a handsome child with a heart-shaped face, expressive blue eyes, and well-shaped lips. Circumstances had made her more of a mother to him than a sister, and she loved him dearly.

Anna glanced up at Jordan Kent and saw that he was watching her. She quickly turned back to Terence, but not quick enough to keep those warm feelings from curling inside her stomach.

"But you must come straight home afterward. Be sure to find me and let me know when you return so I won't worry about you."

Terence gave her a big smile and looked up at Jordan. "Do you have a horse?"

"Yes. He's tied out front."

"It's only a short walk to Mr. Dudley's house. I can stable your horse when I return, if you'd like?"

Jordan laughed lightly. "Yes, I would like that, Terence. His name is Thad. Talk to him gently and he will go with you without problem."

"Follow me, Reverend Kent." Terence ran out the open taproom door.

Jordan's gaze swept Anna's face once again. "Thank you for your help, Anna."

As he turned and hurried after her brother, Anna noticed the tapering width of his chest and broad shoulders beneath his black coat. She saw the proud tilt to his head and the gentle sway of his shoulders. Most of all, she liked the way he said her name, softly, with special emphasis on the first A.

When the door shut behind him she headed for the back of the tavern. She rubbed the tight muscles in her shoulders and the new sore spots from where Benjamin had gripped her arms.

There were too many things to deal with just

now, and the least of them should be the new minister. A woman wanted to sell her berries, Glynis needed help in the kitchen, and Anna's mind was waiting to mull over her conversation with Benjamin.

"Oh, God," she whispered to herself. "Why has everything suddenly gone wrong?"

Later that night, when Jordan had finished his notes on all the people he'd met during the day, he leaned back in his chair, propped his feet on the small desk that had been moved into his room sometime that afternoon, and sipped the brandy he'd hidden in his satchel. It'd been a long time since he'd drunk from a bottle, but he hadn't thought to ask for a cup. That wouldn't have been a good idea anyway. He didn't want it known about town that the new minister was drinking in his room.

Jordan wiped his mouth with the back of his hand. Levi Lowell was still at the top of his list, even though the man was now dead. He had to find out more about Levi's death. It could be connected to the mysterious John Anderson or a simple robbery which had turned into murder as the villagers believed. If Levi had been the contact person for the British, they'd be looking for someone to take his place. His daughter, Anna, would be a good choice.

Beside the tavernkeeper's name he'd written the words "beautiful, strong, sad." That nasty bruise on her face didn't hide her loveliness, and now that he knew how she'd been hurt, he had even more compassion, more admiration for her.

37

He'd been in town less than six hours but he'd heard Anna's story from three different people, each with a different account of what had happened in the tavern that night. He would probably get the most accurate story from Anna, but for the time being, he wouldn't press her to talk about it. Eventually he'd have to. If her father had been aiding the British, she might be approached to carry on his duties. For now, though, he felt comfortable dismissing her as the person he was looking for.

The next person he'd met was Glynis, the cook. He wasn't convinced she was as reserved as she seemed. He'd caught the sharp look she'd given Anna's back. Glynis was a Welsh name, and with the trouble England and Wales had been having, he doubted Glynis had any loyalty to the Crown. But he'd watch her just the same.

Moss was a man he felt comfortable eliminating. The old man had made it quite clear he had no love for the redcoats. Next on his list was Eli Dudley, the man Virgil had corresponded with about this position. As a trapper and a hunter he was definitely in a good position to gather information and pass it on to others. Jordan decided Eli was someone to watch carefully.

Then there was Althea Jarvis. Jordan grunted and took another sip from the bottle. After the hour he'd spent with the woman, it was easy to label her the town gossip. She could very well be the person he was looking for. She certainly seemed to know everything going on in and about town and could quite possibly be an informant.

Jordan stretched his arms up and over his head. The sound of loud talking, raucous laughter, and doors banging shut drifted up from below. Lowell Tavern was certainly a lively place for so early in the evening.

His thoughts drifted back to the owner of the establishment. When he had first seen her, he had immediately been filled with anger that someone had hit such a beautiful woman; then, when she'd reacted with such fear toward him, he'd been puzzled. Now he admired her. She'd killed the man who'd murdered her father and attacked her. And she continued to run the tavern. Most of the women he'd known could not have held themselves together after such an ordeal.

Yes, she was a beautiful woman, inside and out, and that made her dangerous. Jordan wasn't used to ignoring any woman he wanted, and in two seconds he'd known he wanted Anna Lowell.

Jordan let his feet fall to the floor with a thud and rose from the chair. He knew he should spend his evenings downstairs, getting to know the townspeople. The first thing he must do was get to know the regulars and determine which ones had sympathies for the British. Jordan didn't expect John Anderson to walk into the tavern and introduce himself. He was going to have to hunt for him.

A major battle had been fought a couple of years ago in nearby Danbury. It was a well-known fact that the area was crowded with loyalists. This community could have them, too.

Opening the small drawer of the desk, Jordan tucked his paperwork neatly inside and stored his bottle beneath them. It was time to start his first night as the local schoolmaster, minister, and spy.

The taproom was noisy, warm, and smoky when

39

Jordan walked in a few minutes later. He immediately spotted Anna, serving drinks to a table of men. Moss stood behind the bar, and Glynis carried plates of stew to a crowded table. Jordan pulled on the tail of his waistcoat, ran a finger down the collar of his shirt, and headed toward an empty chair at a table where three men sat. One of them he recognized as Parks Winchell, the ironsmith Moss had pointed out earlier in the day. Parks's house was the closest to the tavern. That in itself made the man a prime suspect.

"Do you mind if I join you, gentlemen?"

"Not at all, Reverend. Pleased to have you," Parks said.

Jordan cringed inwardly as he was introduced as the new minister. He'd never get used to the title, even though he knew the Bible as well as most men who had graduated from Harvard. He was also quick when it came to putting words together, one of his main assets as a teacher. Learning came easily to him.

He pulled out the chair and straddled it. Yes, he thought, with a little effort, he could fool the people of this town and have them believing he was called by God to preach the Lord's word — but he'd never like it. He'd need to watch his language, his drinking, and his comments. It wouldn't do for anyone to start thinking he was something other than what he appeared to be. He must listen carefully and commit everything to memory. The least bit of information could be his key to trapping the spy.

As he talked with the men at his table that evening, carefully questioning them about their lives, Jordan's gaze kept traveling back to Anna. He noticed she was careful not to make eye contact with the men she served, and she seldom conversed with customers. He liked her graceful walk. He wondered how her soft brown hair with its auburn glints would look, flowing down her back. Every time he'd seen her, all of it had been tucked in her cap. Her eyes were big, expressive, and blue as the sky at noon on a hot summer's day. She was thin, but now he knew why: she obviously worked too hard and ate too little. Maybe he could change that. He wouldn't mind at all having a meal with her in the early evenings before the tavern became busy.

Someone spoke his name and Jordan returned his attention to the small group of men. He had to be damn careful. The lovely tavernkeeper could very easily make him forget he was handpicked to find a spy and ordained to be the minister of this town.

Throughout the night Jordan made the rounds, talking to everyone at least once, making mental notes about each person he met. By the end of the night he was certain he'd succeeded in passing himself off as a true man of God. He was also confident that if the British had a spy stationed at Lowell Tavern, Jordan Kent would find him.

Chapter Three

Anna asked Moss to lock the doors when the tavern closed for the evening. She tried to be brave about most things, but the thought of going to the door when the taproom was empty was still too chilling for her. The memory of that horrible night faded a little more each day, but she was still fighting a fear of strangers.

"Another good night, Anna," Moss commented, handing her the money bag after he had secured both the front and back doors. "Your papa would be proud of you."

She held up the bag. "Yes, I can tell before I count it." She laid the pouch on the table by the candle. "I meant to go up and check on Terence earlier, but we were so busy I never had the time. Did you see him before he went to bed?"

"No, but he's a good boy. Don't have to worry about him," Moss said as he took off his soiled apron and threw it across the end of the bar. "He can put himself to bed. When he gets a little older, we'll have him staying up to help us until the last man is gone."

Anna smiled wearily and plucked her white cap off her head. "I know, he and I talked about that a couple of days ago. He's tired of helping only in the garden and the kitchen. He wants to work in the taproom." She pulled the pins from her hair and shook it out; it felt so good to set her hair free.

"In time. In time. The boy's trying to grow up too fast, now that his papa's gone." Moss looked at Anna and rubbed his bearded chin. "How long you going to stay up? You've been keeping some late nights."

Moss was right. She had been burning the candle way into the early morning. She could read very well, and her father had taught her a little arithmetic. But not enough, she'd quickly found out. She didn't have enough knowledge of book-keeping to continue her father's accounting system, so she was trying to come up with one of her own. She needed to keep track of the money that was earned and spent at the tavern each day to prove to Benjamin and Althea Jarvis that she didn't need anyone's help.

"Don't worry about me." She smiled to ease Moss's worried frown. "I'm doing very well. You go to bed, and I'll see you in the morning."

Anna pulled the account book from the top shelf behind the bar and sat down at one of the tables while Moss went up the stairs. First she poured all the money out on the table and began sorting the coins and making stacks so it would be easier to count. Then, she opened the jar of ink and the book. Looking at all the numbers in their columns, she resolved that Terence would go to school when the new teacher started his classes. She would gladly turn this part of managing the tavern over to her brother when he could do the job.

43

The new minister and schoolmaster . . . why did he come to her mind so easily and so vividly? She'd heard bits and pieces of conversations throughout the night and had learned that Jordan Kent wasn't married or betrothed. She smiled to herself. By tomorrow evening, every girl between the ages of twelve and twenty-five would be after him.

That thought brought Benjamin to mind. Now he was eligible, too. She closed her eyes tightly and let her head rest in her hand for a moment. She needed Benjamin to hold and comfort her, but everything he'd said that day had come straight from his mother's mouth. Althea must have realized she couldn't make her son or the town believe there had been a rape and had made those heartless stipulations before allowing Benjamin to marry.

To think that the woman wanted her to give up Terence! How could she be so cruel? But was all the blame Althea's? Benjamin was having trouble accepting the fact that she had a man's blood on her hands, and if someone as kind as Benjamin had trouble with it, others would, too. Her prospects for marriage didn't look promising.

With a sigh, she looked down at the ledger; she still had a lot of work to do before she could go to bed. The heat from the candle warmed her cheek as she bent over the book. She had to forget about Benjamin and his mother and concentrate on running the tavern properly. She'd show those two that she could do quite well without them.

"Anna."

Anna gasped and jumped, knocking over the stacks of coins on the table—some rolled to the floor. This was the second time today that Jordan

Kent had startled her. Was he a ghost, that he could come into a room so quietly? With trembling hands she pushed back her chair and turned angrily toward the intruder.

"I told you not to sneak up on me!" Her voice was louder than she had intended.

"I didn't sneak up on you. I called your name to let you know I was coming into the room." Jordan spoke calmly.

"You didn't call out soon enough. You nearly scared the life out of me. And for the second time, I might add."

"You're too jumpy. Have you got a guilty conscience?"

"What? Of course not! What are you talking about?" Her breathing didn't settle into its natural rhythm. He was too close, too tall, and too handsome. She took an unsteady step backward.

"It's been my experience that when people jump every time someone comes into a room, it's because they're doing something they shouldn't be doing and they don't want to get caught."

"That's absurd," she answered quickly. "I just get scared easily since . . ." She broke off her sentence when she noticed a smile twitching his lips and humor in his eyes. Humor? He was teasing her, and that angered her all the more. What right did he have to tease her over something that made her heart leap into her throat? His attitude was completely inappropriate for a man of God.

She brushed loose hair away from her face and ran a hand down her food-stained apron. She didn't have time for humor. There was nothing in her life to smile about.

45

"How *dare* you think it's funny to scare me." Her voice was raspy with indignation.

"Surely you don't really think I deliberately tried to frighten you." His voice was soft, his eyes sincere.

She had to forgive him, of course. It wasn't his fault that she was so jumpy. Anna rubbed her eyes and tried to calm her racing pulse. Her voice tight, she said, "Would you please shuffle your feet when you walk into the room, or loosen the buckles on your boots so that they rattle? Just please do not come up behind me."

The amusement had completely left his eyes as he walked closer. "Is that how the man who attacked you did it? Did he surprise you from behind?"

Memories filled her, and she shivered. "No. He knocked me to the floor—" She crossed her arms over her chest to ward off the offending chill. She looked up at him and saw understanding in his eyes. She softened. "I'm still so troubled about the whole thing. I don't think I'll ever feel safe again."

Jordan didn't take his gaze off her face as he reached up and caressed her bruised cheek. "Did he do this?"

"Yes," she answered, her breathing shallow her chest tight.

Jordan pulled her into his comforting arms and held her close to his chest. Anna relaxed against him. He was warm—no, hot. Strength emanated from him. His large hands rubbed up and down her back, instantly soothing her. She wanted to feel safe again. She laid her cheek against his chest, feeling the smooth material of his jacket, breathing in the heady male smell of him. Contentment surrounded

46

her, leaving her with the feeling that she belonged in his arms. Suddenly it occurred to her that she was receiving from him exactly what she'd wanted from Benjamin. Instead it was the minister who was giving her the solace she wanted and needed.

"Why don't you tell me what happened that night?" he whispered above her ear.

"No." She shook her head as she spoke. "I relive it every night in my dreams. I don't want to think about it." Anna trembled as the image of her father's still body flashed across her mind. She squeezed her eyes shut as once again she felt the sharp blow to her side and the burning pain under her eye.

"You needn't be frightened while I'm here," he whispered in her ear. "I sleep very lightly."

Anna knew he was comforting her the way a parent would comfort a child, but it felt like so much more to her. Why were thoughts of kisses and caresses entering her mind? Why did she want him to hold her tighter?

With the tips of his fingers, Jordan lifted her chin, tilted her head back, and placed a soft kiss on her forehead. At the touch of his cool lips on her hot skin, Anna twisted away from him. The candles were too low, the room too warm. Jordan Kent was too appealing, too kind; and she was too desperate for comfort.

"I'll have to remember that you sleep as lightly as you walk," she said.

He bent to pick up the few coins that had fallen to the floor. "I heard about your misfortune."

"Who told you?" she asked, but she was sure everyone he had met had related the sad story of poor Anna Lowell. Now that her engagement to Benjamin was broken, the gossip would be worse.

"If I had to guess, I'd say Moss supplied the most accurate account of what happened."

"Yes, Moss would have told only the facts," she answered, brushing at her hair, suddenly aware it was uncovered and hanging down her back. The gossips of the small community would have a lot to say about her if they could see her now.

"I'd like to hear the story from you. Did the man rape you?"

Anna turned away as she remembered the unfamiliar hands groping at her skirts. She squeezed her eyes shut for a moment and took a deep breath, determined to put all those feelings behind her. She looked back at Jordan Kent. "No," she answered in a steady voice. "But there are people in town who think he did."

"Your fiancé's mother?"

A bitter smile crossed Anna's lips. "I no longer have a fiancé. Althea Jarvis is a mean-spirited troublemaker. If you're not careful, she'll have you believing she's the only decent woman in this community."

He laughed lightly, with genuine amusement. Suddenly Anna found herself laughing, too. When was the last time she'd laughed, or even felt like laughing? And why was she laughing about the woman who'd ruined her wedding plans?

She sobered. "I guess talk like that doesn't make me sound very Christian."

"I think it makes you sound very strong, and I like that."

48

Anna glowed from his praise. "Thank you, Reverend Kent."

He cleared his throat and looked at the book on the table. "What are you working on?" he asked.

"The accounts," she said softly, and yawned, even though she tried to suppress it. She hadn't realized just how tired she was until the brief moments Jordan had held her. It was as though she'd rested more in those few moments than in the past ten days. With drooping eyelids she looked down at all the work that still lay ahead of her.

"Why don't I help you?" he asked, adding the coins in his hands to the ones on the table.

Anna noticed that no two coins jingled together. He spoke quietly and walked softly. Even when she'd lost her temper he'd remained calm and hadn't gotten upset. What an odd man he was.

She looked up at his face and studied it. His eyes were a beautiful shade of blue, not unlike her own. His nose was straight and well defined; his jawline showed strength. He was clean-shaven which she liked very much, and she especially liked the fact that he didn't powder his hair. What was she doing? It seemed wrong to notice so many things about him. If Benjamin rejected her because she had blood on her hands, so would all other men, including the new minister.

"I'm very good with figures," he said when she didn't answer his question. "Together we can get this finished quickly and you can be off to bed."

She blinked a couple of times to clear her head. He was merely being kind, and here she was, having thoughts that bordered on impure.

"I hate to admit this, but I'm not good with

49

sums. I know very little beyond adding and subtracting."

He smiled at her and she was certain her heart jumped in her chest. She shouldn't have those kinds of feelings for him when she had been so recently engaged to Benjamin. He was just being nice. Jordan was a minister, for heaven's sake! It was his job to offer comfort and to make her feel better.

"I'd be happy to teach you what you need to know."

"Oh, no, I couldn't impose on your time. I'm going to send Terence to your school when it starts so he can learn how to do this properly."

Jordan gathered the money together and put it back in the leather pouch. "You need help now, not a year from now." He gave her the bag. "It's too late to begin tonight. We'll start tomorrow evening."

"Ah—are you sure?" she asked. "I don't want to keep you from your work." But the thought of learning the proper way to keep the books appealed to her.

"It is my work. I'm a teacher," he answered.

She smiled, feeling relieved to know she would learn how to do the book work. "Thank you, Reverend Kent."

He cleared his throat. "Please, just call me Jordan."

"Oh, I couldn't do that. It wouldn't be proper," she answered.

He placed a hand on her shoulder and she didn't flinch. "I insist. My students will call me Mr. Kent. My congregation will call me Reverend Kent, but my friends call me Jordan."

"All right, I accept your offer of help, Jordan."

He picked up the candle. 'Good. We'll start to-morrow night after the tavern is closed."

They walked up the stairs together. Anna's step was as light as Jordan's.

Anna shook out the wet sheet and threw it over the cord her father had stretched between two small trees. It was a warm and sunny Sunday morning, a perfect day to do the tavern's washing. The Lord's day was always quiet because most of the people of Georgetown went to church. There would be those who frowned on her for working instead of going to the services, but she was getting used to the idea of the town gossip being centered on her. Word had gotten out that her wedding had been called off, and once again everyone must be speculating about that. No doubt they'd think washing bedclothes on a Sunday was bound to bring more ill-favor from God.

The last few days had been easier to bear because Anna had spent the late evenings with Jordan. It surprised her how quickly she had started looking forward to their time alone. Since that first night when he'd held her and comforted her, she'd been careful to see that not even their fingers touched when they were working on the books.

Lydia and Terence were the only ones who had questioned her at length about the broken engagement. Terence had said he was glad because he'd never liked Benjamin anyway. Lydia tried to tell her that Benjamin still loved her and in time would defy his mother to marry her and live at the tavern. Anna didn't think so. Benjamin had made it quite clear to her that he would not be an innkeeper and

51

the tavern would have to be sold if they married. And she knew how deeply disturbed he was about the fact that she'd killed a man.

"Anna! Anna!" Lydia called as she came running out of the back door and hurried down the steps. She was breathless when she made it to where Anna was standing, but managed to ask, "W-Why didn't you t-tell me the Reverent Kent was s-so handsome?"

"I was—"

"Oh, I-I know," Lydia interrupted her. "You've had s-so much on your m-mind with all that's h-happened to you."

"Slow down, Lydia, and catch your breath."

Lydia took a deep breath and smiled. Her big brown eyes sparkled. "I'm sorry. I was s-so excited."

"It's all right. Now, what's this you want to tell me about the new minister being so handsome?"

"You p-poor dear, you haven't even noticed him, h-have you?"

Anna started to say, "Of course I have. I'd have to be blind not to," but decided to agree with her friend. "I have been busy. How was his sermon?"

Lydia's lashes fluttered and her eyes rolled heavenward. "He was wonderful. His voice is s-soft and s-soothing. He didn't yell and—and shout, like most preachers do."

Anna imagined Jordan standing in front of the congregation, speaking in that smooth tone she'd come to recognize and respect. A stab of disappointment pierced her. She'd never get to hear him. She had too much work to do. When her father was alive they had tried to go to services each week, but now she had scarcely enough time for eating and sleeping. Church was out of the question.

"Papa s-said we could invite him for lunch n-next week, but he's already received invitations for two — two months of Sundays."

Lydia's news made Anna feel better. Apparently she wasn't the only one who was infatuated with Jordan. An unmarried minister was always the most eligible man in any town. The fact that he was young and handsome, too, only sweetened the pot.

"Well, I'm sure you'll get your chance to entertain him."

Lydia helped Anna stretch another wet sheet over the line and sighed. "B-by the time I get to visit with him he will already have his eye on — on all the pretty girls in town."

"That's nonsense. You're a lovely young lady. Haven't I told you many times?"

"Oh, A-Anna, you know that's not true. My front teeth s-stick out and my eyes are t-too big for the rest of my face, and — and I stutter."

"To me, Lydia, you are lovely. And whoever marries you will be the luckiest man in town."

"Thank you, Anna." She smiled and took another sheet out of the basket. "Benjamin was at ch-church. He didn't look very h-happy."

Anna's stomach muscles tightened. The sun was suddenly too bright, and she looked away from Lydia. "I don't suppose he is. He lost the money he could have gotten from selling the tavern."

"You sh-should be ashamed of yourself," Lydia reprimanded. "H-he only said what his m-mother told him to say and — and you know it, Anna Lowell."

Anna remained quiet. Lydia was quiet. But Anna

53

was beginning to realize she didn't need a man who couldn't speak up for her or for himself.

Later that night after Terence and Moss had gone to bed, Jordan and Anna went over her lessons. She was surprised and pleased at how much she had learned in only a few days.

"You're easy to teach, Anna, a perfect student," Jordan said, as he pushed the book aside.

She smiled at his praise. Their time alone had become so special she hated for it to end each evening. Even though she found the sessions disturbingly intimate, she tried to convince herself he wasn't doing anything for her he wouldn't do for others.

"Before Papa was killed, we were planning a trip to New York to buy directly from the merchant ships. When I learn a little more, I might make that trip myself."

"It's not a good time for a woman to travel alone, Anna, even for so short a trip as New York. Why not Boston? It would take longer to get there, but you wouldn't pass British lines."

"Papa always said the best ships are in New York. Besides, I'm not afraid of the British," she answered quickly.

He smiled. "I can see that." He leaned over the table and placed his hand over hers. His eyes caressed her face. "Your strength is one of your most admirable qualities."

His words made her breath grow short, his touch made her skin tingle. Jordan was a man and she was a woman, and his position in the town couldn't change what was happening between them.

"You have kept your wits about you when so

many other women would have faltered beneath the load you've had to bear."

His mouth was beautiful, she noticed, even though she was sure she shouldn't have. She wanted to feel his lips on hers just once, to feel that pressure. She wanted to feel her body pressed against his. Abruptly she pulled her hand from his and stood up. What was she thinking? This constant attraction to Jordan had to cease.

"It's late. We should be going to bed," she said hastily.

"Wait, Anna, before you go."

She faced him. Her heart pounded against her ribs. Tension knotted in her throat and stomach. She knew what he was going to do, and she wanted him to do it. "I don't think I should stay," she murmured.

"Why not? Because I want to kiss you?"

"Yes," she answered.

"You're right, I shouldn't kiss you. I've been fighting it all week, telling myself not to touch you." He moved closer. "You could prove fatal to my mission here."

"I know," she whispered.

"I don't want to frighten you."

Anna looked into his beautiful blue eyes. "You're not," she answered, and found herself leaning toward him.

Jordan slowly slid his arms around her waist and gently pulled her up against him. The brush of his lips against hers was so warm and sweet her objections faded away.

He raised his head and asked, "Did you like that?"

With her heart thumping wildly in her chest, Anna nodded.

"This time, open your mouth like this." He showed her how to form a flat O with her lips before kissing her again.

His lips were cool, springy. Ooohh, it was good. Anna sighed contentedly. Her hands went around his neck, and his hands slid up her back. The kiss deepened as he slipped his tongue into her mouth. Benjamin had kissed her, but it had never been like this!

Jordan tugged the cap off her head and dug his fingers into the fullness of her hair as it uncoiled down her back. His lips moved softly, sweetly, cautiously over hers.

A loud knock on the tavern startled them. Jordan felt Anna tense immediately, but he continued to hold her as her eyes widened with fear.

"Don't be frightened," he whispered, brushing her hair away from her face. "I'm sure it's only a traveler wanting a bed for the night."

"Don't open it. Maybe he'll go away," she said breathlessly.

He touched her cheek as he took a step away from her. He had to recover quickly, and to do that he had to put distance between them.

"It will be all right, Anna," he soothed her. "I'm here. Nothing's going to happen to you. I promise."

Jordan brushed back his hair and straightened his shirt. He was glad the knock had come. Damn, he'd been careless. A few more minutes with the beautiful tavernkeeper and he would have taken her to bed and blown his cover. He had an important mission, a dangerous one, and he'd been irresponsible. Washington had handpicked him because he was trustworthy. His lack of self-control when it came to this woman worried him. He wouldn't slip again. He'd make damned sure of that.

The brass knocker sounded again. Jordan threw the latch and opened the heavy door only to be rudely brushed aside by a young British officer, who looked him over from head to toe, then swept the rest of the room with a guarded glance. The man's long red-lined cape flared out behind him as he strode with two lesser-ranking officers into the dimly lit room. In one swift movement he swept his cocked hat off his head and threw it across the room.

"John!" Anna squealed as she ran and jumped into the man's outstretched arms. He swung her around, kissing each cheek several times.

"Anna, my lovely young lady, what took you so long to answer?"

"Had I known it was you, I would have run to the door," she replied, delight in her voice. "I'm so glad you came to see me. I wrote to you. Did you get my letter?"

"Of course, milady, that's why I'm here. But a short visit it'll have to be. Many things are happening at this time. But we'll talk of that later. Let me look at how beautiful you've become."

Jordan watched Anna's long, shimmering hair fanned out over her back as the soldier's arms circled her small waist. A knot of jealousy formed inside Jordan. What the hell was this redcoat doing with his hands all over Anna? His hands made fists at his sides, and he took a step toward the enemy.

With the force of a bullet, reality hit him. No, it

couldn't be. But what else? Anna was in the arms of a major in the British Army. A redcoat, for God's sake! He turned away in anger and his fist hit the door. Anna Lowell was the spy he was looking for.

Chapter Four

Anna laughed as John Andre swung her around yet again before setting her on her feet and kissing both cheeks affectionately. She'd been certain he would come to see her, and he hadn't let her down. In all the years she'd known him, he'd been the gentlest, the most understanding of men.

John squeezed her hands and chuckled, looking directly into her eyes, for they were of the same height. "Let me look at you. How beautiful you've become in less than a year."

She smiled, her spirits soaring from his flattering words. "Take off your cloak. I'll get ale for you and your men," she said breathlessly, wanting this moment to go on forever.

"A pint for my men, if you don't mind, Anna. They'll camp out with the horses." He swung his long black cape off his shoulders and draped it across a chair.

"Surely not. I have empty rooms," she argued.

"Your kindness is appreciated, but we'll all feel safer this way. It was easy to slip into Connecticut from White Plains because the woods are dense and the border is poorly patrolled, but now that we're here, we must be cautious." John smiled and reached for her hands, kissing first one and then the other before letting go of her and stepping away.

Brushing her long hair away from her shoulder, Anna swooped down. She picked up her cap and stuffed her hair underneath it once more. As she turned away to walk behind the bar to get the ale, she saw Jordan standing in the dim shadows of the taproom doorway, watching her, his face twisted into an angry scowl. Apparently realizing she'd caught sight of him, his expression changed abruptly before he turned away and shut the door. He didn't have to say a word. She knew what his look meant. Jordan was not happy that she had a British soldier for a friend.

Another thought struck her. The way she'd responded to Jordan's kisses washed over her in an embarrassed wave, and she quickly bent behind the counter to get a jug for John's men. Maybe the fervent embrace they'd enjoyed mere moments ago now was a source of embarrassment to him. Heat rushed to her cheeks and her face flushed with color. Her stomach rolled and quaked.

In God's name, what must he think of the way she'd responded to him and then rushed from his arms into those of another man? What a wanton he must have assumed her to be. He didn't know that Andre was an old friend, a childhood friend. She couldn't explain the abandoned way she'd shared Jordan's kisses, but surely he'd understand the friendship.

Anna set the pint on the counter and pushed it

toward the two lesser-ranking officers who still stood beside John. As she handed them the small clay jug, one of the men thanked her, and after a courtly nod to John, they headed for the door, which Jordan quickly opened once again.

After he'd shut and latched the door behind the soldiers, Jordan turned back to Anna and John. He stood rigidly, his eyes squinting in the feeble light of the lantern and lowering candles.

"Reverend Kent, please come join us." Anna took a deep breath before continuing. Her voice wasn't as strong as she'd wanted it to be. "I'd like to introduce a dear friend of mine, Major John Andre." She looked back at John. "John, this is the Reverend Jordan Kent."

While there was no open hostility between the two men, John and Jordan merely nodded their greeting as Jordan walked over to the bar to stand beside the shorter, impeccably uniformed man.

"I was going to pour wine for John. Will you join him in a bit of wine or ale?"

"Yes, wine, thank you, Anna," Jordan's voice was so pointedly polite it chilled her to the bone.

The two men, standing elbow to elbow, nearly covered the length of the bar. Anna was still shaken by the powerful kisses she'd shared with Jordan, and by his obvious disapproval of her friendship with John. She shouldn't have been surprised. In recent years, not many people in Georgetown had approved of her father's serving British soldiers when they came into town, but John had been a friend since '72, when he was touring the colonies and by chance spent the night at Lowell Tavern. Anna had been only twelve at the time, but she and the young and handsome British soldier had corresponded every few months since then, and John usually managed a visit at least once a year.

With his letters, John would sometimes send her a copy of a poem he'd written. She always shared them with her father and Lydia. On one occasion, he enclosed a sketch of himself which she still kept in a small tin box under her bed. She didn't think of John as a British soldier. He was a gentleman, and that was the only thing that was important.

Anna looked from Jordan to John as she placed clean pewter mugs on the counter. Instead of the ale she'd given John's men, she reached for her father's jug of elderberry wine. When she pulled the cork from the neck, the potent scent drifted through the room and mixed with the smell of burned wood and tallow. She tentatively looked from one man to the other while she poured, not sure where the conversation would go from here.

"John, how long will you be staying?" she asked, when it appeared the two men were not going to look at each other, let alone speak.

"It would not be wise to stay too long away from the safety of White Plains. I ride early on the morrow," John answered. "I was saddened by the news of the death of Levi, a good man, and a good father to you. I know you miss him, and so shall I."

"Yes," she answered, looking into his eyes, reading and appreciating the sincerity she found there.

John's voice was gentle as he said, "When I received your letter telling of Levi's death, I knew it would be risky to come to you, but I had to take the chance. If only for so short a time."

She smiled, then reached over and covered the back of his hand with hers. "I knew you would come."

John was handsome in his white ruffled shirt, his tan breeches and waistcoat and his scarlet-red coat with its many brass buttons and gold roping attached to the shoulders. She noticed that he drank the sack quickly while Jordan looked on broodingly, seldom taking his eyes off the soldier.

"You're up late," John said. "A busy night?"

"Reverend Kent is helping me with the accounts." She motioned to the papers and money bag that still lay on the table by a lighted candle. "Papa had taught me a little, but I soon found out that I didn't know enough to run the tavern properly."

John turned to Jordan. "How kind of you to teach a woman."

"Anna is very intelligent." Jordan's eyes narrowed and he leaned a hip against the bar. "She catches on quickly."

In two more sips the wine was gone from John's cup, but Anna realized that Jordan still hadn't touched his. When he reached for the cup, she noticed that he suddenly withdrew his right hand and looked at it, flexing his fingers as he brought it back to his chest. His knuckles were red, swollen, and scraped as if he'd hit something hard. She wondered what had happened. Surely she would have noticed the scratches when they were working on the figures if they had been there. As she glanced up at his face he saw her looking at his hand and quickly dropped it to his side, lifting the wine in his left hand.

Turning her attention to John, she asked, "Shall I

fill your cup again?" The silence that had fallen on the threesome was so awkward.

"No, milady. It was a long, hard ride to get here tonight, and it's late. We'll talk on the morrow. Come show me where I'm to lay my head."

"Of course," she said as she replaced the cork, leaving the jug on the counter.

"Go ahead and take care of your friend," Jordan told her as she moved from behind the bar. "I'll finish my wine and be up shortly. Don't forget to take the money with you. I'll take care of the candles for you and put the account book away."

His eyes were so cold, Anna felt chilled. "Thank you," she mumbled, her voice scratchy.

"It was indeed a pleasure to meet you, Reverend Kent. Shall I see you tomorrow?"

"Perhaps, Major Andre, perhaps."

Anna didn't like going to bed knowing Jordan was angry. She'd try to explain everything tomorrow.

Jordan hurried over to the bottom of the stairs and listened to the muted voices as Anna and the major climbed the stairs. Their conversation seemed harmless enough, but no doubt they'd have plenty of time tomorrow morning to exchange information while he was at the meetinghouse, preaching to the people of Georgetown. Major Andre must have been certain the inn was a safe haven or he'd never have taken a chance on leaving the safety of the British-held White Plains to come here.

When he heard both doors close upstairs, Jordan walked over to the bar and picked up his wine with his left hand. His right hand throbbed and ached from the blow he'd given the door. It was unlike him to be so emotional. He flexed his fingers and winced. He didn't think he'd broken a bone, but the hand would give him trouble for a few days.

Jordan rested both elbows on the bar. It was unbelievable! Sir Henry Clinton's adjutant was right here in the same tavern with him. Damn it! Virgil was right. Lowell Tavern had a direct line to General Clinton's headquarters in New York. He hadn't thought it was going to be so easy to find the spy. And damn, he didn't want it to be Anna, but what else could he think? He remembered the kisses they'd shared just moments before the major had swept into the room and lifted her in his arms. She was an innocent; he was sure of that. What was her relationship with Andre?

The wine was suddenly bitter on his tongue, and he scrubbed his lips with the back of his hand, hoping to erase the sweet taste of Anna. He was too smitten by her beauty and her strength to be objective. He had to get hold of himself immediately and sort out the facts.

First, Anna had admitted sending a letter to Andre and he had admitted receiving it. Could Andre be John Anderson? But the dates didn't match. The letter Virgil told him about had been intercepted before Levi was killed. If Anna's letter mentioned her father's death, as she'd indicated, the letters couldn't be the same.

Jordan flexed his swelling fingers and winced. He took another sip of wine. It appeared that his original assumption that John Andre was also the John Anderson he was looking for was not correct. Unless Andre's purpose here was twofold. Maybe he was here to see Anna as Andre and here as John

Anderson to see someone else. That was possible.

Andre was sure to be gone tomorrow by the time he finished the church services and dinner at Elder Beacon's house. In fact, if Andre was smart, he'd be heading back to British lines by first light. Jordan popped the cork on the wine and refilled his cup before putting the jug away. He knew he could not sleep tonight knowing that Andre was in the tavern, knowing that the woman he'd so recently held in his arms could be the spy he'd been sent to find.

He picked up a chair and carried it over to the bottom of the stairs, so that he could sit and watch the door Andre had entered. No one would come or go from Andre's room tonight without Jordan's knowing about it.

Anna was up early the next morning, eager to get some of her chores finished so she'd have more time to spend with John. As she started down the stairs, she saw Jordan placing a chair under one of the tables in the taproom. She noticed that his clothes were rumpled, his hair was uncombed, and his eyes were red, as if he'd been up all night.

She was still a little embarrassed by her passionate response to him last evening. What he must think of her she could only guess. If there was any way to hide from him, she would, but that was impossible. She wanted to tell him she'd only been seeking his comfort and she hadn't intended to be so . . . forward. How could she explain that when she didn't really understand it herself?

Her father's death had left her lonely and in need

of many reassurances. But she should have realized that Jordan wasn't the one to give that kind of comfort. She had to explain that she was only taking from him what she'd needed from Benjamin and hadn't received.

"Good morning," she said as she entered the taproom.

"Good morning, Anna." Jordan merely glanced at her as he cleared his throat and smoothed his hair with the palm of his hand.

She looked him over again and asked, "Why are you up so early?"

"I needed to work on my sermon," he answered, and turned to look at her.

Anna's heart quickened. Should she apologize? No, that could make matters worse by further embarrassing both of them. But she couldn't live with herself until she said her piece and got it over with. She walked farther into the room, aware that Jordan's presence reminded her of his touch, his scent, his taste, his sweet words.

"I'm most grateful for the comfort you gave me last night."

Jordan's eyes narrowed considerably. "So this morning it's comfort I was offering you last night, not passion?"

She gasped at his bold statement. His tone left no doubt that he was still angry with her. Stunned, she turned away from him.

"So much has happened in the past two weeks," she said stiffly. "Papa's death and my broken engagement to Benjamin have left me distraught and as ill-tempered as a shrew. I needed someone to hold and comfort me. I wanted to feel safe again.

67

Benjamin didn't—" She met his eyes and saw the anger was still there, so she stopped. Why would he be interested in her problems?

"You mean to say the reason you responded to me the way you did last night was that you were thinking of Benjamin?"

Suddenly she realized he'd given her the perfect explanation for her behavior. Benjamin hadn't crossed her mind last night, but maybe it was best to let him think that. If she let him believe she was using him as a substitute for Benjamin, surely he'd understand her reaction to him. She knew it wasn't right to mislead a man of God, but what else could she do? How could she tell him when he'd touched her last night she'd wanted to melt into his embrace and never leave him?

No, she had to accept all fault and leave him blameless . . . and hope God would forgive her.

"Yes," she whispered, and lowered her lashes over her eyes. "I know it's unforgivable but I pray your forgiveness anyway. I simply wasn't myself last night."

"It's all right. I understand."

Jordan turned away. He thought he'd been the one to arouse the spark of passion that had flared in her last evening. Hearing her admission was like being hit with a pan of cold water.

Hell and damnation! She was a bewitching little devil. If he didn't know better, he'd think she'd been paid to distract him from his real purpose. It didn't do anything for his manhood to hear she'd been thinking of Benjamin Jarvis when he'd held her and kissed her. But it was just as well, he thought, as he stood in front of the fireplace. This was one woman he couldn't have. He had enough confidence in himself to know that with more time he could have made her forget Benjamin, but there was no way in hell he was going to take a British sympathizer to his bed. It was time to forget about her as a woman and think of her only as a suspect. He would forget how naturally she fit in his arms, how eagerly she responded to his kisses, how even now he wanted to hold her once again.

"I'll go make tea and bring you a cup," she said softly.

"Yes, do that," he murmured.

Jordan had no intention of leaving the taproom as long as Moss and Terence were still upstairs. He really didn't believe Moss was connected to Andre, but he had to be sure Moss didn't stop by the major's room on his way downstairs.

Anna hurried into the kitchen and lit a candle that sat on the middle of the table and stoked the fire in the fireplace. Out of habit, she unlocked the door for Glynis, who lived in a small one-room house a short distance away from the tavern.

Next, she filled a pot with water and added a sprinkling of her own mixture of tea leaves before hanging it over the fire to brew. She sliced a loaf of bread Glynis had baked the day before and placed it in the middle of the table. Then she took out some freshly churned butter and a jar of figs she'd picked and packed in sugar a week ago. A few moments later she heard Moss and Terence talking as they shuffled into the kitchen.

"Morning," she said, and each answered her greeting with a mumbled one of his own.

"Did you hear our late-night caller, Moss?" she

69

asked, as she took the ingredients out of the safe to make bread for the day.

"I didn't," Terence answered, taking a slice of bread and smearing it with creamy butter.

"She didn't ask you," Moss scolded the boy before answering Anna, then bent over the fire to check the tea. "I heard the knock and voices. My old bones were so weary I stayed in bed. I knew you'd be all right with the Reverend Kent close by, so I didn't get up to help. Who did we pick up so late in the night?"

"Major John Andre has come for a short visit."

"Did you let that redcoat in the tavern? Is he upstairs?" Moss frowned as he hooked his thumbs under his waistband and lifted his breeches higher.

"John is a friend. He has always been welcome at Lowell Tavern, and always will be. My father's death won't change that," she answered quickly.

Moss sniffed and rubbed his nose on the sleeve of his shirt, his small eyes squinting. "Serving a redcoat was fine, as long as your pa was alive to look after you. But now that he's gone, you can't go around taking in British soldiers. The townspeople won't like it at all. Most of them have sons, brothers, or fathers helping Washington. They won't take kindly to sympathizing with the Crown. Mark my word, it won't be safe for any of us."

"He only came for a visit to offer comfort because I wrote and told him about Papa."

"It's my guess he stopped by only because he was in the area doing mischief and needed a free bed."

Anna gasped and clutched her apron with cold fingers. "That's a horrible thing to say."

"I'm sure it's the truth, Anna," the old man said

with conviction. "Someone has probably already seen the redcoats and is on his way right now to find the nearest group of militia to come capture them." Moss combed his beard with his fingers. "And they'll take us, too."

"No one will hurt Anna, Moss. I'll protect her," Terence said with confidence as he wiped butter from the edge of his mouth with the back of his hand.

Anna rested her hand on her hip and gave Terence a stern look. "No one needs to protect me. I can take care of myself. And so can Major Andre." Anna held out a basket. "Go gather the eggs."

"Glynis is supposed to gather them," Terence answered, refusing to take what she offered.

"She's late and I need the eggs. I have too many things to do today. I can't wait for her to get here. Go." Anna's tone wasn't sharp, but she didn't intend for Terence to argue with her again.

"All right." Terence took the basket from her and left, slamming the door on his way out, making the whole kitchen shake.

Moss took a clean apron from the nail where it hung beside the butterfly shelves and tied it around his waist? "Anna, I've got to make you see the folly in continuing to associate with redcoats. People aren't as tolerant of the British as they used to be. Too many good men have died. It won't be long before you're called a loyalist or a Tory, and that'll have your pa turning over in his grave and you run out of town."

"But I'm neither, Moss, and you know it. I hope the Colonies win the concessions they seek from the British. And you know, we don't get many soldiers

71

in here anymore. John is a friend of the family's. That's not going to change."

"We're fighting for more than concessions now, Anna. We want independence. It's a bloody war!"

"I know . . . I know how terrible it is." She sighed. "Moss, I don't approve of British rule, either. I don't like the taxes and laws England imposes on us any more than you do. But my friendship with John doesn't have anything to do with politics. We've never talked about war or battles or any of those things. We talk about poetry. He shows me his drawings and his writings. I don't want to know about his life as a soldier."

The heavy back door swung open and Glynis stepped inside. Anna's temper was already frayed, and she was ready to reprimand the cook for being late, but when she looked at Glynis, she couldn't. The woman's sun-faded dress hung loosely on her large frame, her fichu draped carelessly about her shoulders. Windblown strands of light brown hair showed from underneath her cap, and her cheeks were flushed from her morning walk.

Anna's heart went out to the careworn woman. "Good morning, Glynis."

"Morning." Glynis nodded to Moss, then glanced back to Anna. "You have two redcoats camping in your barn."

The cook's tone wasn't accusing, but having just defended herself to Moss, Anna wasn't in a mood to take on Glynis, too. "I'm aware of their presence, and it's nothing you should concern yourself with."

"Don't plan to," Glynis mumbled and reached for her apron. "I expect you'll take care of them, as always."

A sharp retort burned on Anna's tongue, but she held it. Glynis had never been downright disrespectful, but she had come close many times. Deciding to ignore her comment, Anna said, "I've already sent Terence after the eggs. You can bring in enough wood for the day while I skim the cream off the milk."

Anna waited until Glynis left before she lifted the churn onto the table and carefully placed a pail of milk beside it so as not to mix the cream and milk again. Slowly she peeled the cheesecloth off the pail and looked at the thick cream; its rich color promised it would make delicious butter. She dipped the ladle into the liquid and poured it directly into the churn.

"I told you the town wouldn't like that redcoat staying—"

"Shh—" she whispered, and turned to Moss. "I hear someone coming. It may be John." She picked up an empty bucket and shoved it toward him. "Go milk the cows. I'll have Terence bring you a cup of tea when it's ready."

"Good morning to you again, Anna, Moss." Jordan said as he strode into the kitchen, his Bible in his hand.

Jordan had stood at the door and listened to Anna and Moss's conversation. He was convinced Moss had nothing to do with Andre's presence, and Anna had done a good job of defending herself. If he hadn't seen her in Andre's arms, he'd have believed every word she said. Her actions belied her words.

"The tea's not ready," she told Jordan as she continued the skimming.

"I'll wait," he answered. "I have some last-minute preparations to do before services today. Will you be joining us?" he asked.

She glanced up at him. "Oh, no, I can't," she murmured. "I know it's not right, but I have too much work to do here." She quickly looked away.

"Anna reads her Bible, Reverend."

Anna liked the way Moss took up for her. It was a small thing, but she appreciated it very much. Moss never went to church, although he seemed to be a religious man. He'd use strong language occasionally and didn't mind arguing to prove his point, but she'd never known him to cheat anyone.

"I'll go start the milking while that tea brews. Have the boy bring me a cup when it's ready," Moss said, as if the idea had been his own, and walked out the door.

With Moss gone, Jordan took the opportunity to question Anna about Andre. "Was your father a Loyalist?" he asked.

"No," she answered, confusion showing in her eyes.

"A Tory?"

"Of course not. Whatever gave you that idea?" Anna walked over to the fire and using the tail of her apron to wrap the hot handle, picked up the pot and poured tea into the cups. "He frequently gave food and money to the militia who camp around our town. When Lyon raided Danbury, he sent most of our supplies up to the battlefield to help the Continental Army." She hung the pot back on the rack, and pushed a cup toward him. "He's never helped the British in any way."

Jordan watched her carefully, feeling certain she

74

was telling the truth. "If that's the case, Anna, I'm confused about the presence of Major Andre. I don't understand your association with the British officer."

"John Andre?" She took a deep breath. First Moss, then Glynis, and now she had to suffer the questions of Jordan Kent. It was her own business whom she welcomed into the tavern. She would not answer any more questions about her friend.

"I'm afraid this is one subject that is none of your concern. My relationship with John is not one I care to discuss with you or anyone." She went back to skimming the cream.

Jordan winced inside. She didn't know it, but her words were confirming his suspicions. Not wanting to talk about Andre was a sure sign she was hiding something. But what? Was she merely a pawn who passed information from one hand to another? As he watched and listened, he still found himself wishing someone else had been seen with Andre. He'd managed to stay awake the entire night and no one had entered Andre's room. So far, Anna was the only one Andre had spoken to at Lowell Tavern. He had to assume she was the one the officer came to see.

"I don't think it's a good idea for you to allow British soldiers to stay here, even for a short time. You could easily be mistaken for a Loyalist, and some of the things that are done to them aren't pleasant." He picked up his cup and sipped the steaming liquid. His right hand had swollen more during the night and he was going to have a devil of a time explaining the injury.

"I'm not a Loyalist," she answered firmly. "It's

not up to you or anyone else to tell me whom I can or cannot serve or be friends with." Her ladle hit the wooden table with a bang, and cream splattered across it. Their cold eyes met.

The door swung open and Terence came in carrying a basket filled with eggs. Anna took a deep breath and turned away from Jordan. "Terence, I'll let you put the eggs away. I'm going to take Moss a cup of tea and start a fire under the washpot." She picked up a loaf of bread and a small jar of fruit and faced Jordan with a defiant expression. "After I take this to John's men." She whirled and hurried out the door.

By the time Anna had delivered the food to the men, they already had a small fire going and a pot sitting in the red-hot coals. She didn't tarry with them, or waste any time before starting her own fire under a large black kettle.

With those chores finished, Anna walked over to the vegetable and herb garden. They'd had a good spring. The garden was green with the promise of a bountiful harvest in the coming weeks. In another week the corn would be ready to pull and the beans ready to pick. And if the good weather held, she could expect travelers on the stagecoach to stop for a meal four to five times a week to eat the pickings. Her father had taught her well. She would make the tavern work — without Benjamin.

Dew clung to the leaves, sparkling like crystal. The low heels of her boots dug into the soft earth around the green plants. Anna inhaled deeply, taking in the fresh morning air. The sky was beautiful, with its soft blues and light dusting of violet and purple where the sun was just breaking above the horizon. An early morning bird chirped happily in the distance behind her.

"Anna?"

She spun around and saw John walking toward her. He looked so handsome in his military suit, his hair lightly powdered.

"Good morning, John. You arrived so late, I didn't expect you up so early."

"I slept too well. That's what a soft bed does for you. If I'd been on the ground with my men, we'd already be on our way."

"Do you have to leave so soon? We haven't talked."

"These are busy times for me, my dear. Many things are happening. I must not tarry. I see my men have the horses saddled and are ready to ride. Come, let's take a short walk before I go. I'm taking great risk in being here, so far from any regiment, but I had to express my sympathy over Levi's death. He was a good man. And you, my beautiful Anna, I had to see for myself that you are all right, that you've come through the horrible experience as strong as you've always been."

"I'm doing very well," she said as they walked further into the garden. "And I'm so glad you took time out from your duties to come see me. It makes me feel very special."

"You are special. Tell me, this man who killed Levi . . . did he harm you?"

"Only a few bruises, and they are almost gone. Everything happened exactly as I told you in my letter. He attacked me and I hit him with a cuspidor. I didn't mean to kill him. I only wanted to get him off me so I could see about Papa. Papa was bleeding very badly. I didn't know that he was already dead."

"You are a brave woman, Anna. I'm sure your father would be proud of you for avenging his death."

"I would rather have left that to the men of the town."

"There are times, milady, when we have no choice but to kill or be killed." He stopped and smiled at her. "Now there'll be no more talk of sad and disturbing memories. When I last heard from you, you were to be married in the fall. Tell me about that."

Anna felt a tightening in her chest. "I'm no longer betrothed. After Papa died, Benjamin wouldn't agree to work at the tavern. He wanted me to sell it and give Terence away to strangers. I couldn't do that."

"You're right. How could a man who says he loves you ask you to give Terence away?" John yanked his gloves from underneath his wide belt and pulled them on. "You're better off without him. Surely he could not have made you happy."

"I don't know if any man will ever want me, now that I've killed a man."

John laid his hands firmly on her shoulders and looked deeply into her eyes. "Why ever not? You're strong and beautiful. If things were not as they are, with you an American and I a soldier committed to the King, I would surely marry you today and give you all the pleasure you deserve."

Looking into his eyes and seeing his sincerity, Anna laughed easily. "You say that every time you visit, John."

"And I always mean it, milady." He placed his

arm through hers, and when they resumed walking, they were on their way back to where his men stood by the barn, waiting with the horses. Dew dampened the skirt of her dress as they passed between the plants.

"You need help in the tavern, Anna. You work too hard. Now that your papa's gone, I'm sure there's even more for you to do."

"I have Moss and Glynis, and Terence does more work each day."

"Ah—yes, I wanted to speak to you about that. I think you should consider having a woman come stay in the tavern with you. You are still single, Anna, with your reputation to uphold. And it's not proper that you don't have an older woman in the house with you."

Anna sighed. "At one time, I had thought about asking Glynis if she'd consider the idea, but she's so quiet. I don't know if she'd agree. She's never been very friendly, even when I try."

"She is your cook? Does she have a husband and children?"

"No, she's alone," Anna answered.

He stopped walking again. "Then she's the perfect one to come stay with you. Why don't you ask her? I feel certain it's the best thing for you."

"I suppose I could ask if she'd like to move into the small room off the kitchen. It would help if she were here earlier in the morning and if she didn't have to leave in the evening."

"Do you think it would make Benjamin come to his right mind and reconsider if I suggested I will marry you and take care of Terence as well?"

Anna laughed lightly. "No, I think it would make

people run me out of town. They are angry enough that I accept you into the tavern."

"It's difficult for them to believe we can be friends despite the war, isn't it?"

"It's never been a problem for me," she said huskily.

"Nor me. I want it to stay that way. And I want you to come to New York for a visit. I have friends you can stay with. I'll have gowns made for you and we'll go to all the parties together. You need to get away from the tavern for a while. How about August or September? Yes, make it September."

Anna was pleased with his invitation, but knew she had to say, "Oh, I couldn't possibly leave the tavern at such a busy time."

"You can if you hire all the help you need. Try," he said as they stopped a short distance from the barn. "I shall speak to Richard Sommerfield and tell him to expect you in late August or early September. Will you let me do that?"

Giving in to the excitement of traveling to New York, she said, "All right, I'll think about it—on one condition."

"And what is that, Anna?" He returned her smile.

"I want you to take me to a merchant ship so I can buy cloth, brandy, and lace."

Laughter pealed from his throat. "Is that all? I shall be happy to escort you to the harbor. It's a promise." He carried her hand to his lips and kissed it.

"Then tell Mr. Sommerfield if all goes well, I shall see him in September."

"Until then, this is for you." He pressed a piece

of parchment in her hand. "It's a poem I wrote especially for you. Read it after I've gone, and remember me."

His expression was the gentlest she'd ever seen. "Thank you, John. I shall always keep it."

"And we will always remain friends, dearest Anna."

As they stood in the early morning light, he lifted her chin and briefly pressed his lips to her forehead. He then quickly walked away and mounted his horse.

"Remember, Anna Lowell, someday I will come for you, and we will be married." He whipped his horse around and the three men galloped away.

Anna stood in the dust the horses left behind, clutching the paper to her breast, letting the early morning sun warm her cheeks. She would wait until she returned to her room to read the poem. Maybe the verse would help put to rest the nagging suspicions Moss had left in her mind that John Andre wouldn't have risked coming to see her if he hadn't already been in the area doing something for the British. What he did as a soldier had nothing to do with their friendship. She was sure of that.

When the riders were out of sight, she turned to go inside for a cup of tea and saw Jordan standing by the side of the house, staring at her. Anna suddenly felt a chill. Had he been watching her, listening to her conversation with John? No. She dismissed the idea. He must have been on the way to get his horse. But surely he'd heard John say he was going to marry her. Jordan would have no way of knowing it was a private joke. She hoped he wouldn't say anything about it to others. No one in Georgetown would like that idea. Not one.

Anna quickly stuffed the poem in the pocket of her dress and hurried up the back steps, seeking the security of the kitchen. She was extremely fond of John Andre. It didn't matter that the townspeople and the new minister didn't approve.

Chapter Five

Later that afternoon, on the back porch of the tavern, Anna churned the cream she'd skimmed that morning. She sat on a short stool with her back straight and the wooden churn caught between her knees. Each thrust of the paddle showed her skill. She mulled over her feelings for Jordan Kent. She had never felt such a mix of emotions about anyone.

Usually a visit with John gave her much to think about for weeks afterward, but this time, as soon as he was gone, so were all thoughts of him. She'd returned to the kitchen and when she was alone she'd taken the poem he'd given her out of her pocket and read it. In a matter of moments she'd memorized the four short lines.

Love me not for comely grace
Love me not for pleasing face
Love me not for any outward part
Love me, dear Anna, from the heart.

But now, hours later, John's visit was fading, and Jordan Kent was on her mind again.

"Good afternoon, Anna."

Startled, Anna stopped the churning and looked up. She hadn't heard Althea Jarvis approach. Anna watched as the older woman pulled up the hem of her coarse muslin skirt and hurried up the steps, a determined expression on her pinched face.

"Shouldn't you be at home, preparing Benjamin's dinner?" Anna asked sharply when Althea stood before her.

"We've already eaten, thank you." She rested her hands on her ample hips and looked down on Anna. "I came to talk some sense into you, foolish girl."

Anna pushed the churn away from her legs and rose, knocking the stool over with her skirts. She was a little taller than Althea, but by no means a match in bulk. "Am I foolish because I don't want to sell my house and give up my brother to strangers?"

"We'll get to that later, young lady. First, I've come to make you see the folly of your ways. Just this morning at church I heard you let British soldiers stay the night in your barn. Shameful, shameful." Althea squinted her eyes and pointed a straight finger at Anna. "Have you so little respect for Washington and his men that you would aid the enemy? Have you no decency left, now that your papa is gone?"

Anger twisted and grew inside Anna with each word that spewed from Althea's wide mouth. She clenched her fists at her sides and spoke back to the woman. "The soldier you're referring to is Major John Andre. He is my friend, and a gentleman. He's visited this tavern many times. My father al-

84

ways welcomed him as a guest, and I intend to do the same whenever he comes to town."

Althea tapped her booted foot and swung her hands up to outline her thickened waist. "It's a sin and disgrace to the people of this town for you to give those redcoats a bed for the night. Had the militia known in time, all of them would have been captured."

Anna drew in her breath with a sharp gasp, and Althea continued.

"You simply must sell this tavern and marry Benjamin. Get out from under this curse that plagues you and makes you do these evil things. The devil himself is after your soul, Anna Lowell."

"What evil things have I done?" Anna's voice rose and her lashes blinked rapidly. "You're the evil one for spreading lies about me."

Althea harrumphed loudly. "Why would I spread lies about the girl my son wants to marry? I'm trying to help you and Benjamin. I've tried to talk some sense into him, but by God's grace only, he still wants to marry you."

"You want me to sell the tavern because of the money it would bring," Anna declared hotly.

Anger heightened Althea's ruddy complexion, and her chest swelled with indignation. "How dare you accuse me, a Christian woman, of such tactics?" She took a menacing step toward Anna.

"If what I say is not true, then go away and leave me alone. I will not sell this tavern, and I most certainly will not give up my brother. And furthermore, I will house anyone I see fit, no matter the color his coat."

"Benjamin couldn't make you see the way of it,

but I intend to take proper care of you, the way your papa would have wanted it. He went to his grave thinking you were to marry Benjamin, and I'm going to see to it. I've made some inquiries for you and have secured a buyer for the tavern. It's a good sum, one that would have pleased your papa and *should* please you. Now you can bring a good dowry to Benjamin."

Anna couldn't believe what this woman was saying. How many times did she have to tell her she wasn't going to marry Benjamin or sell the tavern? What would it take to get through to her?

"You leave Papa out of this," Anna said, a distinct coolness edging her voice.

"Mind how you speak to your elders," Althea shot back quickly. "Your father would be ashamed of you for using such a tone."

Her mouth and chest tight with anger, Anna said, "My father taught me how to recognize people who were out to make trouble for me, and you, Althea Jarvis, are one of those people. Now, leave my tavern. You are not welcome here."

Althea reared back and held her ground. "I'll not let you make a mockery of Benjamin or this town and what it stands for. I'm going to talk to the township. Something has to be done about you."

"I know what the people of this town think about me — and what they think about you." Anna's voice started shaking, and that made her angry with herself. She glanced around the porch and saw a short birch broom. She grabbed it and raised it as a weapon. "I won't marry Benjamin so you can berate me every time I turn around. I don't need you or Benjamin, and I intend to continue to manage Low-

86

ell Tavern. You can tell your buyer you made a mistake! Now, get away from here before I—"

"You're a madwoman!" Althea shouted, then turned and ran down the steps, holding her skirt and calling for Benjamin.

Shaking, Anna dropped the broom and leaned heavily against a post while tears of frustration ran down her cheeks.

Jordan's booted feet kicked up dust as he hurried toward the Jarvis house. A young lad had delivered a note to him at Elder Beacon's house. Althea had summoned him to her house as soon as possible so he excused himself and hurried over. He'd been trying to get away from the elder and his family, but the man kept him talking about the Bible most of the afternoon. Elder Beacon was caught up in the story of John the Baptist. Jordan knew the story as well as any churchgoing man, but he didn't have any specific knowledge on the subject. Elder Beacon didn't seem to notice. The man was more than pleased with every answer Jordan gave.

Jordan wanted to see Anna, too, but first he needed some time alone with his thoughts. With his early morning preparation for the sermon and dinner at Elder Beacon's house, he hadn't had time to reflect on what he'd heard Andre pronounce earlier that morning. The news that Andre intended to come back and marry Anna had hit him like a fist in the gut. He'd bet his last coin that the paper Andre had given her was information she was to pass along to someone. But to whom?

He wondered if Levi had been in on the spying,

87

too. Or had Levi been the spy whose duties Andre wanted to turn over to his daughter? That could be the reason he had told her he would come back and marry her, now that she was no longer betrothed to Benjamin. In any case, Jordan had to find out what was written on the paper Andre had given her.

If the tavern had a busy night, he intended to slip into Anna's room and search for the paper. If business was slow, he'd have to wait until tomorrow morning, when everyone was outside. Prowling through her personal things wasn't something he wanted to do, but he didn't have a choice. All signs indicated that Anna was aiding the British. He hadn't found one other person in town who even sympathized with the redcoats.

He'd find the damning evidence against her and turn her over to Virgil. Then maybe at last he'd be free of her. Damn it! He wanted someone else to be the spy.

Tomorrow he had to send a message to Virgil to come at once. They must find out more about John Andre. If Jordan was right, Andre had recently been appointed adjutant to General Clinton in New York, and if that was true, things didn't look good for Anna.

Thoughts of Anna's connection to the British renewed the pain in his hand. Writing a note to Virgil wouldn't be easy. The swelling was no worse than it had been that morning, but he had a devil of a time trying to move his fingers enough to hold a spoon. If it wasn't better by morning, he didn't think he'd be able to grasp a pen. He'd have to write with his left hand. Anger at himself and Anna coiled and roved restlessly inside him. Next time he hit a door with his fist, he'd make damn sure the woman was worth it.

A few minutes later, Jordan rapped lightly on the front door of the Jarvis home. Althea's message had seemed urgent. Jordan wondered if her dear son Benjamin were dying.

"Oh, Reverend Kent, I'm glad you got here so quickly." Althea gave him a big smile, swung the door wide, and stepped back for him to enter.

"Is someone ill?" he asked, as she showed him into the small parlor with a blue-covered settee and matching chairs.

"Oh, no, no," she said sweetly, motioning for him to sit on the sofa. "But it's on a matter of extreme importance that I asked you to stop over."

"Asked," Jordan thought. It had been a command. "Then why not tell me what it is you need?" He took a seat, trying not to sound or look as irritated as he felt. He should be at the tavern doing his job, not playing nursemaid to this woman.

Althea clasped her hands in front of her and looked at him, a wide smile stretching her pinched face. "Oh, please let me get you something to drink."

He gave her a placating smile. "Mrs. Beacon has been doing that all afternoon. Come sit down and tell me what is so important that you sent an urgent message."

Clearing her throat discreetly, Althea lowered herself into a beautifully carved wheelback side chair and placed her hands in her lap. "It's that Lowell girl," she managed to say in a quiet voice, as the smile she'd worn since opening the door started to fade. "She's shamed the whole town."

89

Jordan tried not to appear eager for information. "Anna?" he questioned, pretending he wasn't certain about whom the woman was talking.

"Yes, yes," she hurried to say. "I spoke with her just this afternoon. I felt it was my duty to make her see the error of her ways. But there's no making her see reason. She's gone mad, and we're going to have to do something."

Jordan remained outwardly calm. "Does this have to do with her refusing to marry Benjamin?"

"No, no. In some ways I'm quite pleased about that." Althea scooted to the edge of her seat and laced her fingers together. "It's her shameful behavior in allowing those British soldiers to stay at the tavern."

Jordan tensed. This woman might have information he needed. "Why do you think she allows it?" he asked.

"Heavens!" She threw her hands in the air and let them plop back into her lap. "How should I know? As long as I can remember, her father would give any man a meal and a bed, and that didn't stop when the war started. But people are up in arms now. What she's doing could cause a band of militia to ride in and burn half the houses in town." She squared her shoulders. "We can't let that happen."

Jordan felt a mixture of relief and disappointment. He was confident Althea had no new information about Anna, but he decided to bait her to be sure. "And you have an idea as to how we can keep this from happening?"

A satisfied smile crept across her lips, and she lifted her chin. "Yes. I think the whole town should come together and force her to sell out. I just happen to know someone who's interested in buying the tavern, but I can't keep him interested for too much longer."

"I see. You think we should run her out of town." Jordan rubbed his chin thoughtfully, wondering just how far he should lead this woman with his questioning. "But you don't think we should turn her in to the proper authorities for aiding the enemy?"

Althea reared back in her chair. "Of course not! I've heard how those soldiers treat sympathizers. And mark my word, they wouldn't stop at Anna. No, they'd harass everyone in town and probably destroy half of it before they left."

Jordan hesitated, choosing his next words carefully, knowing he could be making a mistake telling this if Anna was innocent. "What if Anna is a spy? What if she's obtaining information from our men and supplying it to the British when they visit?"

Althea's deep brown eyes narrowed with surprise, and her full lips formed an O. She bent forward. "Do you think she's doing that?" she asked in a breathy voice.

"Do you think she's capable of it?" he queried.

"Ah — I — I'm not sure."

It was the first time he'd seen the buxom woman flustered. At least he knew by her reaction that she'd never considered the idea that Anna might be giving or selling information to the British. And chances were that if this woman hadn't thought about it, no one else in town had either. He had to consider what that bit of information revealed about Anna. If the town hadn't considered her friendly behavior to the British in this light, did it only mean she was damn good at her job, or was she truly innocent of spying? That last thought left him with the hope he could be wrong.

"Well, it's best we not make any unfounded accusations against our fellow man. Since I'm living at the tavern, why don't you let me handle this? I'll see if I can get to the bottom of why this young woman has jeopardized her safety as well as that of the town by consorting with the British."

Althea rose, her eyes avid. "You know, Reverend, I think you may be on to something. I think I should—"

"Mrs. Jarvis," Jordan interrupted as he rose to stand beside her. He had to put a stop to her gossip. "We have been merely speculating as to possible reasons for certain actions. I must ask you not to talk about this with anyone, no matter how tempting it might be," he cautioned as they walked to the door.

Her brown eyes rounded in horror and her color heightened. "Oh, I won't breathe a word of it. I promise."

"Good. This isn't something the town should gossip about. Innocent people can get hurt. For now, this has to be between the two of us." Jordan wasn't sure she wouldn't tell the first person she saw, so he decided to add a little threat. "If what we've talked about today gets out, I'll know who started it. And I won't look too kindly on you for it."

Althea sniffed, her sharp nose reddening at the implication. "I won't say a word. I've given my promise." She leaned closer to him. "But you will let me know if you learn anything, won't you?"

92

Jordan nodded and walked out the door. Had he said too much? By tomorrow he would know. If Althea talked, the whole damn town would be ready to hang Anna for spying.

The tavern was quiet as Jordan walked into the backyard a few minutes later. The townspeople seldom came to the tavern on Sunday, but the busy traveling season had started. In the last two weeks, there had been men in the tavern who didn't care that it was the Lord's day; they wanted a pint of ale for their dry throats and a plate of stew to fill their empty stomachs.

Jordan took the back steps two at a time and hurried into the kitchen. Anna was seated at the table alone, eating a plate of stew. If he had to make a guess, it was probably the first time she'd eaten all day, and it was already late afternoon. The fact that she worked too hard and didn't take proper care of herself irritated him. He didn't want to care about Anna. He didn't want to look at her and see a strong, beautiful woman. He wanted to see and feel for her what he would for any man he thought was passing information to the British.

Anna rose when he entered and wiped her hands down the front of her stained apron. Long tendrils of hair had fallen from her cap and curled about her neck. "You're back early," she said. "May I get you a plate?"

Her voice was so soft and lilting, her face so pure and innocent-looking, that his tension melted away, leaving him defenseless in the wake of her beauty. She wasn't a big-bosomed woman, the kind he was usually fond of, but he knew she had enough to fill his hand.

"Thank you, no, Anna. I've already eaten. Go ahead. I'll get a cup of tea and join you, if you don't mind."

Anna moved to get him the tea, but he caught her arm with his good hand and stopped her. He looked into her eyes and said, "Go back to your food, Anna; it will get cold. I can serve myself."

When she looked up at him with those beautiful blue eyes, all he wanted to do was pull her into his arms and kiss her again and again. He never tired of looking at her. Her skin was soft and fair, not a freckle or blemish to mar its perfection. He wanted to taste those rosy pink lips once again. He wanted to feel her pressed gently, lovingly against him.

Jordan realized where his thoughts were leading. It was foolish, he knew, but damnation, he wanted her. "Go back to your food, Anna." His voice was harsh as he turned to the fireplace to get the tea. He had to be. She could bewitch him with a single look, and that made her far too dangerous to his mission.

He picked up the pot and poured tea into a silver luster cup. It wasn't easy to do with his left hand, but he managed. The tea was weak; obviously the leaves had already been boiled more than once that day. For a moment he wondered if Anna was having trouble getting supplies, then chided himself. Of course she was; everyone was feeling the effects of this blasted war. He admired her for being so frugal.

"Will you have some sweet bread Glynis made? It's still warm from the oven." She pushed the plate toward him, and the jar of figs that had been on the table since morning.

He shook his head. Elder Beacon had forced more than enough food on him for one day. He really hadn't wanted to do anything but lose himself in a bottle of good brandy since John Andre had walked through the taproom door last evening. But he knew the insanity of such action. Maybe he'd feel better if he promised himself a week of nothing but drinking and heavy-bosomed women when he returned to Boston. That should force him to take his mind off the woman sitting so modestly at the table . . . but it didn't.

"Did your British guests leave?" he asked.

She looked up from her plate. "Yes. I thought you were there when John and his men rode away."

"That's right — I was." He sipped the tea. She had seen him, then. She wasn't easily fooled, and that impressed him. "It's been such a long day, I'd forgotten. Is his regiment nearby?"

"I have no idea. We don't talk of the conflict between the Colonies and the Crown. He mentioned only that many things were happening right now."

Yes, Jordan thought, he'd make a wager that many things were happening and that she knew about them, too. At the very least she'd know what was written on that paper Andre had given her. It was probably in ciphers, but he'd always been fairly good at figuring them out. He'd always astounded Virgil at how quickly he could break a code. The best thing to do would be take a pen and paper with him, copy the message, and work on it in his room.

There was a knock on the door and it opened. A man Jordan didn't recognize as a local stood in the doorway. He snatched his hat off his head and held it in front of him. "Uh—I'm looking for the owner of this establishment." The stranger nervously worked at his hat and looked at Jordan as if he'd expected him to answer.

"Yes, how may I help you?" Anna rose, but remained close to the table. She held on to the corner of the table so tightly her knuckles whitened. A glance at her eyes told Jordan the man frightened her.

"I have some pelts out in my wagon." His gaze darted from Anna to Jordan. "I was hoping you might look through them to see if you wanted to buy any."

Anna cleared her throat and said, "Yes, I'll have a look."

"But not now." Jordan moved between Anna and the peddler, surprised at his sudden surge of protectiveness. "The lady was just finishing her supper. Could you come back in an hour? She'll have more time."

"I beg your pardon," Anna said from behind Jordan. She grabbed his arm, trying to force him to look at her.

Jordan ignored her and pulled away from her hold. He walked toward the man. As he advanced, the stranger stepped backward until he was on the porch. "Yes, an hour should be plenty of time," he said, and closed the door on the fur peddler.

"How dare you speak for me!" Anna rebuked him as he faced her.

Jordan understood that she wouldn't want him to know the stranger had frightened her, so he said, "I dare because you won't speak up for yourself. Do you ever get to eat a meal without an interruption? Do you ever get to enjoy your food?"

"That's none of your concern," she answered, but her voice wasn't nearly as sharp. "I have to take care of the tavern first," she argued.

"No," he said angrily. "You come first. The peddlers with all their wares can wait and let you have a decent meal."

Jordan was surprised he'd spoken so harshly. By the stunned look on her face, he'd startled Anna, too. Damn it, she had the right to finish her meal — but did he have the right to be so concerned?

Anna returned to the table and took her chair. "I'm used to interruptions," she said softly, then picked up her spoon and dipped it into the stew. "He probably won't return," she added.

That would be just fine with Jordan. He knew it took a woman a long time to get over the fear of being attacked. He wished she didn't have to deal with strangers at the tavern.

Over the top of his cup, as he drank, Jordan watched Anna. Now that he was cooling down, he realized she was right. He had no business taking over her life. There was no way she could avoid strangers at the tavern, and he shouldn't care if she never ate another bite. But he did. He rubbed his forehead and sighed.

"How long did you say you've known the British major?" Jordan asked, deliberately keeping his injured hand in his lap. He didn't want her asking any questions. It had been simple enough to tell Beacon he'd caught it in the door. Anna had already shown she wasn't easily duped.

She glanced up at him as a spoonful of stew went into her mouth. Jordan couldn't help but notice what beautiful hands she had. Even though she tilled soil in the garden and scrubbed clothes in hot water her hands looked soft, her nails clean and well cared for.

"I really don't want to discuss him, if you don't mind," she answered. "I feel as if I've been lectured by half the town just because I gave a good friend a bed for the night." She pushed the plate away and wiped her mouth with a piece of cloth. "I won't tolerate it. This is my tavern, and I'll serve whom I wish." She waited for their eyes to meet. "And I'll decide what to buy and when," she added.

"As it should be," he said. Jordan was suddenly sure of one thing: Anna had the strength and independence to be a spy.

He watched her closely. He needed some definite answers. Was her letter to Andre the one Virgil had spoken of? He really didn't think so because of the dates. He felt confident in dismissing that idea. Were John Andre and John Anderson the same man, or was more than one person at the tavern connected to the British? He had to be patient and continue to take one step at a time. Later, when he found that note, and after he'd talked to Virgil, he'd have more answers.

In the two weeks he'd been at the tavern, Anna Lowell was the only one he'd found who had any fondness for the British, but did that simply mean Anna was the only one willing to let it be known?

"Did you see my friend Lydia at church?" Anna asked. "She usually comes on Sundays for a visit, but she didn't come today. I was afraid she might be ill."

"She was there, and she didn't look ill. Of

course, I have no true knowledge as to why she didn't visit today, but could it have been that her father heard that you entertained redcoats last night? The whole congregation was talking about it."

"I suppose that could be it, but John has visited the tavern many times over the years. It's never troubled them before. I don't think anyone in town has sympathies for any British soldier."

"When was the last time he visited?" he asked. She'd said she didn't want to talk about him, but that wasn't going to keep him from asking. He had to be careful, though; he didn't want her becoming suspicious of him.

Anna thought for a moment. "At least a year, but during that time I received two letters."

"And you recently wrote to him about your father's death?"

"Yes."

She was about to say more when the back door swung open and Glynis and Terence shuffled through, each carrying an armload of clothes and several tin pots. Glynis had a slatback chair strapped to her back.

"This is all I have," the older woman said.

"Let me help," Jordan answered. He and Anna hurried to take the clothes and pots from Glynis.

"Glynis, you should have made two trips, or asked me to help. There was no need to carry everything at once," Anna said as she helped the woman untie the rope that held the chair to her back.

"No trouble. We made it," she answered, and took her things from Jordan.

"Is this the whole of your possessions?" Anna

asked, looking at the woman's meager belongings, wishing she'd known Glynis had so little. Her heart immediately went out to her. She'd always thought her father paid a good wage, but it must not have been enough. Anna was ashamed of herself for not asking Glynis to stay with them sooner.

"I had a straw bed but left it." Glynis's gaze darted from Anna to Jordan. "It wasn't much good."

Anna smiled warmly at her. "Well, you have a new home now. And a good bed to sleep on. Terence, I'll take care of what you have. You stay and have a piece of sweet cake with the Reverend Kent while I help Glynis get the rest of her things in her room."

Terence filled Anna's arms with Glynis's things, and she and Glynis walked into the next room.

"I didn't know Glynis was moving in." Jordan turned to see the boy biting into a large piece of cake. Crumbs dropped to the floor, and he immediately stooped to pick them up. Jordan liked the fact that Terence had been raised to have good manners, another reason to admire Anna.

"Anna asked her to come live with us." He looked up at Jordan. "I told Anna we didn't need her, but Anna said with so many men in the tavern she needed another woman living here."

Jordan had mixed feelings. He thought it was a good idea for Anna to have another woman in the tavern, but he wasn't so sure Glynis was the right one. She had some peculiar ways. She didn't speak unless spoken to. And not once in the days he'd been here had she looked him in the eye. Her unusual silence didn't seem natural to Jordan. The one time he'd tried to question her, she'd said she couldn't talk and work at the same time. That certainly made her different from everyone else in town. It also made her suspect. He decided to watch her closely.

What was he doing thinking about Glynis? He could do that later. Right now he had the perfect opportunity to question Terence.

"With Glynis living here at the tavern, she'll be able to take on more chores and take some of the workload off you and your sister. Don't you like that idea?" Jordan asked.

"She's too slow to help me. The only thing she's good at is cooking, and she eats most of what she cooks," Terence said, and put another piece of cake into his mouth.

Jordan laughed, feeling some of the tension leave. He liked Anna's brother. He was smart and intuitive for his eight years.

"One day I'm going to take over managing Papa's tavern," Terence said with confidence. "Then I'll make the decisions."

"And you'll do a good job, just like your sister," Jordan praised him.

"When do you plan to open school, Reverend Kent? I've many things to learn."

"I think it's best to wait until later in the year. Besides, Anna needs you here at the tavern for the summer, and all the other young men are needed to help their families."

"I guess so." Terence's voice had an unhappy ring to it.

Jordan watched him pick up the cloth Anna had used as a napkin and wipe his mouth. He then brushed all the crumbs into one hand and took them over to Anna's empty plate and dropped them in it.

"Your sister is doing a good job of running the tavern. I know for a fact that the most successful taverns in Boston are managed by women. When it comes to managing a house, food, and drinks, no man can do it as well as a woman."

Terence looked up at Jordan as if he didn't believe him. "I'm going to manage this tavern as Papa did. He took care of the money, drinks, and stables, and Anna and Glynis did the cooking, cleaning, and emptying the chamberpots."

Jordan laughed yet again. Anna's brother was a welcome change from the intense day he'd had. Not only was he bright and quick; he was also humorous. Jordan decided he'd better ask a few personal questions before Anna returned.

"Tell me, Terence, how long have you known the British soldier who stayed here last night?"

"I was a babe the first time he came. He's Anna's friend, not mine. Papa never liked him, either, but he didn't say anything because of her. But when I get older, I won't let any redcoats stay in this tavern." Terence picked up the plate and dunked it into a pan of water, then swirled it around.

Jordan smiled. "Perhaps we'll have chased all of them from the Colonies by the time you are older. How do you know your papa didn't like the officer? What did he say about him?"

"He said he had no business over here trying to run our country and tell us what to do. He didn't like serving redcoats, either. Papa said he did it because he could take their money and give it to our

102

army." Terence walked back over and stood before Jordan. His big blue eyes were bright with knowledge. "Papa thought the King didn't have the right to punish Boston for dumping the tea in the harbor and taxing us. Papa said the King should let us have our own government."

"Are you sure you didn't hear Moss say that?" Jordan asked, because it sounded very much like what Moss had said to him earlier in the week.

Terence laughed. "Moss says a lot of things about redcoats, but I'd best not repeat them to a minister. He'd take a strap to me for sure."

"No doubt he would." Jordan laughed. "Tell me, do you agree with your papa?"

"Yes, sir. And as soon as I'm bigger than Anna, I'm going to tell her we're no longer serving redcoats."

Jordan saw pride in the young man's eyes, and his chest tightened. Why couldn't he find this same loyalty in the beautiful tavernkeeper? "Tell me about Anna. How does she feel about the conflict between the Colonists and the British?"

"She wouldn't know anything about fighting wars and battles. Girls don't know about those kinds of things. They cook and sew and clean. You just wait. When I get older, I'm going to take Papa's musket and help run the redcoats out of Connecticut. She won't be serving redcoats in this tavern when *I* get through with them."

Jordan patted the young boy's shoulder. "That's good, Terence. You're a smart young man. I never met your papa, but I have a feeling he'd be very proud of you."

Terence smiled. "Thank you, sir. I'd better go

help Moss milk the cows." Terence opened the door and ran out, slamming it shut behind him.

Jordan remained seated at the table, thinking over all the conversations he'd heard and had today.

"You'd have learned as much if you'd questioned me instead of Terence," Anna remarked behind him.

Startled, Jordan turned to see Anna leaning against the door frame. She was beautiful standing there, taking him to task about his conversation with her brother.

A slow, easy smile formed on Jordan's lips. She was one smart woman. He'd have to be more careful. Not only was he listening to her conversations, she was listening to his.

"When I tried to question you, you told me you didn't want to talk about the British major," he reminded her.

"Then you were wise to question Terence for information I wouldn't give. But tell me, why are you so interested?"

Jordan rose from his chair and leaned against the table. He crossed one ankle over the other and folded his arms across his chest. It wouldn't be wise to tell her he suspected her of siding with the British, but he could warn her. "I don't want to see you get hurt, Anna. You're playing with fire."

Anna lifted her chin and straightened her back. "And you are meddling in something that is none of your concern. I can run this tavern very well without you, and I'll thank you to stay out of my affairs."

He took a step toward her. "All right, I'll agree you can manage the tavern, but what about Andre? Before the major rode away I heard him say he was going to return and marry you."

She blinked several times. "Yes, John did say that, but he always does, and has since I was a young girl. I know he has no intention of doing so."

"I see." He picked up his cup and took a drink, convinced that her answer was truthful. "Do you want him to come back and marry you?"

Anna was thoughtful for a moment. "No. I couldn't be happy with John Andre for a husband. Our views of things are too different."

At least she was being realistic, Jordan thought. "What kind of things?" he asked. Now that he had her talking he had to press his advantage. He had to know her true relationship with Andre.

Anna walked over to the fire and lifted the tea pot. "Not only is he a British soldier and I an American, John is very fond of many women. I'm not the only one he writes to and visits." She refilled their teacups and returned the pot.

As Jordan watched Anna, he could see that she was not in love with John Andre. A woman had a certain look when she talked about the man she loved, and by the sparkle in her eyes, he knew Anna was very fond of Andre, but that was all. He was glad to see she had no illusions about marrying the man.

He also had to take into consideration her admission that Andre was British and she an American. She wasn't nervous when she declared her allegiance to her country. Neither was she edgy when she declared Andre's allegiance to the British. That counted for quite a bit, but it didn't mean she wouldn't aid his cause.

The mixed signals she was giving him were making him doubt his abilities. Was she a spy pretending to be a patriot, or was she as innocent as she seemed?

Jordan wasn't going to jeopardize his mission at the tavern, but he wanted to touch her just once more. He reached out to caress her face, but Anna caught his hand between both of hers and looked at the bruised and swollen knuckles.

"What happened?" she asked, concern in her voice.

"I closed a door on it. It's nothing to worry about. In fact, it's much better today."

"It doesn't *look* much better. Did it happen last night?" she asked.

He hesitated, and for a moment she thought he was going to deny what she knew to be true. His gaze swept across her face before he answered.

"Yes. I was so stunned to see a British soldier burst into the taproom and swing you around in his arms with so much familiarity that I failed to be careful."

She looked up into his eyes. "Perhaps Moss should take a look at it." Her voice was suddenly husky, and she was very aware that she held his hand in hers. As their gazes locked together she was reminded of last night, when he'd kissed her. She remembered the soft caresses of his hands on her shoulders and back and how they tangled in the length of her hair. She remembered the smooth feel of his jacket against her cheek, and the warmth of his strong arms holding her close.

It would be so very easy to slip her arms around his neck and lay her head on his shoulder. Instead, she turned his hand over and kissed the palm.

Roughly, Jordan pulled her to him and sealed his arms around her. "Oh, Anna, you tempt me as no other woman has. You've bewitched me. I can't get you out of my thoughts."

"No!" she whispered, struggling to free herself.

Jordan saw fear in her eyes and realized he'd frightened her. "Anna, I'm not going to hurt you."

He held her firmly, but she felt no pain at his touch.

He smiled. "That's better. See? I won't hurt you. It's just that you're so beautiful I can't stop looking at you, can't stop thinking about you, can't stop wanting you." Jordan moved his lips closer to hers.

"It's wrong," she whispered.

"No." He kissed her cheek, letting his lips glide over her jawline and back again. "Not if you're feeling what I'm feeling. I swear to God it's not wrong."

He covered her mouth with his, slipping his tongue gently inside, sipping her sweetness and easing the ache that had consumed him all day. The very touch of her soothed him while it provoked him. He groaned with pleasure and kissed her deeply, sensing her untapped passionate response, wanting to teach her how to accept love as well as give it.

"Please," she murmured when his lips left hers. "Someone may come in."

Her voice was so gentle yet so compelling it penetrated the fog of desire that had engulfed him. What was he doing? For a few moments he'd forgotten everything except his need to possess her. Spy or not, Anna wasn't a trollop to be used so carelessly. With another brief kiss, he turned her loose.

"I'm sorry, Anna. You're right. I shouldn't have kissed you." Jordan turned away and headed for the stairs. He had to get away from her. He needed some time alone and a shot of brandy to help ease the ache in the pit of his stomach and the throbbing in his hand. The more quickly he recorded his thoughts about Anna and what had happened during the day, the better he'd feel.

As soon as he shut his bedroom door, he opened the bottom drawer of his desk and reached for his bottle of brandy. He poured the amber liquid into the silver luster cup he'd carried upstairs with him a few days ago. Whew! It had a bite and warmed him immediately, but it did nothing for the pain in his hand or the ache Anna had created in the pit of his stomach. He took another swallow and wiped sweat from his forehead.

He scribbled a few notes about Anna and Andre with his left hand, then wrote two lines to Virgil asking him to come at once. He couldn't wait around for Virgil to decide to visit on his own. He needed Virgil's help to find out more about John Andre and what the adjutant to Clinton was doing in this part of Connecticut.

He must get into Anna's room to search for the note Andre had given her. If the taproom got busy enough, he could do it tonight and not wait until morning. Damn, he didn't want to believe that Anna was in league with the British. She said all the right things, but he couldn't erase the image of her in Andre's arms. How had it happened? He was sure now she hadn't been bought with the promise of marriage or better supplies.

If Terence, Moss, and all the others were right, Levi had no love for the British, so Levi couldn't have been Andre's counterpart. Eli Dudley had confirmed that the man who'd killed Levi was wanted for robbery in Danbury, which led him to believe Levi's death wasn't connected to British spying, either. Could Anna be the only one involved with Andre? He didn't like that idea. Damn, he didn't like it!

Chapter Six

Anna carried a tray filled with pewter tankards and cups into the taproom to stack behind the bar for the evening crowd. She was pleased that she'd taken John's suggestion and let Glynis move into the tavern. They were getting the work done faster, the tavern's chores went more smoothly, and Glynis seemed happier, too.

The pain of losing her father and Benjamin was easing with each passing day, though Terence had become a problem of late and Anna was concerned. Since Levi's death, he no longer wanted to be treated like a boy. Terence had always been willing to do his share of the work. Anna was the one who'd wanted him to play. She still had a tendency to treat him like a small child. She knew he wanted to take on more responsibility in the tavern, but she thought that at eight years of age he was still too young.

While she worked, Anna mentally reviewed the latest set of sums Jordan had given her. She found that was the easiest way to learn what he was teaching her. If she practiced during the day, the lesson didn't take so long. Sometimes her biggest problem was keeping her mind on the sums and not on his eyes, or his lips, or his pleasantly cultured voice.

After stacking the last tankard, Anna had started on the smaller cups when the door to the taproom opened and Benjamin walked in. He stood in the doorway for a few moments, looking at her. No doubt about it, he was a handsome man, tall and so erect.

Benjamin stood quietly for so long that Anna became uncomfortable and suddenly realized he wasn't just looking at her, he was judging her. His white ruffled shirt and embroidered waistcoat were impeccably clean, while her muslin dress was faded and her apron badly stained from berries, vegetables, and tea. His hair had been neatly powdered and pulled back with a black ribbon, hers fell in tangled wisps from under her cap.

Forcing herself to refrain from brushing at her hair and straightening her apron, Anna spoke first. "Good morning, Benjamin. How good of you to stop by. It's been a while since I last heard from you."

Anna realized she didn't have real depth of emotion where Benjamin was concerned. Her despair at losing him came from the fear she might never marry and have children of her own.

"You don't look well, Anna. You look tired and — "

Whatever else he was going to say, he must have thought better of it, for he didn't finish his sentence.

"Perhaps a little," Anna responded. His constant staring made her feel dirty and unkempt. Even though she didn't want to, she found herself tucking her hair under her cap and running a hand down her apron. "As you know, we're very busy this time of year. Thank you for inquiring."

"I wasn't inquiring about your health. I was making an observation. You're working too hard."

"Actually, things are easier now. Glynis moved into a small room off the kitchen yesterday. She's a great help to me. With her living here, I'll get to bed much earlier in the evening and I won't have to rise so early in the morning. I've also sent word to Mrs. Dudley to see if she can help during the day because the stagecoach comes so often now. Travelers expect a warm meal no matter what time they arrive."

Anna realized she was talking too much and stopped herself. She didn't have to account to Benjamin for anything. She squared her shoulders and took a deep breath, then continued with her task of putting the cups on the shelf. "So you can see, Benjamin, I'm doing quite well."

"Anna, stop putting those blasted cups away and look at me. I want you to marry me. I love you. If you love me, you'll sell this tavern and marry me at once. You don't have to work this hard. I can take care of you and make your life easier."

Anna's spirits and shoulders sagged as she turned back to face him. "I think I did love you at one time, Benjamin. Or maybe I loved the thought of getting married and having children. I only know I don't love you enough to give up Terence or my father's tavern." Her eyes found his and didn't waver. "I don't love you that much."

Ignoring her statement, he took a step toward

her. "That's precisely one of the things I want to discuss with you. I've persuaded Mama that we don't need to send Terence away. When we add rooms to our house, which we'll have to do once you and I have children, we can make a room for Terence as well. Until then, we'll put him a bed in the attic. During the day he can help tend the garden and do other chores."

Anna was shocked. She didn't know what to say, how to react. "I—I don't believe this."

"It's true." Benjamin hurried behind the bar and seized her hands. His eyes were filled with excitement. "I'm trying to tell you that if you sell the tavern and marry me, we'll keep Terence with us."

Anna was confused. "Ah—what is Terence to do when he's older?"

"I'll teach him to be a clockmaker." His voice was punctuated with urgency.

She couldn't think straight. Here at last Benjamin was saying the things she'd wanted to hear weeks ago. He still loved her, and wanted to marry her and let her keep Terence. All he asked now was that she sell the tavern. Oh God, what was she going to do? This might very well be her only chance to marry. Should she agree, knowing that she didn't love him?

"What about the man who murdered Papa and tried to rape me, the man I killed? How do you feel about that now?" she asked, almost afraid to hear his answer.

Benjamin's heavy-lidded gaze wandered over her face. He rubbed his thumb across her cheek. She knew he must have been wiping away a smudge of dirt. As clean as he was, she was surprised he even wanted to touch her.

"The gossip about you lessens each day. I want the people of this town to forget that you killed that man. The best way to do that is to sell the tavern. I don't want anyone to think of you in connection with this bloody place ever again." His voice was soft, yet unemotional.

"Have you forgotten that night?" she asked.

Their eyes met and he didn't have to say a word. Anna knew the answer. He loved her, but not enough to forget she'd killed a man. Her gaze left his and she looked at the hands that held her arms. She didn't even feel his grip. How was it that Jordan Kent could make her tremble with just a look and Benjamin was holding her in a viselike grip, and she didn't feel anything?

She looked back into his brown eyes. "I can't sell the tavern when it's as much Terence's as it is mine. He loves it here, maybe even more than I do. I don't think he wants to be a clockmaker, Benjamin. I don't think he would want me to sell his home so he can live in your attic."

"It won't hurt him to live in the attic for a time." His hands tightened and his voice grew tense. "There are children who have less. At least he wouldn't be in the streets or with strangers."

"Here he has his own room, plenty to eat, a garden to work, and a business to run, once he gets older. I won't take that away from him. I won't sell this place and give the money to you and your mother."

Benjamin pulled her close in one jerky movement. "Anna, I'm trying to meet you halfway. I've talked Mama into taking Terence into our home; now you must marry me as we planned."

There was anger in his eyes, and that frightened Anna. "No, I don't have to marry you, Benjamin. I'm doing quite well on my own. I don't need you. I'm sorry."

"For heaven's sake, you're only eighteen! You need my name to quell the gossip about why you killed that man and about your harboring redcoats. Anna, you need the protection I can offer."

"You're the only one having a problem with this, Benjamin—you and your mother! The men of this town still come and spend their evenings here at my tavern talking, playing checkers, throwing darts, and buying my ale. The women still sell me their berries, butter, and cloth. You and your mother are the only ones who are not willing to accept what happened that night and forget it. Your mother is the only person who is gossiping about me."

"You don't know what the people say behind your back. You never leave this place!" His voice was intense; his nose flared and his eyes darkened. "I don't want my wife managing a tavern, working as hard as you do, taking in strangers as you do. I expect more from my wife. I want one day to move to New York, or Boston."

Anna took a deep breath and tried to break away from his hold. "Then I'm not the wife you need. I'm sorry, Benjamin."

"I can make you change your mind," he said, and slid his hand to the back of her neck and brought his lips down on hers with fierce pressure.

115

Stunned for a moment, Anna accepted his ardent, unrelenting kisses. Benjamin had kissed her before, but now there was nothing familiar about his touch. She waited for that all-consuming feeling of sweet pleasure to fill her as it had the night Jordan had kissed her.

Benjamin's lips left hers and traveled over her cheek and down her neck. He murmured her name softly under his breath as he covered her face with kisses.

With her eyes closed, Anna tilted her head back, wishing that wonderful feeling of rapture would take control and lift her out of the ordinary and into bliss. She had loved Benjamin. Surely she would experience it soon. She let Benjamin push her to the wall, holding her hard against it with his body, pressing intimately close. His kisses grew rougher and his hand sought her breast, squeezing and pulling at its softness.

Anna's eyes shot open. The only thing she felt was pain from Benjamin's roughness. She realized she wasn't going to feel with him what she had with Jordan, so with both hands flattened against his chest she gave a hard push and Benjamin stumbled backward against the bar. His breathing was ragged, his deep-set eyes wide.

"Benjamin, I don't feel the way I used to. I don't want you ever to touch me again," she whispered, angry with herself that she'd allowed him to be so free with her.

"You wanted it," he muttered in return, as he wiped his reddened lips.

"I wanted love," she said, her throat hurting. "If you come back to Lowell Tavern, all you get is a plate of stew and a tankard of ale. Our engagement is broken, Benjamin."

Her body relaxed and she felt stronger. If Benjamin, whom she'd once loved, couldn't make her feel as Jordan had, she knew no other man could. Her worst fear might come true. She had to accept the fact that she might never marry if she rejected Benjamin again.

"Yes, it is," he answered testily as he jerked on the hem of his waistcoat and smoothed the crown of his hair with his hand. "I don't want to marry a woman half the town considers a whore." He pivoted on one foot and walked proudly out the door.

Anna winced at the sting of his words.

Jordan stayed later than usual in his room, waiting to be sure no one was in the tavern before he slipped into Anna's room. He'd remained in the taproom last evening, watching Anna, should she try to pass Andre's note to anyone. He went to bed certain she had distributed nothing but drinks.

From his window he'd seen Terence feeding the chickens, and Glynis and Moss were in the garden. Anna was the only one still in the tavern. He felt certain she'd check on the others soon, and that would be his time to sneak into her room.

He'd positioned himself at his open door so he could hear when all was quiet downstairs. Only a few minutes had passed when he heard the taproom door open. He stepped out further onto the landing and listened to see who'd come. From his post he heard Benjamin Jarvis. What luck. He was sure to keep Anna busy for a few minutes, probably longer than he'd need to find that piece of paper.

Jordan took his chance and eased across the hall. He remembered that Anna had accused him of walking quietly. If only she'd known how many times he'd practiced being so quiet. It came in handy for the work he did for Washington.

He couldn't help but wonder why Benjamin had come over, but he didn't have time to dwell on the reason. He didn't have time to listen to their conversation, either, although he'd have liked to. If it was true that she hoped to marry Andre one day, it was no wonder she'd jilted the staid clockmaker for the toffee-nosed British major.

With his left hand Jordan slowly twisted the handle. The door opened without creaking and Jordan stepped inside, leaving it ajar so he could hear the muffled voices below. He hated invading Anna's privacy, but her meeting with Andre yesterday left him no choice.

The room was obviously hers. It had her feel, her scent. Coarse cotton curtains parted to allow an abundance of sunshine into the room. A small bed, the covers neatly arranged, stood against the far wall. Beside it a small table held a candlestick. On the other side of the room there was a beautifully carved chest of drawers with brass handles. A scrollback lady's chair stood to the other side of the bed. His eyes traveled once again to the bed with its colorful quilt. For a moment he envisioned her lying on the bed with her hair fanning out over her creamy white shoulders,

118

beckoning him closer with her small hands, with her beautiful eyes, with her silky body. Jordan blinked and swallowed hard, then hurried to the chest.

He opened the bottom drawer first. After pushing aside aprons and shawls, he was rewarded with a stack of letters. He laid the correspondence on the floor beside him and opened the drawer above it. In this one he found only undergarments and two cotton gowns. Looking through her things and touching them made him feel guilty, but it roused him to be so close to her clothes, to hold them in his hands and think about her.

He picked up a gown and carried it to his face, inhaling the enticing scent of freshly washed clothes. He knew the fabric to be cotton, but because it was Anna's, the material felt as luxurious as silk. His fingers closed around the gown, bunching it tightly in his grip. He smelled it again, burying his face deeper into it, closing his eyes, rubbing his nose against the fabric, inhaling deeply the scent of the woman he wanted so very much.

"Oh, damn!" he whispered, and gently laid the gown back in the drawer.

The lure of Anna Lowell was almost more than he could bear. He ached to touch her again, to probe the recesses of her mouth and taste her sweetness. He was stimulated at just touching and smelling her clothes. What kind of woman was she that she excited him so without even being in his presence?

Quickly Jordan shut that drawer and opened

another and another until he'd checked all five. No other papers were found, so he picked up the stack of letters and untied the string.

One by one he opened the letters and skimmed the writing. He noticed the voices downstairs were growing louder than when he'd first entered the room. Benjamin and Anna were arguing, and he wondered if it was because of the British major.

He returned his attention to the letters. All were from Andre, but none contained any information that would be helpful to him. They were all very short and very sweet. He didn't find anything that might be coded for military information. There was no sign of the single sheet of parchment Andre had given Anna the day before. Had she already given it to someone before he'd returned to the tavern yesterday? He doubted it. She had to have a hiding place, but where? He looked around the room while he hastily retied the letters.

Of course, he thought suddenly, she'd put it in the safe where she kept the money, but he didn't know where it was or how he'd open it once he found it.

He looked at the bed again and realized that should have been the first place he looked. A quick glance underneath it revealed a tin box. He pulled it out and was surprised to find it had no lock. Jordan remained on his knees beside the bed and carefully opened the box. Pushing aside two pouches of money, he picked up a single sheet of parchment like the one Andre had given Anna yesterday. On it was a four-line poem which he read several times and put to memory. Further rifling of the box turned up a sketch of Andre, an aged handkerchief, the tavern documents, and a length of black ribbon.

Jordan felt a knot growing in his stomach. Could it be that the only thing Andre had given her was a love poem? He shook his head to clear his mind. Was he to believe that Anna was simply what she appeared to be, a young woman who had a British officer for a friend? Or was that poem a coded message?

He heard the taproom door close and knew Benjamin had left. Anna could decide to come upstairs at any time to see what was keeping him, so as quietly as he entered, Jordan left Anna's room.

Jordan hurried down the back stairs and into the kitchen a few moments later, and heard the stagecoach pull up to the stile. Maybe it carried a letter from Virgil. Looking out the small windowpane, Jordan saw two well-dressed men and an elderly woman step down from the stagecoach by the well. He watched as Anna greeted them and asked them in for refreshments while Moss started drawing water for the horses. Jordan wasn't in the mood to face Anna, so he went out the back door as she headed for the taproom.

Going through her personal things had heightened the private war raging inside him. Hell and damnation! She was a spy for the British, and he was tired of telling himself so. All he needed was tangible evidence linking her to Andre or Clinton.

Jordan approached the driver and asked for the mail. There were only five letters, and not a one was addressed to him. He'd been at the tavern over two weeks, with no word from Virgil. He should have heard something by now. Jordan took his own sloppily written letter from his coat pocket and gave it to the driver to deliver to Boston.

Later that afternoon Anna was in the kitchen, sliding bread out of the oven, when Lydia came into the room. Lydia spoke to Glynis, who was cutting up a cleaned rabbit for stew. Glynis nodded a greeting and went back to her task.

Anna was happy to see her friend. Lydia was the bright spot in her long days, and she missed her when she didn't stop by for a visit. "Let me put this other loaf of bread in the oven, Lydia, and I'll have time for a talk."

"Do you n-need help?" Lydia asked.

"Thanks, but I'm almost finished. I was filling a food basket to take to Mrs. Potter when I realized Glynis needed help in the kitchen. There's so much work to do I've been thinking about hiring someone to help Glynis."

A few minutes later, Anna had washed her hands and dried them on her apron. She was glad to get out of the kitchen for a while because it was so hot with the fire going. As they walked into the taproom, Anna said, "That letter your papa's been wanting came today." Anna went behind the bar and got it for her.

Lydia took the letter and looked at it. "I-I wish I could read a-as well as you."

Anna smiled at her friend. "Papa knew I had to be a good reader to work the tavern. Come, let's go sit in the parlor, where it's cooler. I hope it's good news and not bad," Anna offered as they settled themselves on slatback chairs with braided rush seats.

"M-me too." Lydia folded the letter and put it in the large pocket of her brown muslin skirt.

"C-can we go to old Sib Pond t-tomorrow? Like we used t-to?"

Anna rubbed her forehead and leaned her hand back against a slat. Why not? She was tired. She needed to get away from the tavern, away from all the responsibilities, away from Jordan Kent. "Yes, if we go late in the evening, before the taproom gets busy. We'll take our shoes off and wade in the shallow water, like we used to."

"I-I don't like cold water," Lydia reminded her.

"It's July. The water will be warmed by the sun," Anna insisted. After spending hours baking bread in the hot kitchen, wading in the cool water with her bare feet sounded wonderful.

"H-how are things b-between you and Benjamin?"

Anna sighed and stretched her arms over her head. "He came over this morning. He's decided we can keep Terence now, but he still wants me to sell the tavern. I won't, Lydia. I won't give up Papa's tavern."

"S-so the engagement's off for g-good?" Lydia's big brown eyes filled with sadness.

"Yes. I don't see marriage in my future at all." Her voice carried a ring of regret.

Lydia sprang from her chair and knelt before Anna, a worried expression on her face. "D-don't s-say that! Y-you know it's not t-true!"

"Calm down, Lydia." Anna grabbed Lydia's hands and soothed her with comforting words. "It's all right. Shh—I didn't mean that. I don't want you upset. I was just feeling sorry for myself. Both of us know that I will marry one day and our children will play together. Don't be upset, all right?"

"I-I'm sorry. I know you d-don't l-like it when my s-stuttering gets bad."

"Oh, Lydia, it's not that." Anna squeezed her hands. "You can talk as well as anyone when you don't rush your words. I just don't want people to make fun of you. And they won't, if you remember to take your time even when you get excited."

Lydia rose. "I'd b-better go. Papa wouldn't w-want me to t-tarry with this letter."

"All right." Anna hugged her friend. "I'll see you tomorrow afternoon. Let's make a promise not to talk about anything that upsets us. We'll wade in the water and pick flowers for our hair. We'll act as if we don't have a care in the world. Doesn't that sound wonderful?"

"I can't wait." Lydia's face brightened with a smile, and she squeezed Anna's hand affectionately before letting go. "I-I'll s-see you tomorrow."

Anna hurried back into the kitchen. The rabbit was in a pot of water hanging over the fire, but Glynis was gone. Suddenly an odd feeling washed over her. She'd noticed that Glynis had a way of disappearing whenever she prepared a food basket for Mrs. Potter. Could it be that she didn't think Anna should share with the woman? Or maybe it was just that she was afraid Anna would ask her to take the food to the widow, as she had once before. She remembered that Glynis had talked her out of making her go. Well, she didn't have time to worry about it now. Besides, the walk would do her good.

Jordan was in the backyard helping Parks Winchell put a wheel on his wagon, when he saw Anna leave the tavern with a covered basket on her arm. He'd never known her to leave the tavern, and wondered where she was going. Jordan tensed. Why did she have to decide to leave just now? He couldn't throw the wagon down while Parks was struggling to get the wheel on the axle, but he needed to follow Anna and see what she was up to.

Since the night he'd seen her in Andre's arms, he was suspicious of every move she made.

"I can't hold it much longer," he told Parks, hoping the man would tell him to put it down and that they'd finish when they had more help.

"I've almost got it, Reverend. Hold her steady," Parks said, in between gasps for breath.

Jordan grunted and strained, giving the iron-smith the extra minute he needed to fasten the wheel while he watched in frustration as Anna disappeared from sight. He had tried to stay close to the tavern so he could watch Anna closely, but the people of Georgetown expected a lot from their minister.

"That does it," the older man called. "You can let it down."

Shaking from the exertion, Jordan wiped sweat from his brow and neck with a handkerchief. If he hurried, he might catch up with Anna. "I just remembered an appointment I have to keep. Think you can manage the rest by yourself?" he asked, stuffing the handkerchief in his pocket.

"Sure enough, Reverend. I'm indebted to you."

"Glad I could help," Jordan answered with a wave of his hand as his long strides took him down the road in search of Anna, chiding himself for letting her slip away.

Chapter Seven

Later that same night Jordan made his rounds of each table, talking with the men of the town in the fashion of a minister when all he wanted to do was get as loud and drunk as most of the patrons in the smoky room.

By the time he'd managed to get away from Parks Winchell that afternoon, Anna had already disappeared down one of the side streets. He had no way of knowing whom she had gone to see or what she had in the basket she carried, but he'd made a vow to stick closer to her.

Since the first time a woman had caught his eye when he was a young lad, he'd never had one affect him as Anna Lowell did. Something more than her lovely face drew him to her. She didn't have big breasts or full, rounded hips, like most of the women who caught his fancy. It hadn't mattered to him whether or not the woman was intelligent, so long as she satisfied him. Anna wasn't suggestive or provocative in her manner or speech. Now that he thought about it, he realized he not only wanted to take her to his bed, he liked and admired her. That was certainly a change for him.

But how could he admire her for doing a good job of managing the tavern at such a young age, when he also believed she spied for the British? It didn't make any sense. It only confused him and made him want to bury himself under the covers of a soft bed with a willing woman and a bottle of good brandy.

Jordan was still brooding over a tankard of ale when the gait of a man caught his eye. Virgil? Suddenly, he was watching the stranger carefully. Yes, hell and damnation! It was Virgil Chadsworth, in the flesh, with his hair unpowdered, and dressed in peasant garments. Who would have thought the dandified Virgil would have succumbed to posing as a commoner? Jordan smiled but quickly hid his expression from the other men at his table by taking a long swig of his ale. It wouldn't be wise to show any recognition of the man he was about to welcome to the community as a minister should.

He watched as Virgil took a table close to the small bar. Their eyes met and glances were exchanged. Jordan would make his move when Virgil's tankard was almost empty. It was about time the man showed up to find out what was happening!

While Jordan waited a few minutes to approach his contact, he walked over to a couple of men and watched a checkers game that was almost finished. As he stared at the wooden board and corncob pieces, Jordan remembered the first time he'd met Virgil, one of his teachers at Harvard. The man was highly intelligent and extremely proper in every way, and actually stiff at times. It

128

hadn't taken Mr. Chadsworth, as Jordan had addressed him in those early days, long to figure out that Jordan didn't have to study in order to make excellent marks.

For a time it appeared to annoy Virgil that Jordan could study so little and still do so well on all the examinations. At the end of his second class with Virgil, Jordan's grade was much lower than he expected, so he confronted the teacher, who told him that a person of his talents should be accomplishing much more. Jordan argued long and hard, but Virgil never backed down from his stand, and Jordan never forgot. He had a greater respect and appreciation for the man after that, and they soon became friends.

Virgil had taught him much more than the classics and the Puritan beliefs of the school — he'd taught him how to use what he'd learned. After Jordan's formal schooling, Virgil had recommended him for a teaching position at Harvard. Much later Jordan met General Washington through Virgil's acquaintance with John Adams.

When the call for help came from Washington, Virgil and Jordan were among the first to offer assistance. Jordan didn't mind being a master at Harvard, but sometimes he had the urge to get away from the strict codes at the college, have a little fun, and maybe get into a little trouble along the way. Working for Washington was just the extra activity he needed. He welcomed the challenge. Now it appeared that Washington or Adams had talked Virgil into disguising himself as a poor man. That was quite a feat.

Jordan looked up and saw that his friend's ale

was almost gone, so he made his way over to Virgil's table. "I'm the Reverend Kent. Do you mind if I join you?" he asked loudly enough so that anyone could have heard.

"Not at all, Reverend."

Jordan couldn't hide his smile as he pulled out the bow-back armchair. Not only had Virgil discarded his fancy clothes, he'd lost his polished voice. If the mission hadn't been so important, Jordan would have lost control of himself in a fit of hilarity. He had no idea Virgil could be so versatile.

"I expected to hear from you—not see you," Jordan said in a quieter tone. He tried to appear nonchalant as he looked around the room, but his eyes immediately found Anna and he was once again very aware of her.

"I'm not averse to a game of adventure," Virgil said, rubbing his hand over several days' growth of beard.

"I can see that. I posted a letter to you just today." He spotted Anna by the kitchen door taking two plates of stew from Glynis. It was hard for him to keep his mind on the conversation when she was in the room.

"Have you a lead?" Virgil took a long drink of his ale, then wiped his mouth and nose on the cuff of his dirty sleeve.

"Perhaps. I need you to see what you can find out about a British soldier, Major John Andre."

"Clinton's adjutant general? I know the name." He kept surprise off his face but not out of his voice. He looked around the room as if expecting to see the British officer.

"Careful, you'll give yourself away," Jordan cautioned his older friend. "He's not here now. Just send me all the information you can — quickly. I may be on to something."

"Certainly. I'll do it posthaste."

Virgil cleared his throat and Jordan realized his attention had been captured by Anna once again. He'd been in a state of frustration since he'd been in her room, touching her clothes, inhaling her scent. She was driving him crazy.

"I'll be careful, and you do the same," Virgil warned. "I've noticed you can't keep your eyes off that serving wench. Really, Jordan, you're on an important mission."

"She's not a wench," he mumbled in an annoyed tone. "She doesn't give extra favors to her patrons."

"By the looks of you, you wish she did."

Virgil was making fast work of shortening Jordan's temper. He didn't want anyone, including his friend, talking about Anna as if she were common. He tried to keep his voice level as he said, "She's the tavernkeeper. A thief had killed her father by the time I arrived."

"I'm sorry to hear that. Does his death have anything to do with the reason you're on to Andre?" Virgil asked, before finishing off his ale and landing his tankard on the table with a loud clatter.

"I don't think so." Jordan rubbed his chin. "You said the ink had been smeared on the letter you intercepted. Could the name have been Andre rather than Anderson? Did the letter say anything more?"

"No to both. I saw it before it was delivered to Washington. But Anderson could quite easily be Andre's alias."

"Yes, I've thought about that, but I'm still not sure."

Virgil leaned closer, his green eyes determined. "Come, Jordan, you're being too secretive."

"I'm being cautious, which is what you taught me. The only thing I'm ready to say is that the British major made contact with someone here at the tavern. I want you to see what Lafayette's New York men can find out. They may know something we don't."

"Whom did Andre contact?" Virgil remained cool but insistent.

Jordan leaned back in his chair, but kept his voice low. "I'm not going to say more. I have no proof yet. Just get all the information you can. I don't think this is something we should sit on."

Every time Jordan thought of Anna's being involved with Andre and Clinton, a knot formed in his stomach. He didn't want to believe Anna was in league with the British, but what else could he think when Andre had risked being captured to come and see her? He didn't know any other patriot who had direct contact with Clinton. The only piece of evidence he'd dismissed was the note Andre had given her. After trying several codes, he'd decided there was no message hidden in the poem.

Damn, it wasn't fair that after all these years of wanting a woman who commanded his respect and admiration, as well as his love, he'd found one who was forbidden to him. And he didn't know what he was going to do about it.

Jordan gave himself a mental shake. As much as he wanted to believe Anna's innocence, he had to be practical. He'd seen evidence of her guilt. He had a job to do, and he'd do it. He would accomplish what was required of him and not let her keep him from it, no matter how appealing she might be. A woman could be a turncoat as easily as a man.

"I agree." Virgil placed both elbows on the table and leaned toward Jordan. "I'll see what I can do."

Jordan nodded. "Is there anything going on that I should know about?" he asked, forcing his gaze to remain on his friend.

Virgil's eyes took on a glow of satisfaction. "Rochambeau just landed in Newport with more than five thousand men."

Jordan's chest swelled. France had come through! Jordan felt like clapping Virgil on the back and shouting it to everyone in the taproom. This was damn good news. "I'm glad to hear it. Any word on the French Navy?"

"Just that they're expected. This should make Clinton rethink his position."

"It will, I know it," Jordan said with confidence. "The British have been quiet since the fall of Charleston, but we can look for that to change now."

"Yes. I'm sure he's calling in all his advisers."

"Will you be staying the night in the tavern?" Jordan asked.

"No, we've made a small camp about two miles

north of town. We're going to patrol the Post Road as a band of irregulars for a time. I'll send someone out on the morrow for the information on Andre. I'll be back in town in a week or so to see if you've any news and tell you what I've learned about him."

"Don't look now," Jordan said, as he watched a man on the other side of the room, "but I think that's Spivy Brown who just walked in."

Virgil pretended to scratch his head as he looked around. "Does he have two fingers missing on his left hand?"

"Yes," Jordan answered as he saw the man wave for Anna to bring him a drink. "Isn't he the one who helped William Demont obtain the plans of Fort Washington in '76?"

"That's what some of us believe, but again, there was no real proof, so he was never court-martialed. He bears watching, Jordan. Just as the person in contact with Andre should be watched closely," Virgil added.

"I know what I'm to do," Jordan answered in a clipped tone. "Keep your head low when you leave. He may recognize you." Jordan rose from the chair.

"I'll be careful. You do the same."

Virgil left unnoticed and Jordan made his way toward Spivy's table. No one had joined the man, but Jordan decided to stay close to him in case any one showed up to talk to him. Just because he'd been under suspicion before didn't mean he was at the tavern for any reason other than a hot meal. So far the only person Jordan had any reason to suspect of consorting with the British was

134

Anna, and he hoped desperately that he could find another suspect.

Jordan threw darts with one of the locals while keeping an eye on Spivy, who seemed content to ignore the chatter around him and eat his meal. A short time later Anna swished by him and suddenly Jordan had an idea. Why not mention Rochambeau's landing to her and see how she took the news? Her expression might tell him where her sympathies really lay. The French arrival wasn't top secret; in fact, the Americans would want Clinton to know the French troops had arrived. Riders were probably already on their way to New York to deliver the news to him. If Anna wanted the British to succeed in stopping the rebellion, surely this news would upset her.

Keeping his eyes on Spivy, Jordan walked over to where Anna was stacking empty tankards on a tray.

"I haven't seen you slow down all evening," he said, his voice soft and laced with concern.

"No time," she answered, and continued her chore.

He touched her arm and her gaze flew to his face. Too late Jordan realized he shouldn't have touched her in front of the townspeople. Slowly he lowered his arm and said, "Can you take the time to hear some good news?"

Anna stopped and smiled. "I would love to hear some good news. I don't hear enough of it these days."

Jordan kept his voice low, his eyes on her face. "The French have landed in Newport with more than five thousand troops."

Her eyes lighted up and her smile grew. She picked up the tail of her apron and wiped her hands. "That is good news, wonderful news for us."

Jordan watched her closely and was pleased with her reaction. She seemed genuinely happy, but Jordan was beginning to wonder if he was too besotted with her to be objective.

"Did someone tell you this tonight?" she asked, looking around the room.

"Yes. I talked to a traveler who'd just heard. He's already gone."

"I wonder why he didn't share the news with all of us."

Moss called to Anna, and she turned her attention to him. "Oh, I have drinks waiting. Excuse me." She started to walk away and suddenly looked back at Jordan and smiled at him once again. "Thanks for sharing this. It is good news."

A wave of relief swept over him, easing the tenseness he'd felt. Jordan nodded. Seeing her smile, knowing she was happy the French came through, elated him. He glanced at Spivy. The man had been there about half an hour and no one had joined him. Maybe he was just passing through and had no plans to meet anyone. Maybe he was as innocent as Anna appeared at times. Sometimes people were just in the wrong place at the wrong time.

Just as Jordan was about to indulge in another tankard of ale, he saw Anna walking over to Spivy's table. He hated the doubt that nagged at him but couldn't help it. He inched his way closer and listened.

"How about another ale?" she asked with her usual friendly smile as she picked up his empty plate.

"Not for me," the well-dressed man answered. "I've a long ride ahead of me. But tell me, is there any news of the war these days? It seems quiet of late."

"We don't hear so much since the fighting moved south. Oh, but just tonight I heard that the French have arrived at Newport with five thousand men."

The man's eyes rounded with surprise, and he rubbed his lightly whiskered chin. "Hmm. Doesn't sound good for the British. I would think they would want to know this."

Anna nodded. "I'm sure this news won't make them happy. I don't think they expected to fight the French here and at home," she replied.

"I'm sure you're right. Well, I must be on my way." The man rose from his chair. He reached into his coat pocket, pulled out more than enough coins to pay for the meal, and laid them on the table. "The stew was good, and thanks for the information." He gave Anna a smile and walked away.

Anna scooped up the coins and placed the man's empty tankard in the plate. As she turned toward the kitchen, she noticed that Jordan was staring at her. She shivered lightly before walking away, not understanding why she sometimes found Jordan watching her with an expression of doubt on his face.

It was late by the time the last person left the tavern. The warm weather and numerous travelers kept the men there longer each night. Anna and Moss wiped the tables clean while Glynis stacked the empty mugs, tankards, and cups onto large trays.

After she said good night to Moss and Glynis, Anna went to get the account book, pen and ink, and a candle to light the table where she and Jordan would do the bookwork. By the time she had the coins separated for counting, Jordan was walking into the room, shuffling his feet, which made her smile. Being so near to him was never easy for her. She wanted to reach out and feel his warmth. She wanted to curl into his embrace and wind her arms around his neck.

Jordan walked past Anna, leaned one hip on the round table, and looked at her with annoyance. "Anna, tonight, the man with the missing fingers—did you know him?"

She stood on the opposite side of the table from him and opened the ink jar. What an odd question, she thought. "No. Was he familiar to you?"

"Maybe," Jordan hedged. "I couldn't help but overhear you tell him the news of Rochambeau's troops."

Anna dropped her arms to her sides and asked, "Was it secret?"

Jordan shook his head. "I'm just puzzled as to why you would tell a man you don't know."

"He asked if I had news of the war. That's why I told him." She took a step toward him.

"But why tell that man?" he insisted. "And why did he leave such a large amount of money for his meal?" he asked harshly.

Anna gasped at his tone. She straightened her shoulders. "I frequently tell strangers news, if I have any, just as a stranger told you about the French troops." It took a moment for his accusation to sink in. Her voice grew louder. "People come to a tavern to talk, to tell what they know and to hear from others. And I'm often paid well for the food I provide."

Jordan rubbed the back of his neck as if taking the time to think about her words. "Of course, you're right. Forget I mentioned it."

She placed a hand on his arm and looked into his eyes. "No. Tell me why you're unhappy that I told that man about the troops. Why are you questioning me this way?"

He took a deep breath. "That stranger could have been a spy for the British just waiting to hear news such as this."

Anna laughed lightly. "Surely you jest."

"No, Anna, I'm deadly serious." He took hold of her arm and suddenly winced, pulling his hand back.

Anna noticed his hand was still swollen. Her displeasure of his questioning faded quickly and she said, "Your hand doesn't look any better. Perhaps Moss should take a look."

Jordan held the hand to his chest. "No, I'm fine."

"It doesn't look fine. Let me see it." She took his hand in hers and examined the bruised and swollen knuckles. "I have some salve Moss made up for me when I—when I thought my ribs were broken."

She looked away from him. If Benjamin wanted

to forget the night she was attacked and her father killed, everyone else probably did too, including Jordan. She shouldn't have mentioned it.

"I assure you, my hand is much better." Jordan's voice softened. "When did you have cause to think your ribs were broken?"

His expression was so tender she couldn't deny him an answer. "The man who killed my father hit me here." She reached up and caressed her cheek just below the eye. "And here." Her hand moved from her face to her midriff. "For a long time I couldn't breathe without it hurting."

Jordan leaned forward and gently placed his hand over hers as it rested on her ribs, just below her breasts. "It may help you to talk about what happened, Anna."

She would have liked to confide her fears and troubles. He was kind, gentle, and easy to talk to. It would be so easy to lay her head on his shoulder, slip her arms around his neck. But instead she said, "There's still too much pain when I think of that night."

He rubbed his hand back and forth across hers. "If you talk about it the pain won't be so bad because you'll have shared it with me."

Anna was tempted to pour out all her fears, but if she did that, she'd have to relive that night, and she didn't want to do that. His concern, his generosity, the casual intimacy, were more than she could bear, feeling as she did about him.

Jordan bent down and gently kissed her on the mouth. He raised his head just enough to look into her eyes for a moment before kissing her a second time.

His lips were warm and inviting; his hand covering hers was smooth. It would take so very little for Anna to circle his neck with her arms and pull him close. She realized now she'd never truly loved Benjamin. It was Jordan she loved, wanted, and dreamed about. Jordan knew how to comfort her and make her feel better about herself. Jordan knew how to make her body come alive with a mere touch. And Jordan was the man she could never have.

Regaining her composure, Anna stepped back and pushed his hand away. "Now, where did we leave off?" Turning her attention away from him, she picked up the pen and stuck it in the inkwell.

As they worked, Anna hoped Jordan didn't notice how being so close to him made her tremble. His warmth floated the short distance between them to cover her with a longing to touch him, to taste his lips once again. Anna rubbed her forehead as they worked, trying to erase the feelings that assaulted her every time Jordan's sleeve brushed her arm. She could never have a life with Jordan because of her past, and she had to reconcile herself to that fact and forget any notion of love and marriage.

The next morning Anna was on the back porch cutting potatoes when Glynis walked out the door, holding some pieces of coarse paper. "I thought I'd cut up the vegetables for you today while you make candles. I noticed that we don't have many left," Anna told her.

"I'll get started right away." Glynis fingered the papers she held and looked back at Anna. "When

I was cleaning the Reverend Kent's room I found this lying on his desk." She extended several sheets toward Anna.

Anna was surprised at first, but quickly recovered herself. She dropped the knife and took the papers. "Did you take these from his room?" she asked, and the older woman nodded.

"Glynis, why would you take his papers? I don't understand. Why bring them to me?"

"He has the name of most every person in town listed, including mine and yours."

Anna gasped. "Let me see." She set the pan of potatoes aside and rose from her chair as she glanced at the top sheet. Her name was at the top of the page. Beside it she read the words "beautiful, strong, sad." The next name was Glynis's; by her name he wrote, "Welsh — not as harmless as she acts." Anna continued down the page of names: Moss, Eli Dudley, Parks Winchell, and Althea Jarvis.

"Did you read this? I didn't know you could read," Anna answered before giving Glynis the chance to speak.

"Some," she admitted reluctantly, and rolled her shoulders in a shrugging manner.

Anna looked from the paper to Glynis, not really knowing what to say. She never dreamed Glynis might read something that belonged to another. "Did you say this was on his desk?"

Glynis nodded.

"Why did you pick it up and read it? Why did you bring this to me?"

"I thought it might be important," she answered in a defensive tone. Her upper lip curled upward, showing the space left by a missing front tooth.

"To whom?" Quickly glancing on the back, Anna felt her temper rising. Somehow she doubted Jordan had left the papers on his desk. She'd never seen any papers lying loose when she'd cleaned his room. That meant Glynis had been deliberately prying into his affairs, and that angered her. "How could it possibly be important to me *or* you what the minister writes about his congregation?"

"He wrote 'No sympathies for redcoats' by every name but yours and mine," she stated flatly. "Why's that?"

"I have no idea," Anna said in a tone that didn't conceal her annoyance with Glynis. "I don't know why he's seen fit to list everyone's name and a description of each person, but I'm sure he has a just and fair reason." Anna took a deep breath. Although she liked having Glynis live at the tavern, she couldn't accept this kind of behavior. "Glynis, we don't pry into anyone's personal papers or their business here. Especially the Reverend Kent's. I'm sure he needs to keep a record of these things so he can know better how to serve the needs of this community. I'm ashamed of you and embarrassed by your actions."

"Harrumph."

Glynis's disregard for privacy bothered Anna. "I suggest if you find other writings on the Reverend Kent's desk, or *anywhere* while you're cleaning his room, you don't read them."

"I thought he might be hiding something."

She couldn't be serious. "What could he be hiding? What's wrong with you, Glynis? If he were hiding anything, would he have left his papers on the dresser for someone to read?"

Anna shoved the papers at Glynis. "Now put these back exactly where you found it. From now on, I will clean the Reverend Kent's room."

Glynis stood quietly and listened to Anna's reprimand, then opened the door and went back inside without saying another word.

Anna left the potatoes, and walked to the edge of the porch, fuming. She was not at all happy with Glynis's behavior or that she had come forward with the papers. Still Glynis had a point. Why had Jordan listed everyone in town? And why were Glynis's political sympathies in doubt? Maybe because Jordan had never heard Glynis express her sentiments. She seldom spoke, even when spoken to. But why would the minister be interested in whether or not a person was a British sympathizer? That was odd. Now that Anna thought about it, there were many things about Jordan that puzzled her. The uneasy feeling she'd had the morning John Andre left rose in her again, and she remembered the way Jordan questioned Terence a few days ago. Surely it wasn't necessary for him to know so much about her. Anna rubbed her arms to ward off the chill of the unknown. Was Jordan watching her? No, she decided . . . it had to be her imagination.

Staring out on the hot day, Anna hoped Glynis hadn't picked up on her overprotectiveness of Jordan. She'd risen so quickly to his defense that Glynis could easily have caught on to her true feelings. Anna leaned forward against the porch post and pressed her cheek against the sun-

144

warmed wood. The hardness, the warmth of the wood reminded her of Jordan's hard, warm body pressed ever so tightly against hers. She remembered the way his lips felt against hers and how his touch quickened her breathing. A quiver of longing trembled through her as she thought about him.

Anna took a deep breath and backed away from the post. There was nothing about Jordan Kent that suggested he was a minister. He was too enchanting, too handsome, too young, but by his very words Anna knew that he was a minister. And in order to stay true to his faith, his God, his congregation, he'd have to take as a wife a woman who would be considered above reproach, one who had no blemishes in her past, a woman unlike Anna Lowell.

What she needed was some time away from the tavern, she decided. She'd had eggs left over the last two mornings. She'd take some to Mrs. Potter. Since her husband was killed, the poor woman never had enough food to feed her three children.

It took only a few minutes to pack the eggs in a basket and to ask Glynis to watch the tavern. She walked briskly until she neared Mrs. Potter's house, and a familiar figure on the porch slowed her steps. Jordan was hammering on the front window shutter. A prick of surprise rose up in her. At first she started to turn around, trying to leave before he saw her. She didn't want him to know it bothered her to see him helping the widow. But Anna remembered the pretty young widow's three little blue-eyed boys and knew she had to leave the eggs. She took a deep breath and continued, reminding herself that what Jordan did for others was none of her business.

"Hello," she called when she reached the bottom step.

Startled by Anna's voice, Jordan missed the nail and hit his thumb. "Damn," he whispered under his breath as he dropped the hammer and held his injured thumb in his other hand.

Anna hurried up the steps and placed the basket on the floor. "You're careless when it comes to your hands. Let me see what you've done," she said, and took his hand in hers. She examined it closely. "The skin isn't broken. Maybe it's just bruised." She looked up and found him watching her rather than looking at his thumb. His fingers closed around her hand and squeezed gently. Anna drew in her breath as she recognized the look in his eyes. It was the way he'd looked just before he'd kissed her the other night. Her heart thudded with anticipation. Without realizing what she was doing she tilted her head back to get ready for his lips, then remembered they were out in the open, where anyone could walk by and see them. She dropped his hand as if it were a hot poker and stepped back, embarrassed by her forwardness.

"I—I didn't expect to find you here," she said, a nervous edge to her voice. She looked away as a faint blush warmed her cheeks.

"I can say the same thing about you." He shook his hand a little trying to lessen the pain in his thumb, and the overwhelming desire to kiss her.

"I—I try to bring food once a week." Why was she stammering? And why did it bother her to find that Jordan was helping the young widow too? She moistened her lips and tried again. "I had extra eggs. I knew Mrs. Potter could use them for her children."

Jordan smiled. "That's very kind of you, Anna. I'm sure she appreciates you thinking of her. She's not home right now, but I expect she'll be back soon."

Anna didn't want to be around when Mrs. Potter returned. She didn't want anyone to know how Jordan affected her. Mrs. Potter might wonder why her face was flushed and her tongue tied. "I'll just leave them. I don't want to keep you from your work." She placed the basket in front of the door and turned to go.

"Wait," he said. "I'm finished. I'll walk back to the tavern with you." He picked up the hammer and placed it beside the egg basket.

Anna tensed. "Won't she expect you here when she returns?"

He shook his head as they walked down the steps together. "I told her I'd be gone as soon as I put a few nails in the shutter. And I gave each of her boys a ride on my back before they left."

"She's a very pretty woman and nice, too. She does beautiful work with a needle. And her boys are good boys. I'm sure she's very happy you spent time with them."

Jordan touched Anna's arm and they stopped walking. "Anna, Mrs. Potter is pretty, and her boys are a good diversion for me, but I'm not interested in her. Do you understand?"

147

He was so adamant Anna felt her spirits rise. "Yes." But as soon as they started walking down the dusty road once again, Anna remembered she wasn't right for Jordan, either.

"I've helped Mrs. Potter with some of her chores, as a lot of the men in town have, because I feel sorry for her. In another year her oldest son should take on most of the responsibilities. Besides, right now, I like to play with her sons because they remind me of my childhood."

"Where was that? Your childhood," she asked, enjoying the feel of the warm sun on her back as they strolled back toward the village.

A wagon passed by them and Jordan waited for sounds of the horses' hooves and the creaking of the wheels to fade before he answered. "Boston. I have two brothers, and we used to play in much the same way Mrs. Potter's boys do."

"Your brothers — are they still in Boston?"

He nodded, swiping at the fine film of dirt the wagon left flying in its wake. "Yes. And my mother and father."

Anna felt a tightening in her chest. "You have both your parents. It must make you sad to be away from them for so long."

Jordan stopped again and looked at her with sadness in his blue eyes. "I'm sorry. I shouldn't have spoken so freely about my family."

"Don't be ridiculous," she smiled. "I want to hear about them. I'm happy you still have them with you." Her voice softened. "I wish you could have met my father. You would have liked him."

"I'm sure I would." He smiled. "You know, if

we weren't standing out in the middle of the street, I'd kiss you right now."

Her breath became little gasps. "It's not right that you should kiss me," she answered.

Jordan looked up and saw Eli Dudley walking their way. "Maybe not," he said and took a step away from her. "But that doesn't keep me from wanting to."

Chapter Eight

The first of August brought hot days to Connecticut. The vegetable garden was producing bountiful food for the tavern and its guests. The stagecoach came every other day, and Anna was kept busy from early morning until late at night. Terence and Moss handled the stable, cows, and chickens, and picked most of the vegetables. Mrs. Dudley came in to help with the cooking every day the stagecoach was scheduled.

Things were running smoothly, but Anna knew the real reason was Jordan: if he didn't help her with the books each night she didn't know how she'd keep up with the incoming and outgoing money. As it was, her savings grew larger each day. She still talked of a trip to New York to buy from the merchant ships, but Jordan always discouraged her, reminding her that the British occupation of New York made that too dangerous.

As Anna chopped onions for a stew, the three-day trip to New York was on her mind. Although the British controlled the city, she had no fear of the soldiers because John was her friend. And he'd given her the name of the family she was to stay with when she made the journey.

With watering eyes, Anna glanced up from the strong-scented onion when she heard Lydia call her name from the taproom. "In the kitchen," she answered. She looked around for Glynis, then remembered she'd asked her to clean the pheasant she'd bought earlier that morning. Terence had gone fishing in Old Sib Pond, and Moss was in the barn working on the bullace wine he hoped to sell in the tavern.

Lydia walked very slowly into the kitchen. Anna noticed at once that she'd been crying. Her eyes were swollen, her nose red, and strands of hair were hanging out of her cap. "Lydia, you're pale as death. Come sit down." Anna wiped her hands on her apron and helped Lydia take a chair at the big kitchen table.

She knelt in front of her friend and took Lydia's hands in hers. They were as cold as snow. Fear gripped Anna. Had something terrible happened? She swallowed hard. "Did you have word on your father's brother?" Anna asked, but knew if there'd been word she'd have seen a letter, and the last one had come a few days ago.

Lydia shook her head but refused to look at Anna or speak to her. Even though Anna held her hands, Lydia twisted her fingers nervously.

"What's wrong?" Anna pleaded. "Tell me what has you in this state."

Lydia looked at Anna with her big beautiful eyes, her long lashes hooding their roundness. She took a deep breath and slowly pronounced each word. "P-Papa's arranged a marriage f-for me."

Anna felt relief wash over her. She was afraid someone had died. Although Anna didn't approve

151

of them, an arranged marriage could turn out very well. She swallowed and cleared her throat before she spoke. "Lydia, why are you crying? This is wonderful news. I'm so happy for you." Anna smiled and squeezed Lydia's hands affectionately. "You *should* be married. You'll be a caring wife and loving mother."

Lydia looked at Anna. Big tears rolled effortlessly down her cheeks. "No! I-I don't want t-to."

"Of course you do," Anna reasoned. "Remember how many times we talked of marriage and children? Oh, Lydia, you're so lucky. You'll have a husband to love you and children to care for. Don't be unhappy."

"It's Benjamin!" Lydia said in a rush without a hint of a stutter. Tears continued to tumble down her dampened cheeks and drop onto her muslin apron.

Anna's eyes grew wide with disbelief, filled with denial of her friend's words. Her mouth was open, too, but she was too stunned to close it. Lydia's hands suddenly burned against hers like hot coals, but she couldn't let go. She couldn't think or move. Not Benjamin, not Benjamin, her mind kept saying as Lydia cried. In a whirl of skirts, Anna rose and turned her back on her friend. She rubbed the back of her neck to soothe her tightening muscles. How could this have happened when she was so recently engaged to Benjamin?

What am I thinking? Why shouldn't Lydia marry Benjamin? *Because it hurts!* Only my pride. *But it still hurts.* Do I love him and want to marry him? *No, I just didn't think he'd marry*

152

so soon and my best friend. That's selfish. *I know.*

"I — I'm s-s-sorry, A-Anna, I-I told P-Papa no."

Trembling, Anna turned back to Lydia and wrapped her arms around her, holding her close. "Shhh — Lydia — it's going to be all right." She calmed her although her own pulse was racing with repudiation.

As Lydia sobbed, Anna realized her friend was taking this harder than she was, and that immediately made Anna want to comfort her. Why shouldn't Lydia marry Benjamin? she asked herself again. He was a fair man who made a good living. He was handsome and well mannered. Anna kissed Lydia's forehead and held her tightly. Of course she should marry Benjamin.

"Lydia, listen to me." Anna turned her loose and lifted her chin, forcing Lydia to look at her. "Dry your eyes." Anna reached for the hem of her apron and helped Lydia dry her face. "Come, let's sit down. I want to talk to you."

"I-I d-don't —"

"Shh — Lydia, calm down. Remember, you can talk as well as anyone, even when you're upset. Now prove it to me."

"I don't want t-to marry Benjamin." Her wording was slow but almost perfect.

"Sit down and tell me why." While Lydia pulled out a chair, Anna took her cap off, releasing her long hair to fall across her shoulders and down her back. Now that she had a minute to think about it, she was happy that Lydia was going to marry Benjamin, although that didn't take away the shock.

153

"Because he loves you and you love him." Lydia took her time and said the words without a stutter.

"Not any more." Dropping her hands listlessly into her lap, Anna searched for an explanation her friend could understand. "Benjamin wants a wife above reproach, and I am no longer that."

Lydia started to speak, but Anna stopped her. "No, listen to me. It's not only that. He couldn't understand why I wouldn't agree to sell the tavern. In fact there are many reasons we're not going to marry, things I don't want to talk about right now." She looked at her friend's solemn face. "But we will someday, when we're older and things are more settled. Benjamin is a good man and he will make you a fine husband. But watch out for his mother." Anna knew it wasn't right to talk about the woman, but she had to warn Lydia about Althea Jarvis.

"She and P-Papa arranged the marriage."

Anna smiled. "It's a good arrangement for you, Lydia. You're sweet and kind, and Benjamin is a very lucky man to get you."

"I-I don't want t-to marry him. I'm a-afraid."

"Don't be." Anna took her hands once again. "I know Benjamin will love you and be a good husband to you. You'll have many beautiful children and you'll bring them to the tavern to play while we talk and visit. Our relationship won't change. I promise you."

At last Lydia gave a hint of a smile and Anna felt relieved. How loyal Lydia was. She could not be happy until she was certain that Anna didn't oppose her marrying Benjamin.

"Papa's giving him p-part ownership of the c-carriage shop."

"Then Benjamin is doubly lucky." But to herself Anna thought that if Althea Jarvis couldn't sell the tavern and get all the money, she'd take half the income from the carriage works. Benjamin's mother was a shrewd woman. She could easily dominate Lydia, and that worried Anna.

Glynis came hustling noisily through the back door, and Anna and Lydia rose. Anna knew Glynis needed help in the kitchen, but she couldn't face anyone right now. "Come on, you'd better get back home. Your mama will be worried about you."

The two girls walked arm in arm through the taproom and out onto the front porch. The sun hung low, but the heat of the day hadn't subsided.

"Are you s-sure we'll s-still be friends?" Lydia asked, looking deeply into Anna's eyes, wanting confirmation.

Anna hugged her tightly. "Oh, yes, we'll be friends forever. I'll be at your wedding, and I'll come when your first child is born. We'll always be friends, Lydia. Always."

Anna was glad when Lydia walked down the steps so she could have some time alone. She hurried back inside and stood in the middle of the parlor for a moment, trying to decide where she should go, what she should do. She had meant what she'd said when she'd told Lydia she was happy for her, so why was she shaking so badly? It was just the shock, she reassured herself.

Too much had happened. Her father's death, killing that man, Benjamin's rejection, the arrival of Jordan Kent, and now this marriage. At last she was going to lose control and fall apart. She couldn't hold herself together any longer. Her chest heaved.

"Hello, Anna, are you in there?"

Anna jerked around as Althea Jarvis sauntered out of the taproom and into the parlor. How was she going to cope with this woman right now? Her breathing was so ragged her chest hurt. No, she couldn't break down, not in front of this woman. Anger would be her salvation, she told herself. Yes, she'd make it through this if she got angry.

"Oh, there you are. Your, ah, cook told me you were in the taproom, but I see she was wrong. Here you are in the—what do you call it, the ladies' parlor?"

Althea knew very well this room was considered the ladies' parlor. Women who traveled on the stagecoach didn't want to be subjected to the company of strange men drinking and gaming in the taproom, so they were furnished a separate room where they could have their tea and knit or sew while waiting for the stage to leave.

"I was probably in the taproom when last she saw me," Anna answered, fighting to control her emotions.

"My, my. You do seem to be in a state." Althea advanced further into the room, smiling. "I guess Lydia told you of her forthcoming marriage to Benjamin."

"I'm happy for Lydia," Anna said softly, lifting

156

her shoulders and chin a little higher, in a self-protective effort.

"Delighted to hear it, my dear. I know you want only the best for your dear friend and for Benjamin, too."

Anna knew Althea was here for a reason and she wished she'd go ahead and say what was on her mind and leave. If she'd come to gloat about Benjamin's good fortune in marrying Lydia, well, Anna was simply too tired to listen.

"What do you want?" Anna asked, her voice cold.

"I bring, shall we say, a small request from Benjamin." Althea walked closer, swinging her broad hips from side to side.

It was clear she wanted Anna to ask so she obliged. "What favor does your son ask?"

"That you be kind enough to him and Lydia not to see his bride again before the wedding and that you not attend the ceremony." Althea didn't try to keep the smile from lifting the edges of her full lips. She fairly beamed with pleasure.

Anna sucked in her breath. "He has no right to ask such a thing of me."

"He has every right," Althea said in a loud voice, snapping her hands to her rounded hips. "If you continue to see Lydia you'll no doubt fill her head with lies about my son, and I won't have it."

"I'd never do that," Anna argued, her voice shaking with hurt, anger, and disappointment. "I spoke highly of Benjamin to Lydia. I'm happy for them." Anna's hands closed around her skirt, bunching the material into an unsightly wad. She

157

couldn't believe this. She and Lydia had been friends all their lives.

"Save your lies, I don't want to hear them. I've never been fooled by you, Anna Lowell. I thank God He plucked my son out of your clutches when He did. It's only a matter of time before you bring shame on the entire town. Someone else is on to you as well."

"What are you talking about? You don't know what you are saying." Anna's voice rose in anger to match Althea's. "I don't want to hurt Benjamin or Lydia. You're doing this to hurt me, and I won't let you. You can't keep me from their wedding. I won't listen to you."

Althea laughed with husky pleasure. "Oh, my dear, you are no match for me, no match at all. I've just come from speaking to Lydia's mother. She agrees with me that you could spoil her daughter's happiness. If you come to the ceremony, we've arranged to have you carted away, if necessary."

"No! No," she whispered, suddenly feeling defeated. "Lydia's mother likes me."

"Not anymore," Althea proclaimed triumphantly.

"Why are you doing this?" Anna took an imploring step toward Althea. "I've never done anything to you. Why do you hate me so?"

"Because my son loved you more than me," she shot back quickly. Then as if realizing what she'd said, quickly added in a softer tone, "for a time."

Suddenly the anger and fight left Anna. This woman was pathetic. Althea must live in constant fear that she would lose her son's love. How sad that she didn't realize that love could be shared. Lydia would be the one to suffer the most. Even though her papa could provide a handsome dowry, Lydia didn't have much hope of a good marriage. Because of her stuttering and protruding front teeth, the young men of the town hadn't given Lydia a chance to show them that she was a warm and caring person. Anna was sure Althea didn't see Lydia as a threat. She must have enticed Benjamin into the marriage with the money Lydia would bring in order to get him to agree. Poor Lydia.

Anna closed her eyes, unable to bear the sight of this conniving woman. "Go away," she whispered passionately.

Althea's face reddened. "Ah! How dare you speak to me that way. You should be ashamed of yourself, but of course, you're not. But have no fear, Anna Lowell, you will get your due. Someone is watching every move you make, and in time, justice will be served."

Althea's last sentence sent a chill up Anna's back. She opened her eyes and looked straight into Althea's. Her voice deadly cold, she said, "If you don't leave now, I won't be responsible for what I might do to you."

Althea opened her mouth, then promptly closed it without uttering a sound. She picked up her skirt and swiftly walked past Anna and out the side door as Terence came running in from the taproom.

"Anna, come see the fish I caught!" Terence's bright blue eyes shone with happiness as he spread his hands to show her how big the fish was.

He didn't wait for an answer but grabbed her hand and started pulling her toward the kitchen. Anna tried to share his enthusiasm, but the venom of Althea's attack had been the last straw. All she wanted was to be left alone.

Later that night Jordan lay quietly on his bed. The township kept him busy visiting the elderly and the sick and talking about the Bible. These people might have never studied at the Puritan-founded schools of Harvard and Yale, but they knew their Bible. If he hadn't such good recall for what he had read and were not so quick with an answer, he'd have been run out of town as an impostor weeks ago. But he wasn't fooling himself: this mission wasn't keeping him wide-eyed tonight. It was Anna Lowell.

She had told him early in the evening that she wasn't feeling well and wouldn't be taking her lesson with him. When he'd tried to question her, she'd quickly slipped away and then avoided him the rest of the evening. She did look pale, and she moved more slowly than usual, but something about her told him that whatever was bothering her wasn't physical.

If he wasn't going to sleep, he'd have a drink. Jordan rose from the bed and stepped into his breeches, not bothering to button them. Quietly, he opened his desk drawer and took out his bottle of brandy and a cup. Maybe he could drink Anna off his mind.

As he sat brooding, staring into the darkness, he heard something. He set the cup aside, quieted his own breath, and listened. The noise was faint, vague. He eased to his door and opened it. For a moment he didn't hear anything, then it came again, a sound like a low whimper. He moved out onto the landing and closer to Anna's door. The floor had no rug, and the wood was cool to his bare feet. The air smelled of tallow and burned wood. He put his ear to her door and listened. He squeezed his eyes shut. Damn! She was crying.

Jordan had two choices. He could walk away and forget about her, or slip inside and comfort her. No, he couldn't go into her room. He'd been good of late. He hadn't touched her in over a week. The damn problem was that he was afraid to go into her room and endure the temptation he suffered every time he was near her.

Besides, she frightened too easily. If he tried to enter her room, she'd scream the tavern down. Anyway, it wasn't any of his damn business why she was crying. Still, the longer he stood and listened to her softly sobbing, the more he knew he had to go inside. God help him, he didn't have a choice.

He had to be careful not to alarm her. Should he knock and let her know he was coming in, or try to get to her bed before she realized he was there? Knock, he concluded.

Taking a deep breath, he rapped gently on the door and opened it at the same time. by the shadowed moonlight he saw her bolt upright at his intrusion. He opened the door wider so she would not be frightened. "Anna, it's I, Jordan," he whispered.

He closed the door behind him and hurried to her bed before she had time to think or scream. With care he lowered his weight onto the edge of the bed and whispered, "Don't be afraid. I heard you crying and came to check on you."

She sniffled, wiped her eyes with the back of her hands, and pulled the sheet up to her neck. "I wasn't crying," she protested. "You shouldn't be in here."

"How can I sleep, when I heard you sobbing?"

Fear registered in her eyes. "Was I so loud that I awakened the house?"

"Only me, I'm a light sleeper. Moss is snoring contentedly and Terence is resting like a babe."

Jordan wished there were more light in the room. The feeble moonlight didn't let him see her as he wanted to. Her eyes glistened with tears in the dimness, and he could see that her hair was tangled about her shoulders. A quick glance told him she was wearing one of the sleeveless cotton gowns he'd seen in her drawer.

"Don't worry about the others. Tell me what has you weeping in the dark night." He reached out and brushed her hair away from her shoulder so he could see her creamy skin.

She backed away from him. "I told you I wasn't crying," she whispered, though her sniffling belied her words.

"Anna."

"All right, but it was only for a moment," she admitted reluctantly.

"Why?"

She lowered her head, letting her chin rest on

her chest. Jordan gently lifted her chin, but she wouldn't let her eyes meet his. "Tell me, Anna."

"Lydia came to see me today. Her father has arranged for her to marry Benjamin."

Jordan squeezed his eyes shut for a moment. "I'm sorry, Anna. I know it must be hard to hear your best friend is going to marry the man you love."

She sniffled. "It's not that. I don't think I really loved Benjamin—not as I should have." She looked at him then. "I want Lydia to marry Benjamin. He's a good man—most of the time. And I think Lydia has always loved him, but she'd never admit it. I was cry—I mean, I'm upset because Benjamin's mother told me I couldn't come to the wedding." Her voice broke, a soft sob escaped from her lips, and Jordan pulled her into his arms, pressing her cheek to his bare shoulder, letting her tears wash his skin and her heat dry it. He was relieved to hear that she didn't love Benjamin. Damn, that made him feel good.

"Surely she didn't mean it," he offered, wanting to comfort her. She felt so wonderful here in his arms like this.

"Yes, she did," Anna mumbled. "She's a mean and spiteful woman and I hate her."

"No, you don't," he said softly. "You couldn't hate anyone, even if you tried."

Jordan brushed her hair down the length of her back. It was soft, yet it teased the palm of his hand. He savored the feel of her in his arms. She was tall for a woman, but slender. Holding her so close, he could tell just how thin she was—too thin. She worked too hard and ate too little.

Right now he'd like to put his hands around Althea Jarvis's neck and scare the devil out of her.

"Have you talked with Lydia and her parents about this?" He let his hands glide lazily up and down her back, enjoying the smooth, silky feel of her gown.

"No," she said and shook her head, rolling it back and forth across his chest. "Althea has already talked to Lydia's parents. Benjamin didn't want me there and Lydia's parents agreed. If I show up, they'll have me removed by force, if necessary."

"Do you believe they'd do it?" he questioned, loving the way her hair tickled his chest when she moved her head.

"Benjamin's mother can talk him into doing anything she wants."

She sniffled again and slid her arms around his neck to hold him tighter. Jordan knew she didn't know what she was doing to him, but holding her against his bare chest reminded him he was a man and she was a woman he wanted very badly.

He kissed the top of her head. Her hair smelled fresh washed. "Then it doesn't sound like he'd have been a good husband for you. You need a stronger man than that."

Anna raised her head and looked up at him but didn't remove her arms. "I doubt I'll ever marry."

"Why?" He kept his hands on her back and enjoying the feel of her arms around his neck, wanting to kiss her. He didn't want to stop touching her. She was so warm and so close.

"You're a beautiful woman, Anna, and you've proved you can run the tavern without your father. As soon as your mourning has passed you'll have men begging you to marry them. Benjamin is a fool for not marrying you when he had the chance."

"I'm glad Lydia is going to marry him. He's a good man. It's his mother she will have trouble with."

"You were willing to marry Benjamin with his mother in tow," he reminded her as he pulled her a little closer and caressed her gently. He knew that at any moment she would calm down enough to realize he was in her room, undressed, on her bed, and touching her as if he might never have another chance.

"But I always felt I could handle her. Papa taught me early not to let any man touch me or get the best of me, and I feel the same about women. I will stand up to anyone, but I'm not so sure Lydia will."

Jordan lifted her hair off her shoulder and pushed it to her back. She'd dropped the covers when he'd taken her in his arms and hadn't picked them back up. The gown she wore had a scooped neckline, and the soft moonlight enhanced the beauty of her neck and throat. Jordan wasn't thinking about comforting her anymore. He wasn't thinking about Lydia, Benjamin, or spying. Anna filled his thoughts completely.

"You can't manage her life for her any more than she can yours. You'll have to have faith in her and Benjamin. Lydia will take care of herself. You have to take care of Anna Lowell." As he said the words, he knew he was the one who wanted to take care of Anna. He knew it was irrational, illogical, impossible. But in the pale light of late night, alone with her in this room, none of those things mattered. None of them. He wasn't mad or crazy. He knew what he wanted. She needed him and he needed her.

Slowly, so as not to frighten her, Jordan slid his arms around her and pulled her close to him once again, letting his hands massage the muscles in her back. She moaned her pleasure and fitted her face against his throat so naturally that it made him tremble. Her breath fanned his heated skin. Jordan warred with himself. He should let her go; he had no right to pursue this course when her emotions were running so high. But God help him, he wanted her. He'd just hold her like this and be content, he told himself. He wouldn't kiss her. No, he couldn't do that. It would put him over the edge. He was too close as it was. But then her lips parted and pressed a moist kiss to the base of his throat and he was lost.

He lifted her chin and kissed her yielding lips tenderly at first, still afraid she'd bolt. She was so soft, so good, so warm and enticing. He grew hard quickly — an ache started in the pit of his stomach and spread to his loins. It had been too long since he'd been with a woman, and he was throbbing with expectation. Her silky hands slid up and down his bare back, sending shivers of desire coursing through him.

"I want to touch you, Anna," he murmured against her lips. "I know it's not right to want you, but you tempt me with every move you make."

When Jordan touched her, Anna couldn't think.

She became a part of him, hearing his words before he spoke, feeling him before his touch, seeing him, smelling his scent, tasting him. In his embrace she found all the solace she needed.

Anna had never felt a man's bare skin before, and it thrilled her to be able to touch him. His skin was smooth and slightly moist. His kisses became hard and demanding, but she felt no fear. Her weariness left and she knew she would rely on this man no matter what came next.

She moved her hands upward and touched the hair at the back of his neck. Her fingers curved around and through it, then she slid her hands over his ears, letting her fingers learn their shape. She heard him moan softly and it pleased her greatly. She let her hands rest on the sides of his face and felt the roughness of newly growing whiskers. They tickled her palm. Every part of him felt wonderful to her exploring fingers.

Jordan had to feel her body beneath him just once, then he'd walk away. With his lips pressed hungrily against hers, he leaned her back on the bed and settled himself over her. A moan of intense pleasure escaped his lips. Damn, she felt good, fit his body so well. How could he stop now?

Passion flared and his lips left hers, kissing, lightly biting his way down her neck until he found the soft mound of one breast. His hand covered it while his mouth sought the other through the thin cotton material. Her breasts were small yet firm, and she lifted them unconsciously in response. He groaned again. God had never been this good to him. He'd never wanted a woman this desperately.

"Jordan." He heard her whisper his name huskily, and he lifted his lips from her breast to her mouth and kissed her with all the desire he was feeling. Her mouth was like a flower opening to the sun. He knew she wanted him to show her how to love him, and it excited him. She wanted this as much as he did.

Jordan reached for her gown and shoved it up past her waist, wanting to see those round breasts that tempted him beyond sane reasoning.

Anna slid her hands down his chest to where his pants lay open at the bottom button.

He was suddenly aware that she didn't have anything on under her gown.

She was suddenly aware of what lay below that last button.

Once the gown was gone, there was nothing to stop him.

Once her hand slipped farther, she'd no longer wonder what a man felt like.

She was a virgin and he didn't seduce virgins.

She wanted to know. Just once. Her hand moved downward.

To hell with that, he'd make her his.

She stopped.

He froze.

Had she forgotten everything her father had warned her about?

What was he doing?

May God forgive her! They weren't even engaged!

She was a spy for the British!

Jordan jumped off the bed.

Anna pulled down her gown.

When Jordan's feet hit the floor, he didn't stop until he was once again lying on his own bed. He panted from the sheer fright of what had almost happened. He was no good for this assignment! He suspected Anna was a spy, and he still couldn't keep his hands off her. How could he want a woman who was a traitor to her country? Damn it, she was born here! This was her country.

What had the British offered her? He had to find out. She was making him crazy. He had to get out of the tavern a while. Tonight he'd ride north and find Virgil's camp. He needed the fresh air, the distance. Once he had the evidence, he would turn her over to Virgil and be free of her.

Jordan rose from the bed and finished dressing. Quietly he eased down the back stairs and out the back door.

Upstairs Anna lay curled under her quilt, though the room was quite warm. She rocked back and forth, hugging herself. She was so embarrassed she didn't want to come out of hiding. How could she have behaved so wantonly with Jordan? Benjamin had kissed her many times, but had never touched her as Jordan had. She'd never wanted Benjamin to.

Jordan knew they could never be together, just as she did. There was only one reason why she wanted to kiss him and let him kiss her. Only one reason why she was willing to let him complete what they started. She loved him. It had to be love. She didn't know if Jordan loved her or merely wanted her—not that it really mattered.

He couldn't have her in either case. He was a minister and he wouldn't take her as a mistress, nor would he marry her.

Anna continued to rock. She'd lost so much. Her father, her reputation, Benjamin, Lydia, and now Jordan. "Oh," she groaned into the depths of the covers, feeling physical pain from the toil of the day and the experience of the night. Would God never smile on her again?

Chapter Nine

The first rays of morning were breaking across a dark sky when Jordan saw evidence of Virgil's camp, a thin trail of smoke. The fresh air had cleared his head, but he still had a tightness in the pit of his stomach. His lack of control where the lovely tavernkeeper was concerned angered and worried him.

His old friend probably wouldn't be too happy to see him for fear that Jordan's visit might expose him; but if any of the townspeople saw the minister at the camp, he could easily explain that it was his Christian duty to visit the small camp of militiamen. He wouldn't be able to tell Virgil the real reason why he had to get away from the tavern. How could he say Anna Lowell was driving him crazy and he couldn't keep his hands off her? That admission wouldn't make Virgil very happy.

"Halt, and identify yourself!"

Jordan pulled his horse to an abrupt stop at the loud command. He turned to look behind where the voice had come from, but saw no one. Whoever the voice belonged to stayed hidden behind a large tree, with only the barrel of his bayonet-tipped musket showing.

"Jordan Kent, asking to speak to Virgil Chads-worth," he responded in a calm tone. He heard the shuffling of feet and mumbled voices, but no one stepped from behind the tree. His hands closed around the leather reins and his feet were poised to dig into Thad's sides if it proved he had stumbled upon some other camp. He wasn't armed, and could not defend himself if he was.

He waited in the semidarkness, listening for sounds of danger, but all he heard were feet running in the distance. He relaxed a little, hoping that whoever was running away was going to Virgil for confirmation.

"Take your hands off the reins and you're a dead man," the disembodied voice said.

They were smart to be so cautious. Jordan smiled to himself and lifted his arms a little higher.

Virgil would be angry that he had come to the camp, and he'd probably be angrier still at being awakened before full daylight. He would probably be grumpy, too, from spending so many nights on the hard ground. Jordan smiled to himself. When this damned war was over and the Colonies were free of the British and any other country that held claim to the land, he and Virgil would laugh about two such unlikely men spying for their country.

Within a matter of minutes the man came running back through the bushes and trees, calling softly, "It's clear, send him in." At that point Jordan turned around to see a bearded man with a cocked feathered hat step forward and motion with his musket for Jordan to continue. Jordan nodded his head and prodded Thad to a slow walk.

The camp was small, just as Virgil had indi-

172

cated. As Jordan rode up, Virgil hurried out of one of the two tents, buttoning the flap of his well-worn breeches. His shirt had been hastily thrown on and hung off one shoulder.

"By all that's holy, Jordan, what are you doing here? You were to wait until I came to you. I hope the risk you're taking is worth the information you have."

Virgil's shoulder-length hair fell across his face as he bent his head to find another buttonhole. Jordan had never seen his friend so flustered or in such a state of undress. He laughed heartily as he climbed down, handing his reins to the man who'd followed him into camp.

"Finding you in this undignified state is most rewarding. Well worth the short journey."

"Hold your vulgar humor, it's most unbecoming under the circumstances. It's not safe for you to be here. Whatever got into you? Should you be caught here—"

"Slow down, Virgil." Jordan sobered. "No one followed me. I made sure of that, and I have a ready explanation should any of the townspeople wander into camp. I've found that many things can be brushed aside or completely forgotten with the simple words 'It was my Christian duty.' "

"They do come into camp, the hunters and trappers," Virgil said, and started buttoning the other side of his breeches.

"I'll be careful," Jordan promised, stretching his arms above his head, hoping to ease the tension in his tight muscles. "I had to get away from the tavern for a while, away from the town." And away from Anna, he added to himself.

He walked over, picked up the pot that sat on a bed of coals, and looked around for a cup. He found one on a log and poured it full of the steaming liquid.

"I'm used to a little more diversion than I've had the last few weeks." As soon as the words were out he was angry with himself. Why did he have to defend himself? He'd get the accursed job done, and then make sure it would be a hell of a long time before he accepted another.

"At least you have a bed to sleep in and properly cooked food. Don't expect me to feel sorry for you." Virgil rubbed his back before reaching into the tent and pulling out an extra stool for Jordan to sit on.

Jordan sipped the hot liquid and wondered what it was. It certainly didn't taste like coffee, tea, or rum. "What's this stuff?" he asked, wondering if he should continue drinking it.

"A plant the Ramapo Indians told us about. Go on and drink it. It won't hurt you, and it takes the chill off."

Jordan sipped the slightly bitter brew again and decided he could tolerate it.

"I didn't expect it to be more than a week before I saw you again," he grumbled a few moments later.

"You knew I'd come when I had word. My messenger to New York returned only last evening."

"And what does he have to say? What do we learn of Andre?" Jordan asked, not sure that he really wanted to know.

"John Andre was born in London in May of '50. He first came to America in '72 and later spent

174

some time in prison in Pennsylvania. He's known for his charm and his literary talents, as well as his efficiency and willingness to work tirelessly. The word is that he is responsible for deciding what intelligence goes to Clinton."

"Interesting. Who speaks so well of him?" Jordan asked in an irritated voice. This glowing report of the man didn't make him feel any better about Andre's connection with Anna.

"Informants in New York," Virgil answered. "He started as an intelligence officer to Clinton, but recently he was appointed Clinton's adjutant general and purchased a commission as major, which I believe you already know. There's talk, however, that he is the intellectual power behind Clinton."

The knot in Jordan's stomach grew and his chest tightened. It appeared that when Anna got involved she went straight to the top. Damn her!

"It's my opinion that when you saw Andre at the tavern he was on his way to Newport to check personally on the arrival of Rochambeau's troops. He wouldn't be the kind to leave such an important matter to others."

"You're right, if what Lafayette's men say is true. He'd want to know exactly what they were up against."

"I'm sure he'd want to know the number of men and ships. I have no idea what his sources may have told him, but Rochambeau brings with him six ships, several frigates and transports, and six thousand men to join the Continental Army. Of course, Clinton would find the information useful and probably pull his forces closer to New York, thinking we'll try and regain the city. Rochambeau will wait in Newport for the French Navy, which I hear is on the way."

"Clinton knows he'll be in trouble once the navy arrives. They must be planning night and day."

"And so should we. I think they may try to control the Hudson. That would hurt us greatly."

Jordan nodded his agreement. "We must guard against that. Where is Washington now?"

"Morristown, last I heard. He's constantly on the move and doesn't keep me apprised of all his plans." Virgil sipped his drink like a gentleman, though he looked like a beggar.

"What else did Lafayette's men have to say?"

"The usual rumors: the Continental Army grows weaker every day while the British grow stronger; there's an impending defection of a high-ranking American officer; and of course, there's jubilation because of the fall of Charleston."

"You know what I think of rumors," Jordan answered.

"Yes, you've told me many times. But we're not in a position to take any bit of news lightly. Now, tell me, what brought you here before the break of day? Have you seen more of Andre?"

"No, only that one time." He wasn't hedging but knew it sounded as if he were.

"Come now, Jordan, surely you didn't travel all this way because you miss me?"

Virgil's sarcasm was well founded, but Jordan still didn't like it. "I told you I had to get away for a while."

"Well, let's at least make this trip count for something. Tell me who you saw in a covert alliance with Andre."

Jordan didn't answer.

Virgil rubbed his lightly whiskered chin and sighed. "Are you protecting someone, Jordan? A certain woman, perhaps?"

"No," he responded with all honesty. "I'm beginning to believe the person I saw with Andre is innocent of any wrongdoing. I won't say anything until I have proof one way or the other." He drained his cup and got up and poured more. This whole business wasn't to his liking. If he'd never agreed to this plan, his stomach wouldn't be twisted in knots at the thought of Anna being a loyalist, or worse, a turncoat.

"What kind of proof do you need? What are you doing to get this proof? Damnation! Andre showed up at the tavern. How much more evidence do you need?"

Jordan turned angry eyes on Virgil and tossed the contents of the cup into the bushes. "Andre's appearance is all I do have. I was in the taproom when he first walked through the door. I stayed up the whole damn night watching his room so I'd know if anyone came or went. I was there when he rode away. Damn it, Virgil, I'm beginning to believe his visit to Lowell Tavern was as innocent as it appeared to be and that I need to return my concentration to finding out who John Anderson is and who asked him to come to the tavern." Jordan sighed and sat back down, stretching out his legs.

"You make me grow weary, Jordan. Whom are you protecting?"

Jordan's head snapped up and their eyes met. Virgil was too smart. He should have known he couldn't fool him. "At this point, I'm not protecting anyone. I have no proof of anything, although my eyes and ears are always open."

"Very well." Virgil sighed, then continued. "I have a feeling something big is going to happen soon. I can feel it. The British are not going to sit around quietly and wait for the French Navy to arrive and join forces with Rochambeau. They're making plans, charting courses, and regrouping. We must do the same. We can't discount any bit of information that may be afforded us."

Jordan looked away from Virgil to the beautiful shading of an early morning sunrise. Taking the subtle reprimand to heart, he answered soberly, "I don't intend to."

Anna paced across the back porch, watching for Terence. She'd sent him to watch Benjamin's house more than an hour ago. He was to come tell her the moment he saw Althea leave for her daily afternoon gossip rounds.

Anna hadn't slept at all after Jordan had left her room last night. After fighting to calm down, she gave up and used the time to think and plan. One of the decisions she'd made was to talk to Benjamin about Lydia. That had to be done without Althea present. The other decision came about after no small argument with herself.

She knew very little about what went on between a man and a woman in the dark of night, other than what Jordan had taught her. However, she had picked up a certain amount of knowledge simply from working in the tavern. She now knew enough to be aware that she loved Jordan and

178

wanted to be with him. It was doubtful that, as a minister, Jordan would take a mistress, and she was smart enough to know that while the people of Georgetown readily accepted her as the tavernkeeper, she'd never be approved of as their minister's wife. At daybreak, she had come to the conclusion that she loved Jordan and didn't want to give him up.

Of course, she didn't plan to walk up to him and announce that she would be his mistress should he need or want one. But should the occasion arise again, she would be ready to give herself to him completely.

Anna was about to give up hope that Althea was going to leave for the day when she saw Terence running toward her, his queue bouncing from shoulder to shoulder, his arms pumping. She smiled at how fast he ran, how surefooted he was for his age.

"Has she left?" Anna asked, meeting him by the barn.

"Just now," he answered breathlessly.

"Good. You stay in the kitchen and help Glynis and Mrs. Dudley. If they ask where I've gone, tell them you don't know."

"That's lying, and Papa doesn't want us to do it," he reminded her, a stern look on his young face.

Anna thought quickly. "You're right. Tell them it's none of your concern, and shouldn't concern them, either. How's that? Would Papa approve?"

Terence smiled broadly. "Yes. May I serve drinks if you're not back in time?" His bright eyes sparkled at the prospect.

"I'll be back, don't you worry. You just make sure all the checkers are on the boards and the darts are in place," she said, then headed for the Jarvis house.

Anna hurried along the dusty road. Benjamin and Althea's house was the next to the last on the right. She took the back road to ward off being seen going into their house lest it cause more gossip.

When she came to the back of Benjamin's house, she ran up the steps and took a long, deep breath before giving the wood three loud raps.

Benjamin came to the door. "Anna," he said in surprise.

"May I come in, Benjamin? I need to talk to you." Her voice wasn't as steady as she would have liked.

He opened the door wider and stepped back, allowing her entrance into the kitchen. The room was clean but hot. A low fire burned in the fireplace and a pot of stew simmered over the flames.

"Let's go into the parlor, where we'll be more comfortable," Benjamin suggested.

"No," she said nervously, knowing that she couldn't back down now that she was here. "I can't stay that long and I'd be more comfortable in here." Her stomach was shaking and her voice was light. "I came because I'm worried about Lydia."

Benjamin scrutinized her as he leaned a hip against the rectangular table. "You came because you're worried about Lydia?" His tone and the quirk of his eyebrows questioned her more than his words.

"Yes. I want you to know that I'm very happy

that you're marrying her." Anna took a step closer to him. "She's such a lovely person. She's kind and gentle. She'll be a loving wife for you and a caring mother for your children."

"Are you sure you're speaking for Lydia and not yourself?"

"What?" She knew she hadn't gotten to the real reason for her visit, but what was he thinking? "I don't understand. Of course I'm talking about Lydia."

"I think not," he said, reaching out to pull her to him as he continued to lean against the table.

Anna tried to keep her balance, but she hadn't expected him to grab her. She fell hard on his body, and his arms slipped around her waist to hold her firmly against him. She squirmed and pushed against his chest until her eyes met his. His look told her he didn't intend to let her go. She ceased struggling. "Benjamin, don't do this. I came to talk to you."

"You are so beautiful, Anna," he whispered, his eyes caressing her face.

"Lydia is beautiful, too," she hurried to say. "Benjamin, one of the reasons I came was to make sure you realized just how lovely she is and how she will make you the perfect wife if only you'll let her."

"No, you came here to tempt me, to show me your beauty and remind me that I could have had you."

His hold tightened and a small pebble of fear rolled inside Anna. She was no match for his strength, so she had to try and reason her way out of his arms. "Benjamin, let me go and we'll talk about this."

"Let you go?" His smile was crooked, his eyes lit with mischief. "Now that I have you you want me to let you go? No, you came to me for this." A chuckle rumbled deep in his chest as he bent his head and kissed her cheek, letting his lips travel down her neck with ease.

Anna closed her eyes. She wished she felt something. If Benjamin's kisses had stirred her as Jordan's had, maybe she'd have thought twice about selling the tavern and becoming his wife. Now that she knew she loved Jordan, she hated being this close to Benjamin.

"Let me go! I came only to ask you to watch over Lydia and not let your mother hurt her." She pushed against his chest, harder this time.

Snapping his head up, Benjamin's arms tightened so Anna could hardly breathe. She felt as if he were going to crack a rib. His expression looked diabolical and her fear grew larger. "Benjamin, you're hurting me." She pushed at his arms.

"Why did you mention my mother? She has nothing to do with this."

His tone of voice carried with it a heavy warning, but Anna decided to ignore it. "She has everything to do with why I'm here. I'm afraid she'll be mean and cruel to Lydia, and you must not let that happen!"

"Get out!" Benjamin shoved her so harshly she stumbled backward. She gasped and tried to catch herself with her hand, succeeding only in wrenching her wrist as she fell to the hard floor.

Before she could gather her wits, Benjamin

grabbed the bodice of her dress with both hands and hauled her to her feet. "You leave my mother out of this, whore." He brought her face dangerously close to his. "I didn't ask you to come around here, flaunting your body. You came to me!" His hot breath fanned her cheeks, his nostrils flared with anger. For the first time Anna saw how much Benjamin looked like his mother. And now he had started to act like her.

Anna was afraid he was going to beat her. If he did, no one would blame him. He was right, she had come to him. Oh God, what a horrible mistake that was!

"I-I only wanted to talk. I was concerned for Lydia," she whispered desperately, trying to pull away from him.

"You wanted to tease me and tempt me. You're of the devil, just like Mama said. She's right. I'm lucky to be rid of you." He pushed her away once again, but this time she kept her footing.

"I'm not of the devil! That's not true and you know it." It was foolish of her to argue with him, knowing he was dangerous.

"Get out and don't come back," he yelled as he took a menacing step toward her. "And if I hear you've been near Lydia, I'll run you out of town!"

Anna felt degraded and scared as she ran from his house. Tears filled her eyes as she left the main road and ran into the woods. A limb caught her sleeve and tore it, scratching her arm. She took no note of it and kept running. It would take longer to reach the safety of the tavern this way, but she didn't want to take the chance of anyone seeing her crying.

How could she have been so foolish as to think Benjamin would listen to her? Althea had filled his head with too many lies. Poor Lydia. All she had wanted to do was help.

What was wrong with her? Jordan said she tempted him beyond his control. That she had tempted Benjamin was obvious. The man she'd killed . . . had she in some way lured him into attacking her, too?

"No!" she muttered vehemently as her booted feet pounded the hard earth. She'd never have anything to do with a man again. Never! She was an idiot to think that Jordan would take her as a mistress.

In despair, Anna sank to the ground and gave way to the sobs she'd been containing for so long.

Jordan was in no hurry to get back to the tavern. He let Thad slowly pick his way down the road, past the wooden houses of the town.

"Reverend Kent! Reverend Kent!"

Cringing inside, Jordan pulled Thad to a stop while Althea Jarvis hurried to catch up with him. He'd kept a watchful eye on the woman, thinking she might talk about their discussion of Anna. But he soon realized that she liked the idea of the two of them sharing a little secret.

"What can I do for you, Mrs. Jarvis?" he asked politely as he looked down at her from his horse.

"I haven't talked with you in several days, and I was wondering if you'd found out anything more about what we discussed last week."

Jordan rubbed the back of his neck. "What exactly are you referring to?" he asked, though he knew.

"Well, Anna Lowell, of course. I've been thinking about what you said about—" She looked around to see if anyone was near enough to hear. "About her spying for the British."

"I've asked you not to talk about that." Thad shifted and snorted, causing Althea to step backward.

"Oh, I haven't, but I just wanted to make sure you had the matter under control."

Jordan looked down at her and forced a smile. "Yes, I'm keeping an eye on her. If anything happens that I think you should know about, I'll get in touch with you at once."

She smiled, and her ample chest heaved with satisfaction. "Splendid. Now, I want to talk to you about Benjamin and Lydia's wedding." Her full lips pursed. "Because of all that's happened of late, her parents and I think the marriage should take place as quickly as possible. Are you in agreement?"

Jordan just stared at the woman for a moment. He was well aware that a wedding was to take place, but he hadn't realized he'd be expected to perform the ceremony. Hell and damnation! What would come up next? Preaching from the Holy Book was one thing; he believed most of what it said—but marrying Lydia and Benjamin was an entirely different matter. Surely Virgil didn't expect him to go that far.

"Does this Saturday fit into your schedule all right?" she asked, a wide smile on her face.

Of course Virgil expected him to do it. That's why he had had that elder from the Congregational Church in Boston lay hands on him. If anything like this came up, it had to be legal.

"Reverend, are you all right?" she asked.

Jordan turned his attention back to the woman gazing up at him. He cleared his throat. "I'm sure that date will be fine."

"Good," she said with a satisfied smile. "Now, I want you to—"

In an instant Jordan had ceased to listen. If he could get his hands on Virgil right now, he'd bloody his blasted nose and dare him to make a sound in his own defense. He'd get Virgil Chadsworth for this. He'd get Washington and Adams, too.

Chapter Ten

The taproom had been quiet for a Monday night. Most of the townsfolk were at the meeting-house for Benjamin and Lydia's wedding feast. Anna had been outwardly cheerful all evening, but on the inside she was sad. Even though she was glad she wasn't marrying Benjamin, she was offended that she wasn't allowed to attend the wedding. And if she were truthful, she was disappointed she wasn't the one getting married. She'd be nineteen soon, well on her way to being too old to make a good marriage.

Anna was also still disturbed by Benjamin's behavior the last time she saw him. His treatment of her could have been prompted by anger over her refusal to sell the tavern and marry him; but he'd shown her a side she'd never seen before, and she now worried whether he might be cruel to Lydia. She would hate to see Lydia endure ill treatment from an unloving husband. Althea was bound to make enough trouble for Lydia as it was. She didn't need Benjamin being mean to her as well.

"Kitchen's clean," Glynis said as she shuffled

into the taproom, wiping her wet hands on a soiled apron.

Anna looked up from the checkerboard and smiled. "Glynis, please come join us in a game."

"No. I'm too tired," Glynis said, her tone matching her words. "If there's nothing else to do, I'll say goodnight."

Anna was disappointed she couldn't talk Glynis into playing with them. Her work was fine and she was a good cook, but she refused to participate in what little fun they had. Maybe Glynis hadn't forgiven her for the reprimand concerning Jordan's room. "All right, Glynis. Maybe next time. I'll see you in the morning. Have a restful night."

When the woman was gone, she turned her attention to Moss and asked, "Why do you suppose Glynis refuses to join us for a friendly game?"

Moss sat across the table from Anna with Terence in a chair between them, patiently waiting to play the winner. The old man rubbed his bearded chin and made a rumbling noise in his throat. "She's just a private person. I expect it's best to leave her alone and let her keep to herself. Some people don't take to others."

"I suppose you're right, Moss," she said, picking up the small piece of corncob and making her next move.

Suddenly Moss snapped his game piece across the board and picked up her remaining three men. Astonished, Anna complained, "Wait, you moved so fast I didn't see what you did."

"You should've been looking," he answered.

"I was. You're just too quick for me. How do I know you weren't cheating?"

"Because I don't cheat. I'm good. I don't have to cheat, like some people I know." He looked directly at Terence.

"I don't cheat," Terence said defensively, his eyes widening. "Ask Anna. I don't cheat, do I?"

Anna and Moss both laughed, and Anna patted Terence's arm. "Of course you don't cheat. Moss is only teasing you to get you fired up and ready for the next game. You're a good player, just as Moss is. Here, take my chair so you can play. I've got to count the money we made tonight and record it in the book."

"I can count. Let me do it." Terence jumped up from his chair and stood beside his sister.

Anna rose and smiled down on Terence. He was growing. By next spring she had no doubt his crown would reach her shoulder. He was going to be tall and broad-shouldered, like their papa. "Not tonight. But I will let you help me when you start school. Now help Moss set up the board. You have time for one more game, and then it's off to bed."

Terence continued to grumble as Anna walked over to the bar to get the account book and the small bag of money. It wouldn't take long to do the work tonight. Few people had stopped in for drinks, and she'd served only three plates of the rabbit stew Glynis had cooked.

Instead of going back to the table where the light was better, Anna continued to stand at the bar and as quickly as she could, filled in the proper accounts. Occasionally she'd look over at Moss and Terence when an argument erupted, but for the most part she remained quiet and let them settle their differences. As their game wound down, Anna realized she'd be glad when they finally went to bed. She'd like some time alone to wash and change before Jordan came in from the wedding.

They hadn't talked much since that night he had come into her bedroom. She knew he was angry with himself for what had happened. She'd tried to ease the awkwardness by calling off her lessons in the evenings. Jordan had actually seemed relieved to hear that she was too tired at night to continue with them. He'd mumbled something about starting them again later in the year when the tavern wasn't so busy and she'd agreed.

It might make him unhappy tonight to come in and see her waiting for him, but she intended to ask him about the wedding. She wasn't interested in Benjamin, but she was desperate for news of Lydia, and she wanted very much to spend some time alone with Jordan. She had missed their time alone in the evenings more than she'd thought she would.

The wedding party was a change from the strained atmosphere Jordan had endured at Lowell Tavern the past two weeks. Everyone seemed delighted at the opportunity to have some overdue fun for a few hours.

Jordan left the jovial group he was standing with and slipped outside for some fresh air. A large moon and twinkling stars brightened the sky. The revelers, filling their bellies with drink and food, would have no trouble finding their way home tonight. The August nights were getting cool, but he didn't mind the brisk air as he walked to the back of the meetinghouse, trying to distance himself from the noisemakers inside.

Several days had passed since he'd had a real conversation with Anna. She was apparently avoiding him as much as he was avoiding her. After he'd returned from Virgil's camp and excused himself from the talkative Althea, he'd gone back to the tavern and been surprised to find Anna gone. It had been easy for him to slip upstairs and back into her room to make another search for incriminating evidence.

Once again the only things he found were documents that concerned the tavern, the money, and the other treasures she kept in the tin box. The love poem was also still there, which was a good indication it was never intended for anyone else.

As the days passed, he found nothing to hold against Anna except her association with Andre. Was that enough to label her a spy?

"Hello, Reverend Kent. It is pleasant out tonight, isn't it?"

Jordan turned quickly to see Molly Henderson gliding up behind him. He was usually more alert to the sounds around him. He blamed his failure to hear her approach on the fact that she was still so far away when she called to him, not the possibility that he was so deep in thought about Anna that he probably wouldn't have heard a horse galloping his way.

Molly's hair was piled high on her head in a fashion that looked ridiculously uncomfortable. He knew the style was fashionable, but he preferred hair like Anna's—long and clean. Molly's dress was expensive, but showing age. The low-cut bodice revealed an expanse of ample bosom. A band of wide lace at the neckline had been sewn in to partially conceal her breasts.

"Good evening to you again, Mrs. Henderson." He bowed stiffly in her direction.

"You performed a beautiful ceremony. Just made me cry, remembering my own husband. I thought about the day he left to fight in the Continental Army more than a year ago. I know he was listed as having died on one of those prison ships docked in New York Harbor, but I still have hope they were wrong and that he'll return one day."

Jordan watched her expression. She said all the right words, but she didn't look or sound the least bit concerned about her husband dying in prison. Maybe it was because she told him about it so often that it no longer bothered him or her. He knew she wanted him to feel sorry for her, and in a way he did. He was sorry about every life lost in the battles with the British. And he also knew that Molly wanted him to be more than sorry for her. She wanted him to have a covert relationship with her, and following him outside meant she was no longer being modest about it.

As she stepped closer to him, the moonlight brightened her face. She was a pretty woman but by no means beautiful. She was giving him a look he knew well, the look he always received from Boston's wenches when they were ready for him to meet them. As he watched her closely he decided that perhaps she was just what he needed tonight. He hadn't had a woman since he'd left Boston. He

TO GET YOUR
4 FREE BOOKS
MAIL THE COUPON BELOW.

Heartfire Romance

FREE BOOK CERTIFICATE

GET 4 FREE BOOKS

Yes! I want to subscribe to Zebra's HEARTFIRE HOME SUBSCRIPTION SERVICE. Please send me my 4 FREE books. Then each month I'll receive the four newest Heartfire Romances as soon as they are published to preview Free for ten days. If I decide to keep them I'll pay the special discounted price of just $3.50 each; a total of $14.00. This is a savings of $3.00 off the regular publishers price. There are no shipping, handling or other hidden charges. There is no minimum number of books to buy and I may cancel this subscription at any time. In any case the 4 FREE Books are mine to keep regardless.

NAME _____

ADDRESS _____

CITY _____ STATE _____ ZIP _____

TELEPHONE _____

SIGNATURE _____

(If under 18 parent or guardian must sign)
Terms and prices subject to change.
Orders subject to acceptance.

HF 111

GET 4 FREE BOOKS

HEARTFIRE HOME SUBSCRIPTION
SERVICE
P.O. BOX 5214
120 BRIGHTON ROAD
CLIFTON, NEW JERSEY 07015

AFFIX
STAMP
HERE

couldn't count the nights he'd twisted and turned in bed, frustrated, wanting to go to Anna, who lay just a couple of doors away from him. Could this woman who stood so willingly before him ease his frustration and make him forget about Anna?

Before he had time to consider the idea further and possibly talk himself out of what he was about to do, he took her arm and said, "It's such a pleasant evening, Molly. Why don't we go for a walk?"

She smiled up at him with sparkling eyes and pressed her body against his. "I'd love to, Reverend."

Maybe this wasn't a smart thing to do, he thought as they started walking, but he wasn't feeling very smart right now. In fact, in all his twenty-eight years he'd never been so unsure of his feelings. He'd never felt as if he needed to forget about a woman because he'd never remembered the taste or feel of one until he'd met Anna.

The laughing and talking faded as they walked deeper into the woods behind the meetinghouse. Jordan looked back several times to make sure no one watched from the window. It wouldn't do for anyone to see the minister walking into the woods at night with a widow. If a man and woman were willing, he didn't think it was wrong or anyone else's business, even for a man who preached from the Holy Book. However, he doubted the town would look upon his tryst with Molly Henderson as he did. If he wanted a woman, he wanted her. He didn't want anyone questioning him, pointing a finger at him, or telling him no.

Suddenly Jordan grabbed Molly around the

193

waist and shoved her up against a tree. She groaned her disapproval at his roughness as his lips found hers with hard, demanding pressure, but she responded eagerly. He didn't have time to do this properly. He was desperate to prove to himself that Anna hadn't spoiled him for the taste of other women. He slid his hand beneath the low-necked bodice and cupped her full breast all in one easy motion. With his other hand he grabbed hold of the tree so tightly the bark cut into his palm, and pressed his lower body against her. Jordan wasn't loving; he wasn't easy or kind, either. He pressed harder, trying to elicit a response from his manhood.

Nothing was happening.

He kissed her harder, thrusting his tongue deeper into her mouth, waiting for the first threads of desire to catch hold and spread throughout his body and heat him. He squeezed and pulled at the peak of her breast while his tongue plundered her mouth. He listened to her soft murmuring. A woman's pleasure at his hands usually heightened his arousal.

His response to Molly was dry and unmoving.

He moved his lips down her neck, lightly biting as he went, and buried his face in the wealth of her breasts, pushing them up and out of the confines of her dress. He nuzzled and suckled while Molly cupped his head with her hands, moaning with pleasure, whispering words meant to increase his performance.

There was no physical reaction in him.

Jordan knew the problem, but he refused to admit it. He wanted Anna. *You can't have Anna,* he told himself, and tried harder to enjoy the ever-so-willing woman in his arms. He thought of Anna, tried to tell himself it was her breasts he was kissing and caressing, but his body and mind wouldn't be fooled. He knew the feel of Anna. He knew her taste. And he also knew he wanted no other woman.

After another frustrating moment Jordan left Molly so suddenly it was as if he'd been yanked away from her. This had never happened to him before. His head was spinning with self-disgust and embarrassment and shame. He wanted simply to disappear, but that wouldn't happen. Never before had he not been able to complete what he'd started. He stood with his back to Molly, his breathing ragged. The palm of his hand burned from the scratches caused by the tree. He had to do something to save his pride and hers, too. He rubbed his lips hard with the back of his hand, trying to erase her taste and the whole damn incident.

He doubted she would talk about this to anyone in town. It would ruin her reputation as well as his. Right now, he had to come up with some damn good words for what he'd done to her. Turning to face her, he quietly and calmly said, "Molly, you are a beautiful woman and you tempted me, but by the loving grace of God I was able to stop in time before forgiveness would have been impossible. My apologies, Mrs. Henderson."

"But Reverend, I don't mind. I mean, I wanted you to do those things. I miss my husband." She grabbed the front of his jacket and pulled him toward her.

Her dark eyes glistened and Jordan knew she meant it. He was sorry that he hadn't been the one who could ease her pain. "I'm sure you do. But I can't be a substitute."

He grasped her wrists and held them, waiting for her to let go of his coat. When she did, he turned and headed for the tavern at a brisk pace.

After going upstairs to put the money away and seeing Terence to bed, Anna took a plain but new dress from her chest and carried it back downstairs with her. In the kitchen she took a kettle and placed it on the table, pouring fresh water into it. She then added a little cinnamon and a dash of cloves to the water and mixed it with her hand. Stepping out of her work dress, she took a small cloth and dipped it in the spice-scented water. The cloth was cool and refreshing as she washed her face, her arms, between her legs, and then her feet. After she was finished with her body, she let her hair down. Bending over the table, she rinsed the length of it in the kettle of water. She squeezed what moisture she could out of her hair and the cloth, then brushed the cloth through her hair so it would dry quicker.

She knew she was taking extra time with her bath this evening, and she tried to tell herself she wasn't doing it for Jordan, but she was. She wanted him to notice her. When she'd combed through her hair with her fingers, Anna stepped into the new dark blue muslin dress. It was simple, with a rounded neckline and long, straight sleeves. The bodice fit tightly at the waist, and the gathered skirt made her hips look fuller than they actually were.

She remained barefoot while she poured out the bath water and hung the cloth up to dry. There was still no sign of Jordan when she went back into the taproom, so she did something she'd never done before: she went behind the bar and took out a jug of her father's elderberry wine. Lifting a pewter measure off the shelf, she poured herself half a gill of the wine, then sat in front of the unlit fireplace to wait for Jordan.

After she'd settled on the high-backed rocker, she took a deep breath and sipped her first taste of the wine. She swallowed it quickly, hoping it wouldn't have time to burn her tongue, but it did. It burned all the way down into her stomach, spreading warmth as it went. She wiped her mouth and coughed as tears rushed to her eyes. The smell of the strong wine mixed with the ever-present scent of burned wood permeated the air around her. She fanned her mouth with her hand and breathed deeply.

A year or so ago her father had let her taste the wine. She didn't remember that it was so strong, and she surely didn't remember its burning like a fire in the pit of her stomach. Maybe she had had too much at one time. Perhaps she should try it again. After all, she was the tavernkeeper now and ought to be able to judge what she sold. This wine must be good or so many men wouldn't drink it.

Squeezing her eyes shut, Anna took another taste and swallowed it just as quickly and it burned just as badly. A heat spread up her neck and over her cheeks, giving her the feeling she was standing in front of a roaring fire. No wonder men especially liked to drink on cold nights. This sack would take the chill off the coldest midwinter day. She sipped from her cup again and realized she wasn't going to like it no matter how many times she tried. Cup in hand, she leaned her head back against the rocker and rested, waiting for Jordan to come in so she could talk to him.

Just as her lids grew heavy and closed, the Deerfield door swung open and Jordan stepped inside. It was clear he hadn't expected her to be up so late. Well, she had waited all this time. She wasn't going to let his brooding expression keep her from asking about Lydia.

"You're still up," he observed as he shut the door and slid the latch home.

Anna rose from the rocker trying to hide the light-headedness she felt. For a long moment he just looked at her, his gaze caressing her face. The heat returned to her cheeks, so she sat back down as he continued into the dimly lit room.

"I waited up to talk to you. I wanted to hear about Lydia and the wedding — that is, if you don't mind taking the time to tell me about it." Her voice was soft, breathy.

"Not at all. Do you mind if I get myself a drink?" He took off his black coat and threw it over a chair.

Anna had never noticed his looking tired before, but he did tonight. His hair was mussed attractively and his waistcoat unbuttoned. "No, of course not. I have the elderberry wine out, if you'd like that. I was having a little myself."

He looked back at her. Blue eyes met blue

eyes. "I didn't know you had the inclination."

She gave him equal measure from her gaze. "I don't. I mean, I didn't until tonight."

She watched as he took a cup like hers down from the shelf and filled it. He carried it closer to his eyes and peered inside, then carried it up to his nose and smelled it. Next he tasted it, but kept his gaze on her.

When he brought the cup down from his lips, a smile stretched across his face. "Did you say this was elderberry wine?"

"Yes, Papa and Moss made it about a year ago."

He laughed lightly as he started toward her. "Well, either your papa and Moss made a mistake and made some very expensive brandy, or you've mixed the bottles."

"Brandy?" She looked at the cup she still held. In the pewter cup and dim light she couldn't see the color and she hadn't noticed when she poured it. "No wonder my head is spinning." She touched her forehead.

Jordan came over and knelt on one knee in front of her chair. Taking the cup from her, he looked inside. "There's less than an ounce in here. How much did you pour?"

"About half a gill."

"Then you've had little more than an ounce. I don't think that's enough to make you drunk."

He was so close she wanted to reach out and touch his face, draw him to her. The fire in her stomach spread between her legs and suddenly she wanted nothing more than his touch and his kisses. No, she didn't feel drunk. She wasn't. She felt languid. She knew what she was saying and what she was doing, and she also knew what she wanted.

Anna forced her eyes away from his face and looked at the low-burning candle. "After the wedding, did Lydia look happy?" she asked.

"Very happy," he answered, then sipped his drink. "How does that make you feel?" he asked, looking into her eyes.

She swallowed hard under his close scrutiny. "I want her to be happy. I told you that, and I meant it." She lowered her lashes for a moment. The last time they'd discussed Lydia they'd been on her bed and Jordan had comforted her. No, it was more than comfort. He'd been making love to her.

Anna looked back at Jordan. "Did you talk to her?"

"Yes, she asked me to give you a message." He sighed. "She said she will come to see you as soon as she can. She doesn't understand why her parents and Benjamin are keeping her from you, but first chance she gets, she will come see you."

Anna smiled warmly, feeling unnaturally pensive. "I'm glad. That means she doesn't believe all those things Benjamin and his mother must be saying about me."

"No, she doesn't believe them, and neither does anyone else in town. In time, everyone will forget their gossip."

"Do you think Lydia still wants to be my friend?"

"I'm sure of it." He took a long drink and winced when he brought the cup down.

"You are especially lovely tonight, Anna. The

color of your dress makes your eyes glimmer like the most beautiful of sapphires."

Jordan took another big swallow of the brandy. Why had he said that? Just because she had on a new dress that matched her eyes perfectly. Just because she had that fresh-scrubbed look he found so appealing. Just because her hair was damp and curling temptingly about her small shoulders. Just because her eyes were bright and her lips a shade of pink that looked so kissable was no reason for his body to betray him now and give him what he had needed when he had Molly Henderson backed against that tree.

"Was Lydia lovely tonight? Did she look beautiful?" Anna asked.

Jordan cleared his throat and tried to clear his thoughts. "Indeed she was," he answered, and relied once again on the brandy. *But not as lovely as you are right now.* He knew he should get up, leave her alone, lock himself in his room. Shoot himself if he tried to come out.

But he couldn't. He was still raw from trying to assuage himself with another woman. He'd thought about Anna all night, and he wasn't going to pass up the opportunity to sit with her, look at her, be with her. He wanted to push from his mind the disaster that had happened earlier that evening.

"I hope she has six children and that she'll bring all of them to the tavern to play."

"With your children?" he asked, still on one knee in front of her rocker.

Her smile faded. "No, I doubt I shall ever marry now."

"Anna, you're a very beautiful woman. Of course you'll marry."

Their eyes met and she whispered, "Not if I can't find someone whose kisses make me feel the way yours do."

Jordan's even breathing changed to choppy gulps in an instant. "Don't say that, Anna," he whispered. He tilted his head back, closed his eyes, and finished off his brandy. When he brought the cup down and opened his eyes, she was staring at him. He contemplated pouring more brandy, but he knew that wasn't what he needed or wanted.

He'd managed to control himself the last two weeks: not touching her, refusing to say more than what was required for politeness, even when he wanted to pull her into his arms and kiss her. Now here she was, telling him that she'd never have anyone kiss her the way he did. Did she know that was just the thing he wanted to hear? Did she know he felt the same way about her? Did she know he was aching inside for want of her?

He set his empty cup on the floor beside hers as his other knee went down to steady him. "Anna," he whispered her name as his arms slid around her waist, as her arms slipped around his neck.

Looking into Anna's eyes, he knew why he didn't want Molly tonight, why he didn't want any other woman but this one. He'd fallen in love with her. He didn't know how it had happened or when or why. He'd certainly fought it every step of the way. And as she gazed into his eyes, he knew she loved him, too.

There was no need to keep himself from her,

now that he'd admitted he loved her. He winced. Tomorrow would be filled with recriminations, but tonight there was only Anna. He rose and lifted Anna from the chair and wrapped his arms around her. Then he reached over the table and blew out the candle, leaving them surrounded by only pale moonlight. He lowered his mouth to hers. Soft and gentle was the kiss at first; then, as desire kindled, the pressure grew. Oh yes, this was Anna, this was the woman he wanted, the woman he loved.

Reluctantly, he lifted his head. "Anna, do you know what I want?"

She nodded.

"Do you want it as well?" he asked quietly, letting her know she could stop everything with one word.

"I know what I'm doing and what I want. I have no doubts." Her answer was clear, though her voice was a whisper.

Jordan didn't wait for more to be said. He picked her up as if she weighed nothing, and started quietly up the stairs. When he stood in front of her door, she reached out and opened it for him. Inside, he lowered her to the floor and quietly closed the door, slipping home the latch. He kept his hand on the bolt for a moment and realized he was shaking. He didn't remember being this nervous years ago when it was his first time with a woman. The brandy should have calmed him, made him confident, but it didn't. This woman was too special. He was too afraid of hurting her, scaring her. She touched his arm and he turned back to her.

Moonlight illuminated her face, and her loving expression took his breath away. Should he question her again? Did she really know what it meant for him to be in her room right now?

When he turned from the door and faced her, Anna saw his hesitancy. She understood. He was a minister, and what she was asking him to do was wrong, no matter how badly they both wanted it. Tonight might be the only time she ever had the courage to tempt him into doing this. And she knew that tonight might be the only time they could be together. He'd told her the last time he'd held and kissed her that fate had chosen different destinies for them. After tonight, he'd berate himself for being a fool, hate her for tempting him, swear to God he'd never do it again, and beg His forgiveness. Knowing all this, Anna still wanted him to love her tonight. She couldn't give up her one chance to know the completeness of being with the man she loved.

She reached her hand out and touched his cheek. He took her hand in his and lifted it to his lips, kissing it fiercely. Then suddenly she was in his arms, his lips pressing hungrily upon hers. Anna moaned her surrender.

"You're so beautiful," he breathed, then tenderly he kissed her cheeks, her eyes, her nose, and her lips once again. He tasted the brandy on her mouth and it excited him even more. "I've wanted this since I first stepped inside the tavern."

"Oh, Jordan, so have I," she whispered into his mouth as he claimed her for his own.

"Let me undress you. I want to look at you." His hand caressed the delicate curve of her cheek and slipped down her shoulder to lightly caress her breast. Her whole body quivered, wanting his touch to go on forever.

"Yes," she answered as she felt his hand move to the buttons at the back of her dress. As he fumbled with the buttons, she pulled at his cravat. She didn't have the courage to say it, but she wanted to look at him, too. She wanted to know all of him, to have nothing hidden from her touch or her eyes. As he unfastened her dress, she pulled his shirt free of his breeches. When her hands touched his bare skin she heard him gasp and she kissed him harder, sliding her hands up his hard-muscled back, letting her fingernails lightly scratch him. She felt him tremble and wanted to give him more pleasure.

Jordan tried to pull away, but she held him securely, possessively, not wanting to let him go. She didn't want him to stop, she didn't want him to think about what they were doing. She only wanted him to love her.

"Let me take your dress off," he mumbled between moist kisses.

Slowly, Anna stepped back and Jordan pushed her dress off her shoulders, down past her breasts, over her hips to drop to the floor. He grasped her shoulders and turned her body until her length was flooded with pale moonlight. From this moment on, there could never be another woman for him. Anna was his.

"Oh, God, you're lovely," he said huskily, his gaze traveling the length of her body, lingering at all the places designed for love.

At the sound of the name God, Anna reflexively

crossed her arms over her chest and started to turn away. Jordan quickly pulled her to him. "No, don't hide from me. I didn't expect you to be this beautiful." He brushed her hair away from her face and loved her with his eyes. He lifted her chin and gazed into her eyes. "You're the woman I want. I desire no other."

That his vow had been so recently tested and proved Anna must never know. She had no idea that just an hour ago he'd been trying to capture this kind of desire with another woman. He would never tell her. He didn't want anything to lessen what he was feeling for her right now. Hungrily he kissed her, tracing with his hands a path of passion from the nape of her neck, across her shoulders, down to the small of her back, over the firmness of her buttocks and up to her hips without ever lifting his hands from the delicious feel of her body.

Effortlessly, he swung her off her feet and into his arms and laid her on the bed. She looked up at him with questioning eyes. Did she think he was going to leave her? Never! He smiled and reached for the buckles of his boots. Anna relaxed. Impatiently he discarded them. He stood, and once again had buttons to contend with as he stripped away his breeches and the rest of his clothing. When at last he was free of his clothes, he straightened before her and stood quietly and let her look at him. Her gaze started at his knees, and he watched as it went higher until she found what he could no longer hide, his complete arousal, his desire only for her.

Her lashes lifted. She skimmed the rest of his

body until their eyes met. She whispered his name and extended her arms, beckoning him into her embrace.

He lay down beside her, gathering her against his body, and their legs automatically, naturally entwined. Gently, gently, he reminded himself, he couldn't risk hurting this woman. His love for her tempered every movement.

Jordan lifted her chin and looked into her eyes. "Anna, do you know what you're doing?"

"Loving you," she answered, her voice tremulous.

Her honesty tightened Jordan's muscles. His pulled her closer, holding her tightly in his arms. "Do you know what I'm doing?" he asked.

"Loving me," she answered without a moment's hesitation.

"Oh, yes, my beautiful, sweet Anna. That's right. And I'm going to love you all night long."

Their lips met with unrestrained desire. Jordan's hands wandered over her heated skin, leaving a warm, burning sensation in their wake. His breath fanned her cheeks as his lips pressed against hers. The peaks of her breasts hardened as his hands caressed her body from her waist, down and over her slightly rounded hips, gently stroking to incite and satisfy.

Her desire was every bit as intense as his. Her breath came in short little gasps, indicating her pleasure, her awe at these new sensations he evoked. His tongue traced a pattern of moisture on her taut skin as his lips slipped down her slender neck, over her creamy-tasting shoulders, down to settle over her breast. She tasted of a spice he didn't take time to identify but knew he'd never forget.

Anna's stomach muscles contracted exquisitely. His mouth was warm, enticing her to moan with pleasure. Every inch of her burst into life at his touch. So this was loving! Lying so close to him, feeling him beside her, she knew it was right. It would always be right. There would be no regrets in the morning, only precious memories.

His fingers traced her outer thigh, then pressed inward to feel her warm softness. Her body was firm everywhere he touched, so enticing and desirable. Her slender hips were enough, her small breasts were enough, the touch of her trembling, untutored hands were enough to set him on fire.

Jordan rolled her on her back and gently lowered himself on top of her. As their bodies met, as their hearts met, he knew he would never want any other woman. He was too complete with this one.

Anna jerked beneath him. He soothed and petted her with words and caresses until she moved freely once again, arching to meet him. When her fingers dug into his back and her teeth sank into his bottom lip, he surrendered to the spasm that rocked his body into a frenzied few moments of glorification, gratification.

When the tempo of his breathing slowed, when the buzzing cleared his ears, he lifted his head and allowed himself the weakness of admitting he was in love with a woman who might well be a spy for the British. He groaned from the pain it caused him. He opened his eyes and found Anna watching him.

He moved his lips very close to hers and whispered, "No matter what happens tomorrow, I want you to know that I love you." He brushed her hair away from her face. "Do you understand what I'm saying?"

Anna moistened her lips. She understood. She'd known from the beginning that tonight would be all they would ever share. Even though he loved her tonight, tomorrow they would pretend this never happened.

She swallowed hard. "I understand what will happen tomorrow," she said with a heavy heart. But tomorrow hadn't come yet. She wet her lips again as her hand slipped around his neck. "Must tonight be over so soon?" she asked.

"Oh, no, my beautiful Anna, my love. The night has just begun."

Chapter Eleven

When Jordan left Anna's bed it was near sunrise. Through the parted curtain she'd watched the black sky give way to shades of purple, pink, and gray while she lay with her cheek pressed against his shoulder, her breast warm against his arm. When the time came for him to leave, Jordan remained silent as he caressed her cheek and kissed her lips briefly, tenderly, before slipping from the bed and pulling on his breeches. Moving as quietly as always, he left her room.

Anna stayed in bed for only a few minutes more, savoring the aftermath of their lovemaking, putting to memory the sweetness his loving had left with her. Time would not erase the sensation she'd experienced during the night; Jordan's hands on her body, his lips pressed against hers, his body joining hers. The hunger that had reached into her soul defied propriety.

After she forced herself to get up, Anna quickly drew one of her work dresses over her head, slipped her feet into her work boots, and hurried down the stairs and into the kitchen to wash before Glynis awakened. Her breasts were sore, but she didn't mind the ache. Jordan had awakened her body; even without sleep, she felt good, alive. Her night with Jordan had been so much more than she'd expected she was already wondering how she could have ever thought one night would be enough.

Anna stoked the fire and hung a small kettle of water over it long enough to take the chill off the water. She hummed to herself as she washed, knowing no matter how many times she bathed, she'd never wash away the feel of Jordan, never wash away his touch or taste. There would always be Jordan in her heart and in her memories, just as she had wanted.

When she was through, Anna set a pot of tea on the coals to steep, then sliced a loaf of bread. She spooned some butter into a dish and set a jar of sugar-packed figs in the middle of the table. By the time she finished her first cup of tea, Glynis came shuffling into the kitchen, her faded dress hanging loosely about her large frame, a straggling strand of gray hair showing from beneath her worn cap.

"Good morning, Glynis," Anna said, feeling cheerful, content for the moment with what little fate had given her.

"You're up early," was the older woman's response as she dipped a cup into the milk pail and filled it.

"I couldn't sleep any longer."

"Because it wasn't your wedding night."

Anna's head snapped around at Glynis's statement. What did she mean by that remark? Was it a question or a statement? Was Glynis referring to the fact that Lydia's wedding night could have been her own? Surely the woman had no idea that Jordan had spent the entire night with her.

Anna rubbed her forehead and continued to watch Glynis, who seemed to be more interested in drinking her milk than returning Anna's gaze.

"What do you mean, Glynis?" she asked finally, not really knowing how to respond to the cook's bold statement.

Glynis set the cup down and wiped her mouth with the back of her hand. "I thought you might have had trouble sleeping because your best friend married your fiancé. She stole your wedding night."

Anna gasped. "That's a horrible thing to say, Glynis. You're much too forward," Anna rebuked in a stern voice. "Benjamin and Lydia's wedding had nothing to do with why I didn't sleep any longer this morning. Besides, I'm the one who decided not to marry Benjamin. And I happen to be very happy for Lydia, not jealous of her."

As usual, Glynis accepted the reprimand without comment. She reached for her apron. Feeling relief because Glynis hadn't suspected she'd spent the night with Jordan, Anna turned away from her and set out cups for Moss and Terence. It wasn't like Glynis to make a comment of a personal nature, and Anna wondered what had caused her to breach her silence today.

Anna poured herself a second cup of tea, determined not to let Glynis or her odd behavior distract her or make her angry. This day was too special. She wished she could be left alone so she could mull over all that happened last night. She didn't want to ever forget one little kiss, caress, or word from Jordan. She wanted to remember everything about him and his loving.

She turned back to Glynis and said, "Why don't we roast chicken on the spit today? We've had too much rabbit stew and pork lately. I'll have Terence catch them, and Moss can help you kill and dress them. Make a thick barley soup to go with the chicken. The stagecoach doesn't come today, so three chickens should be enough. I'll start the bread while you gather the eggs." Anna moistened her lips. "And, Glynis—" Anna waited for her to look at her. "I'm sorry I snapped at you. Maybe I am a little upset."

Glynis nodded her head once. "Appears to me you would be." Without saying another word, Glynis put on her apron and tightened the knot in her fichu. She picked up the egg basket, unlocked the door, and walked out.

Pleased to have a few minutes to herself, Anna watched the low-burning flames in the fireplace. A vision of Jordan's long, lean body, stretched out on her bed, moonlight bathing his skin, leapt to her mind. Oh, how she would love to have the time to go down by Old Sib Pond and lie in the cool grass and do nothing but relive last night, starting from the time he laughed at her for drinking brandy instead of wine. No, starting from the very moment he walked into the tavern all those weeks ago and observed her so closely, noticing the ugly bruise that had covered one side of her face.

She had been very much aware of Jordan Kent the first time she saw him. Although she knew, understood, and accepted the fact that all of her to-

213

morrows would only be memories of last night, this morning she was already wanting to change that. How could one glorious night last a lifetime? How could she live so close to him and not touch him, not want him?

The pounding of running feet disturbed Anna's daydreaming. She looked around in time to see Terence burst through the kitchen door like a spent musket ball.

"Slow down and walk," she scolded impatiently. "You know you're never to run in the tavern. You could knock something over or push someone down."

"Who?" he asked, a big smile rounding his cheeks, clearly indicating he was in a teasing mood. "No one's up."

"I am. Am I no one?"

"You're just a girl." He grinned as he answered and took a piece of bread and started coating it with creamy butter.

"I'm a woman, not a girl," she suddenly insisted, feeling it was her right. "And I certainly don't want to be toppled from my feet by you." Her face softened and a smile curled her lips. "Where's Moss?"

"He said his old bones didn't want to move this morning. He's got to have extra time to get them going. He was mumbling something about his neck being stiff as a corn cob that's been dried for three winters."

Anna laughed. "His bones aren't that old. He's obviously feeling lazy this morning. We won't get much work out of him today. Not so much butter," she said as she brushed his dark brown hair with her hand and smiled affectionately.

When Anna turned away to get Terence a cup of milk, she saw Jordan standing in the doorway, quietly watching her. He was nicely groomed, showing no obvious wear from their passionate night. As usual, she hadn't heard him approach, but his sudden presence didn't unsettle her as it always had in the past. She didn't think he'd ever startle her again. It was as if he was a part of her now, and she'd always be expecting him.

"Good morning, Jordan." Her voice was soft and pleased her with its clarity, its steadiness.

"Good morning, Anna." He'd never said her name more beautifully. His eyes, his expression, told her that he, too, remembered every moment of last night, and that it wouldn't be forgotten. But his expression also told her something else. From this day forward, she was the tavernkeeper and he was the town's minister. There would be no repeat of last night, no matter how much she might want it.

Jordan cleared his throat and stepped soft-footed into the kitchen. "I wanted to let you know that I'll be gone most of the day. There's a camp of soldiers about two miles north of here. I thought I'd ride out and see if they need anything in the way of supplies." He looked briefly at Terence and asked, "Would you be interested in earning two pence?"

The young boy's eyes brightened, and he looked up from his half-finished bread, butter smeared across one cheek. "How?"

"Saddle Thad for me and bring him around to the front. I'll be out in a few minutes." Although

215

Jordan spoke to Terence, Anna could feel his eyes on her face.

Terence ran to the door, but suddenly looked back at Jordan as he swung it open. "Do I have to give one of them back to the church?" he asked.

This time Jordan looked at him and smiled. "No. Save it all for yourself."

Terence ran out, slamming the door.

"Anna."

"Jordan."

Their names mingled together as surely as their breaths, their eyes, the same as their bodies had joined the night before. They stared at each other, neither wanting to stop what was happening between them. Neither wanting to resume yesterday's pattern of living.

Anna was afraid to take her eyes from his, afraid that if she did, she might never see him again, but she knew she had to look away. God might forgive her for last night, but He wouldn't forgive her for giving in to the same sin twice.

Jordan's heart pounded in his chest. Anna was more beautiful this morning than he'd ever seen her. Her eyes were bright, her cheeks tinted with a soft shade of pink. Last night he had made her a woman, and it showed. His manhood tightened; already he wanted her again. He loved her, but would she ever truly be his?

Anna picked up the teapot and poured a cup for Jordan, then returned the pot to the fireplace.

Keeping a safe distance from him, she spoke. "I want you to know that I don't hold you accountable for anything that happened last night. I take full responsibility. I lured you into my arms and

216

into my bed. God will not hold you answerable for what only I am guilty of."

Jordan felt the fine hairs on the back of his neck stiffen. That little speech of hers didn't sit well with him. Her willingness to accept the blame for his weakness angered him. He was the first for her. How could she bear the responsibility for last night? She should put the blame on him, where it rightly belonged.

He had never let a woman lead him to her bed when he wasn't willing. He had always initiated any involvement he had with women. He'd never let a woman take the credit or blame for an evening together, and he wasn't about to start with this one. Anna was too special. He'd been the first for her, and that changed everything, as far as he was concerned.

Breathing unevenly, he took a step toward her. "You were a virgin, Anna. I doubt God will hold me blameless for taking what I had no right to." He didn't intend for his voice to sound harsh, but it did. Her first words to him had immediately put him on the defensive. He'd come into the kitchen wanting to tell her they needed to talk about their feelings for each other as well as her true relationship with Andre.

Anna's back straightened, her chin tilted upward. "It was mine to give and I gave it freely."

Jordan's heartbeat increased. She had been free with her love, and he loved her all the more for it. "I'm not untried, Anna. You were an innocent. I knew better and you didn't."

She couldn't let him take the blame. "I knew exactly what I was doing when I bathed and dressed for you last night. I wanted last night to happen."

Damn it, this wasn't going the way he wanted it to. She wasn't saying the things he expected her to say. She should be angry with him, but she wasn't.

"All right, Anna, if you seduced me last evening, why did you do it? Why did you want me in your bed so much you were willing to give up what should only have been taken on your wedding night?"

His temperament changed so quickly Anna flinched. She took a stumbling step backward and he caught her wrist.

"Answer me, Anna. I know why I wanted last night to happen, but why did you?" His voice lowered as he moved closer to her. Right now he was tempted to prove to her that he was the one who controlled their coming together last night, not she.

Anna didn't know how to lie, and she doubted that Jordan wanted to hear her claiming undying love for him at this moment. As he moved forward, she stepped backward. Her throat felt dry and brittle as she took a deep breath. "I don't intend to part with that information," she answered, choosing her words carefully. "It's important only to me."

He laughed huskily. "You're incredible, unbelievable, and—irresistible." He moved his face closer to hers, letting his breath fan her face seductively. Oh, yes, she seduced him with every move she made and he loved it, wanted it, but . . . "That's what makes you so damn dangerous," he said finally.

Anna's inhibitions were slipping away. He was so

close she felt his heat. She had to move away before she melted into his arms again.

She cleared her throat. "You have no cause to fret. No one will ever hear about last night. I'll tell no one. Your reputation is safe with me." She spouted the words hurriedly, hoping he'd drop the subject and forget about it.

"My reputation?" He chuckled lightly. "I'm not worried about my reputation at the moment, but what about yours? What will you say on your wedding night when your husband takes you to bed and finds he is not the first man for you? He'll know."

Anna tried to twist her wrist out of his hold, but he was too strong. She swallowed hard and backed up still further. An awkward flush crept up her neck to her cheeks. Why did he have her on the defensive? He should be angry with her. He should hate her and shame her. "I don't intend to marry," she answered quickly.

"Not marry!" He gave another short laugh. "With your beauty and the tavern, you are the pick of this town. How can you say you will not marry?"

Anna had had enough of this. She didn't want to argue with him. He was trying to spoil what they'd shared last night and she wasn't going to let him. She wanted to remember only soft caresses and sweet kisses. She turned away from him but just as quickly was jerked around to face him once again as he grabbed her other arm. Her gaze flew to his eyes.

"Anna, what we're discussing isn't even important. We need to talk about—" He cut his sentence off as a grumbling, complaining Moss tramped into the kitchen, pulling his breeches up and over his rounded belly, not looking at them. Jordan let her go and stepped away.

"If these old bones of mine get any stiffer, I won't be able to move before evening."

Anna breathed an unsteady sigh of relief that Moss hadn't seen Jordan holding her.

Anna watched as Jordan picked up the cup of tea she'd poured for him and drank it thirstily, not bringing the cup down from his lips until it was empty. He set it on the table with a clatter. "Anna, we'll talk later. Moss, I'll see you tonight for a game of checkers."

"I'll be looking forward to it, Reverend."

Moss laughed and scratched his unkempt beard as Jordan walked out the door. "Now, there's a worthy opponent for a game. He's teaching me moves I never knew about. I thought I knew them all, but he's a sharp-minded player—"

Moss continued to talk, but Anna's mind drifted back to Jordan. She'd caused him to fall from grace. He had every right to be angry, to hate her, to vow never to forgive her, but he didn't. He was a most unusual minister, an unusual man. She wouldn't take back last night even if she could. No, she would remember the man who gave her her heart's desire and made her a woman.

Later that same afternoon, Anna had just finished a piece of well-cooked chicken when she heard a commotion outside. There were shouts and jubilant cries mixed with the sound of horses' hooves on the hard-packed road in front of the tavern. She picked up a cloth and wiped the chicken grease off her hands and mouth as she went into the taproom to look out the window. Six or eight men and women as well as several children surrounded an approaching carriage which appeared to be heading directly for the tavern.

Anna opened the door and stepped outside as Moss and Terence came from behind the building to see what was going on.

"It's General Arnold!" she heard someone shout.

Anna was delighted. General Benedict Arnold had stayed with them on many occasions in the past few years. Lowell Tavern was usually his last stop before he went home to Norwich. Anna looked up and saw that the sun was hanging low in the western sky. It was too late in the day for his arrival to be a refreshment stop. General Arnold would be staying the night.

The carriage and group of well-wishers stopped in front of the tavern. Anna caught a glimpse of the general as he was helped out of his carriage before he was lost in the admiring crowd. Never mind, she thought, she could see him later. His visit meant the tavern would have a very busy night. Every man in town would come out to hear the battlefield stories the general had been telling the past five years. She turned and rushed back inside, calling to Glynis as she hurried through the taproom.

"Yes, Anna?" the older woman responded when Anna entered the kitchen.

"Prepare three more chickens, and get a pone of sweet bread in the oven," she ordered in a breathy voice. "General Benedict Arnold is here, and the whole town will come out tonight. I'm going upstairs to check rooms for the general and his aides, then I'll be down to help you."

"So, he's here at last," Glynis said to herself before turning back to the pot she was stirring.

"I'm sorry. What was that, Glynis? I didn't hear you."

"Nothing. Just talking to myself. Don't mind me." Glynis waved Anna away.

"Very well. I'll be back as soon as I can." Anna called as she hurried to check that the rooms were in readiness.

A couple of minutes later she was back downstairs, waiting to welcome the heroic general into the tavern. The crowd dispersed when General Arnold asked that he be allowed to rest uninterrupted for a couple of hours and have a private meal. He told the people he'd join them in the tavern for a drink afterward and a few hours of the latest news of battles and tales of past heroics.

Closing the Deerfield door, Anna shut out the trailing voices. It was always an exciting time for Georgetown when any of the American generals came to town, and this man was one of their favorites.

Anna told the aide in which room to deposit the bags and turned to properly greet the general, who stood not much taller than she. He was broad shouldered with a big chest, but not an ounce of fat showed beneath his well-maintained clothes. His black coat with its white trim was as immaculate as his buff-white breeches and stockings. His dark hair had been expertly powdered, a detail he

222

hadn't had attended to the last time he stayed at the tavern.

"It's a pleasure to have you stay with us again, General Arnold." She greeted him with a smile and a light curtsy.

"Anna, my dear, it's been a long time, but you are prettier every time I see you. Why is Levi not here to greet me as well?" He reached for her hand and gave it a perfunctory kiss.

Anna's eyes clouded for a moment. "Papa is no longer with us. He was killed by a thief over two months ago."

He clucked his tongue in sympathy. "I hadn't heard. Such a tragedy for you, my dear. My deepest regrets."

"Thank you for your kind words." She gave him a little smile and changed the subject. "What time should I have your meal ready?"

General Arnold grunted and shifted his stance. "A couple of hours. I need to rest my leg. Perhaps you'll join me at dinner. I do hate to eat alone."

"I'd be honored," she responded with a smile as General Arnold's aide came back down the stairs.

Even though Anna had just finished eating, she readily agreed to join the general for a meal. Not only would he help keep her mind off Jordan, she couldn't pass up the chance to have dinner with the man who was so highly praised by the Continental Army. She'd heard talk that as a leader he was better than the Commander-in-Chief, George Washington.

Anna watched as two aides helped the general climb the stairs. He had trouble maneuvering the steps because his left leg had been wounded twice and he had gout in the other. But even with his injuries, Anna considered General Benedict Arnold an impressive man.

Chapter Twelve

Jordan halted his horse down the road from the tavern and stopped to listen to the sounds coming from the brightly lit building, wondering what was going on. He didn't believe he'd ever heard such lusty bursts of laughter and loud talking coming from the taproom. He rode on to the barn and took his time stabling Thad.

He hadn't planned to see Virgil today, and now wished he hadn't gone. Most of the men in the camp were suffering from dysentery and stomach cramps. Had he known that, he'd never have ridden into camp. The men had been too weak to post a sentry, and Jordan was in the midst of them before he realized the sickness was there. But at least the journey had given him the time he needed to decide how to approach Anna. They couldn't go on this way any longer. He had to tell her what he suspected and once and for all clear up his nagging fear of her involvement with Andre.

A few minutes later Jordan entered the taproom and stood just inside the doorway, assessing the smoke-filled room, his eyes searching the crowd.

What had happened to put the town in such a lively mood? Since there was standing room only, he eased the door closed and leaned against it. After several glances around the room, he found the source of all the celebrating.

General Benedict Arnold, who had led the first charge that defeated the British at Saratoga, was sitting in the middle of the tavern, his left leg resting on a cushion in the seat of a ladderback chair. So the hero of Saratoga, the new commandant of West Point, had arrived at Lowell Tavern. A grin crossed Jordan's face as he remembered the man's considerable achievements.

Time and time again with his daring strategy he had outmaneuvered and outled the British generals. Arnold was well known as an expert sailor and fencer, sharpshooter and horseman. He was frequently hailed as one of the most brilliant soldiers in the American forces.

Jordan smiled to himself as he watched Arnold drink from his tankard. He knew Virgil would have come into town with him had they known Arnold was to be here. It was too bad Jordan couldn't talk with the general. They'd met once, more than a year ago, and Jordan couldn't take the chance Arnold might recognize him. He decided to walk a little closer and just listen. He was certain that once Arnold started talking, the crowd would quiet. Everyone wanted to hear the firsthand accounts of Arnold's victories.

As Jordan situated himself behind a large man, he saw Anna come scurrying into the room with two food-laden plates balanced on each hand. His heart beat faster. Damn it, would he always react to her with such intensity? No question, he'd fallen in love with her. And today he'd decided to do something about it.

After placing the plates in front of two men, Anna stopped to talk to Terence. The boy wasn't usually allowed in the taproom, but tonight he was picking up empty plates and tankards and hurrying back to the kitchen with them. Jordan watched Anna walk to the bar where Moss was pouring drinks, moving as gracefully, as always. He rubbed his eyes. His mind was foggy from all the thoughts of her. But tomorrow he and Anna had to talk. Now that he was sure he loved her, he had to find out the truth about her and, if necessary, do everything in his power to protect her—even if she was guilty.

Jordan turned his attention from Anna as the General's voice rose above the crowd and the room grew quiet.

"Of course, Gates had ordered me to remain in my tent all day. I couldn't bear it, listening to the cannon and muskets, the cries of falling men. So I climbed on my white mare and rode like all the hounds in hell were after me. I'd tried to tell Gates he couldn't command men in battle while sitting in that clapboard house he called headquarters. No! A general must lead his men into battle and not rely on couriers to bring accounts of what is happening and then send in the next set of orders. A commander can't sit by and just listen to the roar of the cannon and musketry in the distance. He has to be close enough to see the fire that lights the powder and charges the flint." His voice calmed. "So I did what I had to do, what I've done many times before and since: I took charge. I rode right into the middle of our regiments and ordered the men to follow me." He laughed softly for a moment, then added, "They did."

A roar of shouts and praise rose from the crowd and Jordan was impressed with the power with which Arnold spoke. He was mesmerizing the crowd with this personal account of the battle of Saratoga.

After a drink from his tankard and a groan when he shifted his leg, Arnold held up his hand and the hubbub stilled once again. "I knew immediately upon arriving at the battlefield that the only way to defeat the British was to storm them like a demented devil and not give them time to think or plan. I took the four regiments I'd gathered and we charged the front of Balcarres' redoubt, forcing them to take refuge behind the log-and-mud barricades. This redoubt was difficult to penetrate but we were weakening it, so I decided to aid Daniel Morgan's riflemen in attacking another redoubt as well. From past battles I knew the British redoubt usually had a rear opening—a sally port—so I led a band of soldiers around it and came in through the back door. Unfortunately, I took another ball in my left leg and went down."

Arnold patted his elevated limb. "But all was not lost. Within ten days General Burgoyne surrendered. We had a battlefield victory."

Cries and shouts rent the air. Tankards, mugs, and cups were lifted, slaps on the back echoed throughout the dimly lit room, and hands clasped in joy. The heroic Benedict Arnold was performing at his best.

"Tell us about Tyron's raid on Danbury when your horse was shot!" one man shouted above the roar.

"No, tell us about Quebec," came another voice.

"Lake Champlain!" still another cried out.

"No! Fort Ticonderoga and Ethan Allen's Green Mountain Boys!"

Jordan remained quiet, leaning against the wall. He was amused by the scene. Each man had a favorite story he wanted Arnold to relate. Jordan chuckled to himself when he remembered that his choice would be Arnold's march to Quebec, the one that had impressed the members of Congress enough that they'd made him a brigadier general. Any man who could hold together a starving group of men and lead them over hills and rocks and through bogs and woods in snow and freezing temperatures had Jordan's admiration.

When the crowd's laughter died down, Arnold continued. "Let me finish one story before you ask for another," he lightly admonished the crowd. "As I said, ten days later Burgoyne surrendered to Gates, but Gates didn't see fit to give me my due in his report to Congress because I'd gone against his orders." Boos and quarrelsome chatter were heard about the room. Arnold waved his hand for silence. "However, thanks to my colleagues and my men, Congress and Washington were appropriately informed."

Jordan listened to the man he'd heard described as mercurial and possessing a reckless bravado. In battle he was sure it was true, but tonight the general appeared to be somewhat embittered. Jordan admired Arnold's leadership abilities. That's what

229

made him a damn good general, regardless of the charges that currently surrounded his ability to keep accurate records and the rumors that he'd misused government funds and supplies. Even though Washington continued to praise him, it seemed Congress had decided not to trust the crippled general.

Arnold's recent appointment to command West Point would be one of Washington's most brilliant moves, Jordan thought, as he rubbed his chin. There were rumors that Arnold was a great general but a poor administrator, but that could be said of many officers in the Continental Army. This new appointment would be his chance to show Congress he could do both. Jordan hoped Arnold would strengthen the garrisons and build up the forts of West Point, giving the Americans an unbreachable hold on the Hudson. Whether or not the general was ready to admit it, his bad leg meant his days of charging the British were over.

"Tell us about Lake Champlain," someone yelled from the midst of the crowd.

Arnold held up his hand and nodded. He wasn't shy when it came to talking of his numerous exploits. Jordan listened.

"The fog was so thick, visibility was limited to merely a few feet, as those of you who have seen the fog that covers the northern end of the lake can bear witness." Several men responded and attested to his facts with amens and yeses. "Had it not been for that and God's blessings, I would not be here today. I knew the only way to escape Sir Guy Carlton's fleet was to sail our ships between the British forces and the west shore. After much thought, I suggested to the others that we hang a single lantern in the stern of each ship and cover it so that only the ship behind it could see the dim light. Later, when we sailed, we were so close to the *Maria* and the *Carlton* that we heard hammers and the pumps and talking, and by God, we glided through the water, the mist, and the fog and slipped by the whole damned British Armada."

The crowd roared their approval but Jordan simply listened. Arnold hadn't finished the story. He remembered that Arnold was directly responsible for the four galleys and nine gondolas which had been built in less than six months that year, but later Arnold was also responsible for setting fire to the American ships at Buttonmould Bay when the fog lifted and Sir Guy Carlton caught up with them.

Jordan saw Anna out of the corner of his eye and immediately turned his attention to her. She was hurrying by with a tray filled with tankards of ale. She looked tired. He knew she was. Neither of them had had any sleep the night before, and she was working as hard as a slave. Jordan leaned heavily against the wall and let it support him. Never before had a woman caused him so much misery, but neither had he ever been so blessed as last night in her arms. Complete was the best way he knew how to describe being with Anna. Nothing was missing . . . nothing. Yet he didn't know how that could be when he suspected her of aiding the enemy. Last night he'd admitted he loved her. He'd made her his and realized he could never give her up. Today he'd decided he had to know the truth about her, even if it meant confirming she'd aided the British.

What was her involvement, her connection to Andre? Was the answer as simple as what was happening here tonight? It would be so easy for Arnold to let some valuable piece of information slip out. With the help of a strong man and a fast horse, Anna could get the information to Andre in less than two days.

He squeezed his eyes tightly shut for a moment and remembered the feel of her satiny skin on his. Damn, he wanted to be wrong about her. How was he going to help her if she was truly a spy?

Anna couldn't sleep. She was so tired when she finally lay down she thought she'd go right off, but she couldn't get the scent of Jordan out of her mind. For a few moments she thought she was trying to somehow will him into her room, until she realized his scent was on her pillow, on her sheets. And it was driving her insane. Her meeting with him that morning had left no doubt in her mind that a repeat of last night would never happen. She rose from her bed and paced barefoot back and forth across the cool wood floor. A short time later she heard the sound of a voice coming from the next room. Thinking General Arnold must be restless and talking in his sleep, in need of something for the pain in his leg, she put her ear to a large crack in between two boards in the wall and listened.

"Yes, I've had recent word that your son is still alive. If all goes according to my plans, I'll have him out of Newgate before winter comes."

"He may not last that long in that Connecticut hellhole—"

Anna didn't hear what came next because she jerked away from the wall as if it'd been a hot kettle. It was Glynis talking! Why was the tavern cook talking with General Arnold about the Connecticut prison camp for British soldiers? Anna didn't know Glynis had a son! Apparently he was in an American prison. Anna's heartbeat increased, and her breathing became shallow. She had no choice now but to listen to the conversation. Laying open palms to the wood, she flattened her body against the wall and placed her ear back to the hole.

"I've not forgotten you introduced me to John Stansbury, who put me in touch with Major Andre. Your help has been immeasurable. When all is finished, I assure you I will not forget you for giving me his name when I was here last year."

"I want my son out of that prison before he dies. He's not a strong man. You promised to do this in return for my help."

"And I will. Things are moving quickly now, my dear woman. Major Andre suggested I secure the West Point command which I now have. It is my intention to weaken the fort by separating the garrisons and leaving it open to British attack by putting into the major's hands a map of the area. I hope to meet with Andre within the month to finalize the plans."

"This may be what you're waiting for."

"How long have you had this letter from Andre?" Arnold asked in a sharp voice.

"One of his men slipped it to me when he was

233

here three weeks ago. I'd written General Clinton and asked him to send John Anderson, same as always. Now what about my son?" Her voice rose.

Arnold sighed. "You must be patient. All things in due course. I will make some inquiries about your son while I'm in Norwich and try to see that he is released. I suggest you hold your tongue before you wake the house. Your job now is to make sure no one realizes your loyalty to the British or you'll be joining your son instead of his joining you. Now go so that I can read this letter and rest my leg. It pains me."

Anna kept her ear to the wall long after Glynis crept from the room, long after General Arnold lay down on his bed with a groan. When she finally pried herself away from the wall she found she was sick to her stomach, weak-kneed with fear. Clutching her nightgown with balled fists, she walked over to her bed and sat down, gently rocking back and forth. What was she going to do? General Arnold wanted to weaken West Point for John and the British. There was no doubt in her mind that she had understood the conversation and its import.

She must do something, tell someone. But whom? Was there anything she could do to spoil General Arnold's and John's plan? And what of John's friendship? Would she be betraying him by trying to stop him? She brushed her hair away from her face and lay down on her bed, pulling the covers around, feeling cold.

Obviously, she couldn't tell anyone in town what she'd heard. Who would believe her after hearing Arnold's heroic tales earlier that night? They'd think her mad to suggest the man was contemplating treason. She didn't understand all the ramifications of West Point's falling into British hands, but she knew enough to realize that it shouldn't happen. Even though John was a dear friend, America was her country. She had to stop him.

A plan started to form in her mind. John liked her, trusted her. Maybe the best thing for her to do would be go to New York and discover for herself the details of the British strategy. And she had to go at once. John had asked her to come and stay with his friends, the Sommerfields, so it wouldn't be as if she were unexpected. But what would John do if he found out she was betraying his friendship? She sighed thoughtfully. She must prepare herself for that, but right now she had other arrangements to make. There were many things that had to be done before she could travel to New York on tomorrow's stagecoach.

Before she could leave, she had to get rid of Glynis and hire someone else. Moss could take care of Terence, and the two of them could manage the tavern if she hired someone else to help them. Glynis . . . Anna sighed softly. When Glynis had talked to General Arnold she'd sounded well bred, intelligent. She'd been putting on an act the whole time she'd been at the tavern. No wonder Anna always felt a little uneasy around her.

As Anna's plans took shape she pressed her arm over her eyes, resting her head on her pillow, and was reminded of Jordan. Maybe she could tell him, she thought for a moment, then dismissed the idea completely. No, she'd tell no one. This was something she had to handle by herself.

Anna closed her eyes and groaned softly. She still loved John as a friend, but she couldn't let that friendship stand in the way of helping her country. Just as John had to correspond with General Arnold to help the British, she had to do everything possible to aid her country.

Chapter Thirteen

"Anna? Anna, are you awake?"

Anna's eyes popped open and she sat up quickly in the bed and looked around as Terence opened the door and peeked into her bedroom. She must have fallen asleep sometime during the early morning hours. She wiped sleep from her eyes and brushed her tangled hair away from her face. If Terence was up, that meant she'd overslept. Sunlight from the window indicated it was at least an hour later than her usual rising time. Heavens! She hadn't overslept in years.

Suddenly Anna remembered what she'd overheard last night. General Arnold was going to give John a map of West Point so the British could capture the fort. And Glynis was in on the whole thing! No wonder the cook was such a private person, never letting anyone get close.

Anna moaned and dropped her head into her hand, rubbing her forehead, then pushing her hair away from her face. It all came rushing back to her. Sometime last night she'd decided to go to New York and find out when and where this treasonous act was to take place and stop it. What was she doing oversleeping at a time like this? In order to save the Americans a stunning blow from the British, she would have to betray a friendship that was very dear to her. She would have to become a spy.

"Anna, are you all right?" Terence's voice was low, unsure.

She lifted her head and tried to give him a smile. "Yes, Terence—come in. I'm awake now." She could hardly speak, her mouth and tongue tasting as if they had been smeared with aged tallow.

"Moss sent me up to check on you. He said he couldn't remember a time he came downstairs and you were still asleep. Are you ill?"

"No, no . . . I'm just very tired." She finally managed a smile, but knew it was a weak one. She tried to moisten her lips and clear her throat. "We had a very busy night, remember?"

"I remember. General Arnold is here, and it was my first time to work in the taproom. Did I do a good job?" He stepped further into the room, his expressive eyes locked on her face, looking for approval.

Her smile came easier this time. "You did a wonderful job. I'm very proud of you." She patted the bed with both hands. "Close the door and come and sit beside me." She gave a quick glance toward the wall where she'd heard voices last night. Her chest tightened with apprehension. If she could overhear General Arnold and Glynis, they could hear her. She lowered her voice. "I want to talk to you about something important."

Terence, taking advantage of the situation, leapt

238

onto the bed, landing with a big bounce and a bubble of juvenile laughter.

"Was that necessary?" Anna asked, not really angry with him for having a little fun. It was just that there were so many things to do today and she was angry with herself for already wasting an hour.

"Yes." He clasped his hands together behind his head to form a pillow and laughed again.

Looking at her brother lying on the foot of her bed with his feet hanging off the side, Anna was suddenly unsure about the trip she'd planned to make. She'd never left Terence, and she wasn't happy that she had to do so now. She'd taken care of him since he was six months old. But taking him with her was out of the question. Because of the fighting, the roads were dangerous, and she had no idea what awaited her in New York. She wished she'd never heard Arnold's plans. She didn't really know how to go about stopping this scheme to hand over a map of West Point. But if she could find out from John when and where he was to meet the General, maybe she could prevent the transfer.

Anna rubbed her lips with the back of her hand. "I have something important, something serious to talk about. Come closer." She wanted to make sure no one else could hear.

Terence shot up, his eyebrows drawn together in a line, his eyes narrowing. "I don't want to hear it. The last time you said that was when Papa was killed."

Anna winced. That was true. She should have been more careful with her wording. "This is nothing like that, Terence," she said in a soothing voice.

He crossed his arms over his small chest with elaborate emphasis and pursed his lips to their fullest extent. "I still don't want to hear it. If it's serious, I won't like it."

"But this is a secret," she said, changing her tactics. "And only you and I will know about it. Now, lower your voice to a whisper or I won't tell you." She had a feeling he wouldn't pass up the chance to hear a secret.

She was right. His blue eyes sparkled with a hint of interest, but he wasn't going to give in completely until he heard the whole thing. "A secret?" he asked very softly, and moved closer to her. "All right, what is it?"

"What I'm going to tell you must not be discussed with anyone, not even Moss. Do you understand?"

He nodded. "It will be our secret."

"That's right. You must remember to whisper. We can't have anyone overhear us." She took a few moments to collect her thoughts and decide just how much she was going to tell her brother.

"Now, one of the first things I'm going to do this morning is dismiss Glynis. I have reason to believe she's no longer to be trusted."

He gave her a satisfied look. "I never liked her anyway, Anna. I'm glad she's going. How can that be a big secret? How can you keep that from Moss? All he has to do is go to the kitchen and see she's not there."

Anna smiled. "You're a bright young man. The part of this that's to be kept secret is that I don't think she can be trusted. If anyone asks why she's gone, you simply say we needed someone a little friendlier, which is also true. All right?"

He nodded again. "I understand." He gave a soft sigh, letting her know her big secret wasn't anything new to him.

"I'm going to ask Mrs. Dudley to take over Glynis's job and come in every day and cook and clean, not just on days the stagecoach is due. You like her, don't you, Terence?"

"She's nice," he continued in his whispery voice, his face full of expression. "Mrs. Dudley talks to me and smiles at me. I'm glad you're getting rid of Glynis. She never does."

"I know. She treated me the same way, but now I think I know why." Anna picked up Terence's hand, feeling the need to touch him and reassure herself that she had to leave him and undertake this mission.

"Terence, what I'm about to tell you is the big part of this secret. I have to go away for a few weeks."

His bright eyes widened. "Going away? Like Papa?" He threw himself into Anna's arms. "No, Anna, don't go. Don't leave me!"

"Shh—no, no, Terence, I'm not leaving you for always." She held him tightly, her arms easily reaching around his slight body. She hated reminding him of that time, of those horrible feelings of emptiness and loss.

"Don't go," he cried softly into the curve of her neck.

Anna's arms trembled as she held him close. "Terence, listen to me. Papa died. He is never com-

241

ing back. I promise I'll come back to you." She kissed the top of his cheek just below his eyes.

"There, now, raise your head and look at me." He did. Tears had collected in his eyes, and one slipped over the edge and ran down his cheek. He caught it with the back of his hand and whisked it away. She took a deep breath. "I've received some important information, and I need to see my friend John Andre. I have to go to New York to do this. I'm telling you this much because you're my brother and you have a right to know where I'm going, just as I would want to know if you were leaving for a time."

His lips formed a pout once again. "Why—"

His voice was too loud, so she put her finger to her lips and said "Shh—we must speak softly?"

"Why do you have to go away? Why do you have to talk to the British?" he whispered. "I don't like that man."

"I know you don't, but I don't have time to go into that. Just believe me when I tell you that I have to do this." She glanced at the wall again. "It's very important."

"Then why leave me here? I could go with you. I know how to ride."

Anna brushed at his hair lovingly. She smiled. He was such a good young man. "You ride very well, but I'll be taking the stage when it comes this afternoon. I need you to look after things for me here. As soon as I talk to Glynis, I'll be going over to Mrs. Dudley's to ask her to take over Glynis's work. I'm also hoping her husband, Eli, will help you and Moss in the taproom in the evenings. You like Mr. Dudley, too, don't you?"

He nodded, then asked, "You mean I'll still be helping in the taproom?"

"Of course. That's why you must stay here. Moss will need you. And when I return, you'll start school and begin helping me with the account books in the evenings."

"Who's going to do them while you're gone?"

Anna pulled in her bottom lip and held it with her teeth. She hadn't thought of that. Moss wasn't good at all with figures, and Terence didn't know much, either. Jordan . . . she hadn't thought about him in the last few minutes, but now that he came to mind, she found herself wanting to spend some time thinking about him. She swallowed hard.

The thought of Jordan would always warm her. She wished she could tell him what General Arnold was planning and ask him what he thought she should do with the information she'd overheard. She remembered Glynis going through Jordan's belongings. Why? Was she looking for something in particular? Did Glynis have reason to suspect Jordan had found out something about her relationship to the British? If she could be sure Jordan suspected Glynis of something, she'd go to him with her knowledge. Anna rubbed her forehead and remembered how Jordan had stood against the far wall last night and listened to the general tell of his many exploits. No, she decided. The American officer's popularity was too great. No one would believe her, especially Jordan.

Anna moistened her lips and said, "After I'm gone, ask Reverend Kent to help. He's a nice man and I'm sure he will take care of it. Tell him I will pay him for the work when I return."

Terence twisted his hands together nervously. "Moss isn't going to like you going away."

"Probably not. In fact, I think he'll be furious, so I'll not tell him until it's time for the stage to leave. Don't mention this to anyone."

The teasing light returned to his eyes. "You're going to leave and I'll be the one who has to hear his grumbling and complaining?"

Anna smiled. She didn't want to rush this time with Terence, but she had many things to do. She cupped his chin with her palm. "That's what you get for being the youngest. Besides, you can handle Moss very well. You'll be nine years old in a few weeks. You're big for your age, and you're also very smart. I'm not worried about leaving the tavern with you and Moss. Now, go tell Glynis and Moss I'll be down in two minutes." She paused as a thought struck her. "Has General Arnold left?"

"He hasn't come down."

Anna winced and sent another anxious glance toward the wall. How could she face the man, knowing what he was planning? Knowing that last night he'd paraded himself as an American hero while treason was in his heart.

"You run along, I have to dress. And remember, don't tell anyone what we spoke of."

"I won't." He smiled confidently but hesitated. "Are you sure you have to go away, Anna? Do you have to talk to the British?"

Anna took a deep breath. "I have to do this, and you're going to have to trust that I'm doing the right thing. Now go. I need to hurry."

When Terence had gone, she realized she was shaking. It wasn't easy to leave her brother. It wasn't going to be easy to get information from John, either. How did one go about obtaining military secrets? She'd just have to think about that on her trip, she told herself as she threw on a dress and stuffed her hair under her cap. She'd brush it later, when she dressed for the journey to New York.

Her most difficult task would be dismissing Glynis. She knew that Glynis must be helping General Arnold in order to save her ill son. Anna could understand that and was sure she would do the same if their roles were reversed. She just hoped Glynis understood her motives if she ever discovered the real reason she was going to let her go. Anna was an American, and she couldn't let General Arnold hand over West Point to the British.

A few minutes later, Anna was downstairs cutting cheese and bread when General Arnold, relying heavily on his cane, and his aide walked into the kitchen.

"Good morning," she greeted them, and hoped her smile didn't look as insincere as it felt. "Take a table in the taproom and I'll be right out with your meal."

"No need for that, Anna," the general replied. "We'll not tarry long this morning. I have urgent business to attend to in Norwich. I'm selling some property that's become too burdensome to carry." He pulled out a chair and sat down at the kitchen table.

The aide mumbled something about making sure the carriage was ready, and then he left. Anna glanced around the room. Since Glynis was gathering the eggs and Terence and Moss were milking the cows, she must face General Arnold alone.

"So you're going home to attend to business?"

"Yes. I've left it to others for too long as it is. And of course, I want to see my sons."

Anna's heart pounded as she watched him, her breathing choppy. He seemed so innocent, talking about his sons. Could it be that she'd only dreamed last night? Yes, that was it. Of course she'd dreamed it. This man was an American general. One of the bravest, one of the best! How could she have thought he was going to betray the Continental Army? Trembling inside, she placed a plate before him and pushed the platter of bread and cheese toward him.

"Would you like tea or milk?" she asked, willing her voice to stay under control.

He looked up at her and smiled. "Tea, Anna. Milk is for babes, not soldiers."

Anna returned his smile, but her lips felt brittle. It must have been just a dream, she told herself again as she poured the tea—a silly dream. She set the cup before him and asked, "Your sons, are they well?"

"Very well, thank you for asking. Big boys, all of them," he said, and continued eating.

On weak legs, Anna moved away from the table. She was eager to have the general out of the tavern, out of Georgetown, out of her life. Suddenly it didn't matter if what she heard was true or not. She just wanted him to go away so she wouldn't have to look at him and worry about dreams and reality.

While she was trying to think of something to say, the back door swung open and Glynis stepped inside. Anna saw recognition in General Arnold's eyes as he looked up at Glynis. Their acknowledgment was brief, but it was there. She knew for certain she hadn't dreamed that conversation, and she wasn't going mad. Anna backed away slowly, scarcely daring to breathe. It pained her to look at the general, knowing what he contemplated. It broke her heart to know that John Andre was involved, and that now, so was she.

Right behind Glynis came the aide, announcing that the carriage was ready. General Arnold rose from his chair and limped over to Anna, taking her hand and pressing several coins into it.

"Again, I'm sorry to hear about Levi, but I know he'd be proud of you. You're doing a fine job of managing the tavern." He patted her arm. "I'll stop again."

Anna wasn't sure whether or not she mumbled a response. All she knew was that the coins in her hand burned her skin like hot coals. As soon as the door shut behind the general and his aide, Anna hurried into the taproom and threw the coins into the money box behind the bar. It was the first money of the day, money from a traitor; she wiped her hand down her apron. She wiped it again and again, but couldn't get rid of the heat, the heaviness, the burning sensation those coins had left in her palm.

She didn't know how long she'd stayed in the taproom before she was able to gather her wits and prepare to talk to Glynis and then Mrs. Dudley. So much of the morning had been wasted. She would have to hurry back and pack a satchel and dress before the stage arrived at three.

Weary and worried, Anna approached Glynis with caution. She was nervous, a slight quiver of fear crawling up her back that she might slip up and say too much. How would Glynis react? Her palms were sweating and her body was stiff as a poker as she walked back into the kitchen.

"Glynis." Anna waited for her to turn and look at her.

"Yes, Anna?"

Tension knotted her throat, but she finally took a deep breath and said, "I've decided to let you go. I'll give you a months' wages to take with you. I want you to leave as soon as you can get your belongings together." Her tone rose higher in pitch the more she said. Oh God, that had been difficult to say. Anna remained with her shoulders back and her chin lifted, watching Glynis. The woman's expression didn't change. It was almost as if she'd expected this to happen. Surely she didn't know Anna had been eavesdropping last night.

Anna hurried on to say, "I've decided I need someone a little friendlier to work here at the tavern."

"I do my work. Why do I have to be friendly?"

It was a legitimate question. Anna had to think fast. "It's better for business, Glynis. Your work has been good. You're an excellent cook, but I want someone who will greet people with a smile and a kind word. I have a month's wages here in this bag for you. You should be able to find a place to stay before nightfall and a place to work within a couple of days."

The older woman continued to look at her, and Anna thought she saw resentment and possibly vindictiveness cross her aging face before resignation settled on her features. "I didn't know you had to be friendly in order to do a good job."

Anna felt sorry for the woman. How could she be friendly to the very people who held her son in prison? Anna rubbed the back of her neck and responded, "Then perhaps you'll know for future reference that it does make a difference and try to do better next time."

Glynis eyed Anna carefully as she took the money from her hands. "With this much money, I think I'll travel north and try to find work up toward Hartford."

Anna tried not to react, but relief flooded through her. She hoped she'd given her enough money to travel to Newgate to find out about her son's condition. She understood the woman wanting to free her son from the prison, where many men either starved or froze to death. Still, she couldn't condone what Glynis had done.

Taking a deep breath, she whispered, "I'm sorry it didn't work out here for you. Godspeed."

Glynis turned away without speaking and headed for her room, and Anna let her face drop into her hands as soon as the woman was gone. She was shaking. Why had she been the one to overhear this damning information? She didn't want to get involved in this. If she thought there was a chance anyone would believe her, she'd give this information to a member of the Continental Army. But why would they believe her, when she found the whole thing so hard to believe? The general was a hero! The Americans' only chance was for her to go to John and find out where this meeting was to take place and stop it.

"Anna! Anna!" Terence came running through the back door and slid to a grinding halt in front of her.

"Heavens! Terence, slow down and don't shout for me. You know I'm always close by," she snapped, but immediately regretted her display of temper.

"I'm sorry, but I knew this was important. I had to find you. This is for you." He held up a small piece of paper.

"No, I'm sorry. I've so much to do, I'm cross with everyone." She took the folded note from him and looked at it. "Who gave it to you?" she asked.

"Lydia."

Anna's heart quickened. Her fingers fumbled clumsily with the stiff paper as she opened it. Lydia's writing was crooked and difficult to read, but she finally made out the message.

Anna, meet me at Old Sib Pond at half past three this afternoon.

Lydia

"Oh, no," she said, desperation in her voice. "Not now. Not today."

"What's wrong? Let me read it?" Terence asked.

Anna gave him the note. What was she going to do? The stagecoach would arrive at three, and it usually left by half past. She moaned aloud, not knowing what to do. She wanted to be on that stage, but she also knew Lydia might need her. If she missed the stage today, she'd have to wait two days for it to come again. She had to get to New

York, but she desperately needed to talk to Lydia, too. What if Benjamin or his mother had been cruel to her? What would she do if Lydia needed her to stay?

"Are you going?" Terence asked.

Anna couldn't think. "I don't know. I didn't want to miss that stage. I just don't know what to do right now." Her voice became raspy. "I have to go see Mrs. Dudley, and I can think on the way. You go get Moss and ask him to come watch the taproom for me."

An hour later Anna was on her way back home and feeling calmer about what she had to do. Mrs. Dudley and her husband, Eli, had said they would be happy to earn the extra money by working in the tavern during her absence. Anna decided she had to stay and talk to Lydia, but she'd send letters by the stagecoach today, informing the Sommerfields and John of her pending arrival. That would be much better than just showing up at their door, anyway. Her problem was that she didn't want to wait until the day after tomorrow to leave.

She'd thought of the carriage for hire they had in the barn. If she could find someone who knew the way to New York, she'd hire him to take her in the carriage. She could leave early on the morrow and save a whole day.

Instead of turning into the tavern's yard, she walked on down to Parks Winchell's house. He knew all the roads between Georgetown and New York as well as between here and Boston. He might know of someone willing to take her to the Sommerfields. If not, she'd have to bide her time and wait for the stagecoach day after tomorrow.

By three o'clock that afternoon Anna was at the pond waiting for Lydia. She had left the tavern before the stage arrived so she wouldn't get caught up in working and be late for the meeting. She didn't know how long Lydia would be able to stay. Besides, this would give her an opportunity to see how well Mrs. Dudley could handle things without her.

Sitting on a large rock, Anna lifted her dress above her knees and took off her boots. She rubbed her feet in the long-bladed grass. It tickled. The day was warm, quiet. She looked up at the clear blue sky and let the heat from the sun wash her face with its warmth. That was the way Jordan had felt that night she'd lain with him, warm as sunshine.

With her face lifted to the sun, Anna closed her eyes and let memories take her back to that blissful night. What part of their time together had she liked best? His hands softly yet firmly caressing her breasts? *Oh yes, that had been wonderful.* His tongue exploring the inside of her mouth? *Oh yes, that had been delicious.* His deep, gentle strokes filling her? *Oh yes, that had shown her a glimpse of heaven.* His kisses? *Yes.* His touch? *Yes.* His words? *Yes.* His body stretched out beside hers, his cheek pressed against her breast, his breath cooling her heated skin?

"*Yes, yes, yes!*"

"Anna?"

Startled, Anna's eyes flew open. She looked up and saw Lydia standing over her, a worried expression on her face.

252

"A-are you you all right? You were m-mumbling."

A flush of heat ran up Anna's cheeks as she scrambled off the rock and hugged her friend affectionately. She'd best leave her dreaming of Jordan until the evening, when she was in bed.

"Lydia, I'm so happy to see you. I've missed you terribly. How've you been?"

"I—I was afraid you w-wouldn't come. That you'd b-be angry with me."

Anna stepped away from her embrace and looked at Lydia. She looked wonderful. There was a sparkle in her eyes. Her cheeks had a rosy glow, and she had on a new dress. It seemed as if marriage agreed with her. "Why should I be angry with you? Lydia, you're my friend. Sometimes I think you're the only friend I have. I love you. I've been worried about you."

Lydia hugged her again, tighter. "I tried to p-persuade them to let you c-come to the wedding. I-I wanted you there."

"I know." Anna smiled, took Lydia's hand, and led her to the large stone. "Come, take off your shoes and we'll wade in the pond."

"I d-don't have long," she said, but took off her shoes anyway.

"Reverend Kent told me your wedding was lovely. That you were beautiful."

Lydia smiled. "B-Benjamin wouldn't l-let you come."

"It's all right. I understood why. I think in time he will change his mind and want us to be friends again. Until then, we'll just meet like this whenever we can."

253

They both gasped, then laughed as their toes touched the cool water. Within minutes their skirts were hoisted up and draped over their arms and they were knee-deep in the water, letting the muddy bottom ease up between their toes.

"Are you happy, Lydia? Has Benjamin been good to you?" Anna asked, after a few friendly splashes.

"Oh, yes," she answered, and Anna could tell by the expression on her face that she was. That pleased Anna greatly. After her last visit with Benjamin, she'd thought he might take his anger out on Lydia, but it was apparent he hadn't.

"B-Benjamin is kind and good to me, but like you, h-he doesn't like for me to stutter. I'm trying t-to do better."

"You're doing much better. And I'm glad you're happy with him. It sounds as if he will take very good care of you." Anna reached down into the water, cupped some in her palm, and washed her face. The water felt wonderful. "How about his mother? Is Althea kind to you?"

Lydia laughed and this startled Anna. It was a genuine laugh, not nervous, anxious, or bitter. "Lydia, how can you laugh about Althea Jarvis?"

"Sh-she's not nice."

Anna laughed a little, too. She didn't understand Lydia's carefree response to Althea. Anna considered her the meanest woman in town, and that was no laughing matter. "No, she's not. That's why I've been so worried about you. She hasn't been cruel to you, has she?"

Still smiling, Lydia shook her head. "Sh-she says she c-can't abide my stuttering. It gives her a headache. She s-spends a lot of time in her room and s-stays away from me."

Anna laughed and hugged her friend. She dropped the tail of her skirt and it landed in the water, but she didn't mind. This was wonderful news. She was so happy for Lydia. Althea didn't worry about what she couldn't control, and she couldn't control Lydia's stuttering. Maybe Benjamin's mother had at last met her match. It seemed as if things were going very well for Lydia, and Anna couldn't be happier. She felt better knowing she could make her trip to New York and not worry about her friend.

When Anna and Lydia parted later that afternoon, Anna walked back to Parks Winchell's house to see if he found someone willing to take her to New York. He'd found a family who'd been staying at a tavern on the other end of town who were willing to let her travel with them for an enormous price which she had to pay in advance. She agreed to the sum only because she felt it would be safer traveling with a large family than with only one man. She hoped the wagon wouldn't be any slower than a carriage. She knew it would be safer traveling by stagecoach, but she didn't want to spend another full day at the tavern.

Anna entered the tavern from the kitchen and spoke to Mrs. Dudley. The woman was much friendlier than Glynis, but Anna still felt a pang of sorrow for Glynis because of her son. Anna took the time to go over certain instructions with Mrs. Dudley once again, and then left the kitchen to go upstairs and pack for her trip.

As she entered the taproom, she saw Jordan sit-

255

ting at a table. His long legs were stretched out in front of him, his riding boots on but unbuckled. He'd discarded his jacket and waistcoat and rolled up his sleeves past his elbows. She found his languid appearance very appealing, but she knew she couldn't show how he affected her.

He'd obviously heard her approaching, for he was looking directly at her. She walked a little further into the room and noticed a cup on the table in front of him and immediately wondered if it was tea or something stronger. "Good afternoon, Jordan. How are you today?"

"Not very well, and you know it."

He didn't move a muscle, but continued to stare at her. She cleared her throat as a feeling of unease crept up her spine. "How could I possibly know you're not feeling well? I haven't seen you today, but it appears you're in the same temper as when I saw you yesterday."

"Very good, Anna, considering nothing was settled between us before I left."

His sarcasm stiffened her back. She didn't have time for this. She had to pack and be ready to leave for New York at first light. She walked closer to him, not wanting anyone who might walk in to hear what she was going to say. "I told you I've taken all the blame for what happened between us. I've asked God not to fault you for something that was completely my doing." Her voice was sharp, her words clipped.

In one fluid motion he rose from the chair and towered over her. He looked down into her eyes and said, "Unless you set out to seduce me the minute I first walked into this tavern, you can't take all the blame because I wanted you in my bed the first time I saw you. You can't take any of it, for that matter. It's mine." He struck his thumb to his chest.

Anna's breathing quickened, her eyes widened. She remembered that she had been instantly drawn to him that day but hadn't known he'd felt the same way. She remembered clearly the fit of his breeches, his broad shoulders and narrow hips, his clean-shaven face. Standing so close to him, she knew all it would take was one small movement and she'd be in his arms again, begging him to love her just once more before he was lost to her forever.

"We must forget that night happened," she said.

His eyes roamed over her face, caressing her with each sweep of his lashes. "How can I forget that night? How can you?"

Oh no, she'd never forget the way his bare skin felt beneath her hands, the contours of his firm muscles, his weight upon her. How could she forget his body pressed deeply into hers, or the sweet words of affection, or the kisses that stole her breath? She swallowed hard and forced her eyes away from his. "I only know that we must. You and I can never be together," she whispered softly.

"I think we can." He touched her chin with his forefinger, adding pressure until she lifted her face and eyes to him. "You just need to be honest with me." He grabbed her arms and pulled her up close. "I saw that you'd posted a letter to Andre today. Why must you put yourself in danger by continuing your association with the British?"

Anna opened her mouth to tell him that her association with the British was going to save the Americans from losing control of West Point, but just as quickly she decided not to. It was best not to reveal any of her plans. "You have known for weeks that I correspond with Major Andre." His fingers scraped across her skin as she ripped away from his strong hold. "What I do is not your concern. Stay out of my life, Jordan."

"I don't want to be out of your life. I want to help you," he replied in a voice filled with emotion.

Her heart was pounding. This was her chance, if she wanted to share the burden of eavesdropping. But what could a minister do? "Not with this," she finally said, and picked up her skirt to rush past him.

He grabbed her arm and swung her around to face him. "We need to talk about what happened between us."

Anna sighed. She would like that, but there simply wasn't time. "All right, later. Tomorrow," she whispered, knowing that tomorrow she would be gone.

Chapter Fourteen

Someone was pounding Jordan's head and stomach with his fists. Damn, it hurt. He tried to open his eyes, but his lids were too heavy. He reached up to fend off the attacker, but he couldn't grab hold of him. He was too quick, yet he kept pummeling Jordan about the head. Finally, with a jerk, Jordan opened his eyes, raised his head, and sat straight up in bed. His stomach swam sickly, and fiendish cramps attacked his insides. He was seized by an unusual feeling of weakness, and it drenched him in cold sweat.

"Damn," he swore. The pounding continued in his head, but the roaring in his ears was Moss banging on the door. He was afraid if he opened his mouth to answer the old man, something else would come out.

He took three deep, shaky breaths, then said, "Come in."

The door opened and there Moss stood, swaying before him. "Are you all right, Reverend?"

"No, stomach cramps and maybe fever," he managed to say, though he didn't know how. The pain had him doubled over.

Moss walked over to the chest, picked up the

chamberpot, and placed it on the floor by his bed. "Guess you'll be needing this. It's best not to eat anything for the first few hours. But I'll be up later with a toddy for you."

Jordan covered his eyes with a trembling hand. Why was Moss talking about food? How the hell could he eat anything when his stomach was churning like a rain-swollen river? He'd done some heavy drinking after he'd talked with Anna, but this feeling couldn't be caused by an excessive amount of brandy. God damn it, he thought, as a cramp doubled him up again, he'd caught whatever sickness was going around Virgil's camp. He'd been stupid to stay in that camp just to get away from Anna, and today he was paying for it.

"Alone," he whispered to Moss, as he held his head with one hand and his stomach with the other.

"What did you say?"

"Alone, leave me alone." He gulped in air as he spoke, trying to quell the quaking in his stomach.

"Oh, all right," Moss replied. "It's best to just suffer through the worst of it, but later I'll bring up that hot brew. It'll help you. Right now, try to sleep. You're going to be sore as hell—uh, sorry, Reverend. Ah—I'll be checking on you."

When the door shut behind Moss, Jordan eased his body back on the bed. Oh God, he was sick. Really sick. He lay perfectly still, afraid to move his head an inch in either direction. Cramps attacked his stomach again and he drew his knees up to his chest. This was going to be one hell of a day.

It was early evening before Jordan managed to

get out of bed. He still felt weak as a baby, but he needed to go outside and get some fresh air. He'd been in agony most of the morning, but his stomach settled down after downing whatever it was Moss gave him to drink. It must have been heavily laced with laudanum, for he'd slept the rest of the afternoon and even now still felt the effects of the drug. If he'd been any weaker, he might never have awakened.

His conversation with Anna the afternoon before, his anger at himself for taking her to bed in the first place, had caused him no small amount of worry during his wakeful hours. Now all he wanted was to go downstairs and assure himself she was all right. He wanted to take her in his arms and tell her that he'd make things right between them.

He finally managed to put on his breeches and shirt and shoes, knowing he'd have to forgo the boots, waistcoat, and jacket. He was just too damn weak to put it all on. After he was dressed he decided to spend some time sitting in front of the open window, letting the fresh air and the cool breeze clear his head and relax his stomach.

He was surprised that Anna hadn't been up to check on him. Thinking of Anna made him feel vulnerable, and that made him angry with himself. She'd agreed they could talk and that was what he intended to do.

Last night he'd remembered having one lucid thought: confront her. Let her know he suspected she was working for the British and if she was, give her the opportunity to return her allegiance to the Americans. Yes, that's what he'd decided to

261

do. Virgil was after him to catch a spy. Lafayette and Washington were ready to make an example of someone, and he couldn't let it be Anna. He had to tell her what he suspected and not just leave it to her to open up and be truthful. He had to let her know that she could trust him and depend on him to do whatever was needed to keep her safe. It couldn't be put off any longer. Damn it, he loved her.

His stomach rumbled as he looked out at twilight. He wanted to see Anna. He wanted to pull her to him and hold her, lay his head on her shoulder and draw from her strength. She was so beautiful, the most beautiful woman he'd ever seen.

He laid his head back against the chair and remembered the night he'd made love to her. She was so responsive to his every touch. She was so warm and eager to be loved. She was small and tight, but so much a woman that he'd been going crazy to have her again, make love to her again. How could he have turned away from her, knowing how he felt about her? She was so strong and so independent and so damn righteous she had to take the blame for their lovemaking.

As he sat with the cool wind caressing his cheeks he could remember the smell of her, that tantalizing flavor he'd tasted on her skin. He breathed in deeply, remembering the taste and smell of the spice. He wet his lips, wanting desperately to taste her again.

He'd never wanted to touch a woman so badly in his life. She was soft, firm. He'd loved everything about her, everything. He closed his eyes and he could almost feel his palms running up and down her satiny thighs, not an ounce of spare flesh on them. He'd liked the way her breasts filled his hand, the way the dusky pink tip peaked at his touch and hardened when his mouth closed over it. He remembered the feel of her silken hair as he crushed it between his fingers and rubbed it in the palm of his hands. No other woman had ever given him as much as Anna. He'd never been the first man for any other woman. Now he intended to see to it there was never anyone else for Anna, no one but him.

"Oh, Anna," he whispered, aching to touch her once again.

To hell with thinking about her — he had to see her. He rose and held on to the window frame, having to wait a moment to get his strength. Just a few minutes in the taproom, he told himself as he took several deep breaths. He had at least to catch a glimpse of her before he drove himself crazy.

It was well after dark before Jordan made it down the stairs. The smell of ale and smoke in the taproom made his stomach rumble obnoxiously, but it was worth it to see Anna. He was a little miffed that she hadn't been up to check on him. He'd have liked to know that she was a little bit worried about him.

A slow glance around the taproom showed him Moss and Terence, and Eli Dudley was carrying drinks to the tables. What the hell was going on? Why was Eli serving drinks? Was Anna sick as well? Had he passed this fiendish sickness on to her yesterday? He walked over to the bar where Moss stood and leaned against it.

"Good evening, Reverend. You're still looking a mite peaked. Are you sure you should be up and about?"

No, he wasn't sure. He felt like hell, and the smells of liquor, tallow, and unwashed bodies reminded him of just how sick he'd been. "What's Eli Dudley doing working in here?"

"Oh, Anna hired him to work in the evenings till the tavern closes. She wanted me to check with you and see if you'd record the books for her. Said she'd pay you when she returned."

A cold sweat broke out on Jordan and he felt clammy. He wiped his forehead with the back of his hand, leaning all his weight against the bar. He cleared his throat. "What do you mean, when she returns?"

"She left for New York bright and early this morning. Couldn't talk her out of it."

"Damnation!" Jordan swore and hit his fist on the bar. His gaze caught Moss's questioning look but he didn't have time to apologize. With Anna gone to New York there was a good chance the town would soon know he wasn't a minister.

"I told her it wasn't safe for her to go to New York." A wave of dizziness assailed him and he held onto the bar, waiting for it to pass. He rued the day he'd gone into Virgil's camp.

"I tried to tell her but she wouldn't listen. You don't look well, Reverend. I think you should go back to bed."

"Do you know why she went?" Jordan asked in a raspy voice.

"Couldn't get her to say. Just kept saying this was something she had to do. I have a feeling she told Terence, though his lips are tighter than a virgin's — ah — I mean, I can probably get it out of the boy in a few days."

Jordan was trying to think, but the damn room kept spinning and his legs were getting weaker. "How'd she go?"

"All I know is she went by wagon. I don't know who she's traveling with. She never tells me a thing except to work. Parks Winchell found someone to take her." Moss shoved a tray of ale to the side of the bar.

Jordan knew he was in no shape to ride, or he'd head for New York tonight. And if this bloody sickness didn't work its way out of his system soon, he didn't know when he'd be able to sit a horse. Damn it, she could easily get two or three days ahead of him.

"Did she give you a name or place where she'd be?"

"Anna wrote it down for me." He pulled a piece of paper from his pocket and handed it to Jordan. "A lot of good it does me. I can't read."

It took a few moments for Jordan's eyes to focus. "Mr. and Mrs. Richard Sommerfield."

"Never heard of them," Moss commented. "There's something going on that she isn't talking about, Reverend."

Jordan knew. The Sommerfields were well-known Tories. She'd gone to see some goddamn Tories! Then he'd been *right* about her, after all. She was a spy. Arnold had probably let something slip about his recent visit with Washington and she'd hightailed it off to New York to tell her friends. *Jordan's enemies!* With a trembling hand he gave the paper back to Moss. "I'm going back to bed. Fix me another hot toddy, Moss. I need a good night's sleep."

"I'll get it for you, Reverend. You go on up to bed. I'll be up in a few minutes. You'll sleep like a baby."

That's what he hoped because, come what might, he would be on his way to New York tomorrow morning. His legs were extremely weak as he climbed the stairs, and by the time he made it to his bed he was drenched with sweat and trembling like a rabbit caught in a snare.

Jordan lay on his bed, berating himself for falling under Anna's spell, for thinking she'd be truthful about her relationship with Andre. He'd been taken in by her for the last time. He had to put his personal feelings aside and get to New York as soon as possible.

God damn it, he loved Anna, but he wasn't going to let her betray the Americans.

Chapter Fifteen

Three days later, Anna stood in one of the upstairs bedrooms in the most magnificent house she'd ever seen. Richard and Constance Sommerfield's house was splendid and opulent. The bedroom which was to be hers for the next few days was nestled under the gable of the attic and lighted on each side by dormer windows. It had two single beds, and matching slipper chairs sat at the foot of each. A small fireplace had been added to the room and it was decidedly set off-center. The wardrobe where her clothing had been placed by a servant was highly polished, elaborately paneled oak.

In Georgetown, she and her family had been one of the wealthiest, having plenty, but the Sommerfields lived in grandeur, luxury, extravagance. This kind of excessive indulgence must be sinful.

Yesterday, when she'd arrived, Mr. and Mrs. Sommerfield had welcomed her with open arms, but she also had the feeling they considered her an uneducated child. She was trying not to take offense, knowing that their way of life was vastly different from hers. For some reason they assumed they needed to tell her every little thing to do, from when to go to bed to what she should wear the next day. Anna was not used to this kind of fussing, but decided since she was a guest in their house she'd let them have their way.

She wasn't happy that she had to use their house and their kindness while she plotted a way to stop John and General Arnold, but she had little choice.

While the Sommerfields had been lavish in their praise of her beauty and her manners, they were openly unhappy with her clothes. In Georgetown, she was considered a well-dressed young woman, and she had a new dress made three or four times a year. Here, at this house, her clothes were no better than those of the servants who hurried from room to room making sure everyone was comfortable.

When Anna arrived, Mrs. Sommerfield was wearing a beautiful rose pink silk dress trimmed with cream-colored lace. Or at least Anna thought it was silk. She hadn't actually touched the beautiful fabric. Constance Sommerfield's hair had been piled into a ridiculous-looking mound on top of her head with a piece of fine cutwork lace attached to the top.

Mrs. Sommerfield had insisted Anna take dinner in her room last night, suggesting she was too tired to join them downstairs. Bright and early this morning Anna had been measured for new clothes. When she protested, Mrs. Sommerfield assured her that new clothing was not being made for her, but that some old dresses were going to be altered for her which would be suitable for dining and meeting guests.

Later that morning Mrs. Sommerfield explained that one new dress would be made for a ball that was being held Saturday night at the Grand Ballroom. For that, Major Andre himself had commissioned a new gown for her. He was choosing the fabric, the color, the style, and the dressmaker. She was told the first fitting should be ready by the morrow. Not only did she not want to be indebted to John for a new dress; Anna knew how difficult it was and how long it took to make a dress. She told Mrs. Sommerfield that she wouldn't be in New York long enough to use the dress, but the woman simply wouldn't listen to any of her plans.

Now, here she stood in what she believed to be the largest house in New York, dressed only in a borrowed satin robe. Satin, she laughed, and ran her hands down the material, feeling the contours of her body beneath it. Jordan had said her skin felt like satin. She ran her hands over the material again. *No,* he'd lied. Her skin was not that smooth, that slick. For a brief moment she wondered if he'd lied about other things that night but quickly discarded that thought because now it didn't matter. Even though she loved him, they could never be together again. Oh, having him once was not nearly enough. She wanted to be with him again and again.

Suddenly, Anna scolded herself for thinking of Jordan. What she had to do here was very important, and she couldn't accomplish it if she let her thoughts continue to stray to Jordan. She'd had her chance to elicit Jordan's help and decided against it. There was no one to depend on but herself.

Anna stepped away from the window where she'd watched twilight descend over the garden and looked over at the gold-colored silk dress that had been altered for her. She'd been told to wait and a maid would be up to help her dress. She laughed lightly to herself. When had she ever needed anyone to help her dress? Picking up the beautiful gown and holding it against her, she twirled around several times. She'd never had a dress that was such a brilliant color, never had a silk dress. Her first was supposed to have been her wedding gown. She sighed as she pressed the silk against her breasts.

So much had happened since the night her father was killed. Now here she was in New York, ready to put on a beautiful dress, and trying to stop General Arnold from completing his traitorous meeting with John Andre. Because of the general's trip to Norwich, she was fairly certain the meeting hadn't taken place yet.

The only plan she'd come up with during her journey to the city was to visit John's office at British headquarters. She had to do something, and she had to start somewhere. John's office seemed the most logical place to begin. If she could manage a few minutes alone in his office, surely she could find documentation of his meeting with Arnold. Once she knew where and when they were meeting, she'd plan how to stop or at least stall them until the Americans could be notified.

Anna carefully put the dress back as the servant had left it and checked to make sure her father's pistol was still hidden under the mattress. She hoped she would never have cause to use it. She and John had never discussed military matters, and she knew he would be suspicious if she suddenly developed an interest. She had to be very careful how she handled this so as not to give herself away. This turn of events had made her aware of John's life as a soldier, his duty to his King. After all these years of friendship, the war had finally come between them, and John wasn't even aware of it.

Anna sighed and rubbed the back of her neck. Suddenly she wasn't as certain as she'd been when she'd left Georgetown that she could find out where and when the meeting was to take place. Maybe she should have gone to the Americans and told them what General Arnold intended to do. If she could have sent a message to General Washington, would he have believed her? No, General Arnold had fought so many battles against the British (he had been wounded twice) that he was above suspicion.

She didn't know that she was doing the right thing, only that she didn't know what else to do. There was no one to turn to. If she found out where the meeting was to take place, she must do whatever was necessary to stop the general from handing over the map of West Point. She must find the courage to use her father's pistol, if necessary.

A light knock on her door let Anna know the maid had come to help her dress, and an hour later Anna walked down the curved staircase and into the large parlor of the Sommerfield house. Mrs. Sommerfield sat on a small rose-colored sofa at the far end and Mr. Sommerfield in a brocaded wing chair to her left. An imposing painting of Mrs. Sommerfield hung over the mantel at the foot of the room and a larger painting of Mr. Sommerfield hung over a handsomely carved and gilded pier table with a marble top.

"Ah — Miss Lowell, do come join us." Mr. Sommerfield rose from his chair and gave a slight bow before taking her hand and kissing it. "My dear, you look very lovely tonight. Doesn't she, Constance?"

"Indeed she does," Mrs. Sommerfield replied with a bright smile, as her husband seated Anna beside her on the small settee. She reached over and squeezed Anna's hand.

"Major Andre will be delighted to see the change in you. He should be arriving at this very moment," Mr. Sommerfield assured Anna. "A more punctual man I've never met, have you, Constance?" He returned to his seat, flipping the tail of his coat out so he wouldn't wrinkle it.

"No, I haven't," his wife affirmed.

Anna was afraid to move her head. She was certain her hair was going to fall down if she did, although the maid had insisted that it wouldn't. She'd never worn her hair any way other than hanging straight down her back or stuffed under her cap. With it piled high and puffed out on each side, she felt as if she were going to lose her balance.

The dress was too low-cut as well. She usually wore round-necked collarless dresses. This neckline was so low it showed the V of her breasts, and she kept wanting to pull it up to her neck. The sleeves of the dress were straight and tight until just below the elbow, then they flared out and were tipped with white lace. She was so uncomfortable!

Mrs. Sommerfield turned to Anna. "Major Andre has spoken of you on many occasions, my dear. We're simply delighted to have you join us for a stay. It's so seldom anyone new visits us these days. I guess it's because of all the fighting. New York is not what it once was. We never know who will be controlling the city from day to day."

"Things are looking better, my dear, with the recent fall of Charleston. General Clinton is sure to be—ah, here is Major Andre now."

Anna smiled warmly as John entered the room dressed in full military finery, his handsomeness and air of confidence stealing her breath for a few moments. The gold braid gracing the crest of his shoulders ended with three tassels which swung lightly as he walked. Large brass buttons ran up the sleeves and the front fold, giving distinction to the expertly tailored jacket. And, unlike Jordan's, the buckles on his shoes rattled as John walked into the room. He spoke to Mrs. Sommerfield first, then turned his smiling countenance toward her.

"Milady, how beautiful you look tonight." He took her hand, kissing it as he bowed low in front of her. "I have waited so long for your visit."

"John, I'm happy to see you again so soon." Her smile was genuine, but a feeling of unease settled over her the moment their eyes met. She would never be comfortable with him again, although she had to act as if nothing had changed between them. Looking at him now, she realized that she didn't like John any less for what he was doing — after all, she'd known his loyalties all along. She simply loved her country more. After this was over, she'd have to learn how to live with the fact that she'd betrayed John and used innocent people in order to keep General Arnold from betraying the Americans.

He placed his hand on the hilt of his sword, stepped back, and asked, "Tell me, are my friends treating you well?"

Anna smiled again and laughed lightly, hoping her inner fear didn't show. Were they treating her well? What a question! Up to now she couldn't remember eating a meal she hadn't helped prepare. Never before had her bathwater been heated and brought to her room for her. No one had helped her dress since childhood. Oh yes, they were taking very good care of her. She hated accepting their hospitality when she was deceiving them, but the complexity of the situation demanded it.

Anna cleared her throat, not wanting her voice to betray her. "I couldn't be more delighted with their hospitality, John. Mr. and Mrs. Sommerfield are wonderful people." She gave both of them a smile. "I'm pleased to be here for a few days. Thank you, John, for arranging this."

"My pleasure." He bowed again. "I've always wanted you to come to New York. Now that you're here, I intend to see that you have a wonderful time. You may not want to leave."

"Oh, I must get back to Georgetown soon." She swallowed, trying to ease the dryness of her throat. "While I'm here, John, I was hoping I could do some shopping for the tavern. Maybe tomorrow we could go to a merchant ship, as you'd promised, and later you could show me around your office."

"Surely you don't mean that," Richard Sommer-field injected, rising to his feet again. "John, did you promise to escort her to the harbor? I can't believe it."

Constance gasped. "Oh, my dear, we couldn't allow that. It's not acceptable and much too danger-ous for a young lady."

Anna held her breath and watched John, waiting for his reply. Her heartbeat increased and she braced herself for a fight. "I did promise Anna we could visit a ship so that she might buy goods for her tavern. But of course, Richard, your objections are correct. I'll simply arrange for the items she wishes to see to be brought here." He turned to Anna. "Will that satisfy you?"

Anna had to think fast. "But I've never seen New York," she protested, not caring that she wouldn't visit the ship but still determined to get to John's office so she could search it. "I can't be-lieve I would be in any danger with John at my side."

"I'm afraid Richard is right in this, Anna. The harbor is no place for a lady. I wasn't thinking clearly when I agreed to such an arrangement." John gave her a placating smile.

Anna's lips formed a pout. Playing the part of the whining female wasn't to her liking, but she had to force the issue. "Then you must allow me to visit your office. Surely with so many soldiers around I'll be safe."

"It's the soldiers you have to worry about," Con-stance argued, shaking her head in disagreement.

"No," Anna said firmly, turning to face the

275

older woman who still sat so primly on the sofa. "In John's care, I shall come to no harm." She turned back to John and puckered her lips even more. "Surely I can see something of New York."

John took a deep breath and clasped his hands behind his back. "Well, perhaps a short visit to my office. It's highly irregular, and I'll have to make special arrangement, but —" He smiled at her, then turned to Mr. Sommerfield, who stood equal in height but was of a more robust build. "Richard, will you allow Anna to visit me tomorrow if I promise not to take her to the harbor?"

Richard pursed his lips and looked at his wife. "What do you think?"

"I couldn't possibly escort her tomorrow because of the dinner party."

"Oh, I understand," Anna hurried to say, clasping the woman's hand in both of hers. "If I could borrow your carriage, I'm sure your driver will take proper care of me." She reached over and kissed Constance's delicate cheek, hoping to soften her objections and preempt further discussion of the subject. "Thank you for agreeing to this."

"Well, I suppose it will be all right," Mrs. Sommerfield consented with a pleased smile.

"Now that that's out of the way," John said, "I ask that you allow me to escort Anna to the ball Saturday night."

Richard pursed his lips again and rubbed his chin thoughtfully. "I don't know, Major. Constance has planned a small dinner party for tomorrow evening at which we hoped Anna would pick her own escort. We've seen to it that only suitable young men have been invited. As lovely and graceful as she is, we should have them fighting over her before evening's end. Isn't that so, Constance?"

The older woman's eyes sparkled. "Oh, yes, we're very excited about the prospects of tomorrow evening, Major Andre."

"Exactly what I wished to avoid," John commented. "I don't intend to monopolize her time. She will be free to dance with as many young men as she wishes."

Anna looked from John to Mr. Sommerfield, surprised that they would talk about her as if she weren't present. And Anna wasn't the least bit interested in the men she might meet at the ball or the dinner party. There could never be anyone for her but Jordan.

"Nevertheless, Major, you've entrusted Miss Lowell to our care and we won't be derelict in our duty. After tomorrow evening, when Anna has been introduced to some other young men, we'll let you know promptly if she decides in your favor."

"I knew I couldn't go wrong in placing Anna with you, Richard. We'll not speak further of the matter."

As they continued to discuss the ball, Anna settled back in the sofa, her mind already busy planning the trip to John's office.

The next morning Anna lifted the skirts of her puce silk dress and stepped out of the carriage in front of a large stone building. She stood rigidly for a moment and looked up at the imposing structure flanked by well-dressed soldiers. Muskets were pressed against their shoulders and they stood

277

as straight as the wooden soldiers Moss whittled.

Sunshine warmed her cheeks as she stared at the building. Once she went inside, she couldn't turn back. What she had to do was an act of betrayal of a friendship she'd treasured for many years, and she didn't take that lightly. But this wasn't the time to lose heart.

She reached into her drawstring bag, pulled out three coins, then turned to the carriage driver. "Here," she said in the firm voice her father had taught her to use when addressing strange men. "Go have yourself a tankard of ale while I'm inside."

The elderly, toothless man smiled as another carriage passed them. "No, thank you, Miss. I have orders not to leave this spot without you."

She hadn't expected his objection. She smiled sweetly while she thought of a different approach. Her gaze darted from one end of the street to the other. She couldn't search for a young boy with this man watching. There were more men on the street than women and children, but she was sure she could find one. But first she had to persuade the driver to take the money and leave.

She patted underneath her eyes with her gloved fingers before looking back at the man. "I-If you'll notice, there are enough coins here to buy a bottle of b-brandy. I-I'd like for you t-to purchase one for me." She deliberately broke her words and put a wan expression on her face. "I-I use it at night t-to help me sleep. Please don't t-tell anyone I asked you to purchase it. I wouldn't want anyone to worry about me."

The old man eyed her curiously as he scratched

his head. "I don't know. I'm not supposed to leave you."

"Please. There's no one else for me to ask. I'm not sure Mrs. Sommerfield would understand, but I have a feeling you do."

Anna felt tears gather in her eyes when the old man reached for the coins. It hurt her to know she could lie so easily. "You won't tell anyone?" she asked again.

His toothless smile reassured her. "Not a soul, miss."

"Thank you," she whispered, and dropped the money into his calloused palm.

As the carriage pulled away, Anna realized her tears were real—she was frightened. She quickly wiped the tears away and looked up and down the street. There wasn't a child in sight who was alone, and her plan was dependent upon her finding a young boy. Just as she was about to give up she saw exactly what she needed, a young lad walking toward her, whistling and twirling a stick in his hand. He was light-haired and fair-skinned. His clothes were worn and dirty, giving him the appearance of a street urchin. A smile came to Anna's lips.

"Excuse me please, young man," she said as he drew closer.

The boy stopped and looked at her with questioning blue eyes that reminded her of her beloved brother. "Would you like to earn some money?"

He looked her over from head to toe as if trying to decide whether or not she had any money. "What you want me to do?" he asked finally.

Anna glanced around to make sure no one was close enough to hear, then bent down and whispered to the young lad.

He listened carefully, nodding along the way. Finally, when she was through, he held out his small hand and she dropped several coins into his palm. His fist closed around them. Anna took a deep breath and dabbed at her forehead with her gloved hand. The hard part was over. Now all she had to do was walk into John's office and wait. She turned away from the boy and headed for the door before her legs grew weaker.

She didn't expect to be stopped at the large wooden door by the subaltern, but suddenly he jumped between her and the door, holding his musket between them. "I'm sorry, miss, you're not allowed inside."

Taking a step backward, Anna allowed her breathing to slow before she tried to speak. "I-I'm here to see Major Andre. He's expecting me."

The soldier eyed her curiously, then said, "Wait here." He opened the door and went inside.

Anna looked around and noticed that all the soldiers who guarded the entrance were looking at her. Their icy stares chilled her. She rubbed her hands across her arms and looked straight ahead. She'd come this far. She wouldn't accept defeat now. The door was yanked open and Anna jumped. The soldier didn't speak. With the barrel of his musket, he motioned for her to enter. Anna took a tentative step forward.

A few minutes later she was shown into John's office. She kept her back as straight as an iron rod. Her stomach quaked and her eyes twitched with the fear that coiled inside her. She prayed her feelings didn't show.

"John, I never dreamed New York had so many buildings, so many carriages, so many people in the streets."

John chuckled. "The city surprises everyone on a first visit. Tell me, how do you like my office?" He swept his hand through the air.

Anna glanced around the room. One wall was filled with shelves of books. She'd never seen so many in one place. Dark red drapes covered the windows, and to one side of the room was an expensively decorated sitting area.

"It's magnificent," she said softly, feeling no pride. This office, this building, had belonged to someone else until the British soldiers invaded the city and took up residence.

John smiled. "Thank you. I had most of the furniture brought over from London. It helps to be reminded of home."

"I'm sure it does." Anna's throat felt swollen and dry.

Suddenly loud shouts and cries erupted from the street outside. John frowned and walked over to look out the window. "Hmm. It appears some sort of riot has started." He turned back to Anna as a rock hit the windowpane, cracking the glass. John drew his shoulders up straighter. "Excuse me while I make sure someone is seeing to this."

"By all means," she answered breathlessly, knowing the lad hadn't let her down. She sent up a prayer for his safety.

"There's nothing for you to worry about, Anna. It's just some young boys throwing rocks at the windows. Remain here until I return," he said. John walked out the door, closing it behind him.

As soon as the door shut, Anna sprang to her feet and hurried to the window to check on her little champion. A smile brightened her face. The youngster was smart. He'd enlisted the aid of several friends, and the street below was filled with soldiers running around, trying to catch the little beggars. Satisfied with the boy's performance, Anna hurried over to John's desk to look at the papers scattered on top. Her hands trembled, her heartbeat raced as she picked up each sheet and scanned the contents. Not one had anything to do with a meeting.

She glanced up at the door, then opened the top drawer and pulled back sharply when she saw a pistol. The short-handled weapon unnerved her, and seeing there were no papers underneath it, she quickly closed it and opened the next drawer. Anna groaned. It was filled with so many papers she'd never be able to look through them all before John returned. Closing that drawer, she went on to the next, hoping to find a folder or package or something to give her a clue that what she was looking for actually existed. Just as her hand grabbed the handle of the last drawer, the door opened. She froze.

"Anna?"

Dear God, she'd been caught! What would he do to her? Slowly she straightened her back and looked up as her guilty eyes met John's. She had to think fast.

"John, I-I was looking for a quill," she said breathlessly, then followed his gaze to where a pen lay in full view on his desk. "And a clean piece of paper," she added quickly, breathlessly. "All of this has writing on it."

John walked further into the room, his gaze not wavering from her face. "Why did you need paper, Anna?"

Her throat burned from the tension in her body and sharp pains attacked her stomach. Would he believe her? Could she convince him she was innocent when she wasn't? "I-I was going to write you a note that I was leaving. The noise in the street frightened me," she added, knowing that her face must have paled considerably.

"I told you to remain here, where you would be safe."

On shaky legs she walked from behind the desk and stood before him. Her bottom lip quivered. "I wasn't sure of that. I didn't know when you'd come back."

John took her hands. "You really *were* frightened, weren't you?" His expression softened. "Your hands are cold as a fish, and you're trembling." He pulled her into his arms, pressing her cheek against his chest and patting her shoulder. "Dear Anna, don't you know I would never let anyone harm you?"

A sob broke from her lips and she buried her face into his red coat. Mixed with the feelings of betraying John was deep disappointment at not finding what she'd come for. Now what could she do to stop John and General Arnold?

The next night Anna walked into the ballroom

dressed in a gown the color of a brilliant sapphire. A band of white satin circled her waist. The bodice had a heart-shaped neckline that showed the fullness of her breasts, exaggerated by the corset she wore beneath the silk. The short puffed sleeves were made to wear off the shoulders, and the front waistline dipped into a V before the skirt fanned out in yards of soft, rich blue silk. John walked beside her, clothed in full regimentals.

The use of fretwork on the ceiling gave the large, square ballroom the appearance of a circular room. Round tables draped with white linen cloths outlined the perimeter of the room. In the middle of each table stood a small bouquet of late summer flowers, and crystal glasses and goblets sparkled and glimmered as the light from the candles bounced off their rims. In the center of the room hung a huge brass chandelier with the flames of hundreds of lighted candles dancing from it. The smooth smell of beeswax hung heavily in the air.

During the carriage ride John had mentioned that she seemed nervous. She'd quietly insisted that it was because this was her first ball. But that wasn't the reason. Her failure yesterday had left her in a state of uncertainty. Tonight she'd take a different approach, and that had her stomach roiling. If she failed to obtain any information from John tonight, she'd leave the safety of the Sommerfields and follow John. It wouldn't be easy, but she didn't know what else to do.

If she couldn't talk John into taking her into his confidence and telling her about his plan, she'd have no choice but to take her father's gun and follow him until he met with General Arnold.

A few minutes later, Anna gave up trying to remember the names of the men and women she was introduced to as they made their way across the great expanse of the room. John was obviously a well-known, well-liked man. Everyone stopped to speak to them as they passed. The women and young ladies they met didn't try to hide their feelings of love and admiration for Major Andre as they openly flirted with him. It occurred to Anna that if the man beside her right now were Jordan Kent she would be very jealous.

When they reached a secluded corner, Anna knew it was time to begin her act. If she could convince John that she was willing to spy for the British, maybe he would tell her about his meeting with General Arnold.

"John, I've noticed that everyone in New York addresses you as Major Andre. Only I call you John. Is it improper for me to address you by your Christian name?"

He threw back his head and laughed. A light dusting of powder flew from his head and landed on his shoulders, and he promptly brushed it away. "No, you are not being too familiar. I was only a lieutenant when we first met. If you recall, at that time I asked you to call me John, and that is still my desire." He picked up her hand, kissed it, then smiled at her. "I'm most particular in those I allow to call me by my Christian name, and you, milady, are my favorite."

"Thank you," she answered, smiling sweetly. "I've noticed a few disapproving looks when I've called you John."

"Most of the people here address me by title because we are more formal in the city than people in the Connecticut countryside. I've also seen eyebrows rise when I refer to you as *milady,* which is reserved for titled women." He smiled. "There are times when I decide to break the accepted order of things."

The conversation was going just as she'd hoped it would. But now she must talk him into revealing his plans to her. "Here in the city with you, I find that I'm more aware of the war and that you are a soldier. From the comments I've heard tonight, the British seem confident that it will soon be over and they will have the final victory."

"Does that trouble you, Anna?" His voice had a serious ring.

"You mean as an American?" She drew her brows together and frowned. "No, not as it should. I just want the war to be over. I want the killing to stop." Her voice turned husky and her eyes watered with unshed tears. "John, I would do anything to stop the war."

His eyes searched her face. "So would I, milady," he answered in the same husky voice.

"Is there anything I can do?" she asked, knowing she could very well be sealing her fate. "Is there some way I can help?"

John smiled. "What could you do that the British military cannot? We have everything under control." John took her hand and lightly squeezed it. "Listen, the first dance has started. Come, no more talk of such serious matters at a party."

From across the room Jordan watched Anna smile at Andre. The knot that gripped his stomach had nothing to do with the dysentery that had in-

286

capacitated him for two full days, leaving him weak and irritable. He wanted to stomp over to the other side of the room and beat that bloody smile off the major's face.

Anna was so beautiful in the elaborate dress that matched her eyes. Just looking at the two made him angry. Anna and Andre seemed perfectly matched; what a pair they made. He hated to admit it, but the British soldier was the handsomest man he'd ever laid eyes on, and Anna was by far the most beautiful woman he'd ever seen. Jealousy coiled inside him. He couldn't bear the thought of Andre touching the woman he considered his own.

Jordan had worried, planned, and thought on the miserable ride to New York. By mid-afternoon the day after Anna left, he still couldn't sit a horse, so he'd taken the stage. Because of his ill-fated trip into Virgil's camp, Anna had managed to get to New York two days ahead of him, and by the looks of things, she was already well established in the Tory way of life. To judge by how she and Andre were smiling at each other, she had probably already given him whatever information Arnold had let slip.

Knowing all that, Jordan still could not leave Anna to consort with the British. He still had no idea what it was that Andre must have promised her in return for her allegiance to the Crown. Lowell Tavern had no better supplies than other taverns, so she wasn't getting special treatment in that area. If she'd been after the major's love, why would she have come so willingly into his own arms? Why would she have let him be the first man to make love to her? Anna was his, and he didn't intend to let Andre, the British, or anyone else have her.

Jordan rubbed his eyes and turned away. He had to bide his time, but before this evening was out, he'd approach Anna. He couldn't let his country down. That's what he'd come here for, and he'd do it. He'd find out what she knew, what she'd told Andre, and when the time came, he'd decide what to tell Virgil.

Throughout the long evening Anna learned just how popular Major Andre was with the ladies of New York. She was looked upon with envy, scorn, or awe whenever John was by her side. She wasn't good at the dances she participated in, but none of her partners seemed to notice that she didn't really know what to do. The young men seemed more intent on either telling her how lovely she looked or how important they were, neither of which interested her.

Anna couldn't get her mind off how miserably she'd failed in her effort to gather information about the meeting between John and General Arnold. Maybe there wasn't anything on paper. Maybe John had destroyed any evidence. John had made it quite clear that the British had everything under control, and with General Arnold on their side, they did.

After her fifth dance in a row, Anna had to get away from the crowd for a while and collect her thoughts. She pleaded for a few moments of privacy from the young soldiers clamoring for her attention. As she walked under the archway at the front of the hall, she heard her name spoken softly behind her. Anna gasped. No one pronounced her name that way save one man. She whirled and looked into the startling blue eyes of Jordan Kent.

"Milady." He bowed. "I believe that's how you're addressed here."

Anna couldn't move. She was frozen in place as Jordan stepped around and touched her arm. His face was twisted in an angry scowl, which surprised her even more. She didn't know what to say. She didn't understand. To see him again was a dream come true, but he was the last person she'd expected to find in New York.

"Come, let's move over here so we can have a few moments alone before we're discovered."

"Jordan! What are you doing here?" she finally managed to say, her eyes wide with disbelief.

"Following you, Anna. But tell me, what are you doing here?"

Chapter Sixteen

She hadn't expected him to reverse the question, so she had to think for a moment. "I'm here to visit with friends." She paused to catch her breath, to comprehend that Jordan was really here. "I can't believe you are standing before me." Suddenly she was hit with a cold blast of fear. "Is something wrong at the tavern or with Terence?" she asked in a rush of raspy words.

"No, all was well when I left." His face softened a little.

"Then why did you follow me? Jordan, I don't understand."

"Tonight, I'm the guest of Mr. and Mrs. Franklin Parker. And I know that you are the guest of Mr. and Mrs. Richard Sommerfield. You were escorted here tonight by none other than the well received, highly respected Major John Andre, Adjutant to General Clinton, better known in New York as Sir Henry." His voice held scorn. "Quite impressive for a mere tavernkeeper from a small village in the wilds of Connecticut."

Anna didn't understand Jordan's ridicule or his mockery of her friend. Part of her wanted to rush into his arms and cover him with kisses while the other was affronted by his verbal assault. She didn't want to play word games. She'd been too concerned with her quandary over John and General Arnold to fence words with Jordan right now.

"I had no idea you planned a trip to New York," she said stiffly.

"I had no idea you had one planned so quickly, my love."

Her heart skipped a beat at his affectionate words. What was he doing here? She took the time to gaze into his eyes and saw only anger, but why? He was dressed in a jacket of rusty red. She'd never seen him in any color but black. His waistcoat was elaborately embroidered with intricate little stitches of various colors, but his shirt, breeches, and stockings were his usual buff white. Anna didn't know what to think. This was not the Reverend Kent she knew.

"Jordan—"

He lifted a finger to quiet her. "Here, you are milady and I'm Jason Fields, a wine merchant from Boston. If anyone approaches us, you must refer to me as Jason."

Anna was suddenly flustered. She didn't know how to react, what to say. "I don't understand. Jordan, what—"

"Jason."

She took an exasperated breath and let her hands fall to her sides. "Jason. What are you doing here? Why have you assumed another name?"

His expression softened a little once again. "We have many things to talk about, not the least of which are our reasons for being in New York.

However, we don't have the time to discuss them right now."

"We have to discuss them," she pleaded. "I don't understand any of this."

"Not here, not now. I want you to meet me later tonight, when everyone else is sleeping. Come to the garden on the east side of the Sommerfield house. I'll be waiting for you."

Anna crumpled the lace handkerchief she held as her hand made a fist. "What are you suggesting? You're insane." She took a step away from him. "I don't know what you're doing here — why you followed me. And I don't intend to go out into the night to meet you."

"Anna, you must." His voice was urgent. "I'll tell you why I followed you here. Give me the opportunity to explain. Will you do that, please?"

Her back stiffened. "So you truly followed me here. Why? What right do you have to follow me?"

"I have the right, Anna." His voice turned suddenly husky and his eyes caressed her face. "Do you trust me?" he asked.

Anna looked at him. Trust him? Yes, she trusted him. She loved him, too. Her breath leapt. Could it be that he'd come here because he loved her? Her chest tightened at the thought. Yes, he must love her to have followed her all the way to New York, to be willing once again to go against the church's teachings. And now he wanted her to meet him in the garden.

Warmth spread through her. Yes, she trusted him. Yes, she wanted to be alone with him, too. She wanted him to hold her and love her and kiss her the way he had their first night together. She wanted to forget the reason she was here and lose herself in Jordan's arms, in Jordan's love.

She moistened her lips with mounting anticipation. "All right. I'll meet you."

He sighed in relief. "And you won't tell anyone."

"Of course not. That could prove dangerous for both of us."

"Oh, Anna you are the most intelligent, the most beautiful woman I've ever met. I swear to God that in you I have met my match, and I don't know what I'm going to do with you," he added softly.

Anna smiled. His words confirmed that he had come all this distance away from the people they knew just to be with her. She wouldn't let him down. She would meet him and no one would know.

Jordan sighed. "I can tell by the looks we're getting that I should let you go." He picked up her hand and kissed it. "Until later. Come as soon as you can. I'll be waiting."

"Jor—Jason, don't go yet. I—"

He squeezed her hand gently before letting go. "We will be together soon."

In an instant Jordan was hurrying down the hallway, and Anna suddenly felt very much alone. She felt weak and confused. How could she get through the next couple of hours until she could be in Jordan's arms once again?

"I see you have more suitors than you can handle, Anna," John said behind her.

She cleared her throat and turned around and

looked into his handsome face. "No, I can handle them all." She gave him a shaky smile as she realized why Jordan had made a hasty retreat. John would surely have recognized Jordan from the tavern. She hated this deception. She wished it were over but realized it had only just begun. Tomorrow she must don her tavern clothes and follow John until he met with General Arnold. She realized how risky and almost impossible it would be. But if she was right, the letter Glynis had given the general contained a time and place to meet John, and she had a feeling it would be soon.

John laughed. "I like your self-confidence. Tell me what has put that worried expression on your face. Did I not tell you that tonight we dance? Tomorrow we will deal with serious matters."

Anna put her hand up to run it through her hair and all she felt was a horribly stiff nest. She dropped her hand and it brushed the smooth silk of her gown. "It's not so serious," she lied. "I was just thinking that it's unbelievable people should live like this all the time."

"Like what, milady? Ladies with their hair in a neat coiffure, wearing silk all day, having someone prepare their meals and arrange their baths?"

"Yes. I'd have to do something more. I couldn't live the way these women do." She made a sweeping motion with her arm.

"The majority of these women think balls are the most stimulating events of the year. They live for these parties. You would if you'd been brought up to do so. But that, milady, is one of the things that makes you so attractive to men. You know of a different life, and there is nothing wrong with the way you live. You're strong and beautiful, and whoever marries you will be a lucky man."

Anna stuffed her handkerchief under her sleeve, hoping the tears would stay at bay. How like John to be so kind with his words. If he only knew the plans that were circling her mind even as they talked.

Looking around the room at all the colorful clothes, the smiling faces, the abundance of food, Anna agreed with him. "Oh, this is grand for a week or two." She paused. "But I should miss serving drinks in the tavern—"

"There you are, Major Andre, monopolizing Miss Lowell's time once again. I haven't had the pleasure of a dance this evening. You don't mind, do you?"

Anna smiled at Mr. Sommerfield as John reached for Anna's hand and presented it to Richard. "In that case, Richard, please take this one." He turned back to Anna and smiled. "Save the last dance for me."

Anna had debated whether to dress before slipping out of the Sommerfield home or to remain in her cotton nightgown and the borrowed robe the maid had given her. She'd finally decided it was better to stay dressed for bed. If she was seen, it would be easier to explain that she was simply going to take a stroll in the garden because she couldn't sleep. If she was fully dressed, it would be more difficult to explain.

Inhaling deeply, she opened the door to her

room and stepped out into the softly lighted hallway and silently pulled her door shut behind her. All was quiet and cast in semidarkness. An oil lamp burned dimly at the top of the stairs, giving the hallway its only light. The rug beneath her feet kept her steps soundless as she hurried down the corridor. Her heart pounded in her ears and her throat felt thick.

She didn't like slipping out into the night to meet Jordan. The Sommerfields had been extremely nice to her and she didn't want to bring any shame upon their house. If she was caught meeting Jordan that is exactly what would happen. But then she knew she'd risk anything to meet him. What kind of woman had she turned into that she was meeting a man in the garden at night?

No, she wouldn't think about that right now. Not tonight. He had come to her. This time she had not instigated the meeting, she told herself. He'd followed her, and that had to mean that he cared for her. That was a heady thought. Later, when she returned to Georgetown and had to take up life as a tavernkeeper once again, she would have tonight to add to her memories. She couldn't give that up. She'd seen desire in the eyes of every man she'd danced with this evening, but she wanted only Jordan.

Anna picked up the pale pink skirt of her robe and quietly descended the stairs and walked around to the back of the foyer. Under the stairs was a door which led to the back porch and the garden. The ball had gone on until well after midnight, and it was already early morning. They wouldn't have much time to be together before sunrise.

When her feet hit the ground she took a path that soon obscured her amid the tall trees, the bushes, and the flowers. She shivered in the cool air and wrapped her beltless robe tighter. The smell of some flower she didn't recognize drifted past her, and she breathed it in deeply. The night was clear, and a beautiful crescent moon washed her in soft light.

"Anna."

She turned and saw Jordan standing behind her. He'd taken off his jacket and waistcoat and was dressed in only his shirt and breeches. He was so handsome, and her heart was filled with love for him. Anna rushed into his arms and pressed her lips upon his.

Surprised, at first Jordan didn't respond to her kiss. This wasn't why he'd asked her to meet him. This wasn't what he wanted, he tried to tell himself, but his body wouldn't listen as his lips parted. He slid his arms around her waist, pulled her against his chest. His tongue entered her open mouth and plundered its depth. His hands made the satin sing with a delicious sound as they ran up and down her back, pressing her closer, harder.

Anna moaned contentedly as her fingers curled in Jordan's hair. She wasn't nervous, as she'd expected to be. This was what she'd been waiting for. To be with Jordan again was a dream come true. She could never claim him for her own, but tonight he would be hers.

Desperation forced Jordan to kiss Anna harder,

deeper than he thought was possible. She was so eager, so responsive to his touch, to his kisses, to his hands, that he was forgetting his purpose in being here. A storm of sensations and emotions deluged him. This was the woman he wanted more than anything in his life. But he didn't want her like this. Not here in the garden. She was too special.

Her soft murmurs heightened his arousal to a point where he ached. She wanted him to make love to her, and that excited him despite his inner protests. His mind fought her caresses, but his body wouldn't listen. He was so hard he felt the strain on his breeches.

Somewhere in the back of his mind he knew he wasn't supposed to be doing this, but when his hand found the soft mound of her breast, when his finger and thumb brushed the taut tip, he forgot about that and thought only of how much he wanted this woman.

He had to taste her. He remembered the spice on her skin and he had to sample it once again. He parted her robe, reached his hand beneath the gown, and cupping her breast, brought it out of hiding. The robe and gown slipped off one shoulder as Jordan sucked the dusky rose tip into his mouth.

Moaning with desire so intense she thought she might faint, Anna held Jordan's head to her breast while his mouth and tongue made wonderful things happen to her. Her legs were so weak with desire that when Jordan lowered her to the grass, she went willingly. Somehow, he managed to keep the robe beneath her, but with deft hands he pushed her gown up to her waist.

Jordan knew he should be gentle with her; this was only her second time with a man. He knew he was supposed to say soothing words of love, but all he wanted to say was that this shouldn't be happening. He didn't want it like this.

He tried to tell himself this was happening too quickly. He wanted the time to savor her, but she didn't seem willing to delay their union, either. There was urgency in her touch, a hunger in her soul. He knew she was ready for him, and he wouldn't disappoint her. His movements frantic and jerky, he unbuttoned his breeches and with burning intensity joined his body with hers in an explosive union. Within seconds he felt her release, and he instantly followed.

It was too quick, over before it really began. Jordan sighed and sank his teeth into the soft skin at the crest of her shoulder. Oh God, he hadn't wanted it to be this way with her. Damn it, he didn't want to take his pleasure with her in the garden as if she were a common trollop. He loved her too much to treat her like this. But he'd wanted her so badly and she was so willing. He'd done nothing but make mistakes since he'd met her. What a damnable man he was.

His breathing labored, his energy spent, Jordan tried to hold his weight off Anna by supporting himself with his elbows pressed deeply into the soft earth.

Now that he could think properly, this was definitely not what he wanted. By throwing herself into his arms she'd succeeded in seducing him. Damn it, he loved her! She wasn't common. He couldn't have felt worse if the damnation of the world had been placed on his shoulders. He'd treated her like a peasant whore, and now he hated himself for it.

What a hell of a fine mess he was in. It wasn't easy to admit to himself that when it came to this woman he forgot all his training and lost all control. She was the reason he'd been completely ineffective in this mission.

Slowly Jordan raised his head and looked down into her eyes. The moonlight shadowed her face but he could see she was smiling contentedly. His stomach jumped. She'd enjoyed the desperation, the quickness, the forbidden desire as much as he had. She was all woman! But would she ever truly be *his* woman?

"Anna, we have to talk," he managed to say in a hoarse voice.

"No," she whispered, and reached up to press her lips against his, trying to hold him inside her, not wanting, not willing to give him up. They had so little time. In another hour or two it would be sunrise, and morning meant they had to part. She knew this time with him might never happen again. She wouldn't give him up so easily, now that she had him in her arms once again.

"We have to," he insisted, and rolled away, pulling her gown down and his breeches up as he went.

Anna took a deep breath, stood up, and straightened her clothes while Jordan buttoned his breeches. She shouldn't have expected this time to be any different from before. He made love to her and then was sorry. How could she deal with his contradictory emotions toward her? Were those frantic few moments in his arms worth his hating her afterward? Yes. Yes, because she loved him.

But she wouldn't accept the responsibility for their union this time. No, he'd followed her and asked her to meet him. This time he would have to wear the guilt.

She turned to face him, ready to defend herself to him, whichever was necessary. His back was to the moon so she couldn't see his face clearly, but she knew by the tone of his voice that he wasn't happy with her.

"All right, let's talk," she said, pulling the robe tightly around her.

He ran both hands through his hair and tried to straighten it. "Anna, I know why you've come to New York."

Anna gasped. All thoughts of guilt and blame vanishing with his admission. "How could you know that? Did you overhear what I heard?"

"No, Anna, damn it, I didn't hear anything, and I wouldn't have come running to the British with anything I might have heard. Feeling the way I do about you, it's so damn hard to believe you are a spy." His last few words were broken with husky emotional gulps.

She couldn't make a sound. His words robbed her of breath for a few seconds. "What? A spy?" A thread of fear trembled up her back. She moistened her dry lips. "Jordan, what are you talking about?"

"When Major Andre came to the tavern, I feared you were a spy for the British. I didn't want to believe it, but why else would he risk coming through enemy lines to see you? You obviously had some intelligence for him at that time, or he had some for you. I never found out which."

Anna wrapped her arms around her chest and rubbed her arms. So Jordan believed she was a spy. Here she was in New York to stop General Arnold from delivering the Americans into British hands and he was calling her a spy. Anger rose within her.

"How dare you accuse me of such a thing!" she said contemptuously. His insult hit her hard and she was trying desperately to keep her composure. "You think that just because I have a friend who's British, I'm a spy? What kind of minister are you!"

"A damned one!" he shot back quickly. "I know the truth, Anna." His voice grew stronger, firmer. "Your ruse is over, and so is mine."

"You sanctimonious—" She bit her tongue to keep from saying the next word that fought to roll off her tongue. "How can it be over when it's never begun?" She lifted her hand in frustration. "I can't believe we're even discussing this after what just happened between us. I can't believe you truly think I'm a spy."

"It's because of what just happened between us that we have to talk. I can no longer let you play games with your British friends."

"You can no longer *let* me?" she asked indignantly, as her hands curled into fists of anger. "Who my friends are, Jordan Kent, is none of your business."

"It is my business when you give American intelligence to the British. I wanted to keep you from betraying us to the British."

Anna's anger turned to bitter disillusionment. "I won't listen to this. You're wrong. I'm not a spy." Her heart breaking, she turned and ran.

Jordan caught hold of the skirt of her robe as it flared out behind her and pulled it off one arm, wrenching her shoulder, but Anna kept running. She made a few more steps before Jordan overtook her, knocking her to the ground and pouncing on top of her.

The stunning blow of his weight took her breath for a moment before it returned with a groan of pain. The earth was hard beneath her, and a pebble under her chest was grinding into her flesh. She groaned again as Jordan rolled her over on her back and straddled her waist, shoving his hand over her mouth.

His roughness suddenly frightened her, and she tried to scream. Trying to bite his hand, she hit at him with her free hand and kicked and bucked beneath him, but it only caused him to press his hand harder over her mouth. He trapped her legs with his own and held them pinned beneath his. He caught her hands and pinioned them to her sides, all of his body weight upon her.

"Stop it, Anna! I don't want to hurt you," he said harshly between clenched teeth.

She tried to beg him to let her go, but all she could do was mumble an incoherent little sound. Tears burned her eyes as she weakened. She didn't want him to best her. She wanted to be stronger than he. She wanted to win.

"Anna, settle down. Damn it, I don't want to

hurt you." Jordan tried again to calm the hellcat struggling beneath him. Accusing her of being a spy had surely made her angrier than any woman he'd ever seen.

One arm slipped out of his sweaty hand and her fist caught him on the chin. He grunted and quickly recaptured her wrist. One blow from him would put her out cold, but he could never hit Anna, even if it meant a scream from her would bring the British down upon him. He found himself admiring her strength and determination as he held her, waiting for her to tire herself out so she'd listen to reason. She was fighting as if she thought he was going to kill her. Why didn't she realize he'd never hurt her?

Jordan watched the heaving of her chest as she fought him and found it provocative. The movements of her body against his were erotic, and he was having a hell of a time keeping his mind on subduing her. For a moment he let his mind go back to just a few minutes ago, when she was underneath him for a very different reason. Those feelings tempted him to remove his hand from her mouth and replace it with his lips.

Anna squirmed and heaved until she was completely out of strength, too tired to move anymore. Her lungs burned with each short breath, and her body felt bruised and battered. She was angry at Jordan for holding her down and furious with herself for the tears that rolled out of her eyes and fell into her hair when she squeezed them shut.

"Anna."

No, please, she thought, don't say my name

that way. It was too seductive, too romantic, too soft and personal.

She opened her eyes and through her tear-blurred vision saw the remorse in his expression. Her body relaxed. Suddenly she knew he meant her no harm. He merely wanted to keep her from running away from him. She wanted to hate him, but knew she never could.

Jordan swallowed hard, although he'd used no energy to overpower Anna. If the tears were meant to make him feel sorry for her, they worked. He felt like kicking himself.

"Are you ready to listen to me now?" His voice was raspy, but he hadn't intended for it to be.

She nodded.

"You won't scream?" he asked, wanting her promise.

She shook her head.

He watched her eyes for any hint she was trying to fool him. Finally, convinced she meant it, he carefully removed his hand. Placing his palms on the earth, he lifted his weight but remained poised above her. He meant to see that she didn't get away until they understood each other. And the way they were going right now, it would be sunrise before that happened.

Jordan looked down into the most beautiful eyes he'd ever seen. He loved her so much he felt a constant ache in the pit of his stomach.

"I'm not a spy," she whispered.

"I'm beginning to believe you," he answered huskily.

Jordan wanted to believe she wasn't a spy. But he still didn't know what she was doing in New

York at a party with John Andre. "Oh, Anna, sometimes you make me go crazy." His voice was thick, his throat ached from wanting to tell her that he loved her.

A strange little sound came from Anna's parted lips and the atmosphere between them changed. The night air was crisp and the night's sounds were silent. Jordan was suddenly aware of every muscle in his body as he again lay fully on top of Anna. He looked down and saw where her gown had worked off one shoulder, showing her breast. He was immediately aroused. She looked so lovely. The rosebud tip of her breast stared up at him, asking him to take it into his mouth and warm it.

He did. Oh God, it was good. He sucked and pulled, teasing it with his tongue. Anna squirmed enticingly beneath him and he raised his head and looked into her eyes. "Anna, if you don't want this, tell me now. I don't want to do any thing to hurt you."

Anna moistened her lips and reached up and slipped her arms around his neck. The initial urgency was over but Anna was by no means sated. "Love me, Jordan. Just love me."

"Yes, Anna, yes." He traced his hand down her ribs, across her hip, and over her leg. His mouth left her breast and his tongue made biting sweeps across her lips and cheeks. "Yes, I'll love you."

And he did until dawn streaked across the dark sky, bringing forth the birth of sunrise.

Jordan sat with his back against a tree, his arms wrapped around Anna, who sat between his legs, leaning against his chest. Their time was always too short. Even now she should be on her way back to the house before the servants caught her sneaking inside.

She took a deep breath, reluctant to rise from his embrace. "I have to go."

He squeezed her for a moment and quietly said, "Anna, nothing is settled between us. If you're not spying for the British, it's time you told me what you're really doing in New York."

Anna debated what she should do. Maybe it would be best to share her mission with Jordan and get his reaction. Maybe it was time she took him into her confidence. She would, she decided.

"It's not an easy story to tell," she hesitated. "And I'm not sure I can trust you to keep quiet until I've done what I have to do."

"Sweet hell, Anna!" He grabbed her arms and turned her around to face him. "I just made love to you on the ground as if you were a common whore. I didn't like doing that. I want to make it right between us. Stolen moments of love in the middle of the night are not what I want for us. But damn it, I don't know that we'll ever have more, and I won't know until you tell me the truth of your relationship with Andre."

"We're friends."

"God damn it, Anna, I can't help you if you're not going to be truthful with me."

He grasped her arms so hard it hurt and shocked her. "It's the truth, Jordan. I swear to God there has never been anything between us but friendship. Even you know you were the first man for me."

307

"Anna, I know you didn't have that kind of relationship with him." He lowered his head. "Oh God, I'm beginning to believe you don't know that you're spying for him."

"Spying for whom, Jordan?" she asked, frustration eating away at her.

"For Andre."

"I'm not!" she protested, trying to keep her voice low.

"Then tell me why you came to New York the very day after Benedict Arnold visited the tavern."

His words were like a sharp knife. She thought he'd followed her because he loved her. Oh, God! Now she understood. He'd followed her because he thought she had secret information for the British. What a fool she'd been. How could she love a man who didn't love her!

She looked into his eyes and knew at that moment it didn't matter if he didn't love her, she loved him and wanted to share this burden with him. She'd trust him with what she knew about General Arnold and Major Andre.

"It's a long story, but I'll try to make it brief. We haven't much time." She moistened her lips. "The night General Arnold stayed at the tavern I couldn't sleep. It was the night after you and I had — well. I was pacing the floor when I heard a voice. I thought perhaps the general's leg was bothering him and he might need something to help him sleep. I put my ear to a small hole in the wall to listen and recognized Glynis's voice."

"The cook?"

She had his attention. "Yes, she was in General Arnold's room. I continued to listen. Let me just tell you what I gleaned from the conversation rather than trying to reconstruct who said what."

"All right."

"Glynis asked the general to have her son released from Newgate."

"The prison camp in Connecticut?"

"Yes. Apparently she has a son in the service of the British whom she never told me about. General Arnold thanked Glynis for putting him in touch with a man in Philadelphia who in turn put General Arnold in touch with John."

"Andre?" he asked.

"Yes." She took a deep breath. "General Arnold has plans to surrender his command of West Point to the British, and John is the British soldier he is in touch with."

"My God! You're worse than I thought." He pushed her away and stood up. "I can't believe you're trying to smear the reputation of our greatest general."

Anna scrambled to her feet and drew the soiled robe around her shaking body. She shouldn't have expected him to believe her. This was the very reason she hadn't gone to anyone in the Continental army.

The chill of early morning made her tremble. "No, it's true, Jordan, I swear I heard it all. I came at once to try to find out more about the meeting and stop it."

Anna grabbed his arm, but he shrugged it off and turned cold eyes upon her. "Go back to your handsome British soldier. I want nothing more to do with you!"

"Jordan, you must believe me. I swear by all

that's holy, I speak the truth of what I heard. General Arnold intends to weaken West Point and hand over a map of the area to John so the British can capture it."

"You're a lying, whoring bitch!"

Chapter Seventeen

Anna had no problem slipping back into the Sommerfield household and into her bedroom a few minutes later. A quick look at the satin robe and wrinkled cotton night gown made her wince in horror. What would the maid think when she saw grass and dirt stains all over the back of the beautiful robe? "The truth," she said bitterly. That she'd spent the night wallowing on the ground with a man. Anna covered her eyes with her hands, ashamed of the weakness Jordan created inside her, ashamed of herself for tempting Jordan beyond his control.

She'd expected Jordan's disbelief, but she'd been stunned by his insults and accusations. Jordan hated her because he wanted her even though she was forbidden to him by a strict moral code, and tonight she'd added revulsion to whatever else he'd felt for her when she'd told him about General Arnold. No American in his right mind would believe the twice-wounded General Arnold was planning to commit treason.

Anna inhaled deeply and raised her head, wiping away the tears that ran down her cheeks. She wasn't one to sit around and let things happen to her if she could do anything about it. There was no one to rescue her. She had only herself to rely on.

Anna wiped her eyes with the back of her hand and brushed her long hair away from her face. Why did she have to wait for the maid to clean the robe? She could wash it herself. She was good with a needle as well. She could mend the small tear at the shoulder and no one would ever know. A careful inspection showed that the gown hadn't been soiled, so she put it back on and went to work.

The only thing left to do was to find a way to leave the house without arousing suspicion, she thought, pouring water from the pitcher into the bowl.

Anna didn't know whether stains would come out of satin or if the material would shrink. She had needle and thread of her own, so she quickly stitched the small rip. Next she lowered the satin robe into the bowl of water. She decided that if she ruined it, she'd simply say it was time for her monthly sickness and she'd only been trying to be helpful by washing the robe. That should keep the maid from looking at it too closely.

She scrubbed the robe until only shadows of stains remained on the back. She then squeezed the excess water out of the robe and poured the dirty water into the chamberpot. After rinsing the robe with the rest of the water, she hung it over the back of one of the chairs to dry.

By the time Anna had finished, she was shaking so badly she couldn't think straight. This deception was not for her. As she lay down on the clean, cool sheets, she decided to plead a headache when the maid came up and to stay in her room until she decided exactly how she was going to leave the Sommerfield house.

She needed to make plans, but not now, she told herself. Her eyes were too heavy. She'd been up all night and needed to sleep for a while before she could think straight. With that decided, Anna relaxed.

She pretended she felt Jordan's lips upon hers as she closed her eyes and slept.

Jordan did not even try to sleep after he left Anna. He spent most of the morning nursing a foul temper and pacing the floor in his tavern room. He called Anna every repulsive name he could think of and then started on himself for falling under her spell. He'd come to New York expecting to change Anna's mind about consorting with the British. He'd planned to tell her that he loved her and wanted to marry her. Instead he'd been manipulated by her once again. She'd controlled their meeting right from the start by throwing herself into his arms. God, he'd wanted her — but not that way. His hunger for her had forced him to take the momentary pleasure of her embrace. Now he found he wasn't satisfied. He needed, wanted, expected more. He wanted her love.

After an hour of self-recrimination, Jordan calmed a little and started thinking about what Anna had said and realized he had to talk to her again. The story she'd told him seemed incredible, but he remembered there had been a rumor from their men in New York. What was it Virgil had said? A high-ranking American officer was conspiring to commit treason. If there was just the slightest chance that what she'd said about Arnold was true, he must act quickly and swiftly. He had to put aside his personal feelings for Anna and Arnold. This time he wouldn't allow Anna to undermine his mission. He'd get Andre, Arnold—or Anna, whoever was responsible—to preserve the freedom the Americans were fighting and dying for.

If he was willing to believe Anna's fantastic story, he had to consider the full extent of Benedict Arnold's worth to the Americans before he could comprehend the significance of such a betrayal as the surrender of West Point. Virgil had told him that Arnold had asked for the command, but Jordan had naturally believed it was because he wanted to strengthen it, not weaken it for a British invasion. If the British gained control of the fort, they would control the upper Hudson and could possibly split the colonies in two.

As he thought back over the last three years, he realized Congress and the Philadelphia council had never publicly recognized Arnold's true value to the American forces. Arnold had been slighted more than a year ago, when five inferior brigadiers were promoted to major general over him. Washington and Arnold had been furious about that, and Arnold had resigned his duties for a time because of it. Just a few months ago, Congress had denied Arnold payment in full for his expenses in his last campaign and Washington had formally reprimanded him in April for his misuse of funds and supplies.

Jordan wished he could study all the correspondence. He had an uneasy feeling it would show that Arnold was becoming increasingly unhappy with his shabby treatment by the Americans. But was it enough to send the general running to the other side? Jordan didn't know the answer. He spent the rest of the morning thinking over what Anna told him and realized he had to believe her, even though he couldn't have been more surprised if she'd named George Washington. He had to believe Anna because he didn't dare risk the consequences of what could happen if he didn't.

He had his work cut out for him. He also had to recognize that this could be a foul plan by Andre to instill doubt in the eyes of the Americans for one of their best generals. Just what kind of plot was Anna involved in, and how was he going to get to the truth?

At some time during the late morning Jordan's body finally demanded sleep; and after a couple of hours of deep slumber, he awakened refreshed. He went into the taproom and ate a full meal of roasted chicken, potatoes, squash, and green peas. Then he put on his black waistcoat and jacket and hired a carriage to take him to the Sommerfield's house. He'd have the driver let him off half a mile away so he could be sure no British soldiers were looking for him. If Anna felt she was in any danger from him she could have Andre's men searching for him.

By mid-afternoon Jordan stood at the edge of the woods in front of the Sommerfield house, wondering how he was going to approach Anna.

Anna's worries had taken more out of her than she'd realized, and she slept until the maid brought up a lunch tray. While she ate the warm bread and sipped the delicious tea, she decided the Sommerfields had been so kind to her she couldn't leave without saying goodbye, so when the maid came for the breakfast tray Anna asked if she might see Mr. Sommerfield. The maid came back a few minutes later and told her he would see her.

At two o'clock Anna knocked on the door of Mr. Sommerfield's study. Mr. Sommerfield rose from his padded chair behind a dark mahogany desk as she entered. The room was as expensively furnished as the rest of the house, and the air held the lingering scent of beeswax and oil polish mixed with the odor of burned wood.

"Anna, I was pleased to hear you wanted to see me. I trust you had a marvelous time last evening."

"Yes," she answered truthfully. "I shall never forget it."

"You look beautiful, as always. Do sit down. I have news for you this morning."

"Thank you," she answered politely. "But I won't keep you long." Anna took a seat in a chair, knowing that what lay ahead of her wouldn't be easy.

"Very well." He picked up a piece of paper and said, "I just had a note delivered from Major Andre. He asked me to tell you that pressing military matters have called him out of New York for a few days. I'm to take the utmost care of you and continue to see that you are happy and entertained."

Anna's heartbeat increased rapidly. John must already be on his way to meet with General Arnold. She'd waited too long! She had to do something, but what? "Did he say where he's going?" she asked, realizing her voice didn't sound natural. She didn't feel natural, either.

"No, my dear, but he did mention that he'd be aboard the *Vulture,* should an emergency arise. I could contact him there if a life-threatening problem were to arise."

"I see," she answered quickly. What was she to do? There was no time to speak with anyone about help. She had to follow him and stop him. With the decision made, Anna's courage increased. "Ah — the *Vulture,* I assume that's a ship. Does that mean he's about to sail?"

"I would assume so, yes." He gave her a big smile, walked around his desk, and put a fatherly arm on her shoulder. "You're not to worry, my dear. I can take care of anything you might need."

Anna looked into his eyes. He'd been very kind, but now she thought it best not to tell him she was leaving. She would have to sneak away from the house. "Thank you, I'll remember that."

On shaky legs Anna made a hasty retreat from Mr. Sommerfield's study. Her plan was forming even as she climbed the stairs to her room. She had to follow John, and she couldn't afford to wait for the cloak of darkness. She'd leave the Sommerfields' house immediately and somehow persuade someone to take her by boat or ferry up the Hudson to find the *Vulture.* She had to find

317

John and stop him before he met with General Arnold, and she prayed it wasn't already too late.

If Jordan hadn't been watching the house carefully he'd have missed her, she moved so quickly. But he was sure it was Anna who slipped out the front door, dressed in a dark blue cloak. She glanced around, then walked across the road a short distance from him. As soon as she made it to the other side, she darted into the woods, picked up her skirts, and ran.

Surprised by her actions, Jordan took off after her, darting behind the bushes to avoid being seen from the road. He knew why he was trying not to be seen, but why was Anna hurrying away from the Sommerfield's house in such secrecy? He followed for a time, wanting to be sure they were well away from the house before he overtook her. She kept close to the road but far enough into the bushes that no one passing in a carriage would notice her unless they were looking for her.

When the bushes and trees thickened, and no house was in sight, Jordan decided it was time to stop her and find out why she was running. He quickly closed the distance between them and, remembering she didn't like to be caught unawares, called her name.

"Anna."

She stopped dead and slowly turned around. Her chest heaved and her mouth opened to take in gulps of air. "Why are you still following me?" she asked coldly.

He hadn't expected her to be nice to him. He certainly hadn't been nice to her last night. By the look on her face he knew she wasn't going to run away. Her hair was back under her cap, and she had on the simple blue dress that was so flattering to her figure.

Jordan moved closer to her. He wanted to tell her that he was sorry for what he'd said to her. He wanted to tell her that he loved her, but instead he said, "We need to talk."

"I believe that's exactly what you said the last time I saw you. I didn't like what you had to say then, and I seriously doubt I'll like it any better now."

Jordan took a deep breath. She had every right to be angry. Hell, he was angry, too. "I don't blame you. I acted like a fool, but I've had time to think about what you told me." He paused when he saw her hands ball into fists. She was getting ready to give him hell, and he had to calm her down. "Why are you sneaking away from the Sommerfields' house?"

"It has nothing to do with you, and I wouldn't tell you if it did. You made it clear what you thought of me, how you felt about me and what I told you. And quite frankly, Jordan, I don't want to hear it again. Once was enough," she finished on a breathless note, her chest still heaving.

"All right," he said, moving a little closer. He didn't want to spook her and make her run. The time for fighting each other was over. They had to work together on this. "I deserved that lecture. Now, let's start at the beginning."

"No, go away and leave me be. I don't have time for you right now." Her voice grew softer. "I don't know why you're following me, unless you think I have some kind of information for the

British. Well, I don't—so go away and leave me to do what I must before it's too late."

Jordan could see the hurt in her eyes. Damn it, he knew he'd caused that, and it made him angrier with himself. He wanted to take her in his arms and comfort her, but knew it wouldn't solve what was between them right now. If he was going to get anywhere with her he had to be honest. He walked around her and positioned himself between her and the direction she was heading, wanting to be ready in case she decided to run. "I'm prepared to believe what you told me."

The way her eyes widened and her lips parted, he knew she'd weakened, but only for a moment. She gave him a short, bitter laugh before she said. "You're too late. I don't need your help to do what I must." She straightened her back and lifted her chin. "Just as I didn't need Benjamin to help me run the tavern, I don't need you to help me stop John and General Arnold. Now, get out of my way, you're hindering me."

He didn't like being lumped with Jarvis, and he sure as hell didn't want to hear that she didn't need him. Suddenly the rest of what she'd said penetrated. Anna was no longer an adversary. They were allies.

"Anna, we've got to talk this through, and you're not going anywhere until we do. I was angry last night, and that kept me from thinking clearly. I'm going to help you whether you like it or not." His tone was rougher than he'd wanted, but Anna had left him with a desperate feeling in his gut.

She breathed deeply and pressed her hands together in front of her skirt. "I don't have time to talk, Jordan." Her words were a desperate plea. "John is on a ship called the *Vulture,* and I must get to him. I know you don't believe me, but unless I stop John, West Point is going to be invaded or captured. I'm not sure which. I don't know much about military matters, but I know the surrender of West Point would be disastrous to us. I can't let that happen."

Hearing the passion in her voice, Jordan wondered why he hadn't believed her last night. Because he'd already made up his mind that she was a spy. Damnation! How could he have been so wrong? How could he have doubted her?

He grabbed her upper arms and pulled her close to his chest. "Listen to me, Anna. We have to take time because I don't intend to let you go anywhere alone or near anything that could put you in danger. If Arnold and Andre have a conspiracy going, you could be in great danger." She tried to pull away from him, but he held her fast. "Don't be naive, Anna. John Andre is a military man, adjutant to the commander of the British forces. He didn't get that title without stepping on a few dead men along the way. If a high-ranking American officer is going to defect and hand over West Point, Andre won't let anyone stop him, including you."

Jordan's words sent a nervous shudder through Anna, and she went weak. She felt as if she'd just been awakened from a bad dream. Was Jordan right? She didn't know anymore. She only knew she had to try. Jordan caught her in his arms and lowered her to the ground, holding her against his chest. His arms around her felt so right, but she

321

didn't have the time to think about Jordan and what his touch did to her. The first thing she had to do was dislodge herself from his arms. She couldn't think straight when he touched her. Jordan let her ease out of his arms, but he remained very close.

"Anna, listen to me. Let's start over." He spoke softly, quietly. "Look at me." She did. "I believe you. I'm going to help you, but you have to start at the beginning and tell me what you remember from the night Arnold stayed in the tavern. This time, tell me exactly who said what from beginning to end."

Anna glanced away, not ready to put her trust in him again. With the tips of his fingers, he touched her chin and forced her to look at him. "I'm going to help you find John. Do you understand? You're not going anywhere without me."

Looking into his eyes, Anna realized he did believe her. At last she had someone to help her stop this madness. She was so relieved she felt lightheaded for a moment and rested her head on his shoulder, and his arms went around her once again. Thank God, she wasn't alone any more.

"It's all right, Anna, I'm here. Tell me what you know."

She raised her head and wiped her lips with the back of her hand and said, "When I first put my ear to the hole, I heard General Arnold say, 'Yes, I've recent word that your son is still alive. If all goes according to my plan, I'll have him out of Newgate before winter comes. He may not last that long in that Connecticut hellhole.' I didn't hear what was said after this because I realized

322

Glynis was the woman speaking. I was stunned that she was in the general's room and by the fact she had a son I didn't know about, and that he was in prison."

"Go on," Jordan coaxed.

"General Arnold was speaking again. He said, 'I've not forgotten you put me in touch with Stansbury. It's through him that I've communicated with Major Andre. Your help was immeasurable at the time. When all is finished, I assure you, I won't forget you for giving his name when I was here last year.'

"Glynis spoke then. 'I want my son out of that prison before he dies. I did my part of the bargain, now you do yours and have my son released.'

"It seemed as if General Arnold was trying to appease her, because he said, 'Things are moving quickly now. Major Andre suggested I secure the West Point command which I now have. It is my intention to weaken the fort by separating the garrisons and leaving it open to the British Army by putting into the hands of the major a map of the area. I hope to meet with Major Andre soon to finalize our plans.'"

Anna took a deep breath. "She must have handed him a letter, because the general asked her how long she'd had it. Glynis told him one of John's men passed it to her when they were at the tavern. She said she'd written General Clinton and asked him to send John Anderson. Oh, Jordan, it's all so confusing, and we don't have time to sort it all out. We must hurry. I believe John is on his way to meet with General Arnold."

"My God, it's so hard to believe, Anna. So

damn hard to believe." Jordan shook his head and rubbed his eyes. Glynis had written the letter Virgil had intercepted. So the old woman was the spy. His hunch had been right, when he'd thought she was too quiet. He should have acted on his intuitive feeling about her.

"For me, too," she said, wanting to comfort him, but knowing she couldn't. Not now. She wet her lips and continued. "The next morning, I fired Glynis. She left without any trouble." Anna wiped her eyes, not knowing why tears suddenly collected there. "I understood her need to help her son. But I couldn't condone it. I gave her a month's wage, hoping it would be enough for her to travel to Simsbury and see her son." She looked up into his eyes. "Will they let her see him if she goes there?"

"I hope so," he answered as his gaze scanned her face lovingly.

Anna brushed at a leaf that had fallen on her dress. The trees shaded them from the sun, but it was a warm, beautiful September day.

"I came to New York as soon as I could. I wanted to find out when and where the meeting was to be held and stop it."

Jordan chuckled lightly. "How could you have stopped it alone?"

Anna bristled. Last night John had asked what she could do that the British military couldn't, and now Jordan was laughing at her for thinking she could stop this meeting. She opened the drawstring purse that hung from her wrist, pulled out her father's pistol, and laid it in Jordan's hand. Her eyes and voice were serious when she said, "I was going to shoot him in the leg so he wouldn't be able to travel."

Clearing his throat, and feeling pleased about Anna's strength and courage, Jordan took the pistol from her and stuffed it in his jacket pocket. "I believe you would. If there's any shooting to be done, I'll do it."

Anna was relieved to hand over the heavy weapon. "I was on my way to find someone to take me to see John."

Jordan sighed heavily. "It's a good thing I stopped you, Anna. That would have been very dangerous for you."

"I didn't know what else to do."

"Anna, think: if you were willing to use a weapon to stop him, don't you think he'd be willing to use one to stop you? When it comes down to military matters, he's as cold-hearted and bloodthirsty as any other soldier."

"No! that's not true," she protested loudly, but it sounded unconvincing, even to her.

"Anna, he was under the command of General Grey during the Paoli and Baylor massacres. Have you heard of those atrocities? He's a soldier serving his country. He'll use any means to accomplish—"

"Stop!" She rose quickly from the ground, finding that her legs were still very weak. "I don't want to hear any more," she said in a trembling voice. "What else could I do?" She grabbed the folds of her skirt and knotted them in her fist. "If I had approached anyone in the Continental Army, surely they would have treated me just as you did. No one would have believed me. I'm doing the only thing I know to do. If General Arnold succeeded in surrendering West Point and I hadn't done anything, I couldn't live with myself." Her voice fell to a whisper. "I didn't know what else to do but follow him."

Jordan touched her cheek with the back of his fingers. "And I'm so damn proud of you, Anna. But you're no longer alone. I'm going to help you. We'll work this out together."

"Why, Jordan?" she asked, looking up into his blue eyes. "You're a minister. You're supposed to be neutral in this fighting."

Jordan wanted to set her back down and tell her everything about himself, but he knew they didn't have the time. If the *Vulture* was heading north, it was a sure bet that Andre was on his way to see Arnold, just as Anna suspected.

"I need to have a long talk with you about that, but not now. I'll explain everything to you after this is settled. In fact, Anna, I have many things to tell you, but first we have a conspiracy to stop."

The way she looked at him with those big, beautiful eyes melted Jordan's heart. He wanted her as strongly as if he'd never made love to her. But here and now he was making a vow to himself not to touch her again until she was his wife. And this time he wouldn't break his pledge. If he failed this time, he wasn't the man he thought.

"Well," Jordan said finally, "we know Andre is on the HMS *Vulture* and we think he's going to meet with Arnold. The best thing for us to do is follow the *Vulture* and watch Andre to see whom he meets."

"I was on my way to find someone to take me there when you caught up with me," Anna said.

He wanted to take her in his arms and kiss those beautiful lips. He wanted to tell her he loved her, that he was going to take care of her, but instead, he said, "You've found him. We'd best get started. Along the way we'll pick up a spyglass and hire a couple of horses. Can you ride?"

"Yes, of course."

He smiled. "Good." He reached out and took her hand. It was warm, soft. "Anna, I have a lot of explaining to do, and I promise I will as soon as we've settled this business."

Chapter Eighteen

Anna and Jordan galloped across Kings Bridge, which connected Manhattan and Westchester, and rode north to Dobbs Ferry. Still in the guise of a minister, Jordan was able to discover that a young British soldier had been rowed to the *Vulture* and that the ship had pulled anchor and taken a northerly course toward Haverstraw Bay. After some haggling with a boat owner, Jordan persuaded him to row them up the Hudson in chase of the mighty British ship. The horses would have been faster but more dangerous inside enemy lines.

There were many things Anna did well, but fighting the choppy waters of the Hudson wasn't one of them. She spent most of her time with her head hanging over the side. She was so sick Jordan soon decided to go ashore on the east side and follow Andre on the embankment by horse.

At Tarrytown, Jordan had the man row the small boat to shore and help Anna out. He left her to rest in a tavern while he traded for fresh horses. By late afternoon they were on their way again. As luck would have it, they spotted the

Vulture about an hour out of Tarrytown, near Teller's Point.

Anna and Jordan stopped and made camp a short distance down from the ship.

"How are you feeling?" Jordan asked as he helped Anna dismount.

"Better, now that I'm no longer on that boat," she answered, but her stomach really didn't feel better. In fact, she didn't know if it would ever be the same.

"We can't build a fire. It's not safe. Maybe you should try to eat some of the bread we brought along. It may help to settle your stomach. You're still pale."

"No, I don't think I'll try anything until tomorrow," she said, although it pleased her to see the concern in his eyes. It pleased her even more that he was with her, helping her. She still had trouble believing he'd followed her because he thought she had American intelligence for the British. One thing was certain now: Jordan was more than an ordinary minister.

He gave her a warm smile. "Whatever you think is best," he said as he took the spyglass out of his saddlebag. "I'm going down to the river's edge to see how well this thing works. Why don't you lay out a blanket and rest? We could be here for a long while."

"No, I'm fine. I want to come with you. Besides, I need to stretch my legs or they might cramp. I haven't done a lot of riding and none recently."

"All right, but stay right behind me. If I give a signal like this" — he stopped and put one finger to his closed lips—"it means you are to stop where you are and not ask questions."

"I understand," she said.

"All right, let's go. Stoop this way." Jordan bent at the waist and rounded his back, hunching his shoulders, keeping his body low to the ground. "We're not the only ones who have spyglasses, and we don't want to be seen."

Anna picked up her long skirt as she bent forward and followed Jordan soundlessly to the bank. She really had no fear of anyone hearing Jordan, he moved so quietly, so effortlessly. They concealed themselves behind high bushes that hadn't started to lose their foliage with the approach of fall. In the distance, over Jordan's shoulder, Anna saw the big ship *Vulture* with many guns mounted on its deck.

It was a clear afternoon with not a hint of fog or mist, but the wind was high, making the water rough. The great ship looked ominous to Anna as she stared at it and wondered how they were going to get to John. From her vantage point, she could see several red-jacketed men on the deck, but couldn't make out any faces.

"Andre's on the front deck, pacing," Jordan said quietly. "He keeps looking to the west side of the Hudson."

"What? Are you sure? Let me see."

"It's him," Jordan affirmed as he gave the spyglass to Anna and showed her how to work it.

Anna had never looked through a telescope, and she was amazed at how clearly she saw the men. She gasped as she focused on John, dressed in his scarlet coat, tan riding breeches, and shiny black riding boots, with a white scarf wrapped around his neck. He was as handsome as always, she thought.

"Isn't it dangerous for him to be out in the open?" she asked when she handed the spyglass back to Jordan.

Jordan chuckled dryly. "He has no reason to believe anyone is following him or looking for him. Something tells me this man is not worried at all about being discovered. He looks quite confident."

"What do we do now?"

Jordan sighed and leaned against a large stone. "We wait. It looks as though Andre is waiting, too. I think Arnold is probably expected to board the *Vulture* sometime tonight. If he does, we follow the ship until Andre or Arnold disembarks. But we should also be prepared in case Andre takes a boat over to the west side to meet with Arnold. It's unfortunate, but we're going to have to make our plans as we go, depending on what they do."

"What will we do if Andre rows to the other side?" she asked, although she feared she already knew the answer.

"We need to be prepared to row, too." He gave her a questioning smile. "If that happens, I think you should wait here. You didn't take well to the boat."

"No." Though her stomach protested at the thought, she shook her head. "I'll go with you. I'm in this to the end."

Jordan reached out and laid a gentle hand on her stomach, and she immediately felt comforted.

331

She would always welcome his touch. She wanted to lay her head on his shoulder and rest, but now wasn't the time for that.

"This is perhaps the widest section of the Hudson, and the water is not going to be calm tonight. It won't be easy, Anna," he reminded her.

Anna took a deep breath. It wasn't something she looked forward to, but she didn't intend for Jordan to handle this on his own. She had nothing left in her stomach and she didn't plan to eat anything. She looked him directly in the eye and pushed his warm hand away, not wanting to appear weak. "Don't worry about me. I can take care of myself."

Jordan let out an exasperated sigh. "I can't take the chance that you'll slow me down. This is too important. When Arnold and Andre make their move, I'll have to worry about them, not you."

Her back stiffened. She didn't like his words or his tone. "I don't intend for you to worry about me. I'll be all right."

"Damn it, Anna listen to me. This could be dangerous. If Arnold is planning treason he's a desperate man, and I don't want to have to worry about a sick woman."

"A sick woman? If he's planning treason?" The words flew swift and low. Her eyes sparked with anger. "You still don't believe me, do you?"

"We haven't seen anything of Arnold yet." He shot back sharply.

"And you don't think we will," she accused him, a raw tension gripping her. "You told me you believed me."

Jordan ran his hands through his hair and

sighed. "I don't know what to believe right now." His voice was husky with frustration. He tried to take her arm, but she shook it off.

"Don't touch me!" Her words were a mumbled hiss.

"Anna you're asking me to believe the hero of the American forces is going to defect. Do you know what that does to me in here?" He struck his stomach with his thumb.

"You don't believe me. Why don't you leave? I can handle this by myself. I don't need you."

"The hell you don't," he muttered.

"I don't! I started this without you, and I'll finish it without you."

Jordan wiped his hand down his chin and looked deeply into her eyes. Calmly he said, "Damn it, Anna, I wouldn't be here if I didn't believe you. But I keep hoping it's not true. This could destroy what it's taken us six years to accomplish."

"Why do you think I've been trying to do something to stop them?" Emotion slurred her words, and a wave of fatigue washed over her.

Jordan rubbed his eyes, the back of his neck, and his shoulders before he looked at her again. "You've got to let me take it from here. This is not something you should be involved in."

"No. This is my fight." Anna remained firm. "Don't you worry about me, Jordan Kent. I don't intend for you to have a *sick woman* to slow you down."

He deserved her rancor. He was taking his frustration out on her when without her he wouldn't have even known about Arnold's plan. He needed to get away and calm himself.

"All right. You stay here and watch for any movement on the ship. I'm going to see if I can get us a boat."

"I have a few coins," she offered.

"I'll barter with what I have. Save yours. If we have to row to the west side, we may need them later. Don't move from this spot until I return— understand?"

Anna nodded briefly before turning away from him. She wasn't going anywhere.

Later that night, by a half-shadowed moon, looking through his spyglass, Jordan recognized Andre as he covered his regimentals with a dark cloak and climbed into a boat with another man. The lantern hanging at the stern gave just enough light to illuminate the movement on the ship. Jordan's heartbeat quickened. Andre was heading for the enemy line.

Jordan turned to Anna knowing that they had no choice but to cross the Hudson in the small two-man boat he'd bought for several coins. He quietly eased the boat into the water less than half a mile downriver from the *Vulture*. Anna didn't say a word; she didn't have to. He knew she wasn't looking forward to crossing the river again, but he admired her for having the courage to do it. There wasn't anything he could do to make crossing the choppy water easier.

Clouds passed intermittently over the moon, plunging them into darkness and then back into light. A strong wind blew from the north, but it was warm for late September in New York.

Much to Jordan's surprise, Anna didn't get sick on the way over to the other shore, but Jordan hadn't rowed in years and his muscles burned and ached from the exertion. Even though the wind kept him cool, he was soon sweat-soaked. When they were close enough to shore for him to jump out, he found his legs were too weak to hold him, so he held onto the side of the boat for a few moments and rested before helping Anna to dry land.

They moved quietly through the bushes for a few minutes until they heard voices drifting through the firs. Not far from them, he saw a sentry on watch. They moved further toward the water so they wouldn't be seen. They slowly moved closer, then Jordan stopped short, his body stiffening. Arnold and Andre were standing under the branch of a tree. He willed his breathing to stay under control as his stomach roiled from the unbelievable, unthinkable scene he witnessed. God damn it! Anna had been right.

He felt Anna's hand touch his and he whipped his head around. He wanted to tell her he was sorry for doubting her, but the words wouldn't come. He was too sick inside.

Jordan didn't really have a solid plan of action, he realized as he watched the British major and the American general. For the most part he'd have to work on instinct. He'd known that Arnold and Andre would have to meet before he could make a clear plan. And now that had happened.

When Andre was captured it would be important that he be carrying some kind of evidence that this meeting had taken place. If what Anna had heard was true, Arnold intended to give the major a map of West Point. Jordan felt sure that after their meeting, Andre would be rowed back to the *Vulture* with whatever information the general gave him. Jordan needed to come up with a plan to catch Andre before he returned to headquarters, but the chances of capturing him before the *Vulture* took him back to New York were slim.

Before Jordan had formulated a more definite plan, a sentry brought horses around and the major and the general mounted.

Jordan wasn't prepared for the conspirators to ride away. *Hell, Andre was inside the American lines!* He'd expected Andre to go directly back to the *Vulture*. The water must have gotten too rough for the boatmen to row back to the ship; and with dawn approaching, they had decided to take shelter.

With no time to waste, Jordan grabbed Anna's hand and they moved quickly through the woods, running after the sound of the horses' hooves clopping on the ground ahead of them. Jordan expected Anna to falter at any moment, unable to keep up with the cantering horses any longer, but she managed to stay right behind him for a while. But finally their hands slipped apart, and he knew she was weakening.

"Stay—here. I'll come—back for you," he said between gulping breaths.

Anna shook her head and kept up the grueling pace as they chased after the horses. She held her side, panted, but kept her place at Jordan's heels. Her heart pounded in her ears and her lungs

336

burned from the stress. She lost her cap and her hair fell free, but she kept running. If the horses had been any faster, she couldn't have kept up with them. Sheer determination kept her going when her body cried out for her to stop.

Without warning lights of a house came into view. Jordan stopped abruptly, then slowly sank to the ground on his knees as he watched the general and major rein in their horses and dismount. He was so winded he could scarcely breathe. He heard Anna running up behind him and pulled her down beside him.

Anna couldn't have moved if a gun had been pointed at her head. Jordan lay close beside her, the sound of his labored breathing loud in her ears. Her muscles felt as if fifty heavy weights had been tied to them, and her heart thumped as if it would beat out of her chest.

"Why—why did you stop?" she asked in a raspy voice when she could talk.

"There's a house about fifty yards ahead. If we're lucky, they've stopped there for the night. As soon as I can move, I'll make sure."

Now that Anna's heartbeat was slowing, she noticed the air was cold on her sweat-soaked skin. She sent up a prayer that she wouldn't catch a chill on top of the seasickness. As she was thinking about how sick the choppy water had made her, she heard Jordan chuckling. Why? What on earth could be funny at a time like this?

She rose on her elbow and looked over at him. She couldn't see him well, but the shadowed moonlight showed his chest and stomach moving. "What's so funny?" she whispered.

Jordan rose, too, and looked at her, his white teeth gleaming. "Us. You and me."

Anna didn't know how to take what he was saying. That made her nervous. "What do you mean?"

"Trying to keep up with horses. We must be crazy."

"They were only trotting. It wasn't that difficult," she lied, the pain in her side proving it.

"Yes it was, and you know it. One of us could have stepped in a hole and broken a leg. You could have become winded and fainted."

"So could you," she added quickly, smiling at him.

He chuckled again. "We make a good team, Anna. You stayed with me, and we must have run for a good ten minutes. You surprise me, no, amaze me."

Suddenly the mood changed between them and Jordan was very aware of it. They were alone, bathed in moonlight, caressed by a breeze. He wanted to put his arms around her and pull her close. He was tempted to reach over and kiss her, but he knew where that would lead. Now wasn't the time. He had a job to do before he and Anna could talk freely.

"You wait here and rest while I go see what I can find out. I expected Andre to go directly back to the ship. When I know what's going on we'll make our plans."

Taking a deep breath, Anna asked the question she'd been afraid to ask. "What kind of plans?"

Jordan rubbed his chin and felt the two-day

stubble of beard as he rose to his feet. "How to capture Andre and Arnold," he said, and slipped into the shadows.

With a heavy heart Anna pulled her knees up and rested her forehead on them. Betraying John wasn't going to be easy, but when the time came, she'd have to turn him over to the Revolutionary forces.

Shortly after Jordan left, the sun appeared on the horizon and Anna lay down on the hard ground, using her arms for a pillow. She rested on her side and pulled her knees up and within moments slept.

Anna was so tired she didn't awaken until the sound of cannon fire roused her. Alarmed, she scrambled to her feet and ran to shelter behind a large tree The sun was high in the sky and there was no sign of Jordan. Fear possessed her as she clung to the tree.

She didn't know how long she remained behind the tree, hiding even after the shelling stopped. At last she heard the sound of horses approaching. Peeking from behind her cover, she saw Jordan coming toward her leading two horses. Anna leaned against the tree, weak with relief.

Jordan told her that the American forces were shelling the *Vulture* and that it had slipped anchor and sailed downstream, toward New York. Arnold had left the house where he and Andre had spent the remainder of the night, and with the *Vulture* no longer available to Andre, Jordan expected him to leave at dusk. Jordan had found a nearby tavern and traded for horses. For now, he thought it best to concentrate on capturing

Andre. He felt sure Arnold was on his way back to West Point and could be caught there.

Jordan brought with him cheese, bread, and a flask of wine. After they'd eaten, Anna kept watch on the house while Jordan slept. By early evening, both were rested and ready to ride when they saw John Andre and another man mount their horses.

For the duration of the night and until mid-morning Anna and Jordan quietly followed the two men, staying far enough behind so as not to be detected. Jordan realized that Andre was heading back to British-held White Plains and knew he'd have to stop him before he made it to the safety of British lines. He didn't know what to do about Anna. He didn't want her around when the time came to stop Andre.

They had a stroke of luck at midday, when Andre's fellow traveler left his company at Pine's Bridge. This was the break Jordan had been waiting for. Andre was alone.

Jordan took a deep breath, preparing himself for what he had to do, and turned to Anna. "I'll take it from here. You stay over there behind that tree and wait for me."

"No." Anna shook her head. "I've come this far. I won't let you leave me now."

Suddenly Jordan grabbed the reins of her horse. Anna jumped and the horse stomped and snorted at the sudden action. "Anna, I don't have time to argue the point. Just listen to me. There's no reason for Andre ever to know you had anything to do with this. In fact, it's best that he thinks I'm the only one involved."

Her eyes flashed surprise. "No, I can't let you do that."

Jordan curled her reins tighter in his hands as the two horses continued to sidestep. "If he has a map of West Point in his pocket he will stop at nothing to deliver it to Clinton. Anna, we don't have time to argue about this. I can't protect you."

"I'm prepared for whatever may happen," she cried desperately, trying to pull the reins away from him.

"Be still and listen to me." He wrapped his own reins around the horn of his saddle and grabbed Anna's wrists. "I've tried to make you see you're dealing with a ruthless military man. I can't risk his hurting you."

"I won't let you go without me!" Anna squirmed as his hands bit into her flesh, making her cry out.

In one swift movement Jordan stood up in his stirrups and fell upon Anna, knocking them both to the ground, as the horses shied away from them. It happened so fast she didn't have time to scream. Anna landed on her back with only Jordan's arm to cushion the blow. She heard him wince, and she moaned from the pain of the fall. The jolt was so hard the breath was knocked from her lungs. She lay motionless, stunned for a moment, trying to collect her thoughts. Suddenly Jordan was on his knees, rolling her onto her stomach.

"I'll tie your hands if I have to, Anna," he said, his breathing labored. "I can't let you go."

"No!" she screamed, and bucked, trying to

341

move him. She felt his knee press into the small of her back with agonizing pressure. He leaned over and clamped one hand over her mouth. The side of her face was pressed into the dirt and small pieces of gravel bit into her cheek.

Jordan bent over her back and put his mouth to her ear and whispered, "Anna, quiet—lie still! I hear horses. Someone's coming. Promise me you won't scream and I'll let you sit up."

She rolled her eyes around, trying to see his face. Horses? Was John coming back?

"Promise me, Anna," he said huskily.

Having no choice, she nodded, and Jordan helped her sit up. Her cheek burned from the scratches and her right shoulder felt as if all her weight had landed on it. She lifted her head and looked at Jordan. Tears of disappointment and anger ran down her cheeks. Her head throbbed with pain—her hip, too, she realized as the tears rolled unchecked.

"I'm sorry I had to do this, Anna." He helped her to stand as three men rode into view. "If they're militia, we can send them after Andre." He wiped his forehead. "Will you agree to that?" he asked.

For a moment Anna's thoughts were jumbled, then she realized having someone from Washington's army catch John would be best. Anna nodded to Jordan and wiped her eyes with the back of her hand. She didn't like the looks of the three men riding toward them. Fear seized her once again and suddenly she started shaking.

"These aren't Washington's men," Jordan said.

"Let me do the talking. Go along with whatever I say."

Jordan had to think fast. As the men rode closer to Jordan, he took in as many details about them as possible. They wore no insignia, so they weren't militia men, as he'd hoped; but at least they weren't wearing red coats. Two of them had muskets thrown over their shoulders, and the other held a musket in his hands. He laid his hand against the pistol in his pocket and hoped he wouldn't have to use it.

Suddenly he took off running toward the three men, shouting, "Please, you must help us!" Jordan stopped a short distance from the lead horse. "Sir, I need your help."

The man, chewing on a small twig, looked down at him. "What's your trouble, stranger?"

The man took the stem out of his mouth and spat very close to Jordan's boots, then looked past Jordan to Anna. Jordan felt sure these men were common highwaymen, looking for someone they could rob. He had to convince them that they'd already been robbed and send the men down the road to stop Andre.

"My wife and I were robbed not more than five minutes ago." Jordan glanced back at Anna, who was brushing dirt from her dress, to make sure she wasn't going to dispute his word. "He was a well dressed fellow in a claret-colored coat and brown hat. He took every shilling we had. Will you help me go after him? I'll pay you for your services once we've found him."

Jordan didn't like the way the three men were looking at Anna. He was glad she was staying near the horses. If either of the men made a move, he hoped he could stall them long enough for her to mount and ride away.

"You say he took all your money?" the bearded man in the middle asked.

"Yes. We've not a penny to our name." He glanced at Anna again. "The incident has upset my wife, and I was trying to calm her when you arrived. The robber is getting farther away as we talk. Will you help me?"

The front man grinned, showing rotten teeth. "You stay here with your wife, mister. Me and the boys will find the man and get your money for you."

Jordan scowled and grabbed the man's reins. "How do I know I can trust you to bring the money back to me?"

The man put the stem back in his mouth and jerked the reins out of Jordan's hand. "You can't." He turned his horse and the three men galloped down the road after Andre.

Jordan's stomach heaved with relief. He took three deep breaths, then hurried back to Anna. Her hair was a mass of tangles, her dress coated with dust. Tears had mingled with dirt and streaked her cheeks. "Are you all right?" he asked, concern showing in his eyes and edging his voice.

"What if they kill him?" The words seemed to be torn from her throat as her bottom lip quivered.

Jordan took a step toward her and stopped. He wanted to hold her, to say he was sorry, to do something, but knew he didn't have time. "They're robbers, Anna—not murderers."

Her eyes were cold. "How do you know that?"

"Highwaymen are common in this area. They're known for preying on wealthy travelers. When they search him they should find the papers Arnold gave him. I need to follow them and make sure they get to Andre before he gets to White Plains. Do you want to come?"

Anna lifted her chin and wiped her cheeks with a gloved hand. "I don't intend to let you leave me out of it now." She turned away and mounted her horse.

Hurting Anna hadn't been easy for him, but he couldn't let her have anything to do with Andre's actual capture. When Andre was caught, he was sure to hang, and he was afraid Anna wouldn't be able to live with that on her conscience.

Five days later Jordan and Anna were staying in the Harvester's Ring Tavern, less than half a mile from Casparus Mabie's Tavern, where Major John Andre was being held by the American forces. The tavern-turned-prison was surrounded by at least forty soldiers, with six sentries posted outside the door to the major's room. Two soldiers with swords drawn were kept inside at all times.

The glory in capturing the now infamous Major John Andre had been taken away from Jordan Kent. He and Anna had watched from the bushes as the three highwaymen searched Andre and found the West Point papers in his boot instead of money. They had followed the four men as far as North Castle to make sure the robbers didn't let Andre go for a price. Jordan was sure Andre would offer the men money for safe passage to White Plains once they realized who he was.

Because of Anna, Jordan was glad they hadn't been the ones to capture Andre, but for himself, he was sorry to have missed the chance. They followed the men until Andre had been delivered safely to Colonel Jameson.

Upon hearing of the treason, Washington had immediately set out to strengthen West Point and find General Arnold. However, Arnold was swift, and within hours of Andre's capture he had escaped to New York by the *Vulture,* the very ship that had brought Andre to him.

With Arnold out of reach and West Point reinforced, Washington had turned his attention to Andre. Jordan knew that if Andre had been of a lower rank he would have been hanged at once, but because of his status, Washington ordered a board of general officers to investigate the case. Andre was convicted of being an enemy spy and sentenced to hang.

When Jordan told her the decision, Anna took the news quietly. Too quietly. She'd been almost mute for the last three days. It worried him. It was time they had a much-needed talk.

Late in the afternoon of the day of Andre's sentencing, Anna stood on the front porch of the Harvester's Ring Tavern, staring at the blaze of color offered by the trees that lined the Hudson River.

"Anna, take a walk with me. I have something to tell you," Jordan said as he walked up to her.

"There's nothing left to be said between us," she answered in a soft voice.

346

Jordan touched her arm. "I think you'll change your mind when you hear what I have to say. I may be able to help Andre." That brought a little life to her eyes. "Come with me."

Anna walked with him into the woods behind the tavern, just far enough to make sure they would be alone. He couldn't afford to let anyone overhear them. Now that the time had come to tell her about himself, Jordan wasn't sure about the best way to do it or how she might react. She could very well end up hating him more than she already did.

They stopped at a small clearing and Jordan tensed. This wasn't going to be easy, and Anna wasn't helping. She found a large stone and leaned against it, but avoided looking at him. He'd rather have seen her fighting mad, throwing her small fists at him, than have her seem so beaten.

"Anna, damn it, can't you look at me?" he asked in a growling voice.

Her head popped up. "I don't have any trouble looking at you, Jordan. It's myself I'm having trouble looking at."

He swore under his breath. He should have remembered how easily she accepted guilt. "Andre's fate was not determined by you. Don't blame yourself. Andre controlled his own destiny. He had a way out and he didn't take it. If he'd admitted the *Vulture* let him off under the flag of truce, he may have been spared. If he hadn't taken off his uniform and changed into that claret-colored coat and brown hat, he would have been considered a prisoner of war. Andre was responsible for his own downfall, not you."

"If they'd let me talk to him, maybe I could have made him change his mind about that."

He took an impatient step toward her, his eyes squinting as they caught the late afternoon sunlight that found its way through the tall hardwood trees. "How the hell do you think you could have made him change his mind when the commander of the British forces couldn't get him to save his neck by agreeing to say he was under a flag of truce? Damn it, Anna! Look at the facts."

Her eyes widened and her pale lips parted. Maybe he was finally getting through to her. He yearned to hold her against him and show her how much he loved her, but knew he couldn't do that until he'd told her everything. His voice and expression softened.

"Andre took a great risk for his country. There is nothing wrong with that. If our roles had been reversed, I would probably have done the same thing. He made some mistakes that condemned him as a spy; but he was a very brave man, Anna, and you were brave to try and stop him."

Anna took a step toward him. "What *is* a spy, Jordan?"

He looked into her questioning blue eyes. She was trying to understand, and he loved her all the more for it. "As far as the military goes, it's plain and simple: one who obtains information about the enemy."

"Was John a spy?"

Jordan knew she wasn't trying to trick him, only trying to understand. "Yes."

Anna groaned. "Why can't he merely be taken

as a prisoner of war? I don't understand why they must hang him simply because he took a piece of paper." Her voice was filled with anguish.

Jordan's heart grew heavy. He hurt for her. "If spies are detected and taken during war, almost without exception they are put to death. This started with the history of man. It's unfortunate that Andre falls under the penalty. No other verdict was possible."

"The treason was General Arnold's," she said in a tight voice. "What will happen to him?"

"That depends on whether or not we catch him."

Jordan rubbed the back of his neck. The late afternoon was still warmed by the sun, but a cool breeze blew in off the Hudson. He hoped the time was finally right to tell Anna the truth about himself, now that she was talking to him so openly. He moistened his lips and took a step toward her. "Anna, when I asked you to come here with me I said I could possibly help Andre, but there's something I have to tell you first."

She watched him closely, intently.

"I'm not really a minister." She gasped, but he hurried on, not giving her time to speak. "For most of the year, I'm a teacher at Harvard, but on occasion I'm a civilian aide to General Washington. I was sent by him to Lowell Tavern to try and catch a spy who, until a few days ago, I thought was you."

Anna couldn't believe her ears. She placed her hands on the side of her head and rubbed her temples, trying to comprehend what he'd said. She had to take one admission at a time. "You're not a minister?" She dropped her hands limply to her side and looked up at him.

"No," she whispered, and shook her head.

"Yes," he confirmed.

How many more shocks could she take? Her breathing grew ragged and her legs felt watery. "I don't understand. Why didn't you tell me?" So many things rushed through her mind as she tried to assimilate what he had said. All her fears that she'd led a man of God astray, all her self-reproach, were jumping around in her head. Yes! She had trusted him.

"You work for Washington?" How he had deceived her hit her hard. "You lied to me!"

Anna rushed at Jordan, not sure of her intent, only knowing she wanted to hurt him. One hand struck him across the chin before he grabbed her wrists, shoved her up against the large stone, and penned her to it with his body.

His eyes glared into hers. "Stop, Anna. You can beat the hell out of me later for all the things I've said and done to you, but right now, my relationship to Washington may be the only thing that can save Andre's life, and we don't have time to waste."

A rush of hope filled her and mixed with all the other emotions warring inside her. She quieted immediately. "What are you talking about? Washington is the one who wants to hang him."

He continued to hold her, although she no longer needed subduing. It had been days since he'd been this close to her, and he wasn't going to pass up this chance. He let go of her wrists and encircled her in his arms, letting his hands clasp together behind her back. "Washington owes me a favor. I'm going to ask him to stay Andre's execution and merely hold him prisoner."

"Can you do that?" she asked. "Jordan, can you save him?"

"No promises, but I can try. It's not known how widespread this conspiracy is, how many people are involved. Some officials think it's the better part of wisdom to make an example of Andre and Arnold, too, if they can get their hands on him."

"But there's a possibility you can help him? You can save his life?" Her eyes glowed at the prospect.

"There's a chance," he said as he looked deeply into her eyes, wanting to press himself closer, but afraid she'd push him away. He started, tentatively at first, to move his hands lazily up and down her back.

"What will you tell Washington?" she asked, suddenly aware of just how close they were, how safe she felt nestled in his arms. She told herself not to enjoy the light pressure of his hand on her back, but she did.

"As little as possible." Jordan bent his head and kissed her cheek. "I don't want to involve you at all in this if I can keep it from him." He kissed the side of her neck. "Anna, I've missed holding you."

Anna was trying to keep her mind on the business at hand and not the desperation she heard in Jordan's voice or the delicious little tremors he was sending up her spine with every gentle kiss. Just a few more and she'd make him stop.

"Does he know you went to New York and tha
you suspected me of spying?"

Jordan continued a trail of light kisses along
her neck and over her cheeks, staying away from
her lips. He knew once he took those there would
be no stopping him. He wanted her too badly.

"I was stationed in Lowell Tavern because we
had intercepted a letter addressed to Clinton. We
knew only that someone had asked him to send
John Anderson to Lowell Tavern."

"That must have been the letter Glynis was
talking about." The rhythm of her breathing had
changed from even breaths to choppy little gasps.
She was furious with him for deceiving her
but she couldn't deny the desire he created in
her.

"Yes. If Arnold is captured, I'll tell Washington
about Glynis. If not, no one need ever hear about
her. We'll let her stay with her son."

His kindness to Glynis warmed Anna as surely
as if she stood in front of a fire. Anna lifted her
arms and circled his neck. "Do you really teach at
Harvard?" she asked.

Jordan poised his lips above hers and looked
into her eyes. "Yes. Boston is my home."

He stuck his tongue out and touched the tip of
her chin, loving the taste of her. "Why didn't you
tell me this when I told you about John and General Arnold?"

"I wanted to. But I knew it would take a lot of
explaining, and we didn't have the time. We don't
have the time now, either. I need to go to Washington. Before I do, I have one other thing to tell
you, and I have to take time for this." He wet his

352

lips, then whispered, "I love you, and I want to marry you."

She gasped, and her heart skipped a beat as she swallowed hard. "You love me? Jordan, do you mean that?"

"Yes. I loved you even when I thought you were a spy for the British, and I hated myself for loving you. I had one hell of a time staying away from you."

Anna closed her eyes for a brief moment and let the happiness of his words wash over her. He's not a minister, she told herself. She didn't have to worry that the people of Georgetown wouldn't accept her as his wife. "Oh, Jordan, I love you, too." She barely got the words out before his lips crushed hers with sweet urgency. How she'd missed the taste of him, the feel of his strong back beneath the palms of her hands.

"I should be furious with you," she said between kisses. "When I think of all the times I berated myself for tempting a man of God into my bedroom, for thinking I could never be good enough for you . . ."

"Oh God, you did tempt me. Night and day. You still do," he said, just before his tongue slipped into the warmth of her mouth and plundered.

"Jordan, we have to talk," she managed to say a couple of minutes later.

"No, not now," he said, reluctant to let her go.

"There's time for this later." She struggled out of his arms and stepped away, but continued to look into his eyes. "You don't intend to tell Washington that you thought I was a spy?"

"Not unless I have to. I may have to tell the whole damn—" From behind him, Jordan heard the click of a hammer cocking and quickly spun around to stare down the long barrel of a light dragoon pistol.

"Good afternoon, Reverend."

With both hands Glynis clutched a pistol which was pointed directly at Anna's chest. Alarm bells went off in Jordan's head and he tensed.

"Glynis." He heard Anna whisper her name, but he didn't take his eyes off the cook. The look in the older woman's eyes warned Jordan not to rush her. She'd pull the trigger without the slightest hesitation. He knew the accuracy of a single-shot pistol wasn't the best, but Glynis was so damn close, aim wouldn't matter. What in hell was she doing here? Why was she pointing that gun at Anna? Had she overheard what they'd said? He moved his foot, trying to get between Anna and the dragoon.

"Stay where you are! Don't take a step closer." Her voice was low and her tone mean.

Jordan didn't want to scare Glynis into pulling the trigger, so he stopped and lifted his arms away from his jacket. He had to handle her carefully. Damn it! Here they were in the woods with a crazy woman pointing a pistol at Anna, and not much chance of anyone stumbling upon them to help.

"Glynis, what are you doing here?" Anna asked in a tremulous voice.

"News travels fast. I was on my way back to the tavern when I heard that Major Andre had been captured and General Arnold had sailed for

354

New York. I knew you had to be the one who'd spoiled their plans. I had a feeling when you made me leave you'd overheard me talking to the general that night, since his room was right beside yours. I was right, wasn't I?"

Jordan decided to stay quiet and let the two women talk. With any luck, Glynis would forget about him and he could jump her.

"I did overhear you that night," Anna admitted.

That wasn't smart, Anna. Can't you see she has that pistol aimed at you?

"And you went straight to New York so you could interrupt their plans."

"I did go to see Major Andre, but tell me, Glynis, how's your son?"

Good, Anna. Change the subject. Get her mind on something else so I can get that gun!

"I was too late. He was dead of consumption by the time I got there. I knew he wouldn't last long in those damp caves of Newgate." Tears sprang to the woman's eyes.

Wrong subject, Anna. Try something else. Hurry! Glynis's hands were shaking and that made her extremely dangerous.

"Glynis, I'm so sorry about your son."

"You're lying! What do you care about a British boy barely seventeen when he came to America to fight for his country? I followed him over here to this godforsaken land because he was all I had. Now he's gone. He was a good son. It's too late for him, but there are other boys who are rotting in those prisons."

"I have nothing to do with that!" Anna cried, not understanding why the woman was blaming her for a war that took the lives of innocents.

"Glynis, put the gun down," Jordan spoke calmly. "Anna gave you money to go to your son. It's not her fault he died before you got there."

"She was the one who kept General Arnold from surrendering West Point and giving the Americans what they deserve for letting my son die in that hellhole."

Jordan knew by the expression in her eyes that she was going to fire the pistol. He lunged for her outstretched arms and felt a sharp burning pain tearing at his chest as a loud explosion rattled his ears. As he fell, he heard Anna scream. He wanted to go to her, but the blackness enveloped him and he could do nothing at all.

Anna screamed as the gun went off just a few feet in front of Jordan. She reached for him, trying to push him out of the way, but saw the ball strike his upper chest. A vision of her father's death flitted across her mind, but this time the weapon was a gun instead of a knife and the attacker was a woman. Panic and fury filled Anna and she lunged for Glynis, knocking the gun out of her hand.

Glynis landed on the ground with a thud and Anna pounced on top of her and straddled her waist. Glynis slapped her face hard before she could raise her arms to protect herself. Despite the pain, she managed to seize Glynis's flailing hands. The woman was not only large, she was strong. It was all Anna could do to hold the woman's flexing fingers away from her throat. Fear gave Anna abnormal strength as she held Glynis at bay until, little by little, she pushed

Glynis's hands farther away from her neck.

Then Anna heard shouting and booted feet running toward them. Someone from the tavern must have heard the shot. She knew help was on the way, but she mustn't slacken her grip. If Glynis worked free, she was strong enough to snap Anna's neck in seconds.

Suddenly Anna was yanked off Glynis. Her arms were held firmly behind her back. Two other men grabbed Glynis by the arms and pulled her to her feet.

"Let me go!" Glynis shouted, kicking at the men who held her. "I'm going to kill her!"

"She shot Jordan!" Anna shouted to the man who held her. "Please let me go to him," she pleaded.

"I'll kill you, Anna Lowell!" Glynis struggled to free herself of her captors.

"Take her to the smokehouse and lock her up," the man behind Anna told the two men restraining Glynis.

Anna squirmed away from the man who held her and hurried over to Jordan. The front panel of his shirt was soaked with blood. "Oh God, no!" she whispered as she fell to her knees and lifted his head into her lap. Glynis continued to shout insults and spit at Jordan and Anna as she was dragged away.

Anna looked up at the man who knelt beside her, recognizing him as Mr. Bristol, the tavernkeeper. "Is he dead?" she asked in a faint voice.

"No, I see his chest moving. He's alive." The man pulled a folded handkerchief out of his pocket. Pulling Jordan's coat, waistcoat, and shirt aside, he placed it over the blackened and red hole in Jordan's chest, an inch above his nipple. Anna couldn't hold back a small cry of anguish when she saw the wound.

"Hold that tight against his chest," the man said. "Tight!" he said in a sharper voice. "We've got to stop the bleeding. I'll go get my boys to help me carry him to the tavern."

The man hurried away as tears streamed down Anna's face. Despair filled her breast and she sobbed loudly. They'd just admitted their love for each other, and now Jordan was dying.

"Hurry!" she called after the fleeing man. "Hurry! Hurry!" she screamed over and over again, until her voice was only a gravelly whimper in her throat.

Chapter Nineteen

Jordan was a big man, so it wasn't easy for the tavernkeeper and two boys to carry him upstairs to his room. Even though the men tried to be gentle, Anna could see that the movement caused the wound to bleed more profusely. She was thankful when he was laid on the bed at last.

"How soon will the doctor get here?" she asked.

"You're looking at him," the man said, with no boasting in his words. "Got my training on the battlefield in Danbury. Worked on General Wooster myself. 'Course, he didn't make it." The man sighed and lifted his sagging breeches up and over his rounded belly.

Anna shuddered as she looked at Mr. Bristol. "Just keep Jordan from dying," she whispered. "Please."

The man sniffed. "I'll do what I can. I've taken out a few balls in my time. I've saved more than one, American and British alike, but I can't promise you anything. He was hit at close range, and that's not good. The only reason he's breathing now is because the ball had to tear through his clothes first." He fingered Jordan's jacket. "By the looks of this, the ball glanced off this brass button. Now, it could have hit a rib or his lung. We won't know until we open him up and go in and see."

Anna's stomach churned as if she were back on that rocking boat in the middle of the Hudson. "Just do what you have to do and tell me what you need. I'll do anything to help you."

"It would be best if you went downstairs and let me handle this. Mrs. Bristol will help me when I need it. No sense in you putting yourself through this."

"No, I'm not leaving him," she said, and covered Jordan's hand with her own.

"All right, but if you faint, I'll let you lie where you fall. I can't tend to both of you, and he comes first."

Anna summoned up her strength. "You won't have to worry about me. I don't intend to faint."

"Well, I'm going down to get the things I need. Be back in a minute."

Anna was glad that she had a few moments alone with Jordan. Through her tears she could see that his face and lips had paled considerably. He was losing blood and strength fast.

"Jordan, don't die," she whispered in fear as she bent closer to him, her words sounding loud in the silent room.

Suddenly his eyes fluttered open but quickly squeezed closed as a painful groan came from his lips. His breathing was raspy and he labored for each breath.

"Jordan, can you hear me?"

"Damn!" he swore as his face twisted with pain once again.

"Shh—don't talk," she calmed him. "Mr. Bristol is a doctor. He's going to take the ball out and you'll get well." Her voice was husky with tears.

Jordan coughed and tried to listen to what she was saying, but the pain in his chest was so bad he couldn't comprehend much. He was trying to estimate the damage of the bullet. He didn't think it had pierced his lung, he didn't taste any blood in his mouth, but he was almost certain it had struck a rib. Damn, it hurt like hell. The searing, burning pain wouldn't go away.

"Glynis," he managed to say, although his throat felt like a bayonet had scraped it.

Anna caressed his forehead, the only thing she knew to do. "She's locked up. She can't get out."

"Did she hurt you?" he managed to say in a rush of words.

"No, oh, no, Jordan. I'm fine, and you will be, too. Don't waste your strength trying to talk. Just close your eyes and rest. Everything is going to be all right. Just rest."

"I've got to—to get to Washington." He tried to rise, but started coughing and fell back to the bed.

"Jordan, don't! You'll make the bleeding worse. Be still. Please!"

"Washington," he repeated.

"We'll take care of that as soon as you're better," Anna told him, knowing that by the time Jordan could get better, it would be too late for John. She sank to her knees by the bed, leaning against it for support. She carried Jordan's limp hand to her lips and kissed it as tears rolled down her cheeks.

Jordan moaned in pain, turned his head, and lost consciousness again. Anna looked frantically at the door, praying for the tavernkeeper to hurry back before it was too late for Jordan. At last the door opened.

"Is he still alive?" Mr. Bristol asked, walking up to the bed and peering down at Jordan.

"Yes." Anna rose and stepped away. "What do we do first?"

Mr. Bristol looked at her and sighed. "I still say it's best if you leave the room. This won't be a pretty sight. I'll let you know when I'm through."

"I'm not leaving," she said firmly.

"Then build a fire. It's too cold in here. He doesn't need to catch a chill. You'll need to keep a low fire burning at all times. I'll undress him while we wait for my wife to bring up the hot water."

Anna took a deep breath, then took a step toward the bed. "I'll undress him. You build the fire," she told the man, and turned to Jordan.

"All right. I understand."

With infinite care, wanting to disturb his chest as little as possible, Anna eased off the blood-soaked jacket, waistcoat, and shirt. The saturated handkerchief was the only thing that covered the hole in Jordan's chest. She closed her eyes for a moment and prayed for strength before removing the cloth and hurriedly replacing it with one of the clean cloths Mr. Bristol had brought with him. She made short work of his boots and breeches and lowered them to the floor with the other clothes. She'd put them away later.

Jordan stirred, mumbled her name, and groaned. If they didn't get the ball out soon he was bound to take fever, and that scared her far more than the small piece of metal lodged in his chest.

As Mr. Bristol rose from tending the fire, his wife, a small woman, came in carrying an iron pot of steaming water.

They turned three lanterns up as high as possible but the room still seemed too dark. Anna helped Mr. Bristol rouse Jordan enough to get the laudanum in him, then she wiped his forehead with a wet cloth while the drug took effect.

Mrs. Bristol stood on the opposite side of the bed and held a lantern close to Jordan's chest when Mr. Bristol started his job of looking for the musket ball. Fresh blood gushed. Anna wiped the blood as quickly as she could so that he could see what he was doing. She swallowed hard when Mr. Bristol asked her to hold one side of the flesh apart while he dug his fingers into Jordan's chest, searching for the ball.

"I'm going to have to make a cut," he said, giving her a sideways glance. "If I don't find it, we're in trouble, because that's going to mean it's somewhere in his lung."

Anna squeezed her eyes shut and sent up a quick prayer. The tavernkeeper put the knife to Jordan's chest.

"Ah—I think I have it. Hold it back further," he said hoarsely, digging two fingers into the bloody flesh. He dug until slowly he pulled his fingers out with a small piece of warped, misshapen metal held between them.

Anna was close to fainting. Her body was drenched in sweat; her dress clung to her. "Is that all?" she asked, leaning against the bed, afraid her legs alone wouldn't hold her.

"Let's hope so. But I'd better check before I sew him up. It appears this rib stopped it."

Anna averted her eyes this time. She couldn't watch again.

"I think that's it," he said.

She looked down at Jordan. He was as still, as pale as death. The only thing that told her he was alive was the slight rhythmic rise and fall of his chest.

"Do you want to stitch him?"

Her gaze flew to Mr. Bristol's face. "What?"

"Most women are a little handier with a needle than I am. You might make it look a little better."

Anna looked at the incision Mr. Bristol had made. She moistened her lips and said, "No, I'll let you do it." But when she saw Bristol's big hands pushing the needle through Jordan's skin, she changed her mind. She started by guiding him with her gentle voice and soon the needle was in her hand and she was sewing a straight line. After the stitches were finished, Mr. Bristol collected the tools of his trade while Anna placed a clean cloth over Jordan's chest.

"I guess you know we could lose him to fever or infection."

"I won't let that happen," she said, realizing that she didn't know how she could prevent it.

"No, I can see you won't," Mr. Bristol said. "There's not much you can do now. He should sleep most of the night, but when he wakes that bullet hole is going to make him wish he were dead. It's been my experience that the best thing for him now is rest. Try to keep the room warm but his body cool. Keep the window closed and the fire going, and wash his body with a cold cloth—often. That may keep the fever down, but it won't keep it from coming."

"I will. Thank you, Mr. Bristol."

He picked up the pan of water and dropped the used cloths and the knife into it. "I'll send up some fresh water and be up to check on him before bed."

"I'll bring you up something to eat," Mrs. Bristol added, and Anna gave the kind woman a grateful smile.

After Mr. Bristol closed the door behind them, Anna knelt beside Jordan's bed, picked up his hand, carried it to her lips, and kissed it reverently. "Jordan, my love," she whispered, "you must not die. Please get better so that we can have a life together. Please."

She leaned forward and kissed his forehead. Thank God it was still cool.

Remaining on her knees, Anna laid her head on the bed beside Jordan's arm. Now that she had done all she could for him, her other worries rushed back. Glynis had ruined their plans to save John. What was she going to do? She would go to Washington if that would help. But she felt sure Washington would never agree to see a woman whose name he didn't know. She'd try to free John, but she'd seen the number of soldiers who guarded his room. Oh God, she hoped Jordan was right and that she didn't have to bear the guilt for John's death, for surely there was nothing she could do to prevent it.

Anna realized it the moment Jordan awakened near dawn. She was sitting on the floor, her head resting on the bed. Jordan groaned, moaned, and mumbled something. The laudanum had worn off. She touched his forehead and squeezed her eyes shut. He was warm but not hot. She helped him sip the laudanum mixture Mr. Bristol had left and he soon quieted again.

Anna quickly put a cloth in the basin of water and began to bathe Jordan's face, the cloth sometimes catching on his stubble of beard. She folded back the sheet and swiftly but carefully continued to wash his body. She left his face and ran the cloth over his shoulder, down his arms, across his stomach, feeling the firmness of every muscle as she went. When she'd finished with that part of his body, she started down his legs and over his feet. His whole body was warm to her touch, even his toes, as she washed him with the cool cloth. As the water became tepid she refilled the basin with fresh, cool water. Then she started her labor of love all over again, rediscovering every inch of his body as she worked to keep it cool.

By the next morning the fever was down but not gone. She had a feeling it would go higher during the night, if not before. At one point during the day Jordan opened his feverish eyes and looked at her.

"Jordan, do you know who I am?" she asked.

"Dry," was all he said. She held a cup of sweetened water to his lips and helped him drink.

"No, try not to cough," she said, fearful he'd tear the stitches. "Do you remember what happened?"

366

"Shot," he answered with a nod, then winced before his eyes closed in sleep.

At least the fever wasn't high enough to make him delirious. That was a good sign. But Anna was aware that could change at any moment. His color wasn't good and the incision continued to drain. The fever smoldered under his skin, and it was only a matter of time until it erupted again.

About an hour before sundown Anna asked Mrs. Bristol to sit with Jordan while she went out for a walk. Anna knew she had to try to see John. She loved John, too, although not in the same way she loved Jordan. If she pleaded her cause, maybe someone would agree to let her see him.

On sluggish legs she walked the quarter mile down the road to Mabie's Tavern. As she approached the front of the building a first lieutenant stopped her.

"I'm sorry, ma'am, you're not allowed in here," he said, as he pulled his musket from his shoulder and held it in front of him.

Anna straightened her shoulders. "I'd like to speak to the man in charge," she said in a strong voice.

"Right now, I'm in charge. The colonel's having his meal."

The lieutenant was dressed in a dusty black coat with the collar, cuffs, and front border a dirty shade of white. Small tarnished brass buttons ran up and down the front of the jacket. His face was pleasant to look upon, and his eyes were dark and deep set. She decided to be truthful with this man.

"I'd like to see Major Andre," she said in a soft voice.

The man laughed gently. "So would a dozen other women."

That was probably true. "We are friends. I need to talk to him. I'm willing for you to search me." She held out her arms. "I carry nothing but a heavy heart. Please, must I beg you?"

The man must have felt sorry for her, because he said, "Oh, all right. I never could deny a pretty face. If I'm going to slip you in, now's the time to do it, while the colonel's having his meal. But if you ever tell anyone I let you in, I'll deny it."

Her spirits lifted. "I promise I'll never tell a soul I was here."

He led her up the tavern steps and quickly up the stairs. Four men were posted outside John's door and two others at the end of the hallway.

"We can't let her in," a rough-looking, bearded man with two teeth missing said to the lieutenant.

"I've searched her; she has no weapon. If you were scheduled to hang tomorrow, would you want anyone to deny you your last chance to talk to a beautiful woman?"

"No, I guess not," he said, scratching his long, gray-streaked beard. "But I'll have to search her, too."

Anna cringed. She could tell by the look in his eyes how he was going to search her. Her first thought was that she wouldn't let him; she'd appeal to the nice lieutenant — but on second thought, she knew if they argued over her, the colonel would come and she wouldn't get to see John at all. She was too close to him now to get weak in the knees. She'd let the subaltern fondle her.

He stood before her and yanked her cap off her head and threw it to the floor. With both hands he ran his fingers thoroughly through the length of her hair.

"Women have been known to hide things in their hair," he said, although he wasn't touching her hair as if he was looking for an object. His rough hands slid down to her ears, taking the time to run his fingers suggestively around both lobes. Then his hands glided over her shoulders and down the length of both arms, back up her waist, and over her breasts, the movements excessively slow and deliberate.

Anna closed her eyes and bit her tongue to keep from pushing his hands away. If she caused a scene, she wouldn't get in to see John, so she remained silent. The subaltern went down on one knee and lifted her skirt, feeling one leg all the way up her thigh. Anna cringed inside but stood ramrod straight, hoping the lieutenant would put a halt to this lecherous man and his abominable treatment before she started screaming in outrage. When his hand slid over that part of her no one had touched but Jordan, she jumped and stepped back.

"That's enough," the lieutenant said in a low tone that left no doubt she'd been searched enough.

When Anna opened her eyes, she saw that the lieutenant had his pistol pointed at the soldier's head.

"You've had your price. Open the door and let her in."

When Anna walked in, John was sitting at a

desk writing and so engrossed that he didn't look up to see who had entered. The light was poor, but a candle burned beside him. The room was small and warm. One window overlooked a small garden below. And just as she'd been told, two soldiers stood by each wall, their swords drawn.

"John." She called his name with a slight catch to her voice.

He jerked his head up and gave a startled look. "Anna! My God, how did you get in here?"

He rose from his chair, and Anna rushed into his arms. He hugged her warmly, affectionately. She was shaking from the cruel treatment of the soldier, and it felt wonderful to have friendly arms around her.

"I had to come see you," she whispered into his collar.

"How did you get in? I was told I could see no one."

"I met a nice lieutenant who felt sorry for me."

He smiled. "My beautiful Anna. I should have married you when I had the chance. I should have known if anyone could pass through the enemy lines and see me it would be you."

"John, I don't understand any of this. Isn't there something to be done that can spare your life?"

"No, my lovely Anna. This mission and the steps I took to keep it from failing are what doomed me. There is no one to blame but me. I disobeyed orders on three occasions."

"What? How? I can't believe that you would."

"General Clinton instructed me not to enter enemy lines, but I did. He ordered me not to quit my uniform and I did. Last, he asked that I not

370

take any incriminating papers or documents into my possession, but I did." He sighed. "Anna, I've resigned myself to my death. Now you must accept it."

"No! Why did you listen to General Arnold? Why would you want to accept a traitor in your army?" Her voice was clogged with emotion.

"A traitor, Anna? Not so. General Arnold had merely decided to return to his true allegiance. You must not forget that what is treason to one is the return of loyalty to another. Is Arnold any more reprehensible than the many Americans who remained loyal from the beginning?"

Anna could not respond to such a statement, for she knew it to be true and it broke her heart.

"What concerns me over this whole incident is that some will label me a common spy and that is not so. Had I, as personal envoy from Sir Henry, been asked to sneak into the American lines as a common spy, I would have been indignant and affronted. As it turned out, I was powerless over my own actions and that caused me to behave as a spy."

"But you're not a spy. You were *given* that information. General Arnold is the one who should be punished. He should be hanged!" Her voice trembled.

"Anna, don't do this. No one bears fault but me."

She wiped tears from her cheeks and asked, "John, if I had known about the plan, about your meeting with General Arnold, would there have been any way I could have stopped you?"

He looked deeply into her eyes and gave her a

small smile. "No. The glory of an accomplished mission would have been too great." He took her hands in his. "You must understand that it was my duty to accept the general's overtures and, if I could, to profit by them. I may despise the act of treason, but in this instance, I was compelled to act upon it. No one could have stopped me. You can't know the excitement I felt at luring this great general to our side."

Tears slipped down her cheeks once again. Jordan had been right; John would have done anything to see his mission accomplished. "Is there nothing that can be done?" she asked.

"No, Anna. Nothing. No other verdict was possible. I never intended to play the part of a spy, but I now have to accept the consequences."

She had come here with the idea she'd confess to John that she knew of his plan and admit her role in following him, but now she knew she couldn't. It was clear that he would blame no one but himself, and now she saw that he was right. It was a tragically heroic thing to do—exactly what she would have expected from a gentleman.

"You must attend the execution, Anna."

Her gaze flew to his face and she backed away. "No, John don't ask it of me, I can't."

"Would you deny me this last request? It would please me and make it easier to bear if I see your beautiful face and your eyes filled with tears as they are now. Then I will know that someone will miss me."

"I will miss you, John. I swear all the days of my life I will miss you and be so very sorry this happened. I'll be forever grieved that I could do nothing to prevent it," she said with heartfelt regret.

"When you think of me, will you smile?" he asked.

Her eyes closed briefly in a spasm of grief. "Yes," she whispered as her heart sank lower.

"Anna." He lifted her chin with the tips of his fingers.

"Yes." Tears drenched her cheeks and her trembling lips formed a smile.

"Hand me a flower as I pass by."

Chapter Twenty

The walk back to the Harvester's Ring Tavern was not easy for Anna. She stopped along the way and leaned against a tree and wept for John. When she had no more tears to shed, she dried her face with the hem of her dress and hurried back to Jordan. She couldn't save John's life, but maybe with her care and her prayers she could save Jordan's.

"You don't look well," Mrs. Bristol said when Anna entered the room a few minutes later.

"I'll be all right." She walked up to the bed and put her hand on his forehead. Still warm. "Has he been restful?" Anna looked up at the woman.

"Mostly. He woke up and mumbled, but his words made no sense. I gave him a drink and he quieted down again."

Anna gave the woman a kind smile. "Thank you for staying with him. I'll bathe him now."

"All right. I'll bring up some supper later."

"Thank you. Mrs. Bristol, before you go, could I ask that you sit again with Jordan tomorrow at noon? I must—"

"Attend the hanging?" Mrs. Bristol asked.

"Yes," she said softly, sadly.

374

"I'll sit with him. I don't care anything about seeing a man swing from a gibbet. Makes no sense to me why someone would want to watch a man die, though I know people and soldiers are coming from all over the area to see it. They usually bring their picnic baskets and ale and let their children laugh and play. I've even seen boys throw rocks at the swinging body." Mrs. Bristol clucked her lips disapprovingly, then opened the door and went out.

Anna's stomach churned at the woman's graphic wording. She knew that some people enjoyed hangings, and to watch while John was treated that way was more than she thought she could bear. She couldn't go—but she couldn't deny John. Anna sank dispiritedly into the chair beside Jordan's bed and took hold of his hand. Somewhere she had to find the courage to accept John's death and possibly Jordan's.

Anna stayed awake throughout most of the night, resting only for short periods of time. She continued to wash Jordan's fevered body and calm his mumbling. Even though she kept the wound clean, it had swelled and turned red and angry-looking.

Just before noon the next day Anna once again left Jordan in Mrs. Bristol's care and on heavy legs walked up the steep and rocky path that led to the gallows in Tappan. Along the way she saw a scattering of bright yellow flowers growing wild along the embankment. She stopped and picked one for John. As the gibbet came into view she jumped

375

back, startled by the horrible sight of the upright post with a rope hanging from a projecting arm, a horse and wagon underneath it. In the wagon, a coffin filled the bed.

Her grief was immense as she looked at the scene before her. Did she have to watch him die? How could she watch? Was this to be a punishment for her? And if so, for what? For loving Jordan or for failing John? No, she told herself as she searched for inner strength. She was fulfilling a very special friend's last request.

The day was beautiful, with warm sunshine and a cool breeze. A few birds hiding in the many trees chirped in the distance as Anna took a place in the crowd of people who lined the route John had to walk. She was surprised and relieved that there was no loud talking or laughing coming from the crowd. She'd expected to find an angry mob of spectators cheering for the death of the young British soldier. Instead, she saw young women sobbing. Soldiers of all ranks were among the crowd, but the highest-ranking officers sat on horseback a few yards away. A guard of single-file soldiers lined the pathway. The atmosphere was not one of tense excitement. It was one of melancholy and gloom.

In spite of her misery, Anna's spirits lifted. It appeared that the people who came to this hanging did so out of respect, not because they were bloodthirsty. Anna found comfort in this realization. Yes, John Andre was the enemy, but he'd done his best to serve his country well, just as Anna had been forced to betray him to save her country.

Between two subordinate officers Major John

Andre walked from the stone house in which he'd been confined. He was dressed in his royal regimentals and riding boots. He wore a brilliant scarlet coat trimmed in a shade of deep forest green. His hair was held at the back with a black ribbon.

The march to his death was solemn. No one spoke, only the sobbing could be heard. The eyes of the crowd were fixed on John, who looked superior to the fear of death. He betrayed no lack of fortitude as he politely bowed to several gentlemen who respectfully returned the courtesy.

When he passed by, Anna reached between the two soldiers and handed John the yellow flower. He smiled and bowed. Anna returned the smile with quivering lips. Her eyes were wet and a choking sound came from her throat. John continued the walk.

His only sign of dread came as he stepped into the wagon. He shunned the executioner, who had covered his face and hands with tar so he wouldn't be recognized. John took off his hat and stock and laid them in the wagon. He grabbed the rope and slipped it over his head and adjusted the knot firmly behind his right ear. He took a white handkerchief from his pocket and covered his eyes with swift movements. Someone yelled that his arms would have to be tied, so he took off his white scarf and handed it to the provost-marshal, who loosely pinioned his arms above the elbow.

At last someone asked if he'd like to speak.

John cleared his throat. "I pray you to bear me witness that I meet my fate like a soldier and a brave man."

The hangman cracked the whip across the

horse's rump and the cart jumped out from under John.

Anna turned away stumbling and running, not stopping until she was far into the woods and too tired to run any further.

Jordan's fever continued for two more days. There were many times during the forty-eight hours that Anna didn't think he would live. She stayed by his bed, not leaving him again. She kept the fire burning and continued to wash him with a cool cloth. Sometime during the third night Anna fell asleep, her head resting on the bed beside Jordan's still hand.

Anna heard someone calling her name, but she couldn't open her eyes. She was too tired. She wanted only to sleep. Someone was playing with her hair, and she swatted at a hand but still couldn't open her eyes, wanting only to be left alone with her sleep.

"Anna."

Slowly her lashes rose and she looked into Jordan's clear blue eyes. She jumped up. "You're awake," she exclaimed joyfully. "Thank God."

"You must be very tired. I've been trying to wake you for at least five minutes." His voice was husky, but she understood every word.

"Jordan, I'm so happy you're awake." She kissed his forehead. It was cool. "Your fever's gone," she said with a big smile, squeezing his hand affectionately.

"That's good. I need to get to Washington."

Anna's lashes lowered and the pit of her stomach clenched. She went down on her knees beside him again. "It's too late. John was hanged three days ago."

"Damn it, Anna, I'm sorry." He tried to raise himself.

"Don't move," she said, and laid gentle hands on his shoulders and pushed him back on the pillow. "It's all right, Jordan. There was nothing you could do. As you said, his fate was sealed, and neither you nor I could have changed it."

"I wanted to try—for you."

She smiled, knowing that she loved him with all her heart, knowing that he loved her enough to want to save John. Suddenly she felt very lucky and sent up a prayer of praise.

"I know. How do you feel?" she asked.

"Like someone beat the hell out of me." He tried to chuckle, but groaned instead.

Anna kissed his hand. "You're going to be sore for a long time."

Jordan reached up and touched her face. "Have you been here with me all this time?"

"Nearly all." Now wasn't the time to tell him about John and what he'd asked of her. "You were shot five days ago." She looked out the window and saw sunrise on the horizon. "No, six days," she corrected herself as light showed through the windowpane.

"Help me to sit up." He tried to rise again.

"Jordan, don't. You're not well enough." She tried to push him back on the pillow.

"A little," he pleaded. "Just enough to drink water."

"All right, but only for a moment." She positioned another pillow behind his head and helped him to drink fresh water from a cup. "Not too much. You don't want to get sick."

"That's better," he said a few moments later. "Where's Glynis?"

Anna winced and turned back to Jordan. "Hers is a tragic story." She glanced around the room, suddenly wishing so many things had been different. "She was locked in the smokehouse behind the tavern while it was being decided what to do with her for shooting you. Along the back wall a poisonous vine had grown through a crack and into the building. No one knows whether she knew of its deadly effect, but she ate it. She was found yesterday morning when she was taken food."

"What damnable news to wake up to." Regret filled his eyes and his voice. "The British lost two very loyal countrymen this week. Their cause will miss the courage of Andre and Glynis."

"Yes," she whispered, loving him more because of his remorse for the untimely deaths. "And our cause will continue until we are free of all British rule."

Jordan looked up at her and smiled. "Thanks to you, West Point is secure."

"I'd like to think those men would have stopped John even if we hadn't sent them after him."

Jordan squeezed her hand and smiled. "I think that's the best way to look at it."

She returned his smile, then reached over and pressed her lips to his and was rewarded with a sigh of contentment. "You need rest," she said.

"Not yet." He took her hand. "Anna, come over to this side of the bed and lie beside me."

"I'll hurt your shoulder," she protested.

"No, come. I need to feel you beside me. We've come too close to losing each other. Take off your dress and lie here with me while I rest."

"Jordan, what if I should fall asleep and Mrs. Bristol comes in to find me in your bed?"

"We'll send her for a minister. Come lie with me."

Anna smiled again while she unbuttoned her dress and let it slip down her legs, leaving it on the floor. With the greatest care she eased into the bed beside him and pressed her cool body next to his.

With a moan of pain, Jordan turned on his side and faced her. "You feel wonderful. Having you here is bound to speed up my recovery. Come closer," he encouraged. "I need you."

Anna snuggled closer, loving the feel of his skin next to hers, and said, "If I hurt you I'll never forgive myself."

"Do you love me, Anna?" he asked as he looked into her eyes.

"Yes," she answered softly. "I love you."

"Then you can't hurt me. There are many things we need to talk about."

Anna saw he was weakening. "We'll have time, Jordan. I know now that you are going to get well. There will be time for us to talk when you're better," she promised.

"Will you marry me?" he asked.

"Yes," she answered.

"It will mean moving away from Georgetown, leaving the tavern. We'll make a home for Terence in Boston. We can keep the tavern and hire someone to manage it until Terence decides what he wants to do with it."

Anna brushed his damp hair away from his forehead and ran her hand down his cheek, feeling the stubble. "You know, when Benjamin asked me to give up the tavern I wouldn't even consider it."

"And now?" he asked.

"Now the right man is asking." She smiled. "I love you, Jordan."

"And I love you."

Author's Note

I started my research of Benedict Arnold and John Andre with the jaundiced view most Americans have of this infamous duo, but as I studied their lives and their roles in our history, I found my views changing. At the conclusion I felt compassion for Major John Andre and pity for General Arnold, who threw away his heroic place in history.

John Andre's meeting with Benedict Arnold in the firs and Andre's flight, capture, and hanging were taken directly from the pages of history. My only invention was Anna's visit to Andre at Mabie's Tavern, and I changed the number of days from his capture to his death to suit my story.

Historians don't really know who first introduced Arnold to John Stansbury, but most think it was Arnold's second wife, Peggy Shippen. I chose to give this honor to Glynis.

The *Vulture* carried Benedict Arnold to safety, but not to glory. He was later involved in two battles against the Americans before he sailed to London, where he lived in ill health until his death in 1801.

On a final note, I'll add this: if I could have

rewritten the pages of history, Jordan would have
made his appeal to General Washington, and John
Andre's life would have been spared.